A Cornelius Calendar
    comprising –
    The Adventures of Una Persson
        and Catherine Cornelius in
        the Twentieth Century
    The Entropy Tango
    The Great Rock 'n' Roll Swindle
    The Alchemist's Question
    Firing the Cathedral / Modem
        Times 2.0

Von Bek
    comprising –
    The War Hound and the World's
        Pain
    The City in the Autumn Stars

The Eternal Champion
    comprising –
    The Eternal Champion
    Phoenix in Obsidian
    The Dragon in the Sword

The Dancers at the
End of Time
    comprising –
    An Alien Heat
    The Hollow Lands
    The End of all Songs

Kane of Old Mars
    comprising –
    Warriors of Mars
    Blades of Mars
    Barbarians of Mars

Moorcock's Multiverse
    comprising –
    The Sundered Worlds
    The Winds of Limbo
    The Shores of Death

The Nomad of Time
    comprising –
    The Warlord of the Air
    The Land Leviathan
    The Steel Tsar

Travelling to Utopia
    comprising –
    The Wrecks of Time
    The Ice Schooner
    The Black Corridor

The War Amongst the Angels
    comprising –
    Blood: A Southern Fantasy
    Fabulous Harbours
    The War Amongst the Angels

Tales From the End of Time
    comprising –
    Legends from the End of Time
    Constant Fire
    Elric at the End of Time

Behold the Man

Gloriana; or, The Unfulfill'd Queen

SHORT FICTION
My Experiences in the Third World
War and Other Stories: The Best
Short Fiction of Michael Moorcock
Volume 1

The Brothel in Rosenstrasse and
Other Stories: The Best Short Fiction
of Michael Moorcock Volume 2

Breakfast in the Ruins and Other
Stories: The Best Short Fiction of
Michael Moorcock Volume 3

My Experiences in the Third World War and Other Stories

The Best Short Fiction of Michael Moorcock

Volume 1

MICHAEL MOORCOCK

Edited by John Davey

This edition published in Great Britain in 2014 by
Gollancz
An imprint of the Orion Publishing Group
Orion House, 5 Upper St Martin's Lane,
London WC2H 9EA

An Hachette UK Company

1 3 5 7 9 10 8 6 4 2

A CIP catalogue record for this book is
available from the British Library

ISBN 978 0 575 11505 7

Typeset by Jouve (UK), Milton Keynes

Printed and bound by CPI Group (UK) Ltd, Croydon, CR0 4YY

The Orion Publishing Group's policy is to use papers
that are natural, renewable and recyclable products and
made from wood grown in sustainable forests. The logging
and manufacturing processes are expected to conform to
the environmental regulations of the country of origin.

www.multiverse.org
www.sfgateway.com
www.gollancz.co.uk
www.orionbooks.co.uk

Introduction to
The Michael Moorcock Collection
John Clute

H E IS NOW over 70, enough time for most careers to start and end in, enough time to fit in an occasional half-decade or so of silence to mark off the big years. Silence happens. I don't think I know an author who doesn't fear silence like the plague; most of us, if we live long enough, can remember a bad blank year or so, or more. Not Michael Moorcock. Except for some worrying surgery on his toes in recent years, he seems not to have taken time off to breathe the air of peace and panic. There has been no time to spare. The nearly 60 years of his active career seems to have been too short to fit everything in: the teenage comics; the editing jobs; the pulp fiction; the reinvented heroic fantasies; the Eternal Champion; the deep Jerry Cornelius riffs; NEW WORLDS; the 1970s/1980s flow of stories and novels, dozens upon dozens of them in every category of modern fantastika; the tales of the dying Earth and the possessing of Jesus; the exercises in postmodernism that turned the world inside out before most of us had begun to guess we were living on the wrong side of things; the invention (more or less) of steampunk; the alternate histories; the *Mitteleuropean* tales of sexual terror; the deep-city London riffs: the turns and changes and returns and reconfigurations to which he has subjected his oeuvre over the years (he expects this new Collected Edition will fix these transformations in place for good); the late tales where he has been remodelling the intersecting worlds he created in the 1960s in terms of twenty-first-century physics: for starters. If you can't take the heat, I guess, stay out of the multiverse.

His life has been full and complicated, a life he has exposed and hidden (like many other prolific authors) throughout his work. In *Mother London* (1988), though, a non-fantastic novel published at what is now something like the midpoint of his career, it may be possible to find the key to all the other selves who made the 100 books. There are three protagonists in the tale, which is set from about 1940 to about 1988 in the suburbs and inner runnels of the vast metropolis of Charles Dickens and Robert Louis Stevenson. The oldest of these protagonists is Joseph Kiss, a flamboyant self-advertising fin-de-siècle figure of substantial girth and a fantasticating relationship to the world: he is Michael Moorcock, seen with genial bite as a kind of G.K. Chesterton without the wearying punch-line paradoxes. The youngest of the three is David Mummery, a haunted introspective half-insane denizen of a secret London of trials and runes and codes and magic: he too is Michael Moorcock, seen through a glass, darkly. And there is Mary Gasalee, a kind of holy-innocent and survivor, blessed with a luminous clarity of insight, so that in all her apparent ignorance of the onrushing secular world she is more deeply wise than other folk: she is also Michael Moorcock, Moorcock when young as viewed from the wry middle years of 1988. When we read the book, we are reading a book of instructions for the assembly of a London writer. The Moorcock we put together from this choice of portraits is amused and bemused at the vision of himself; he is a phenomenon of flamboyance and introspection, a poseur and a solitary, a dreamer and a doer, a multitude and a singleton. But only the three Moorcocks in this book, working together, could have written all the other books.

It all began – as it does for David Mummery in *Mother London* – in South London, in a subtopian stretch of villas called Mitcham, in 1939. In early childhood, he experienced the Blitz, and never forgot the extraordinariness of being a participant – however minute – in the great drama; all around him, as though the world were being dismantled nightly, darkness and blackout would descend, bombs fall, buildings and streets disappear; and in the morning, as though a new universe had taken over from the old one and the world had become portals, the sun would rise on glinting rubble, abandoned tricycles, men and women going about their daily tasks as though nothing had happened, strange shards of ruin poking into altered air. From a very early age, Michael Moorcock's security reposed in a sense that everything might change, in the blinking of an eye, and be *rejourneyed* the next day (or the next book). Though as a writer he has certainly elucidated the fears and alarums of life in Aftermath Britain, it does seem that his very early years were marked by the epiphanies of war, rather than the inflictions of despair and beclouding amnesia most adults necessarily experienced. After the war ended, his parents separated, and the young Moorcock began to attend a pretty wide variety of schools, several of which he seems to have been expelled from, and as soon as he could legally do so he began to work full time, up north in London's heart, which he only left when he moved to Texas (with intervals in Paris) in the early 1990s, from where (to jump briefly up the decades) he continues to cast a Martian eye: as with most exiles, Moorcock's intensest anatomies of his homeland date from after his cunning departure.

But back again to the beginning (just as though we were rimming a multiverse). Starting in the 1950s there was the comics and pulp work for Fleetway Publications; there was the first book (*Caribbean Crisis*, 1962) as by Desmond Reid, co-written with his early friend the artist James Cawthorn (1929–2008); there was marriage, with the writer Hilary Bailey (they divorced in 1978), three children, a heated existence in the Ladbroke Grove/Notting Hill Gate region of London he was later to populate with Jerry Cornelius and his vast family; there was the editing of NEW WORLDS, which began in 1964 and became the heartbeat of the British New Wave two years later as writers like Brian W. Aldiss and J.G. Ballard, reaching their early prime, made it into a tympanum, as young American writers like Thomas M. Disch, John T. Sladek, Norman Spinrad and Pamela Zoline found a home in London for material they could not publish in America, and new British writers like M. John Harrison and Charles Platt began their careers in its pages; but before that there was Elric. With *The Stealer of Souls* (1963) and

Stormbringer (1965), the multiverse began to flicker into view, and the Eternal Champion (whom Elric parodied and embodied) began properly to ransack the worlds in his fight against a greater Chaos than the great dance could sustain. There was also the first SF novel, *The Sundered Worlds* (1965), but in the 1960s SF was a difficult nut to demolish for Moorcock: he would bide his time.

We come to the heart of the matter. Jerry Cornelius, who first appears in *The Final Programme* (1968) – which assembles and co-ordinates material first published a few years earlier in NEW WORLDS – is a deliberate solarisation of the albino Elric, who was himself a mocking solarisation of Robert E. Howard's Conan, or rather of the mighty-thew-headed Conan created for profit by Howard epigones: Moorcock rarely mocks the true quill. Cornelius, who reaches his first and most telling apotheosis in the four novels comprising *The Cornelius Quartet*, remains his most distinctive and perhaps most original single creation: a wide boy, an agent, a *flaneur*, a bad musician, a shopper, a shapechanger, a trans, a spy in the house of London: a toxic palimpsest on whom and through whom the *zeitgeist* inscribes surreal conjugations of 'message'. Jerry Cornelius gives head to Elric.

The life continued apace. By 1970, with NEW WORLDS on its last legs, multiverse fantasies and experimental novels poured forth; Moorcock and Hilary Bailey began to live separately, though he moved, in fact, only around the corner, where he set up house with Jill Riches, who would become his second wife; there was a second home in Yorkshire, but London remained his central base. *The Condition of Muzak* (1977), which is the fourth Cornelius novel, and *Gloriana; or, The Unfulfill'd Queen* (1978), which transfigures the first Elizabeth into a kinked Astraea, marked perhaps the high point of his career as a writer of fiction whose font lay in genre or its mutations – marked perhaps the furthest bournes he could transgress while remaining within the perimeters of fantasy (though *within* those bournes vast stretches of territory remained and would, continually, be explored). During these years he sometimes wore a leather jacket constructed out of numerous patches of varicoloured material, and it sometimes seemed perfectly fitting that he bore the semblance, as his jacket flickered and fuzzed from across a room or road, of an illustrated man, a map, a thing of shreds and patches, a student fleshed from dreams. Like the stories he told, he seemed to be more than one thing. To use a term frequently applied (by me at least) to twenty-first-century fiction, he seemed equipoisal: which is to say that, through all his genre-hopping and genre-mixing and genre-transcending and genre-loyal returnings to old pitches, *he was never still*, because 'equipoise' is all about *making stories move*. As with his stories, he cannot be pinned down, because he is not in one place. In person and in his work, it has always been sink or swim: like a shark, or a dancer, or an equilibrist...

The marriage with Jill Riches came to an end. He married Linda Steele in 1983; they remain married. The Colonel Pyat books, *Byzantium Endures* (1981), *The Laughter of Carthage* (1984), *Jerusalem Commands* (1992) and *The Vengeance of Rome* (2006), dominated these years, along with *Mother London*. As these books, which are non-fantastic, are not included in the current *Michael Moorcock Collection*, it might be worth noting here that, in their insistence on the irreducible difficulty of gaining anything like true sight, they represent Moorcock's mature modernist take on what one might call the rag-and-bone shop of the world itself; and that the huge ornate postmodern edifice of his multiverse *loosens* us from that world, gives us room to breathe, to juggle our strategies for living – allows us ultimately to escape from prison (to use a phrase from a writer he does not respect, J.R.R. Tolkien, for whom the twentieth century was a prison train bound for hell). What Moorcock may best be remembered for in the end is the (perhaps unique) interplay between modernism and postmodernism in his work. (But a plethora of discordant understandings makes these terms hard to use; so enough of them.) In the end, one might just say that Moorcock's work as a whole represents an extraordinarily multifarious execution of the fantasist's main task: which is to *get us out of here*.

Recent decades saw a continuation of the multifarious, but with a more intensely applied methodology. The late volumes of the long Elric saga, and the Second Ether sequence of meta-fantasies – *Blood: A Southern Fantasy* (1995), *Fabulous Harbours* (1995) and *The War Amongst the Angels: An Autobiographical Story* (1996) – brood on the real world and the multiverse through the lens of Chaos Theory: the closer you get to the world, the less you describe it. *The Metatemporal Detective* (2007) – a narrative in the Steampunk mode Moorcock had previewed as long ago as *The Warlord of the Air* (1971) and *The Land Leviathan* (1974) – continues the process, sometimes dizzyingly: as though the reader inhabited the eye of a camera increasing its focus on a closely observed reality while its bogey simultaneously wheels it backwards from the desired rapport: an old Kurasawa trick here amplified into a tool of conspectus, fantasy eyed and (once again) rejourneyed, this time through the lens of SF.

We reach the second decade of the twenty-first century, time still to make things new, but also time to sort. There are dozens of titles in *The Michael Moorcock Collection* that have not been listed in this short space, much less trawled for tidbits. The various avatars of the Eternal Champion – Elric, Kane of Old Mars, Hawkmoon, Count Brass, Corum, Von Bek – differ vastly from one another. Hawkmoon is a bit of a berk; Corum is a steely solitary at the End of Time: the joys and doleurs of the interplays amongst them can only be experienced through immersion. And the Dancers at the End of Time books, and the Nomad of the Time Stream books, and the Karl Glogauer books, and all the others. They are here now, a 100 books that make up one book. They have been fixed for reading. It is time to enter the multiverse and see the world.

September 2012

Introduction to
The Michael Moorcock Collection
Michael Moorcock

B Y 1964, AFTER I had been editing NEW WORLDS for some
months and had published several science fiction and fantasy
novels, including *Stormbringer*, I realised that my run as a writer
was over. About the only new ideas I'd come up with were miniature computers, the multiverse and black holes, all very crudely
realised, in *The Sundered Worlds*. No doubt I would have to return
to journalism, writing features and editing. 'My career,' I told my
friend J.G. Ballard, 'is finished.' He sympathised and told me he
only had a few SF stories left in him, then he, too, wasn't sure
what he'd do.

In January 1965, living in Colville Terrace, Notting Hill, then an
infamous slum, best known for its race riots, I sat down at the
typewriter in our kitchen-cum-bathroom and began a locally
based book, designed to be accompanied by music and graphics.
The Final Programme featured a character based on a young man
I'd seen around the area and whom I named after a local green-
grocer, Jerry Cornelius, 'Messiah to the Age of Science'. Jerry was
as much a technique as a character. Not the 'spy' some critics
described him as but an urban adventurer as interested in his
psychic environment as the contemporary physical world. My
influences were English and French absurdists, American noir
novels. My inspiration was William Burroughs with whom I'd
recently begun a correspondence. I also borrowed a few SF ideas,
though I was adamant that I was not writing in any established
genre. I felt I had at last found my own authentic voice.

I had already written a short novel, *The Golden Barge*, set in a
nowhere, no-time world very much influenced by Peake and the

surrealists, which I had not attempted to publish. An earlier auto-biographical novel, *The Hungry Dreamers*, set in Soho, was eaten by rats in a Ladbroke Grove basement. I remained unsatisfied with my style and my technique. *The Final Programme* took nine days to complete (by 20 January, 1965) with my baby daughters sometimes cradled with their bottles while I typed on. This, I should say, is my memory of events; my then wife scoffed at this story when I recounted it. Whatever the truth, the fact is I only believed I might be a serious writer after I had finished that novel, with all its flaws. But Jerry Cornelius, probably my most successful sustained attempt at unconventional fiction, was born then and ever since has remained a useful means of telling complex stories. Associated with the 60s and 70s, he has been equally at home in all the following decades. Through novels and novellas I developed a means of carrying several narratives and viewpoints on what appeared to be a very light (but tight) structure which dispensed with some of the earlier methods of fiction. In the sense that it took for granted the understanding that the novel is among other things an internal dialogue and I did not feel the need to repeat by now commonly understood modernist conventions, this fiction was post-modern.

Not all my fiction looked for new forms for the new century. Like many 'revolutionaries' I looked back as well as forward. As George Meredith looked to the eighteenth century for inspiration for his experiments with narrative, I looked to Meredith, popular Edwardian realists like Pett Ridge and Zangwill and the writers of the *fin de siècle* for methods and inspiration. An almost obsessive interest in the Fabians, several of whom believed in the possibility of benign imperialism, ultimately led to my Bastable books which examined our enduring British notion that an empire could be essentially a force for good. The first was *The Warlord of the Air*.

I also wrote my *Dancers at the End of Time* stories and novels under the influence of Edwardian humourists and absurdists like Jerome or Firbank. Together with more conventional generic books like *The Ice Schooner* or *The Black Corridor*, most of that work was done in the 1960s and 70s when I wrote the Eternal Champion supernatural adventure novels which helped support my own and others' experiments via NEW WORLDS, allowing me also to keep a family while writing books in which action and fantastic invention were paramount. Though I did them quickly, I didn't write them cynically. I have always believed, somewhat puritanically, in giving the audience good value for money. I enjoyed writing them, tried to avoid repetition, and through each new one was able to develop a few more ideas. They also continued to teach me how to express myself through image and metaphor. My Everyman became the Eternal Champion, his dreams and ambitions represented by the multiverse. He could be an ordinary person struggling with familiar problems in a contemporary setting or he could be a swordsman fighting monsters on a far-away world.

Long before I wrote *Gloriana* (in four parts reflecting the seasons) I had learned to think in images and symbols through reading John Bunyan's *Pilgrim's Progress*, Milton and others, understanding early on that the visual could be the most important part of a book and was often in itself a story as, for instance, a famous personality could also, through everything associated with their name, function as narrative. I wanted to find ways of carrying as many stories as possible in one. From the cinema I also learned how to use images as connecting themes. Images, colours, music, and even popular magazine headlines can all add coherence to an apparently random story, underpinning it and giving the reader a sense of internal logic and a satisfactory resolution, dispensing with certain familiar literary conventions.

When the story required it, I also began writing neo-realist fiction exploring the interface of character and environment, especially the city, especially London. In some books I condensed, manipulated and randomised time to achieve what I wanted, but in others the sense of 'real time' as we all generally perceive it was more suitable and could best be achieved by traditional nineteenth-century means. For the Pyat books I first looked back to the great German classic, Grimmelshausen's *Simplicissimus* and other early picaresques. I then examined the roots of a certain kind of moral fiction from Defoe through Thackeray and Meredith then to modern times where the picaresque (or rogue tale) can take the form of a road movie, for instance. While it's probably fair to say that Pyat and *Byzantium Endures* precipitated the end of my second marriage (echoed to a degree in *The Brothel in Rosenstrasse*), the late 70s and the 80s were exhilarating times for me, with *Mother London* being perhaps my own favourite novel of that period. I wanted to write something celebratory.

By the 90s I was again attempting to unite several kinds of fiction in one novel with my Second Ether trilogy. With Mandelbrot, Chaos Theory and String Theory I felt, as I said at the time, as if I were being offered a chart of my own brain. That chart made it easier for me to develop the notion of the multiverse as representing both the internal and the external, as a metaphor and as a means of structuring and rationalising an outrageously inventive and quasi-realistic narrative. The worlds of the multiverse move up and down scales or 'planes' explained in terms of mass, allowing entire universes to exist in the 'same' space. The result of developing this idea was the *War Amongst the Angels* sequence which added absurdist elements also functioning as a kind of mythology and folklore for a world beginning to understand itself in terms of new metaphysics and theoretical physics. As the cosmos becomes denser and almost infinite before our eyes, with black holes and dark matter affecting our own reality, we can explore them and observe them as our ancestors explored our planet and observed the heavens.

At the end of the 90s I'd returned to realism, sometimes with a dash of fantasy, with *King of the City* and the stories collected in *London Bone*. I also wrote a new Elric/Eternal Champion sequence, beginning with *Daughter of Dreams*, which brought the fantasy worlds of Hawkmoon, Bastable and Co. in line with my realistic and autobiographical stories, another attempt to unify all my fiction, and also offer a way in which disparate genres could be reunited, through notions developed from the multiverse and the Eternal Champion, as one giant novel. At the time I was finishing the Pyat sequence which attempted to look at the roots of the Nazi Holocaust in our European, Middle Eastern and American cultures and to ground my strange survival guilt while at the same time examining my own cultural roots in the light of an enduring anti-Semitism.

By the 2000s I was exploring various conventional ways of story-telling in the last parts of *The Metatemporal Detective* and through other homages, comics, parodies and games. I also looked back at my earliest influences. I had reached retirement age and felt like a rest. I wrote a 'prequel' to the Elric series as a graphic novel with Walter Simonson, *The Making of a Sorcerer*, and did a little online editing with FANTASTIC METROPOLIS.

By 2010 I had written a novel featuring Doctor Who, *The Coming of the Terraphiles*, with a nod to P.G. Wodehouse (a boyhood favourite), continued to write short stories and novellas and to work on the beginning of a new sequence combining pure fantasy and straight autobiography called *The Whispering Swarm* while still writing more Cornelius stories trying to unite all the various genres and sub-genres into which contemporary fiction has fallen.

Throughout my career critics have announced that I'm 'abandoning' fantasy and concentrating on literary fiction. The truth is, however, that all my life, since I became a professional writer and editor at the age of 16, I've written in whatever mode suits a story best and where necessary created a new form if an old one didn't work for me. Certain ideas are best carried on a Jerry Cornelius story, others work better as realism and others as fantasy or science fiction. Some work best as a combination. I'm sure I'll write whatever I like and will continue to experiment with all the ways there are of telling stories and carrying as many themes as possible. Whether I write about a widow coping with loneliness in her cottage or a massive, universe-size sentient spaceship searching for her children, I'll no doubt die trying to tell them all. I hope you'll find at least some of them to your taste.

One thing a reader can be sure of about these new editions is that they would not have been possible without the tremendous and indispensable help of my old friend and bibliographer John Davey. John has ensured that these Gollancz editions are definitive. I am indebted to John for many things, including his work at

Moorcock's Miscellany, my website, but his work on this edition has been outstanding. As well as being an accomplished novelist in his own right John is an astonishingly good editor who has worked with Gollancz and myself to point out every error and flaw in all previous editions, some of them not corrected since their first publication, and has enabled me to correct or revise them. I couldn't have completed this project without him. Together, I think, Gollancz, John Davey and myself have produced what will be the best editions possible and I am very grateful to him, to Malcolm Edwards, Darren Nash and Marcus Gipps for all the considerable hard work they have done to make this edition what it is.

Michael Moorcock

Contents

My Experiences in the Third World War   1

   Casablanca   3

   Going to Canada   27

   Leaving Pasadena   39

   Crossing into Cambodia   59

The Mountain   79

The Deep Fix   91

The Frozen Cardinal   153

Wolf   165

The Pleasure Garden of Felipe Sagittarius   173

The Real Life Mr Newman   187

The Cairene Purse   229

Acknowledgements   307

My Experiences in the Third World War

Casablanca

We are betrayed by what is false within.

– George Meredith

B EYOND THE DESERTED huts and artificial pools, far out to sea, like a cold wall around our world, a mist had formed. I saw an oil tanker moving through it, coming away from the Gulf, while on the harbour and the unkempt flat roofs, where TV dishes were raised like broken shields, a thin drizzle settled. I turned from the window but found no warmth in the room.

'Well, darling, you told me so! Panos is a complete bastard.' She advanced on me, put her hand on my arm, her head against my shoulder. 'Forgive me?' Her lips anticipated the pleasure of my assent.

Again I resisted the ritual. The effort was considerable. 'I'm tired of what you do,' I said. 'I'm going to leave you.'

'Sweetie!' Her disbelief was turning to fury at the prospect of being denied her usual blessing. I wondered if she had always loathed me and if every betrayal I had so far accepted had been from fear of that one terrible truth.

'Faithless...' I began, but moralising was beyond me. I had known her from the beginning. Any pain she caused was of my own seeking. I felt disgust. I stepped back from the balcony. 'We have to separate, Nadja.'

'That doesn't suit me.' She controlled herself. 'I need you.'

'I've nothing left to give. I'm exhausted.'

'I've been selfish. I didn't think.' But she gave up this approach almost at once, retrieving her dignity and her sense of perspective at the same time. She laughed. I had confirmed her view of the world. Her golden skin glowed like metal and her eyes were ancient stones.

'I'm going,' I said. 'I'm in an hotel on Rue de la Radiance du Sol. We'll be in contact, eh? I shan't want the flat immediately.' I was tempted to touch her hair for the last time; hair as delicate and as coarse as her love-making, as black as her most secret despair.

I turned my back on her. I turned my back on Africa. She went past me and stood on the balcony, deliberately re-entering my field of vision. She let the moisture settle in her hands, combing it into her hair, spreading Casablanca's oily atmosphere over her face, arms and shoulders and cleansing whatever vestiges of sin she imagined to be still visible on her body.

I wish that she had not made an awful sort of choking noise when I left.

My chief met me in the Travel Bureau, which was closed for the afternoon, its plate glass staring onto an almost deserted Boulevard Emile Zola, where a few cars moved in the brightening afternoon light. He was a thin man with a moustache modelled on Georgian lines, I would guess, so he looked like a wolfish caricature of Stalin, something he was unconscious of and would have been horrified to know. His name was Yagolovski. He had been born in Riga and was of that new breed of traditionalist who emerged from the Gorbachev period. We sat together in the empty chairs watching a video of the Barbados beaches reflected in the shop's window. 'You've made your plans?' he asked.

'She and I are finished.'

'And you're happy with that?' Yagolovski became avuncular with approval. 'You're a strong one. Good boy!'

I had not suffered such praise for many years.

All this happened some time ago, before I took up my last post in England and during that prolonged 'phoney' period prior to the outbreak of the World War. After my spell in Athens and before I settled in London, I was working in Casablanca. Most people will tell you that Casablanca is not the real Morocco but she remains my favourite. She was big, even in those days, with a population of around seven million, much of it in shanty towns, had a few remarkable features. Even her medina was sleazy in the way of the most industrial ports. The tourist trade, primarily dependent on the Bogart myth, had established holiday villages along the bleak and dangerous beaches, a series of bathing lagoons and some restaurants with names like *Villa Tahiti* and, of course, *Café Americaine*, which looked even grubbier in the foul weather blowing so frequently off the Atlantic.

The years of rain, following the drought of the '70s and '80s, were, of course, to Morocco's benefit and helped establish her as one of Africa's richest nations, but during my time in Casablanca most people were worried about what the wet weather would do to the vacation business.

If the rain had no serious effect on the port traffic and the factories, it was a relief for the people living in the countless shanties, since it cut down Casa's smog, the equal to Los Angeles', and made the city a little healthier. For a while local entrepreneurs had managed to sell fake Burberry trench coats to tourists determined to milk at least a little romance from a city having more in common with the reality of Liverpool than the fantasy of Hollywood.

As usual I was working as an art dealer, specialising chiefly in North African antiquities, and had been established in the name of Erich Volker, a Czech émigré, in the old harbour quarter's Rue Sour el Djedid, a street becoming fashionable amongst successful Moroccan bohemians, chiefly painters and photographers.

'Women are grief,' said Yagolovski. 'You should know that.' Out of deference to me he did not light the cigarette between his fingers. I was making one of my attempts to stop smoking. 'You're lucky this job came up.' Even in his sympathetic mood he reminded me of a jocular Stalin about to betray some old comrade. 'It will take you away from Casablanca. And, when you return, never fear – she'll have discovered some new supporter.' He cleared his throat and picked up a file. 'They're ten a penny.'

I welcomed his remarks. I did not need comfort at that stage. I was glad to be going.

'You like Marrakech, don't you?'

'For a holiday. Is that my destination?'

'Initially. You'll be staying at the Mamounia. It's well known, of course.'

The Mamounia had remained Morocco's most famous hotel for half a century and, like similar legendary hotels across the world, had never quite lost its romance or failed to disappoint, very slightly, those who had imagined for years how they might get there. I preferred the smaller hotels in the medina, or the Es Saadi, where the French show-people went and which offered an equally magnificent view of the High Atlas. At least I had never been to the Mamounia with Nadja. 'It was Churchill's favourite.' I looked out past the reflected waves and consciously took control of myself. 'He painted in their gardens. And I think de Gaulle, Roosevelt went there. Possibly Stalin. John Foster Dulles. And of course all those emirs and kings from the other side of Suez. It sounds as if I'm to hob-nob with a better class of people.'

When I looked at him Yagolovski was grinning. 'Just a richer class. No Saudi princes or Gulf sultans, I'm afraid.' He outlined the first part of my assignment, which was to make contact with an Algerian agent who would book into the Mamounia as an Egyptian businessman.

Although officially Morocco was no longer at war with Algeria, who had apparently given up ambitions in the old Spanish Sahara and withdrawn support for the Polisario guerrillas, there was still a great deal of political activity under the surface, much of it, of course, in relation to Libya and Algeria's frustration at having no Atlantic seaboard. For that reason we continued to maintain a department in Casablanca and another in Algiers.

'I suppose you want me to leave tomorrow,' I said.

Raising his unlit cigarette to his heavy moustache Yagolovski chuckled as he shook his head. 'Tonight,' he said. 'You meet your Egyptian businessman in the morning. But, believe me, this should take your mind off your troubles.'

The Marrakech plane was full of pale tourists going on to Agadir whose beaches were golden and whose hotels were high and white. A town destroyed by God, they said of the earthquake, restored by Man and populated by Satan. I think Satan was a euphemism for Europe. The nearest thing I had seen to even a simple *djinn* in that Moroccan Miami Beach was a German holidaymaker creeping out before dawn to lay claim to a pool-chair with his towel. The place consisted entirely of hotels, restaurants and tourist shops and was, I thought, an unfortunate vision of Morocco's future.

My own country was also eager for hard currency in those days, so I sympathised with Moroccan policies, even as I regretted the signs of standardisation which threatened to place a Laura Ashley and a McDonald's in every identical shopping mall from Moscow to Melbourne. Marrakech had kept so much of her character through her position in one of the country's richest agricultural areas while the Berbers in particular did not so much resist the evils of capitalism as ignore those aspects of it they did not need.

It was not in my nature to express judgements, but I would have been happy if the tourist industry had confined itself to North Africa's Atlantic coast.

The journey was short. By the time we landed at Minar Airport I was thinking of nothing but Nadja and already, of course, weakening. Walking from the plane to the embarkation building I put on my wide-brimmed panama and drew a deep breath of the relaxing heat, turning my face to a heaven which had something of that dark, moistureless desert blue of skies beyond the High Atlas. The soldiers on duty smoked and chatted, showing us only casual interest. I remembered what I had liked about Marrakech and why I feared her attraction. Of all Maghrebi cities, she possessed the greatest love of pleasure, a carelessness, a good humour, that reminded me of Cairo. The French had never been very secure in Marrakech. Her easy-going confidence derived, I think, from her once superior position as the centre of a great Berber Empire from the Pyrenees to the Sahara, successfully resisting all would-be outside conquerors. I suppose Casablanca's cautious cynicism, developed in the service of a dozen masters, was preferable to me.

After suffering the irritating passport and customs rituals which refused to distinguish residents from visitors, I found a taxi to take me to the Mamounia. I chatted in French with a driver who assumed me to be a tourist and recommended a variety of relatives for whatever goods or services I might require. I did not reveal any knowledge of Arabic. It is my habit to seem unfamiliar with languages. People have a way of revealing much more if they think you have only a word or two of their native tongue.

As we drove along the broad red avenues of the Menara quarter in the new town, I remembered how Nadja and I had wandered these streets when we were first together. I wondered if this were an important job or if my chief, knowing that it was in my interest to stay away from Casablanca as long as possible, had done me a favour. He, like all his kind, possessed a fatherly and sometimes unwelcome concern about the private lives of his officers. It is in the tradition of our Service and goes back long before the Revolution.

For my part, I should have been unhappy without that concern. 'Follow the rules and enjoy the love of the Father,' as the priests used to say in our little town. My mother was fond of the phrase and would repeat it sometimes like a litany. My own father's rules were inviolable but I could not say he loved any of us.

I grew up in the shadow of Stalin and, even though he was dead before my time, the old habits lived on. It makes us slow to take decisions sometimes, even now. But that is often no bad thing.

A case in point was our decision to remain in the Maghreb when almost everyone else removed their agencies altogether, usually leaving one officer at their consulate. An American friend of mine, who had guessed my job as I had guessed his, was amused by it. 'You Russians keep as many staff in warm countries as you can possibly justify. I don't blame you, with your hideous climate, but it's a standing joke amongst most intelligence crews. Your chiefs want to be sure of a few days of sunshine every year.' I was reminded of all the engineers, military experts and technicians volunteering for work in, for instance, Libya, and how Afghanistan with her awful winters had proved such a disappointment to certain colleagues.

We drove through broad streets cooled by tall palms, flanked by red-brown walls, by wrought iron which gave glimpses of villas decorated with bright tile and pastel lime-wash, with vibrant trailing flowers and vines, lush shrubs and trees, the New City, which we used to call the French City, lying outside the walls of the medina. The Mamounia was almost as famous a landmark as the tall, elegant outline of the Katoubia Mosque, the Mosque of the Booksellers, where from the surrounding shops, it was again possible to buy exquisitely printed editions of Ibn Rushd's Aristotle commentaries, al-Khwarizmi's mathematical treatises, as well as any number of editions of the Qur'an. Unlike the mosque, however, the Mamounia, lying just within the high crenellated walls of the medina at the Djedid Gate, had changed to meet changing times. My suitcase was taken from the taxi by a man dressed for a touring production of *The Desert Song* who carried it into a foyer half reproduction deco, half the interior of Los Angeles' *Dar Maghreb* restaurant.

I was a little shocked and at the same time amused. The place was a vulgar Arabian Nights fantasy, an authentic extension of Hollywood. I reflected that as Morocco grew richer she resembled California in all her ways. Perhaps this was the logic of wealth? Perhaps our notions of value and culture and human dignity were old-fashioned? Certainly nobody suffered in modern Marrakech as when the Caids held power.

I went to sleep in a bed whose canopy of red silk, whose massive purple pillows and yellow sheets would have put to shame the ostentation of a Turkish pasha and in the morning was served, on a tray of rosewood, silver and mother-of-pearl, coffee and croissants the rival of anything I had tasted in Paris. I showered in a black-and-silver stall almost the size of the flat I had been born in, then shaved and dressed, started down to the pool to keep my appointment, seemingly a casual meeting, in the shade of some palms.

I remembered when Nadja and I had stayed at a little hotel just outside the medina and seen the dawn rising in a pale mist of pink and blue: the palms and eucalyptus dark green against the red walls of the city. From some shuttered shop came the resonant lute and drum music of Rouicha Mohamed while elsewhere Azzahia sang of metaphysical love to inspire images of birds, animals and flowers as vivid as any picture. This was the perfect life of Marrakech or, at least, a perfect moment, a pause before the day began. The smell of sweet mint tea joined the aroma of baking bread and wood-smoke. She had told me how much she loved me and how she would always love me and I had had her again, as the sounds of the city rose around us like a symphony.

There were already a few Americans and Germans around the pool, distinguished from one another only by the tone of their tanning agents. My man stood smoking under an orange tree, apparently fascinated by the brilliant pinks of a bougainvillaea. He was tall and handsome, reminding me of an Egyptian film star I saw frequently on billboards in Casablanca. About thirty-five, with dark, sardonic eyes, carefully groomed black curly hair and moustache, he wore a grey silk suit which had not been bought this side of the Italian Riviera. His name, even his cover name, was unknown to me, but we had a rather childish conversation code for mutual identification.

'A beautiful morning,' I said.

'Like the first morning in Paradise.' He smiled. 'Have you been in Marrakech long?' He purred his words like a Cairene.

'A matter of hours. I live in Casablanca. I have a business there.' I replied in French.

We walked away from the pool. On the other side of the hotel wall came sounds of the city's ordinary commerce, the muezzin, a radio playing Rai hits.

I yawned. 'I'm still a little sleepy. I arrived late last night. The mountains are magnificent from my room.'

'Unfortunately I have only a concourse. You're in business in Morocco? That's interesting.'

'I deal in antiques.'

'Quite a coincidence,' he murmured in what was virtually

an aside to the tree. 'I sell cotton. I'm at present in Esna but my home's in Alexandria. You know Egypt, I suppose?'

'Fairly well. I do very little buying there now.'

'The export restrictions on that sort of thing are pretty much total. And if they're not there, it's clear what you buy is a fake!'

We talked a little longer, then shook hands and agreed to meet before lunch. At about noon, in a horse-drawn taxi, we toured the city's pink sandstone walls which served, among other things, to protect the medina from fierce winter sandstorms.

My contact smoked constantly. Eventually I accepted his offered Marlboro and, with a sense of considerable relief, lit it. I felt I gave my liberty up to a familiar and not unkind master. I had always understood the basic meaning of Islam, which was 'Surrender'. The Egyptian's name was Tewfik al-Boulekh, he said. We used English, of which our driver had only a few words.

'You'll be wanting to interview the boy?' He tossed a dirham coin towards the group of shouting children now running beside our carriage. Some scrambled for the money while others kept pace with us. I admired their stamina. 'M'sieu!' they called. 'Un dirham! Un dirham!' I was reminded of an English friend telling me how he had pursued American jeeps during the Second World War pleading for gum. Across the road men used materials and methods unaltered for a thousand years to rebuild the walls. The red mud blended with older remains of houses and stables. 'The Maghreb is so much cleaner than Egypt.'

'I know very little.' I thought it wise not to admit my complete ignorance. 'Is he here in Marrakech?'

'No, no.' He turned his head as our driver reined in suddenly to begin a passionate argument with a man whose donkey was almost hidden by a huge bundle of newly picked mint. Clutching at his brown-and-white-striped djellabah in a gesture that was as obscene as it was obscure, the Berber further enraged our cabman and brought another donkey-owner into the argument while passengers boarding a nearby bus, onto which one man was forcing two sheep he had just bought, turned with interest to witness the argument concerning the first donkey's absolute refusal to move from the tarmac to the strip of hardened mud beside it and so give the taxi a clear passage. Meanwhile we were joined by a score of astonishingly lovely Marrakshi children asking us for watches and money. I ignored them until we were on the move again then threw them a cheap Timex and some small change.

Al-Boulekh continued: 'The boy was born in France but his papers are absolutely authentic. There can be no question of his lineage.'

'Are his ancestors well known?'

The Egyptian laughed heartily. 'Oh, indeed!'

'Provenance is so important in my walk of life,' I said.

He dropped his voice. 'There is no question that our young friend is a direct descendant of the Prophet. If anything his blood is better than any ruling Fatimid.'

I hid my surprise and cursed my chief for not warning me of the fantastic nature of the assignment. I regarded the Algerian agent with increased suspicion. Was I to be involved in some bizarre kidnapping? Even during my early days with the Service such schemes had fallen out of fashion.

We went together to Djemaa el-Fna. The great central square of Marrakech was crowded as always with every kind of produce, entertainer and tourist. It always reminded me, I told my companion, of London's Portobello Road. There were spice-sellers and foodstalls, fruit and vegetables, pots and pans, and two great hand-cart displays of Japanese digital timepieces. The modern goods were offered side by side with rugs, pottery and tools in use since the city's foundation when William the Conqueror was making London his capital.

We sat at a table outside the *Café de France*. I had the *simple* and my Algerian-Egyptian had the *filtre*.

'You know where we are going tomorrow?' he asked.

'I believe I am to travel to the other side of the mountains.' I gestured with my cup at the distant peaks.

'We have to be pretty cautious at this moment.' Chiefly because I had no cigarettes myself I refused his offered Marlboro.

After lunch we walked through the souk and then went to the

Majorelle Gardens, the *Bou Saf Saf*, whose entrance was in a little side street in the Gueliz district not far from the Doukkala Gate. As usual the botanical gardens were almost deserted and I was immediately captured by their peacefulness. I am always impressed by the Arab appreciation of zones of tranquillity, little bits of paradise on earth, though this particular garden was the creation of a French painter.

'There's nothing like this in Cairo now.' Al-Boulekh was impressed. 'People have to go beyond the pyramids if they want some space. That city should be a warning to us.'

I told him Cairo was one of my favourite cities. Given her thirty million inhabitants, she was a splendid example of how people of disparate religions and politics could survive together, however tenuously.

This did not suit his own views. Changing the subject, he said he had known a Volker in Munich who ran a little private toy museum there, near the open market. Was I a relative? I told him I was not German but had been born near Prague and emigrated with my parents in the 1950s. He accepted this lie as readily as he accepted any other story from me. He had that way of Mediterranean and African peoples, who seem to judge you not by the accuracy but by the quality of your accounts. For his benefit I next invented a trek across no man's land, guards shooting at us, my little sister being killed.

'Yet now you work again for the Russians?' He introduced a sudden reality into our exchange.

I laughed aloud and he joined me; just, I decided, for the relief of it. Since we demanded no superficial logic of our ancient myths and legends, why should we demand it of our modern ones?

We paused beside a mosaic fountain, under great feathery branches of trees which had covered the Earth before the first fish crawled to land and filled its lungs.

'There's an economic crisis coming here.' He blew smoke towards a sky so blue and still it might have been painted by a New York pop artist. 'Until now King Hassan has been able to control the Left. But with the population explosion, the growth of a restless, newly educated, largely unemployable middle class, the collapse of their European markets, and before the Libyan trouble, the situation will soon become volatile, wouldn't you say?'

I agreed his projection had some basis in truth, though privately I believed Morocco could solve her problems and maintain a stability already making her one of the most progressive countries in Africa.

'The Left on its own has no-one to lead a successful coup. We've nobody in the UNFP. And anyway all the attempted coups have come from the Right. The Left needs a good alternative to Hassan III. His sons won't do, of course. Hassan can't last very much longer. It's at that point we have the chance to win the country over.'

'You expect us to co-operate with you in financing a revolution?' I was incredulous.

'It wouldn't amount to anything hugely disruptive. Not with the cards we have to play.'

'I thought your people had stopped supporting the Polisarios?' The guerrillas of the old Spanish Sahara had been neutralised in their bid for an independent nation controlling the phosphate mines which gave Morocco so much of its hard currency.

'You know the pressure we were under.' He began to walk down one of the brick paths towards a group of sinuous plants whose brilliant, spikey blossoms suggested they had been brought from the continental interior. 'We expected the United States to reduce her aid. Instead she increased it. For a while she was almost as generous to Morocco as she was to Israel. Yet somehow Hassan kept faith with everyone. Largely because of his importance to Islam. There are not many like him left.' He meant, I assumed, that Hassan was a descendant of the Prophet's daughter, Fatima, which many accepted as the purest of all royal bloodlines. 'His survival has proved to many Islamic leaders, even those directly opposed to his policies, that he is Allah's chosen. Well, you know that. His *baraka* has never been more evident.'

This was European logic, of which I was always suspicious if presented by an Arab, yet again I was bound to agree with him.

The word, distinctly Arabic, had a wealth of meaning – a mixture of status, charisma, chutzpah, glamour and good fortune which, in a world whose rulers, even socialist presidents, were regarded as God's representatives as well as the State's, was of crucial significance now that the fundamentalists gained so much power. My chief always complained how our Moscow people refused to understand that to Moslems, even our own Moslems, politics and religion were synonymous.

'The problem,' my companion continued, 'has never been how to overthrow Hassan, but who will replace him.'

Again I agreed. Sentimentally, of course, I could see no possible point in replacing Hassan, whose grandfather had proved himself since 1976 (when, leading his people into the desert, he had peacefully occupied the Spanish Sahara) a brilliant politician. His esteem in the country and throughout the world had never been higher. Moroccan troops had fought bravely beside Syrians in the Golan Heights while at the same time Hassan had encouraged Jews to return to his country, displaying that tolerance for other faiths which his greatest ancestors had exercised throughout their long rule in Africa and Europe. He had demonstrated ethical and pragmatic judgement at least equal to Egypt's and any hint of our interfering with his rule would lose us authority throughout the world.

I wondered why my chief, who knew my admiration for Hassan, had given me this task. Hassan was everything great that Stalin could have been. But Stalin was a failed priest, ever unable to placate his own ghosts or reconcile his past with a future for which he had relinquished his place in heaven. Self-sacrifice is always borne with greater dignity if that sacrifice is proved of value.

The Egyptian again revealed his obsession. 'This boy has Almohad, Fatimid and Abbasid blood. By showing increased support to orthodoxy he could win unprecedented influence through the entire Islamic world. It might be truly united for the first time in history!'

'Under whom?' I asked. He did not reply.

We walked back from the gardens and visited some of the shopping streets of the French Quarter. He paused in the Place du 16 Novembre outside a motorbike showroom. Staring through the display window al-Boulekh was surprised by a poster on which three Japanese women in one-piece bathing suits advertised a new Kawasaki.

'Doesn't it occur to you how behind the times we are in this profession?' I said. 'The Japanese concern themselves with commercial espionage, with the empire of the market place. It makes a great deal of sense.'

He was predictably disapproving. 'It certainly does, if you've something to sell. These days Moscow has very little people want except gas. You relied on exporting an ideal.'

'But that's a bit obsolete now. These days we're trying for the consumer market. We're out of practice.'

He was dismissive. 'If the War doesn't escalate, you'll do it, I'm sure. You still have a low-paid and extremely well-disciplined work-force.'

I found myself unamused by his irony. I remained suspicious of Arab socialists. I was more comfortable with traditional power-seekers.

We returned to the Mamounia and I went to my room, having agreed to see him for dinner. On impulse I put through a call to Casablanca but was told that there was no reply. Trying to avoid thinking of Nadja, I watched a James Cagney movie on television, *Yankee Doodle Dandy* dubbed into French with Arabic subtitles. Eventually I turned the TV off and listened to the radio news. As usual England was justifying some piece of American gunboat diplomacy to her EC allies while Israel accused Syria of arming the Jews for Palestine guerrillas recently allied to the PLO. South Africa's invasion of Mozambique and Libya's 'border dispute' with Tunisia seemed to be taking place unopposed.

These familiar reports were comforting. When the Folklorique performances followed I was irritated and found a Tunisian discussion on the changing face of France. Maghrebis share that complicated fascination with their former rulers which Indians have with the British. Not everyone benefits from colonialism and there are many losses in the name of Western progress, but I cannot dismiss all imperialist expansion as harmful. I was raised in a tradition, old-fashioned in the non-Communist world before I was born, and it is still hard for me not to take a paternalist view of what was once the Third World, especially since paternalism prevails there. We Russians understand and accept the nature of power rather more readily than the ambivalent English, for instance, or those who inherited and developed their particular brand of imperialism, the Americans.

Until I was on the edge of sleep I gave no thought to what al-Boulekh had told me. The Egyptian's story seemed the fantastic concoction of some distant intelligence agency without enough real business. According to the Algerians I was to meet a young man whose Sharifian lineage, just on one strand alone, went back to the seventeenth-century Alouite sultans of Marrakech. With such potent blood, the Egyptian claimed, Hassan and his family could be deposed and a régime more closely aligned to the world be installed in Rabat. To me the scheme, even if the boy's ancestry were perfect, was so pointless and reminiscent of a foolish nineteenth-century Ottoman plot that I was hardly able to stop scoffing at it on the spot. Yet the Egyptian revealed himself as being closely involved with and committed to the scheme. Doubtless he had supplementary ambitions.

'Wait until you meet him,' he had said. 'You'll be won over.'

I had my orders. I had no choice. The next morning we were to drive over the High Atlas to a small town on the edge of the Sahara which had been colonised by Club Med and was primarily patronised by middle-class French people in their late thirties. In 1928 Ouarzazate had been a Foreign Legion garrison town on the site of an old kasbah and was more than once attacked by various bands of determined irregulars, who refused to accept European protection and were still not completely pacified at the outbreak of the Second World War.

At that time Route P31 over the Tizi 'n' Tichka Pass to the Draa Valley was, after the first few miles, somewhat bleak, rising about

8,000 feet amongst peaks still snow-capped and frequently as barren as those parts of the Lake District where as an exchange student I once hiked. Until spring, when wild flowers make them vibrant, they are unremarkable mountains, dotted with ruined kasbahs from which local chieftains, controlling the caravan routes and trails, had raided as successfully as the Scottish robber barons in the Highlands.

Obviously familiar with the range, my companion drove our Avis Renault at headlong speed around the mountain roads, his horn frequently in use, occasionally missing a collision with a truck or a tourist bus. The radio was turned up to full volume. *'Too tired to make it, too tired to fight about it'*, sang al-Boulekh with the Eagles. As we descended towards the Draa we followed the river, the Oued Imini, south-east through shale slopes and grey-black rock occasionally brightened by a little foliage, a narrow strip of cultivated land, a small goat herd or a dusty, broken tower.

For twenty years Old Ouarzazate, the provincial capital, had been the location of so many Hollywood films that it immediately struck a romantic chord. The low, pleasant houses, the crenellated walls, the half-ruined kasbah, the palm trees and oases where nomads came to trade, were familiar to anyone who ever saw *Lawrence of Arabia*. The reality confirmed the fantasy so thoroughly it seemed they were the same.

Al-Boulekh told me a little of his work with the Polisario guerrillas. Until recently he said they had camped not a hundred miles from here. The Algerians were too cautious to involve directly any of their own people, so the contact officers had been, like al-Boulekh, from friendly Arab countries or else were disaffected Berbers, sometimes Moroccan Taureqs considering a career move. Pressured by us, the Americans and the Arab League, Algeria had agreed to stop even her indirect Polisario support. That war drained everyone and had only strategic results for the Polisarios. Ironically, Morocco was at one time forced to put more men and money into that particular field than the French spent maintaining power over the whole Maghreb.

Al-Boulekh was tired by the drive and wanted a drink. I

suggested stopping at a little place called *Zitoun*, the Olive Grove, but he shook his head.

'It's hard now to find a public bar in Ouarzazate. *Zitoun* doesn't sell alcohol. For a while, you know, Club Med had the monopoly. Did you ever try to get a beer in Moulay Idris?'

'That's hardly a good example. It's a holy town.'

He shrugged. Like so many younger Arabs he equated drinking with modernity. He would no more patronise a café which did not sell liquor than he would sit and listen to the love songs of Oum Kalthoum, the classical Egyptian singer I admired. He only listened to American pop, he had said, like Dire Straits. So he preferred, I replied, to hear old millionaires from San Luis Obispo wailing their contempt for microwaves and colour televisions? There had been a familiar note of puritanism in his voice, echoing writers I had known who dismissed narrative, or painters who loathed anything remotely figurative: an attitude which in Europe had seemed radically progressive many years earlier but which I nowadays found embarrassing. We had entered a more conservative phase of our cultural history and I was consoled by it. But at least he had revealed something of his moral view and I felt pleasantly satisfied by this, as if I had mysteriously gained an advantage in an unfamiliar game.

Near the old Glaovi Kasbah we found a pleasant restaurant with rooftop seats looking down onto Ouarzazate's ever-expanding main street, where stalls now sold trinkets, handicrafts and Pakistani brasswork to tourists. In the uncompromising near-desert heat German automobiles manoeuvred for space with donkeys, bicycles, horsemen and ancient trucks whose gaudy decoration was reminiscent of the nomad tents we had passed coming in. Once a detachment of smart Moroccan soldiers marched by. I almost mistook them for paras. Their presence surprised me.

'Is the Sahara trouble starting up again?' I asked as I sipped my Valgrave.

'Who knows?' He had stretched out his long legs and was as relaxed as the hopeful cats who sat politely around us.

'You, possibly?' I was sardonic. I guessed he had high ambitions.

'Oh, we're nothing but intermediaries. You understand that. Messenger boys at best. Even you, Monsieur Volker, in spite of your rank.'

I was mildly amused by this display of knowledge. I had no information about him, but someone had shown him a dossier on me.

'I'm a simple antique dealer,' I said. 'A Czech émigré.'

'I had forgotten.' It seemed a genuine apology.

When he had finished his beer we drove to the Club Med buildings. The great kasbah-style walls looked as if they might have resisted the whole of Abd'-al-Krim's 1920s tribal army. Had it not been for some kind of special pass displayed by al-Boulekh, I think we could have found it impossible to reach the reception area.

The place was decorated in French-Moorish, a rather unhappy combination of two splendid aesthetics, and we were greeted by a pretty young Berber woman stylish in Parisian casuals. Her name was R'Kia and she was the Customer Relations Liaison Officer. She had been told to expect us. Normally, she said, visits from relatives were discouraged by the Club. She was charming. She was sure we could understand why these rules existed.

I told her I too was a great believer in rules, and she was winningly grateful. She led us around the pool where near-naked women stretched themselves on loungers and their men played water-football or lay playing electronic games, through an archway, up a short stair until we stood outside a bright blue door on which she tapped.

During the pause I said: 'You have a world of your own here.' We were all speaking French.

'Yes. You never need to leave, if you don't want to. Everything is provided.' She called through the door. 'Monsieur Maquin. Your uncle and his friend are here.'

The door was opened by a handsome boy of about twenty dressed in shorts and grey silk beach shirt. He was below middle height but had the physique of a body-builder. He shook hands, greeting us in an educated Parisian accent. I guessed that French was his first language. It was immediately obvious why al-Boulekh was convinced and why our Odessa office had given credence to the scheme. The boy radiated *baraka*.

Alain Makhainy knew nothing of my people's involvement and, I would guess, had not been told of any historic destiny planned for him by whatever Algerian Secret Service department had concocted this Ruritanian scheme to replace him at the head of the Moroccan state. Al-Boulekh had described his vision of a shining new monarch coming out of the desert at the head of an Algerian-Russian equipped army to unite the Maghreb, including Libya, into one powerful nation. Wild as the plan was, many people in those days of flux would have given it credence. Myths of hope were in short supply. It was not the most bizarre plan invented by the world's intelligence agencies, nor the most dangerous. Indeed, in retrospect, it has for me a certain innocence. At that time, however, in a very different climate, I was utterly sceptical.

Makhainy took us to a bar with a wide balcony looking out over the battlements to palms and a shallow stream. When I tried to pay for our drinks he laughed and gave the waiter some coloured beads from his pocket. 'This is the only currency we're allowed here.'

The boy believed he was to be interviewed for a sensitive job representing one of the main international banks where his lineage would stand him in unusually good stead with Arab clients.

I questioned him about his parents, who were both second-generation Parisians. His grandfather had come from Lebanon and his grandmother from Sinai. During the War they had lived in Casablanca. His maternal grandparents were both Palestinian Arabs who had emigrated to Lyons after 1947. He had birth certificates, family photographs, documents of every kind from half a dozen French and Arab authorities, including references to his ancestors in a variety of Islamic historical texts. His paternal grandfather was the son of a mutual ancestor of the Moroccan Sultans. They had been a distinguished family of Islamic judges and scholars. In France, as merchants, they had experienced great wealth for a while. I was in no doubt about his bloodlines, neither was I surprised by his family's recent past. Not everyone desires to be a prince or even an eminent holy man. 'My parents are French citizens,' he said. 'My father was a socialist.'

'And you?' I asked casually.

He shrugged. 'I am a child of my age. I need a well-paid job which will make the best use of my talents.'

'You are fluent in Arabic?' I asked in that language.

'A bit rusty,' he told me. 'But practice should take care of that. Eh, m'sieu?' He offered me a wonderful smile. I think he had the measure of his own gifts. 'I am not a practising Moslem.'

The Egyptian and I stayed overnight at a local *fonduk*, rather like one of those pensions you used to find in provincial France, and which had the same air of flyblown cosiness. We each had a single iron-framed bed and the Turkish toilet facilities on the floor below.

Al-Boulekh was elated by what he was certain had been a successful encounter. 'Isn't he perfect?' He had removed his European clothes and sat on his bed's edge wearing a blue-and-white Alexandrian gelabea.

'He's certainly convincing and he has personality.' I carefully folded my clothes and sat them on the tiled floor. 'Let's hope he does well at the doctor's examination.'

He frowned from where he lay with a book supported by his pillows. 'A doctor? What for?'

'Oh, it's one of our rules,' I said. 'You know what bureaucracies are like. Moscow will want it.'

'He doesn't look the type to have a heart attack.' Then he smiled. 'I know. You're worried about AIDS. I'm sure he's fundamentally heterosexual.'

I said nothing to this. Neither did I tell him how much I had liked the young man and, unusually for me, did not wish him to be destroyed by what I considered an already doomed adventure. Algeria had taken the wrong lessons from us. Times and methods were changing rapidly. At that stage we were hoping to avert what the Americans called 'a major conflict'.

'And he can always brush up his Arabic,' said al-Boulekh.

Next morning we returned to Marrakech. The Egyptian was exceptionally friendly on the journey back and even turned off the radio at my request, whereupon he outlined the great benefits of the Maghreb's unification. 'What Hassan did for Morocco, Hamed – his original name – will do for the whole of North Africa. Imagine! A unified socialist Arab alliance the length and breadth of the Mediterranean from the Atlantic to the Red Sea. And what an example for the rest of Africa! Within a couple of generations they could form a bloc as powerful as Europe!' Was this naïveté a display for my benefit?

I envied him, I said, his old-fashioned optimism. In my own country Lenin's great ideal was giving way to Lenin's equally great pragmatism and it was fashionable to describe how Stalin had lost the way, that Lenin had foreseen what could go wrong and thus had introduced the New Economic Policy which, essentially, most well-established former socialist states were now reproducing. There is sometimes nothing worse than being taken for the representative of an ideal – or even a sexual preference – one has discarded in the light of experience.

In Marrakech I tried to phone my flat from the airport while I waited for the delayed plane but my operator was unable, he said, to make the connection, though I insisted I had heard the number ring. I had decided to try one last time to come to an agreement with Nadja and felt urgently she should know.

The plane eventually came in from Agadir. It was packed with sun-reddened tourists wearing locally bought straw hats, Rose Sarkissian shirts covered in rhinestones and gilded cowboy emblems, and cheaply made kaftans. I found a seat on the smoking side of the plane. Moroccans had solved the problem of non-smoking accommodation by simply dividing the plane down the middle. Halfway to Casablanca I bought a packet of English cigarettes from the stewardess but did not light one until I was outside the airport waiting for my car.

I went straight to the office and gave my report to my chief.

'You seem unimpressed,' he said. It was raining heavily. The water poured like mercury down the plate glass. 'This is a little awkward for me.'

'He's a very personable young man. Simply tell him he has to have a medical before we can give him a firm answer.'

'You're not normally so assertive.' Without comment he accepted a Silk Cut from my packet. 'Very well. I'll tell Odessa. And they'll tell Moscow. And we'll hear in a month. You think the scheme's crazy, don't you?'

'And you?'

I expected no reply.

He shrugged. 'Otherwise, you'd say he was what he claims?'

'I think claims are being made for him. All he wants is an easy, well-paid job. But yes – he's kosher.' And I smiled as I picked up my bag. 'I think the Algerians are trying to get back into the game. He's all they have at present.'

He was equally amused. 'Very romantic, Erich. Just like the Great Game, eh?' Typical of his years, he was a keen reader of Kipling and Jack London. 'More like a plot from the turn of the century. Don't you feel nostalgic? Like a character in John Buchan. Or one of those old Alexander Korda movies?'

'Our destinies are just as determined by mythology as were our ancestors'. I used to be frightened by the idea.'

'That girl of yours, by the way, has a new gentleman friend. A Tunisian sardine wholesaler. Named Hafid. You'll be at your hotel?'

'My flat. I have some stuff there I want.'

He said nothing as he watched me leave.

I enjoyed the walk through the rain to the taxi stand. The car took me along the seafront with its closed-down bars and abandoned nightclubs, its waterlogged beach umbrellas and torn red-, white- and blue-striped awnings, its drunks in their filthy European suits, its desolate whores. I was sure the boy would be found to be uncircumcised. An uncircumcised Moslem is a contradiction in terms. If he did not know Arabic well, he did not know the Qur'an and therefore had no prospect of a crown by that route. Without our support, he was not the slightest threat to Hassan or his sons, all of whom were thoroughly educated in Islam. The Egyptian clearly had some sort of financial stake in this scheme.

The taxi dropped me off outside the whitewashed walls of my building. When I pressed the code on the electronic lock there was some trouble with it and I could not get in. I shivered as I put my finger to my own bell and was answered by Nadja's voice.

'It's Volker,' I said. 'I'm back from Marrakech.'

After a short pause she pushed the button to admit me. I walked up the stairs, obscurely thinking I should give her a little time before I reached the door, but she had opened it and was waiting for me as I walked in. Her clothes were unfamiliar. She wore a tight red skirt and a gold blouse. Her make-up had created a stranger. She was already established in her newest rôle.

'I'm leaving in the morning,' she told me. There were a few boxes and suitcases packed. 'I shan't take much.'

'Perhaps you'll let the concierge have my keys,' I said.

'Of course,' she said. 'You look tired. Your trip didn't do you much good.'

'Oh, I enjoyed myself, I think. A little.' I turned to go. 'The department knows about your Tunisian. You'll be careful, I hope. No mistakes. Nothing about me.'

She took my warning without expression and then kissed me gravely. 'For a while,' she said, 'I thought I had worked a miracle. I convinced myself I had brought the dead to life.'

My answering smile appeared to disturb her.

Going to Canada

I WAS ORDERED to Canada; that pie-dish of privilege and broken promises: to Toronto. My chief was uncomprehending when I showed disappointment. 'Canada! Everybody wants to go there.'

'I have stayed in Toronto before,' I told him.

He knew. He became suspicious, so I said that I had been joking. I chuckled to confirm this. His old, Great Russian face, moulded by the imposition of a dozen conflicting tyrannies, made a little mad smile. 'You are to look up Belko, an émigré. He is the only Belko in the phone book.'

'Very well, Victor Andreyevitch.' I accepted the colourful paper wallet of tickets and money. This supply was an unusual one. My 'front' normally allowed me to be self-supporting. I work as an antique-dealer in the Portobello Road.

'Belko knows why you are meeting him. He will tell you what you have to know. It concerns some American planes, I gather.'

I shook hands and descended the green-carpeted stairs into the rain of East London.

During our Civil War many pretended to be Bolsheviks in order to terrorise local communities. After the war these people had continued as commissars. It had been their class which had gradually ousted most of the original Marxists. Stalin became their leader and exemplar. My father had been a member of that embryonic aristocracy.

Like the order it had replaced, our aristocracy had been founded on banditry and maintained by orthodox piety. I was a younger son without much of a patrimony. Previously I might

27

have gone into the priesthood or the army. I went into the modern combination of both, the KGB. The KGB was a far more conventional and congenial profession than most Westerners imagine. There I enjoyed myself first as a minor bureaucrat in a Moscow department, later as a special officer on one of our passenger ships plying between Leningrad and New York, Odessa and Sydney. Later still I became a plant in London where until recently I lived for twelve relatively uneventful years. I flattered myself that my background and character suited me to the rôle of a seedy near-alcoholic dealer in old furniture and overpriced bric-à-brac. It was believed that I was a Polish expatriate and indeed I had taken the name and British passport of just such an émigré; he had returned voluntarily to Poland on a whim and had sold his old identity to us in a perfectly amiable arrangement. We eased his way with the Cracow authorities who granted him new papers and found him a flat and a job.

In spite of changing régimes my own life had remained relatively untroubled. My name in London was Tomas Dubrowski. For my private amusement I preferred the name of Tom Conrad. It was this name, in '30s 'modern' lettering, which adorned my shop. I paid taxes, VAT, and owned a TV licence. Although I had no particular desire to maintain my part for ever, I enjoyed it for its complete lack of anxiety and the corresponding sense of security it gave me. Now that I was to return briefly to the real world, I should have to seek a fresh *context*.

A Russian citizen requires a *context*, because his conditioning makes him a permanent child. Anything will do. Therefore the *context* is often simple slavery. Even I, of Jewish Ukrainian extraction (through my grandmother), need that sense of boundaries. It is probably no coincidence that Kropotkin, founder of modern anarchism, was a Russian: his defiant views are directly opposed to our needs, which are on the whole of an authoritarian nature.

My father had been a naval petty officer. Later he became 'commissar' of a small town in Belorussia. He had eleven other deserting sailors with him when he had arrived in early 1918. They represented themselves as Bolsheviks. He had worn a leather jacket with two Mauser pistols in his belt and he had rarely taken off his sailor's peaked cap. Somehow the civil war did not touch the town much, so the gang made the most of its time.

My father took five young girls from the local gymnasium for himself and gave the rest to his men. He instructed the girls in every debauchery. When the civil war ended and it became obvious who had won, my father did not do away with the girls (as he might well have – it was common practice) but made them read to him from the works of Marx and Engels, from Lenin's writings, *Pravda* and *Izvestia* until he and they were all familiar with the new dogma. Then he formed his thugs into the nucleus of the local Party, sent four of the girls (now fully fledged Komsomol leaders) back to the gymnasium as teachers and married Vera Vladimirovna, my mother.

In time he was praised for his example to the community and was awarded a medal by the State. During the famines of the next few years he and my mother were never hungry. During the purges they never seemed to be in danger. They had two children, a boy and a girl.

In 1936 my father went off on Party business and in 1938 I was born. The young writer who begat me was subsequently sent to a camp and died. I had long considered myself the secret guardian of his blood. My father was in most respects a realist. He preferred to accept me as his own rather than risk the scandal of his name being associated with that of the writer. My older sister was killed in the War. My older brother became a hero during the Siege of Stalingrad. He ran a large power plant near Smolensk on the Dnieper. He was a self-satisfied, right-thinking man.

'A little pain,' my mother used to say to her friends, 'makes good girls of us all.'

My father trained his girls to kiss his feet, his legs, his private parts, his arse. My mother was more wholehearted at this than her rivals, which is how he came to pick her as his wife. Again, she behaved in a Russian way. She was dutiful in all things, but, when his authority was absent, she became irresponsible. The Russian soul is a masochist's wounds. It is a frightening, self-indulgent, monumentally sentimental relinquishing of individual responsibility: it is schizophrenic. More than elsewhere, personal suffering is equated with virtue.

My grandmother was apparently raped by a young Jew and my mother was the result. The Jew was killed shortly afterwards, in a general pogrom resulting from the affair. That was in Yekaterinaslav province in the last years of the nineteenth century. My grandmother never would say for certain that it had been rape. I remember her winking at me when the word was mentioned. My great-uncle, the surviving brother of the dead man, told me that after the Revolution some Red Cossacks came to his shtetl. He was mortally afraid, of course, and would have done anything to stay alive. A Cossack named Konkoff billeted himself in my great-uncle's house. My great-uncle was mindless with terror, grovelling before the Cossack, ready to lick the soles off his boots at the first demand. Instead, Konkoff had laughed at him, offered him some rations, pulled him upright, patted him on the back and called him 'comrade'. My great-uncle realised that the Revolution had actually changed things. He was no longer a detested animal. He had become a Cossack's pet Jew.

In Russia, in those days before the present war, there had been a resurgence of Nationalism, encouraged by the State. Because of the absence of real democratic power, many had turned (as they did under Tsarism) to Pan-Slavism. A direct consequence of this movement was anti-Semitism, also blessed unofficially by the State, and a spirit amongst our élite which, while not so unequivocally anti-Semitic, was reminiscent of the Black Hundreds or the Legion of the Archangel Michael, the early-twentieth-century pogromists. It was obvious that the State equated radicalism with intellectual Jewish troublemakers. The State therefore encouraged – through the simple prejudices of its cunning but not considerably intelligent leaders – a movement in no way dissimilar to that which had followed the troubles of 1905, when Jewish socialists had been scapegoats for everything. Stalin had eliminated virtually the entire Jewish element of the Party, of course, by 1935.

When I was young it had been fashionable to scoff at the trappings of Nationalism – at folk costumes, at peasant blouses and so on. Outside of cultural exhibitions and performances these things were a sign of old-fashioned romanticism. They were not considered progressive. When I returned to Russia briefly in 1980 young people were walking the streets looking as if they had stepped out of a performance of *Prince Igor*. Even some of the younger leaders would on occasions be photographed in Cossack costume. Anti-Semitic books and paintings, even songs, received official patronage. The authoritarian republic had at last, in sixty years, managed to resemble in detail the autocracy it had replaced. Soon there would be no clear differences save that poverty and sickness had been abolished in the Slavic regions of the Union.

These benefits had been gained by relinquishing dignity and liberty, and the nobler forms of idealism which had given the early Revolution its rhetoric and its impetus. There were no longer any private arts. Everything had been sacrificed to formalised ceremonies similar to Church ritual or other primitive affirmations of superstition. The Soviet Union had codified and sanctified this terrifying impulse of human beings to shout reassuring lies to one another while standing with eyes tight shut on the brink of a chasm of reality. The State pretended that it was impossible (or at very least immoral) for such a chasm to exist. Soviet bureaucracy, too, formalised human failing and gave it shape and respectability; it did not merely accept this failing: it exalted it. I was as conditioned as anyone to believe that our lobotomising methods of ordering the human condition were the most sensible. I had found all these aspects of Soviet life comforting and reassuring. I did not have the character necessary for the enjoyment of personal freedom.

Like the Celts, Russians have no ethical system as such, merely a philosophy of life based firmly on the dignity of pain, on fear of the unknown and suspicion of anything we cannot at once recognise. That is why Bolshevism was so attractive an ideology to many peasants who identified it with a benevolently modified Church and Monarchy and for a time believed that Lenin intended to restore the Tsar to his throne; it is why it was so quickly adapted to Russian needs and Russian methods. I do not disapprove of the government of the Soviet Union. I accept it as a necessity. In 1930, as a result of the bourgeois Revolution headed by Kerensky, and the Revolution initiated by the bourgeois Lenin, women and children were starving to death all over Russia. Stalin was at heart an Orthodox peasant. He and other Orthodox peasants saved Russia from the monster released upon the nation by foolish, middle-class idealists. In doing so he punished the Communists who had brought about the disaster; the intellectuals and fanatics who were truly to blame for our misfortunes.

Stalin took on the great burden and responsibilities of a Tsar and all his ministers. Stalin knew that History would revile him and that his followers would become cynical and cruel. He countered their cynicism and cruelty with the only weapon he was able to use: terror. He became mad. He was himself not a cynic. He made factories efficient. He gave us our industry, our education, our health service. He made homes clean and sanitary. He killed millions for the sake of all those other millions who would otherwise have perished. He made it possible for us to round, eventually, on Hitler and drive him back to Germany. He returned to us the security of our Empire. And when he died we destroyed his memory. He knew that we would and I believe that he understood that this would have to happen. He was a realist; but he possessed an Orthodox conscience and his conscience made him mad. I am a realist happily born of an age which countered and adapted Christianity and that is doubtless what continues to make me such a good and reliable employee of the Russian State.

Because of the increasingly strict controls applied to those who wished to travel to and from Canada, it was necessary for me to go to my doctor for a medical certificate. I used a fashionable private doctor in South Kensington who was quick to prescribe the drugs I required. In his waiting room I found three young women wearing the elaborate and violent make-up and costume then favoured by the British demi-monde. They were whispering together in a peculiar way common only to whores and nuns, full of sudden shifts of volume and tone and oblique reference, glances and gestures, so I only heard snatches of their conversation.

'I was doing this job, you know – straight… At the club. He said he wanted me to work for him – you know – so I said I wouldn't – he said to go out with him – but I wouldn't – he was a funny guy, you know – he gave me this –' A bandaged arm was held up. It was a soft arm in a soft dress. 'He had a bottle, you know – they called the cops – they're prosecuting – his lawyer phoned me and offered me thirty thousand to settle out of court…'

'Settle,' advised one of the other girls.

'I would,' said the second.

'But my lawyer says we can get fifty.'

'Settle for thirty.'

'He gave me seventeen stitches.' All this was relayed in a neutral, almost self-satisfied tone. 'What you doing here, anyway?'

'I just came with her,' said the prettiest. 'It's about her pills.'

'I came to get my slimming pills changed. Those others make me feel really sick, you know.'

'What! Durophets?'

'Yeah. They make me feel terrible.'

'What you going to ask him for? Terranin?'

'They're what I use,' said her friend.

'They're much better,' agreed the wounded whore. 'You're looking different,' she told the girl's friend. 'I wouldn't have recognised you. You're looking terrible.'

They all laughed.

'Did you know what happened to Mary?' She put her mouth close to the girl's ear and began to whisper rapidly.

The doctor's receptionist opened the door. 'You can go in now, Miss Williams.'

'… all over the bed,' finished Miss Williams, rising and following the receptionist.

When she had gone the other two began to discuss her in a disinterested fashion, as if they followed some unconscious habit. Neither, it emerged, believed that thirty thousand pounds had been offered. 'More like three,' said one. They, too, were not at all outraged by the event. Most whores are frightened of any demonstration of passion, which is why they choose masters who treat them coldly. I had for a short while been in charge of a whore-house in Greece and had learned how to deal with the girls who were conditioned to confuse love with fear. If they were afraid of their master they thought they loved him. Because they were not afraid of their clients they could not love them and in the main felt contempt for them. But it was self-contempt they actually felt. I remembered with some dismay the single-mindedness of such girls who pursued persecution and exploitation as an anodyne, as their customers often pursued sexual sensation; who learned to purchase the favours of their employers with the very money they received from the hire of their own bodies. My spell as a whore-master had been the only time I had tasted direct power and it had taken every ounce of self-discipline to administer; it was a relief to become what I now was.

Miss Williams rejoined her friends. 'I'm going to have it photographed this afternoon,' she told them, pulling down her sleeve.

The two girls went in to the doctor. They came out. All three left together.

I was next in the surgery. The doctor smiled at me. 'More trouble?'

I shook my head.

'The penicillin worked?'

'Yes.'

'It's funny that. Acts like a shot on you, won't touch me. Well, what's the trouble?' He spoke rapidly in a high-pitched voice. He was a Jew.

'None. I just need a certificate to say I'm not suffering from anything a Canadian's likely to catch.'

He laughed. 'That depends on you, doesn't it?' He was already reaching for his pad of forms. 'Canada, eh? Lucky you.'

He filled in the form swiftly and handed it to me. 'Going for long?'

'I don't think so,' I said.

'Business?'

'Believe it or not, we're buying our antiques from North America these days.' It was true.

'No! Really?' He was amused. He stood up as I stood up. He leaned across his desk to shake hands. 'Well, good luck. Enjoy yourself.'

'I will.'

I left his surgery and began to walk up Kensington Church Street, passing the three girls who were waiting on the kerb for a taxi. One of them looked very much like the girl who had given me the disease. I wondered if she would recognise me as I went by. But she was too deep in conversation to notice, even though I walked to within an inch or two of her shoulder, close enough to identify her heavy perfume.

The morning of the day I was due to take the overnight plane from Gatwick (it was a budget flight) I read the news of a border clash between China and India, but I did not give it too much attention. The Russo-Indian Pact had been signed the previous year, in Simla, and I believed that the Chinese would take the pact seriously. By the afternoon the radio news reported Moscow's warnings to Peking. When I left for Gatwick on the train from Victoria, I bought an evening paper. I had begun to consider the possibility of war between Russia and China. The evening news was vague and told me no more than had the radio news. On the plane, which took off on schedule, I watched a Walt Disney film about two teenage girls who seemed to be twins.

I reached Toronto at eleven o'clock in the evening, local time, took a taxi to a downtown hotel and turned on the television to discover that Confederation troops and tanks were invading China while Indian forces, with some British and American divisions already stationed there, were moving towards the Chinese border. A newsflash brought the information that both CIS and EC countries had lent their support to India and that China and her allies were expected to capitulate very soon.

Early the next day I found myself in a pleasant suburban street of tall, Victorian wooden houses, birch trees and maples and soft lawns, ringing the bell of my contact, Mr Belko. An angry girl, a pudgy seventeen, came to the door. She was wearing a blue dressing gown.

'Mr Belko is expecting me,' I told her.

She was triumphant. 'Mr Belko left an hour ago.'

'Where did he go? Would you mind?'

'To the airport. Hadn't you heard? It's World War Three!'

For a moment I was amused by the inevitability of her remark; the assumption, moreover, of the inevitable event.

'You look beat,' she said. 'Are you a diplomat?'

'Not really.'

She grew to feeling guilty. 'Come in and have some coffee.'

'I accept. Thank you.'

Her mother was at breakfast in the large, modern kitchen. 'Dubrowski,' I said, removing my hat. 'I am so sorry...'

'Vassily's left. Janet told you?'

'Yes.' I unbuttoned my overcoat. Janet took it. I thanked her. I sat down at the table. I was brought a cup of that Western coffee which smells so good but does not taste of anything. I drank it.

'Was it important?' asked Janet's mother.

'Well...'

'To do with the crisis?'

I was not sure. I waved a palm.

'Well,' said Janet's mother, 'you're lucky to be here, that's all I can say.'

'You think there will be a full-scale war?' I accepted sugar from the young girl's hands.

'Let them fight it out,' said Janet's mother. 'Get it over with.'

'It will involve Canada.'

Janet's mother buttered some toast. 'Not directly.'

'Are you Ukrainian, too?' said Janet.

'Too?'.

'We're Ukrainians.' Janet sat down beside me. I became aware of her warmth. 'Or at least momma and poppa are.'

I looked at the woman in the housecoat with her dyed red hair,

36

her make-up, her American way of slouching against the table. I wondered if I were not enduring some kind of complicated test.

'I came over in 1947,' said Janet's mother. 'From England. We'd been deported during the German occupation and when the allies arrived we managed to get to England. Fedya was born here. Are you Ukrainian?'

I began to laugh a little. It was a feeble titter, but it was the first spontaneous expression of emotion I had had in years. 'Yes,' I said. 'I am.'

'We haven't really stayed in touch much,' said Janet's mother, 'with the Community here, you know. Janet's been to some meetings. She sees more of the old people than we do. She's a Nationalist, aren't you, dear?'

'Convinced,' said Janet.

'Canadian,' I asked, 'or Ukrainian?' I was genuinely confused.

Janet took this well. She put youthful fingers on my sleeve. 'Both,' she said.

When I returned to my hotel I found a note telling me to go to our embassy. At the embassy I was ordered to fly direct to Moscow on the next Aeroflot flight. There I would be briefed about my new rôle. By the time I reached Moscow, Allied troops were already withdrawing from China and an agreement was being negotiated in the United Nations. I was given a Ukrainian passport and told to return to London.

My brief stay in Moscow had made me homesick. I would have been grateful for a holiday in the country for a week or two. I have yet to have my dream fulfilled. A month after I got back, the real War broke and I, in common with so many others, began to taste the euphoria of Armageddon.

Leaving Pasadena

I was asked by the woman why I had no pity. She sat on the floor, her elbow resting upon a couch, her head in her hand. She had not wept. Her anguish had tempered her eyes: they glittered with unvoiced needs. I could not touch her. I could not insult her with my compassion. I told her that pity was an inappropriate emotion. Our world was burning and there was no time for anything but rapid action. Africa and Australia were already gone. The clouds and the contamination were a matter of anxiety to those who survived. She told me, in slow, over-controlled syllables, that she was probably dying. She needed love, she said. I told her she should find someone, therefore, whose needs matched her own. My first loyalty was to my unit. I could not reach my hand to her. Any gesture would have been cruel.

The other two women came into the room. One had my bag. 'You still don't know where you're going?' said the blonde, Julia. Her fashionably garish cosmetics appeared to give her face the lustre and texture of porcelain.

I turned my back and walked into the hallway. 'Not yet.'

Julia said: 'I'll try to look after her.'

As I got to the front door of the apartment, the brown-haired woman, Honour, said: 'You pious bastard.' She wore no make-up. Her face was as pale as Julia's.

I accepted her accusation. I had at that moment nothing left but piety and I would not dignify it with words. I nodded, shook hands with them both. I heard her mumbling some despairing question from the room, then I had walked down the white steps of the Pasadena condominium, crossed the courtyard with its silenced fountain, its poised cherubs, brilliant in the sun, and entered the car which had been sent to collect me. I was leaving California. That was all I had been told.

My chief had a rented house in Long Beach, near the marina. We drove to it through avenues of gigantic palms until we reached the almost deserted freeway. Vehicles kept well apart, considering the others warily. Only government people had official driving permits; anyone else could be psychotic or a criminal.

Long Beach was still populated. There were even people sailing their yachts into the harbour. The Pacific threat seemed to bother the people only as much as they had been bothered by the threat of earthquakes. The houses were low and calm, divided by shrubs and trees, with neat grass. I saw a man riding a pony across his lawn. He waved sardonically at the car. Groups of women stared at the limousine with expressions of contempt. We found my chief's house. The chauffeur went to tell him we were there. He came out immediately.

As he stopped to join me, the chief said: 'You look bad. You should sleep more.'

I told him, dutifully, about the woman. He was sympathetic. 'There's a war on. It's how it is in war.' Naturally, I agreed with him. 'We are fighting for their good, after all,' he added.

We drove to a military airfield. Both Soviet and US planes were there. We went immediately to our Ilyushin, and had scarcely settled in the uncomfortable seats before we took off.

My chief handed me a passport. It had my real name and a recent photograph. 'You're officially with the liaison staff, at last,' he said. 'It means you can report either to the Americans or to us. Nothing will be kept back. Matters are too urgent now.' I expressed appropriate surprise.

I looked down on Los Angeles; its beaches, its fantasies. It was like setting aside a favourite story as a child. We headed inland over mountains, going east.

'The Third World War has already been fought,' said my chief, 'in the "third world", as the Americans call it. Why else would they call it that? This is actually the Fifth World War.'

'What was the Fourth?' I asked.

'It was fought in the country of the soul.'

I laughed. I had forgotten his sentimentality. 'Who won?'

'Nobody. It merely prepared us for this.'

There were clouds beneath us. It seemed to become calm as the altitude encouraged deafness. I could hardly hear his next remark: 'It has sharpened our wits and deadened our emotional responses. War is a great relief, eh? A completely false sense of objectivity. The strain to remain grown-up is too much for most of us.'

It was familiar stuff from him. I unfastened my seat belt and walked clumsily along the plane to where a Cossack sergeant served at a small bar. I ordered some of the Finnish vodka we had recently acquired. I drank the glass down and returned to my place. Four high-ranking officers in tropical uniforms were arguing in the seats behind me. One of them was of the opinion that we should begin full-scale rocket attacks on major Chinese cities. The others were for caution. The bombing had, after all, been stopped. Most of the civilised countries were still unharmed.

My chief began coughing. It was that dry noise usually associated with smoke inhalation. He recovered himself and in answer to my concerned expression told me that he was probably getting a cold. 'We should be in Washington soon. All this travelling about is bad for the constitution.' He shrugged. 'But life is never easy. Even in wartime.'

An official car met us at the airport. It bore the arms of the President. We passed the monstrous neo-classical buildings which celebrated that naïve eighteenth-century rationalism we all now regretted and from which we seemed to be suffering at present. We arrived at a modern block of government offices. In the elevator my chief told me not to show surprise at whatever we discussed. He believed that we were thought to know more than we had actually been told.

A bland, smooth-faced man in a light-coloured suit introduced himself as Mansfield and offered us deep, black chairs. He asked us about our journey, about California, and told us of the people living along the West Coast. 'People learn to identify their homes with their security. When something like this happens... Well, we all know about the Jews refusing to leave Germany.'

'Your newspapers contradict themselves,' said my chief. He smiled. 'They say there is little to fear.'

'True.' Mansfield offered us Lucky Strike cigarettes which we accepted. My chief coughed a little before he took a light.

'We think you'll have more success in Venezuela.' Mansfield returned the lighter to his desk. 'They are suspicious of our motives, naturally.'

'And not of ours?' My chief continued to smile.

'They could believe your arguments better. They are not too sure if the alliance will maintain itself. You might be able to persuade them.'

'Possibly.'

'They can't stay neutral much longer.'

'Why not?'

'Because someone will attack them.'

'Then perhaps we should wait until that happens. It would be easier to liberate them, eh?'

'We need their oil. This freeze of theirs is pointless. It does nobody any good.'

'And why do you want us to go?'

'The Russians?'

'No.' My chief waved a hand at me. 'Us.'

'We have to contact their intelligence first. After that the politicians can sort things out.'

'You've made arrangements?'

'Yes. It was thought best not to meet in Caracas. You'll go to Maracaibo. It's where the oil is, anyway. Most of their oil people want to sell. We're not certain of the attitudes you'll find, but we understand that there is a lot of pressure from that side.'

'You have material for us?'

Mansfield lifted a folder from his desk and showed it to us.

Although my chief seemed to be taking the meeting seriously, I began to wonder at the vagueness of its content. I suspected that our going to Maracaibo would have no effect at all. We were going because it was something to do.

I resisted an urge, when we reached our hotel in Maracaibo, to telephone the woman and ask how she was. It would do her no good, I decided, for her to hear from me. I knew that, in other circumstances, I would have loved her. She had done me several favours in the course of my work, so I was also grateful to her. The sense of gratitude was the only indulgence I allowed myself.

My chief walked through the connecting door into my room. He rubbed his eyebrows. 'I have a meeting with a member of their intelligence. A colonel. But it is to be a one-to-one thing. You're free to do what you like this evening. I have the name of a house.'

'Thank you.' I wrote down the address he gave me.

'It will do you good,' he said. He was sympathetic. 'And one of us might as well enjoy the pleasures of the town. I hear the whores are of a high quality.'

'I am much obliged to you.' I would go, I thought, only because I had no wish to stay in my room the whole time. His giving me leave confirmed my suspicion that there was no real reason for us being in Maracaibo.

The town, with its skyscrapers and remnants of Spanish-style architecture, was well-lit and relatively clean. I had once been told that 'Venezuela is the future'. They had been experimenting with different energy sources, using their oil income to develop systems which would not be much dependent on oil. But Maracaibo seemed very little different, save that the lake itself, full of machinery and rigging, occasionally gave off mysterious puffs of flame which would illuminate buildings and create uncertain shadows. There was a stink of oil about the place. As I walked, local map in hand, to the address my chief had given me I saw one of their airships, built by a British firm at Cardington, sail into the darkness beyond the city. Venezuela had been perhaps the last country to associate romance with practical engineering.

I reached the house. It was large and fairly luxurious. The décor was comfortable and lush in the manner of some of the more grandiose family restaurants I had visited in Pasadena. There was a pianist playing similar music to his American counterpart. There was a bar. I sat down and ordered a Scotch. I was approached by a pretty hostess who wore a blonde wig. Her skin was dark and her smile was wide and seemed genuine. In English she said that she thought she had seen me there before. I told her that this was only my second visit to Maracaibo. She asked if I were Swedish. I said that I was Russian. She kissed me and said that she loved Russian people, that they knew how to enjoy themselves. 'Lots of vodka,' she said. But I was drinking Scotch; was I an émigré? I said, from habit, that I was. Her name was Anna. Her father, she said, had been born in South London. Did I know London? Very well, I said. I had lived there for some years. Anna wondered if Brixton were like Maracaibo. I said there were some similarities. We look for familiarity in the most unlikely circumstances before we accept what is strange to us. It is as true of travellers as it is of lovers.

Anna brought a girl for me. She had fine black hair tied back from her face; a white dress with a great deal of lace. She looked about sixteen. Her make-up was subtle. She pretended to be shy. I found her appealing. Her name was Maria, she told me. She spoke excellent English with an American accent. I bought her a drink, expecting to go to her room, but she said she would like to take me home, if that suited me. I decided against caution. She led me outside and we drove in a taxi to a street of what seemed to be quiet, middle-class apartment buildings. We climbed two flights of stairs. She opened a well-polished wooden door with her key and we entered an apartment full of quality furniture in subdued good taste. I began to suspect I had been picked up by a schoolgirl and that this was her parents' home. But the way she moved in it, getting me another Scotch, switching on the overhead fan, taking my jacket, convinced me that she was the mistress of the place. Moreover, I knew that she was actually older than sixteen; that she cultivated the appearance of a teenager. I began to experience a reluctance to go to bed with her. Against my will I remembered the woman in Pasadena. I forced myself towards that belief that all women were, after all, the same, that it satisfied them to give themselves up to a man. The whore, at least, would make money from her instincts. The woman in Pasadena came by nothing but pain. We went into the bedroom and undressed. In the large and comfortable white bed I eventually confessed that I was in no haste to make love to her. I had been unable to adjust my mood. I asked her why she had shaved her pubic hair. She said that it increased her own pleasure and besides many men found it irresistible. She began to tell me her story. She had been, she said, in love with the man who introduced her to prostitution. Evidently she was still obsessed by him, because it required no great expression of interest from me for her to tell me the whole story. It was familiar enough. What she said, of course, was couched in the usual sort of sentimentality and romanticism. She mentioned love a great deal and her knowledge that, although he did not say so, he really loved her and cared for her and it was only right, because she loved him, that he should be allowed to be the way he was. He had many other girls, including, I gathered, a wife. Initially Maria had, in the manner of despairing women, attempted to make of herself an improved piece of capital: she had dyed her hair, shaved her pubis, painted her face and nails. The girl-whore is always highly valued wherever one goes in the world. I gathered that while the man had appreciated the gesture he had told her that he intended to continue seeing other women. All this was depressing, for I was never particularly interested in economics. I found myself moralising a trifle. I told her that maturity and self-possession were in the end more attractive qualities to me. They guaranteed me a certain kind of freedom based on mutually accepted responsibility. She did not understand a word, of course. I added that a woman's attempts to use a man as her context were thoroughly understood by me. I had my loyalties. But, like most men, I was not able to be either a woman's nation or her cause. Maria made some attempt to rouse me and then fell back. She said that it was her bad luck to pick up a bore. She had thought I would be interesting. She added that she did not feel she could charge me much. I was amused. I got up and telephoned the hotel. The chief had not yet returned. I said that I would stay longer in that case. She said that she would enjoy my company, but I would have to be more entertaining. Eventually I achieved a reasonable state of mind and made love to her. She was soft, yielding and foul-mouthed. She was able to bring me to a more than satisfactory orgasm. As I left, she insisted that I telephone her the next day if I could. I agreed that I would if it were at all possible.

My chief was jovial when we breakfasted together in his room. 'We have at least a week here,' he said. 'There are subtleties. These people are worse than the Arabs.'

I reported the girl. He shrugged. 'You have nothing to reveal. Even if it is some kind of strategy, they would be wasting their time.'

I had the impression that he had brought me here on holiday. In the outside world, the news was not good. A bomb had landed somewhere in India and no-one was absolutely certain where it had come from. No major city had been hit. This was not acceptable warfare, said my chief. War was supposed to cut down on ambiguities.

I telephoned the girl from the breakfast table. I arranged to see her for lunch.

We ate in a smart restaurant at the top of a modern tower. There was mist on the lake and Maracaibo was covered in pale gold light. She wore a red suit with a matching hat. She was gentle and obviously amused by what she saw as my stiffness. She had a way of making me relax. Naturally, I resisted falling too much under her spell.

After lunch, she took us to a quay. Several men in tattered nautical clothes called to her. She spoke to one of them and then we had climbed down into a small, elegant motor boat. She started the engine, took the wheel, and we rode out into the mist.

I asked her what her man thought of all this. She became gay. 'He doesn't care.'

'But you are making no money.'

'It's not really like that,' she said. 'He's kind, you know. Or can be.'

The whole episode had the character of a lull in a singularly bad storm. I could not entirely rid my mind of the knowledge of the woman in Pasadena, but I could think of no better way of spending my time. Maria steered the boat inexpertly past a series of oil derricks which stood in the water like stranded and decapitated giraffes. A breeze began to part the mist. I had the impression of distant mountains.

She stopped the engine and we embraced. She suggested that we fuck. 'It's always been an ambition of mine,' she said.

I did my best, but the boat was uncomfortable and my body was too tired. I eventually brought her to orgasm with my mouth. She seemed more than contented. After a while she got up and returned to the wheel. 'You look happier,' she said. 'So do you,' I replied. I was hard put not to feel affection for her. But that sense of affection did me no good because it recalled the woman in Pasadena. I began to tell her a joke about the War. Some Chinese commandos had entered what they thought was Indian territory and completely destroyed one of their own bases. She became serious. 'Will the War reach Venezuela?'

'Almost certainly,' I said. 'Unless a few people come to their senses. But there has been no true catharsis yet.'

She asked me what I meant. I said: 'No orgasm, eh?'

'My God,' she said.

On the quay, we agreed to meet at the same spot that evening. 'I want to show you the lake at night.' She looked up suddenly and pointed. There was a soft sound of engines. It was another airship, white and painted with the Venezuelan military colours. Reassessed technology was to have been the salvation of the world. Now this country would be lucky if it escaped complete destruction. I said nothing of this to Maria.

When I was first ordered to work abroad I felt I was going into exile. The territory was unfamiliar, offering dangers I could not anticipate. I saw Maria to her taxi and walked back to my hotel. For some reason I was reminded, perhaps by a sign or a face on the street, of the strange suburb-ghetto of Watts, where everyone lived better than almost anyone in the Soviet Union. It had amused me to go there. They had food stamps: the young have never known a breadline. One had hoped to match America. Before the War, we were only a short distance behind on the road to discontented capitalism. Beyond that was anarchy, which cannot appeal to me, although I know it was supposed to have been our goal.

I bought a Polish-language newspaper. It was over a week old and I could barely understand the references. The newspaper was published in New York. But I enjoyed the feel of the print. I read it as I lay in my bath. My chief telephoned. He sounded drunk. It occurred to me that he, too, believed himself to be on vacation. He told me that I was free for the evening.

Maria had two friends with her when I arrived at the quay. They were both some years older than she and wore the sort of heavy '40s make-up which had been fashionable a few years previously in the West. Their cotton dresses, one pink and one yellow, followed the same style, as did their hair. They wore very strong perfume and looked like versions of Rita Hayworth. They were far more self-conscious than Maria. She said they spoke little English and apologised for bringing them along. Her explanation was vague, consisting mainly of shrugs and raised brows. I made no objection. I was content to enjoy the close presence of so much femininity.

Once again, Maria drove us out into the twilight. The water seemed to brighten as it became blacker. The two older women sat together behind Maria and myself. They produced some Mexican Tequila and passed the bottle. Soon we were all fairly drunk. When Maria stopped the boat in the middle of the lake again, we all rolled together in one another's arms. I realised that this was part of Maria's plan. Another fantasy she wished to experience. I allowed the women to have their way with me, although I was not of much use to them. It gave me considerable pleasure to watch them making love. Maria took no part in this, but observed and directed, giggling the whole time. The unreality was disarming. The situation was no stranger than the situation in the world at large. It seemed that I moved from one dream to another and that this dream, given the cheerfulness of everyone involved, was preferable to the rest. I knew now that Maria felt safe with me, because

I controlled my emotions so thoroughly and because I was a stranger. I knew that I was proving of help to her and this made me happy. I thought of warning her that in seeking catharsis through her sexuality she could lose touch with the source of her feelings, lose her lovers, lose her bearings, but it did not seem to matter. With the War threatening to become more widespread our futures were all so thoroughly in doubt that we might as well enjoy what we could of the present.

Several days and nights passed. Each time we met, Maria would propose another sexual escapade and I would agree. My own curiosity was satisfied, as was my impulse to believe myself of use to someone. My chief continued to be drunk and wave me on, even when I reported exactly what was happening. As I grew to know her better I believed that she was desperately anxious to become a woman, to escape the form of security in which she now found herself. Her need for instantaneous maturity, her greedy reaching for experience, however painful, was in itself childish. She had indulged herself and been indulged for so long that her means of achieving liberty were crude and often graceless. And yet liberty, maturity might gradually come to her, earned through trauma and that feminine willingness to find fulfilment in despair. There was no doubt that her activities, her attitudes, disguised a considerable amount of despair and emotional confusion. I wondered if I were not exploiting her, even though superficially she seemed to be exploiting me. We were, I determined, merely making reasonable use of one another's time. And in the meanwhile, I recalled, there was the figure of her protector, Ramirez. He presumably knew what was happening, just as my chief knew. I began to feel a certain fondness for him, a certain gratitude. I told Maria that I should like to meet him. This did not appeal to her, but she said she would let him know what I had said. I told her that I would let her know when I was leaving, so that the meeting, if it occurred, could be on my last night. I also warned her that I might be forced to leave suddenly. She said that she had guessed this. On one level, I realised, I was asking her to give up the only power she had. I made some drunken remarks about people who surround themselves with ambiguity in order to maintain their course. They are eventually trapped by the conditions they have created, become confused and begin to question almost every aspect of their own judgement. I felt a certain amount of self-disgust after this statement. I had no business offering Maria a moral education. But political habits are hard to lose.

Puzzled, she told me that she thought Ramirez meant security for her. Yet she knew that she had no desire to marry him. She would not be happy if, tomorrow, he came to her and offered her his all. We laughed together at this. Women marry for security, I remarked, while men often marry merely for the promise of regular sex. The man is inclined to keep his side of the marriage bargain because it is fairly clear. But the woman, having no idea of what the bargain was, is baffled when the man complains.

'Are all marriages like that?' she asked. She had doubtless had many customers who had verified this. I said no, not all. I knew of several very satisfactory marriages. By and large, however, in countries where political or religious orthodoxy held sway, sexual relationships became extremely confused. Again I had lost her. I became bored with my own simplifications. As we made love, I found myself desperately yearning for the woman in Pasadena.

Maria began to speak more and more of Ramirez. I was now a confessor. From what she said I formed an opinion of him. He was tight-fisted but had made his caution and lack of generosity into a creed so that it sometimes seemed he was expressing self-discipline and neutrality, whereas he was actually indulging himself absolutely. As a result he had begun to fail in business (her flat was threatened), partly through an inability to risk capital, partly through the loss of nerve which comes when security is equated with material goods and well-being. His was a typical dilemma of the middle class, but she had no way of knowing that since she had spent most of her life in a working-class or bohemian environment. This materialism extended into his sex-life, as is so frequently the case: he hoped to get something for nothing if he could (his life was a series of deals) but expected a good return on any expenditure. He was attractive, boyish and emotionally somewhat naïve. These qualities appealed, needless to say, to many women, not all of them childless. He was easily understood and fairly easy to manipulate. Moreover, the woman had some sense of control over the relationship, for such men can also be, on certain levels, highly impressionable: they are nearly all ego. However, his inability, ultimately, to accept responsibility either for himself or others made him a frustrating partner and his relationships were inclined to deteriorate after a period in which some reform had been attempted on him and he had become resentful. We are changed only by circumstance, never by will alone. She had, for her part, she said, accepted him gladly for what he was. He was better than most, and more interesting. He was not a fool. Neither am I, I found myself saying. She shook her head. 'No. You are a big fool. It is why I'm fond of you.' I was astonished.

News came from my chief early that morning that we were due to return to the United States the next day. I saw Maria for lunch and said that I should like to see Ramirez. She made me swear that I was leaving and then arranged to meet later at the quay.

From the quayside we went to a nearby bar. It was an ordinary place, dark and a little seamy. Maria knew many of the regulars, particularly the women, whom she kissed. Ramirez arrived. He wore a good suit of dark blue cloth and I was surprised that he was bearded and had spectacles. He shook hands. His flesh was a little soft and his grasp feminine. He said that he was not sure why he had come, except 'I can resist no request from Maria'. We had several strong drinks. We took the motor boat out onto the lake. It was a warm night. He removed his jacket but not his waistcoat and asked me if I sniffed cocaine. I said that I did. As he prepared the drug on a small hand-mirror he informed me that he was Maria's master and allowed her sometimes, as in this case, to play with other men: I should go away now or I might find myself the subject of either blackmail or violence. I was amused when I realised that Maria was deceiving him. I decided to play her game as best I could: I told him that I had run whores in Greece and that I knew he did not possess the character of a true ponce. He was not insulted. We took the cocaine. It was of the best quality. I complimented him. 'You understand me, however,' he said. I did not reply until we returned to the harbour. When we were out of the boat and standing together, Maria on my right, Ramirez beside the open door of his car, I threatened him with death. I told him that I was an agent of the KGB. He became nervous, made no comment, got into his car and left. Maria, on the way home, was disturbed. She asked me what she was going to do. I told her that she was free to take a number of choices. She said she needed money. I gave her some. We stayed together in her flat through the rest of that night and in the morning drove the boat onto the lake again. When Maracaibo disappeared and we seemed alone in the middle of the still, blue water, she took out a small packet of cocaine and, steadying her thin body against a seat, carefully cut two lines on her compact mirror. I took the first, through an American ten dollar bill. She paused before sniffing half the line into one nostril, half into the other. She smiled at me, weary and intimate. 'Well?'

'You'll go back to Ramirez?'

'Not if I can stay at an hotel.'

'And if you stay at an hotel?'

'I can earn some money. Could you help me get to America?'

'At present? You're safer here.'

'But could you?'

'Only on terms I do not wish to make. I repeat, you're better off here.'

'Really?'

'Believe me.'

Her dark eyes looked away into the lake. 'The future is no better than the past.'

I guessed that within a week she would be back with Ramirez; within a year she would be free of him. I started the engine and headed towards the reality of the rigs and refineries. I told Maria that I knew she would survive, if there were any luck in the world at all. She had none of that self-involved sexuality which contains in it a peculiar coldness: the more it is indulged, the more the coldness grows. One meets libertines whose lives are devoted to sex and yet who have gradually lost any sexual generosity. Certain women are the same. They cease to celebrate and come more and more to control. It is the inevitable progress of rationalised romance, as I knew well.

In the hotel my chief notified me suddenly that he was dying. He wanted me, eventually, to go to Kiev as liaison officer with a Cossack regiment. 'I think it's the best I can offer you,' he said. He added that his willpower had failed him. I asked him if he were suffering from radiation poisoning. He said that he was. He would be returning to Long Beach for a short while, but I could stay in Washington if I wished. I would be allowed some leave. I could not begin to guess at the manipulation and persuasion he had exerted in order to gain us both so much time, but I was grateful to him and indicated as much. I had decided, I said, to return to Pasadena.

'Good,' he said. 'We can take the same plane.'

I decided not to telephone ahead but went directly from Burbank airport to Pasadena. Los Angeles was quieter than ever, though there was now some evidence of desertion and vandalism. Most of the cars on the freeways were police vehicles. As I drove my rented Toyota towards the richer suburbs I was stopped twice and had my papers checked. Now, in the current situation, it had become an advantage in America to possess a Soviet passport and KGB identification.

I drove off the freeway onto South Orange. The wide, palm-shaded streets seemed without texture or density after Maracaibo. A thin dream. Pasadena was a geometrical kindergarten vision of security. Only downtown, amongst the bricks and stones of the original settlement, and at the railroad station, was there a sense of complexity at all, and that was the complexity of any small American rural town. I yearned for Europe, for London and its mysterious, claustrophobic streets.

I parked in the communal garages, took my bag from the back seat and walked along the neat crazy paving to the end block of the condominium. Like so much Los Angeles building it was less than ten years old and beginning to show signs of decay beneath the glaring white glaze. I walked up the steps, glad of the shade, and rang the bell on the right of the double doors. I stopped and picked up a folded newspaper, surprised that there were still deliveries. Julia's voice came from the other side of the doors. I said who it was. She seemed delighted. 'You came back. This is wonderful. She's been in a bad way.' I felt as if, unknowingly, I had reaffirmed Julia's faith in the entire human race. Some of us have such a terrible desire for a decent world that we will clutch at the tiniest strand of evidence for its existence and reject all other proof to the contrary. Julia looked tired. Her hair was disordered.

I unbuttoned my light raincoat and handed it to her. I pushed my suitcase under a small table which sat against the wall of the entrance hall.

'Honour went back to Flagstaff,' said Julia. She looked rueful. 'Just as well. She didn't think a lot of you.'

'I enjoyed her candour,' I said.

The woman knew I had arrived but she continued to sit at the easel we had erected together in the large front room. Light fell on a half-finished landscape, on her thinning, ash-blonde hair, on her pastel skin. She was more delicate, more beautiful, yet still I checked myself against the sensation of love for her.

'Why are you here?' She spoke in a low voice. She began to turn, resisting hope, looking at me as if I might wound her afresh. 'The War isn't over.'

I gestured with the newspaper. 'Apparently not.'

'This is too much,' she said.

I told her that I had decided to take a leave. Nobody but my chief knew where I was and he had made up some story about my need to go underground with a group of radical pacifists.

'Your people won't believe that.'

'Our structure is so rigid it can be resisted only by the most audacious means,' I said, 'and then often very successfully. It is probably one of the few advantages of orthodoxy.'

'You're full of bullshit, as ever,' she said. 'You can't do what you did to me a second time. I'd kill myself.'

I moved close to her so that my chest was on a level with her lovely head. We did not embrace. She did not look as grey or as drawn as she had when she had first been given confirmation of her illness. As she looked up at me I was impressed with her gentle beauty. She was at once noble and pathetic. Her eyes began to fill with tears. One fell. She apologised. I told her there was no need. I touched her shoulder, her cheek. She began to speak my name several times, holding tightly to my hand.

'You don't look well,' she said. 'You were afraid you would go crazy, weren't you?'

'I am not going to go mad,' I told her. 'I often wish that I could. This state of control is a kind of madness, isn't it? Perhaps more profoundly insane than any other kind. But it has none of the appeal of irresponsibility, of giving up any sense of others, which the classic lunatic experiences.' I laughed. 'So it has no advantages.'

'What about your duty?'

'To the War?'

'Or your cause, or whatever.'

'Excellent excuses.'

'What's more important?'

I drew a breath. 'I don't know. Affection?'

'You've changed your mind. Your rationale. Your logic.'

'I had to simplify.'

'Now?'

'I am defeated. I can no longer maintain it. Things remain as perplexing as ever.'

'What are you saying?'

I shrugged. 'Love conquers all?'

'Not you!' She shook her head.

'I do not know,' I said, 'what the truth is. It has been my duty to lie and to counter lies. Duty allows this, demands it. The only other truth for me is the truth of my feelings, my cravings, and senses. Anything else is hypocrisy, self-deception. At best it is a sentimental rationale. We are all moved by self-interest.'

'But sometimes self-interest takes on a broader form,' she said. 'And that is when we become human. Why are you here?'

'To see you. To be with you.'

'We'll lie down,' she said. 'We'll go to bed.'

The bed was very large. The place had belonged to her parents. Now they were in Iowa where they believed themselves to be safer. We undressed and I took her in my arms. We kissed. Her body was warm and still strong. We did not make love, but talked, as we always had. I told her that I did not know the meaning of love and that what had brought me back to her was a sense that the alternatives were less tolerable to me. I told her that a mixture of sentimentality and power politics had been the nearest substitute for love I had been able to afford in my circumstances. Altruism was a luxury. She said that she believed it a necessity. Without altruism there was no virtue in human existence, therefore if one rejected it one also rejected the only rationale for the race's continuation. Could that be why I was now on leave from the War?

I praised her for her fine fundamentalism and said that I regretted my inability to live according to such principles. She told me that it was not difficult: one did not take extra responsibility – one relinquished power and in doing that one also relinquished guilt. The very idea, I told her humorously, was terrifying to the Russian soul. Without guilt there was no movement at all! She shook her head at what she called my cynicism, my self-contempt. I said that I preferred to think I had my own measure.

I got out of bed and went into the hall. From my bag I took a pendant I had bought for her in Maracaibo. I came back and presented it to her. She looked at it and thanked me bleakly. She set it aside. 'You'll never be free, then?' she said. 'I believe not,' I said. It was too late for that.

She rose and put on a robe, walking with her hands folded beneath her breasts into the room she used as a studio. 'Love and art wither without freedom.' She stared at a half-finished portrait stacked against the wall. I seemed much older in the picture. 'I suppose so,' I said. But I was in the business of politics which, by definition, was opposed both to lovers and to artists. They were factors which always would over-complicate the game and cause enormous frustrations in those of us who preferred, by temperament, to simplify the world as much as possible.

'You've always found my reasoning stupidly romantic, haven't you?' she said. She discredited my intelligence, I said. We lived in a world of power and manipulation. Currently political decisions (I took her hand) decided if we should live or die – if we should love or create art. My realism, I said, was limited to the situation; hers was appropriate to her life as an artist and as an individual who must continue to hope. 'But I am dying,' she said. 'I have no need for hope.' She smiled as she completed the sentence. She turned away with a shrug which had much of her old gaiety in it. She ran her hands over the frames of the canvases. 'I wish my life to have had some point, of course.'

I could not answer her, yet suddenly I was lost in her again, as I had been during the early days of our affair. I went towards her and I embraced her. I kissed her. She recognised my emotion at once. She responded. There was a great generosity in her, a kindness. I could not at that moment bear to think of its leaving the world. But I should have a memory of it, I thought.

I told her that I admired her tendency to ascribe altruistic motives to me, to all other people. But most of us were far too selfish. We had to survive in a cynical world. She said that she had to believe in self-sufficiency and altruism was the only way by which we could, with any meaning, survive at all. One had to keep one's eye on the world as it was and somehow learn to trust oneself to maintain tolerance and hope. I said her courage was greater than mine. She acknowledged this. She said that a woman found it necessary to discover courage if she were to make any sense of her life as an individual. 'But you pursued me,' I said gently. 'I love you,' she said. 'I want you for myself and will do everything I can to keep you.'

'I cannot change.'

'I would not wish it.'

'You have won me.'

'Well,' she said, 'I have won something of you and for the time being am content. Have I won it honourably, do you think? Did you return simply out of pity?'

'I was drawn here, to you. I have no reservations.'

'You don't feel trapped?'

'On the contrary.'

'You'll stay here?'

'Until you die.'

'It might be – I might ask you to kill me when the worst begins.'

'I know.'

'Could you?'

'I suspect you were attracted to me because you knew that I could.'

She became relieved. The tension between us vanished completely. She smiled at me and took my hand again: in love with her executioner.

Crossing into Cambodia

In homage to Isaac Babel, 1894–1941?

Chapter One

I APPROACHED AND Savitsky, Commander of the Sixth Division,
got up. As usual I was impressed by his gigantic, perfect body.
Yet he seemed unconscious either of his power or of his elegance.
Although not obliged to do so, I almost saluted him. He stretched
an arm towards me. I put the papers into his gloved hand. 'These
were the last messages we received,' I said. The loose sleeve of his
Cossack cherkesska slipped back to reveal a battle-strengthened
forearm, brown and glowing. I compared his skin to my own. For
all that I had ridden with the Sixth for five months, I was still pale;
still possessed, I thought, of an intellectual's hands. Evening light
fell through the jungle foliage and a few parrots shrieked their
last goodnight. Mosquitoes were gathering in the shadows, whirling in tight-woven patterns, like a frightened mob. The jungle
smelled of rot. Yakovlev, somewhere, began to play a sad accordion tune.

The Vietnamese spy we had caught spoke calmly from the
other side of Savitsky's camp-table. 'I think I should like to be
away from here before nightfall. Will you keep your word, sir, if I
tell you what I know?'

Savitsky looked back and I saw the prisoner for the first time
(though his presence was of course well known to the camp). His
wrists and ankles were pinned to the ground with bayonets but he
was otherwise unhurt.

Savitsky drew in his breath and continued to study the documents I had brought him. Our radio was now useless. 'He seems

to be confirming what these say.' He tapped the second sheet. 'An attack tonight.'

The temple on the other side of the clearing came to life within. Pale light rippled on greenish, half-ruined stonework. Some of our men must have lit a fire there. I heard noises of delight and some complaints from the women who had been with the spy. One began to shout in that peculiar, irritating high-pitched half-wail they all use when they are trying to appeal to us. For a moment Savitsky and I had a bond in our disgust. I felt flattered. Savitsky made an impatient gesture, as if of embarrassment. He turned his handsome face and looked gravely down at the peasant. 'Does it matter to you? You've lost a great deal of blood.'

'I do not think I am dying.'

Savitsky nodded. He was economical in everything, even his cruelties. He had been prepared to tear the man apart with horses, but he knew that he would tire two already overworked beasts. He picked up his cap from the camp-table and put it thoughtfully on his head. From the deserted huts came the smell of our horses as the wind reversed its direction. I drew my borrowed burka about me. I was the only one in our unit to bother to wear it, for I felt the cold as soon as the sun was down.

'Will you show me on the map where they intend to ambush us?'

'Yes,' said the peasant. 'Then you can send a man to spy on their camp. He will confirm what I say.'

I stood to one side while these two professionals conducted their business. Savitsky strode over to the spy and very quickly, like a man plucking a hen, drew the bayonets out and threw them on the ground. With some gentleness, he helped the peasant to his feet and sat him down in the leather campaign chair he had carried with him on our long ride from Danang, where we had disembarked off the troop-ship which had brought us from Vladivostok.

'I'll get some rags to stop him bleeding,' I said.

'Good idea,' confirmed Savitsky. 'We don't want the stuff all over the maps. You'd better be in on this, anyway.'

As the liaison officer, it was my duty to know what was

happening. That is why I am able to tell this story. My whole inclination was to return to my billet where two miserable ancients cowered and sang at me whenever I entered or left but where at least I had a small barrier between me and the casual day-to-day terrors of the campaign. But, illiterate and obtuse though these horsemen were, they had accurate instincts and could tell immediately if I betrayed any sign of fear. Perhaps, I thought, it is because they are all so used to disguising their own fears. Yet bravery was a habit with them and I yearned to catch it. I had ridden with them in more than a dozen encounters, helping to drive the Cambodians back into their own country. Each time I had seen men and horses blown to pieces, torn apart, burned alive. I had come to exist on the smell of blood and gunpowder as if it were a substitute for air and food – I identified it with the smell of Life itself – yet I had still failed to achieve that strangely passive sense of inner calm my comrades all, to a greater or lesser degree, displayed.

Only in action did they seem possessed in any way by the outer world, although they still worked with efficient ferocity, killing as quickly as possible with lance, sabre or carbine and, with ghastly humanity, never leaving a wounded man of their own or the enemy's without his throat cut or a bullet in his brain. I was thankful that these, my traditional foes, were now allies for I could not have resisted them had they turned against me.

I bound the peasant's slender wrists and ankles. He was like a child. He said: 'I knew there were no arteries cut.' I nodded at him. 'You're the political officer, aren't you?' He spoke almost sympathetically.

'Liaison,' I said.

He was satisfied by my reply, as if I had confirmed his opinion. He added: 'I suppose it's the leather coat. Almost a uniform.'

I smiled. 'A sign of class difference, you think?'

His eyes were suddenly drowned with pain and he staggered, but recovered to finish what he had evidently planned to say: 'You Russians are natural bourgeoisie. It's not your fault. It's your turn.'

Savitsky was too tired to respond with anything more than a small smile. I felt that he agreed with the peasant and that these two excluded me, felt superior to me. I knew anger, then. Tightening the last rag on his left wrist, I made the spy wince. Satisfied that my honour was avenged I cast an eye over the map. 'Here we are,' I said. We were on the very edge of Cambodia. A small river, easily forded, formed the border. We had heard it just before we had entered this village. Scouts confirmed that it lay no more than half a verst to the west. The stream on the far side of the village, behind the temple, was a tributary.

'You give your word you won't kill me,' said the Vietnamese.

'Yes,' said Savitsky. He was beyond joking. We all were. It had been ages since any of us had been anything but direct with one another, save for the conventional jests which were merely part of the general noise of the squadron, like the jangling of harness. And he was beyond lying, except where it was absolutely necessary. His threats were as unqualified as his promises.

'They are here.' The spy indicated a town. He began to shiver. He was wearing only torn shorts. 'And some of them are here, because they think you might use the bridge rather than the ford.'

'And the attacking force for tonight?'

'Based here.' A point on our side of the river.

Savitsky shouted. 'Pavlichenko.'

From the Division Commander's own tent, young Pavlichenko, capless, with ruffled fair hair and a look of restrained disappointment, emerged. 'Comrade?'

'Get a horse and ride with this man for half an hour the way we came today. Ride as fast as you can, then leave him and return to camp.'

Pavlichenko ran towards the huts where the horses were stabled. Savitsky had believed the spy and was not bothering to check his information. 'We can't attack them,' he murmured. 'We'll have to wait until they come to us. It's better.' The flap of Savitsky's tent was now open. I glanced through and to my surprise saw a Eurasian girl of about fourteen. She had her feet in a bucket of water. She smiled at me. I looked away.

Savitsky said: 'He's washing her for me. Pavlichenko's an expert.'

'My wife and daughters?' said the spy.

'They'll have to remain now. What can I do?' Savitsky shrugged in the direction of the temple. 'You should have spoken earlier.'

The Vietnamese accepted this and, when Pavlichenko returned with the horse, leading it and running as if he wished to get the job over with in the fastest possible time, he allowed the young Cossack to lift him onto the saddle.

'Take your rifle,' Savitsky told Pavlichenko. 'We're expecting an attack.'

Pavlichenko dashed for his own tent, the small one close to Savitsky's. The horse, as thoroughly trained as the men who rode him, stood awkwardly but quietly beneath his nervous load. The spy clutched the saddle pommel, the mane, his bare feet angled towards the mount's neck. He stared ahead of him into the night. His wife and daughter had stopped their appalling wailing but I thought I could hear the occasional feminine grunt from the temple. The flames had become more animated. His other daughter, her feet still in the bucket, held her arms tightly under her chest and her curious eyes looked without rancour at her father, then at the Division Commander, then, finally, at me. Savitsky spoke. 'You're the intellectual. She doesn't know Russian. Tell her that her father will be safe. She can join him tomorrow.'

'My Vietnamese might not be up to that.'

'Use English or French, then.' He began to tidy his maps, calling over Kreshenko, who was in charge of the guard.

I entered the tent and was shocked by her little smile. She had a peculiar smell to her – like old tea and cooked rice. I knew my Vietnamese was too limited so I asked her if she spoke French. She was of the wrong generation. 'Amerikanski,' she told me. I relayed Savitsky's message. She said: 'So I am the price of the old bastard's freedom.'

'Not at all.' I reassured her. 'He told us what we wanted. It was just bad luck for you that he used you three for cover.'

She laughed. 'Nuts! It was me got him to do it. With my sister. Tao's boyfriend works for the Cambodians.' She added: 'They seemed to be winning at the time.'

Savitsky entered the tent and zipped it up from the bottom. He used a single, graceful movement. For all that he was bone-weary, he moved with the unconscious fluidity of an acrobat. He lit one of his foul-smelling papyrosi and sat heavily on the camp-bed beside the girl.

'She speaks English,' I said. 'She's a half-caste. Look.'

He loosened his collar. 'Could you ask her if she's clean, comrade?'

'I doubt it,' I said. I repeated what she had told me.

He nodded. 'Well, ask her if she'll be a good girl and use her mouth. I just want to get on with it. I expect she does, too.'

I relayed the DC's message.

'I'll bite his cock off if I get the chance,' said the girl.

Outside in the night the horse began to move away. I explained what she had said.

'I wonder, comrade,' Savitsky said, 'if you would oblige me by holding the lady's head.' He began to undo the belt of his trousers, pulling up his elaborately embroidered shirt.

The girl's feet became noisy in the water and the bucket over-turned. In my leather jacket, my burka, with my automatic pistol at her right ear, I restrained the girl until Savitsky had finished with her. He began to take off his boots. 'Would you care for her, yourself?'

I shook my head and escorted the girl from the tent. She was walking in that familiar stiff way women have after they have been raped. I asked her if she was hungry. She agreed that she was. I took her to my billet. The old couple found some more rice and I watched her eat it.

Later that night she moved towards me from where she had been lying more or less at my feet. I thought I was being attacked and shot her in the stomach. Knowing what my comrades would think of me if I tried to keep her alive (it would be a matter of hours) I shot her in the head to put her out of her misery. As luck would have it, these shots woke the camp and when the Khmer soldiers attacked a few moments later we were ready for them and killed a great many before the rest ran back into the jungle. Most of these soldiers were younger than the girl.

In the morning, to save any embarrassment, the remaining women were chased out of the camp in the direction taken by the patriarch. The old couple had disappeared and I assumed that they would not return or, if they did, that they would bury the girl, so I left her where I had shot her. A silver ring she wore would compensate them for their trouble. There was very little food remaining in the village, but what there was we ate for our breakfast or packed into our saddlebags. Then, mounting up, we followed the almost preternaturally handsome Savitsky back into the jungle, heading for the river.

Chapter Two

W HEN OUR SCOUT did not return after we had heard a long burst of machine-gun fire, we guessed that he had found at least part of the enemy ambush and that the spy had not lied to us, so we decided to cross the river at a less convenient spot where, with luck, no enemy would be waiting.

The river was swift but had none of the force of Russian rivers and Pavlichenko was sent across with a rope which he tied to a tree trunk. Then we entered the water and began to swim our horses across. Those who had lost the canvas covers for their carbines kept them high in the air, holding the rope with one hand and guiding their horses with legs and with reins which they gripped in their teeth. I was more or less in the middle, with half the division behind me and half beginning to assemble on dry land on the other side, when Cambodian aircraft sighted us and began an attack dive. The aircraft were in poor repair, borrowed from half a dozen other countries, and their guns, aiming equipment and, I suspect, their pilots were in worse condition, but they killed seven of our men as we let go of the ropes, slipped out of our saddles, and swam beside our horses, making for the far bank, while those still on dry land behind us went to cover where they could. A couple of machine-gun carts were turned on the attacking planes, but these were of little use. The peculiar assortment of weapons used against us – tracers, two rockets, a few napalm canisters which struck the water and sank (only one opened and burned but the mixture was quickly carried off by the current) and then they were flying back to base somewhere in Cambodia's interior – indicated that they had very little conventional armament left. This was true of most of the participants at this stage, which is why our cavalry had proved so effective. But they had bought some time for their ground troops who were now coming in.

In virtual silence, any shouts drowned by the rushing of the river, we crossed to the enemy bank and set up a defensive position, using the machine-gun carts which were last to come across on ropes. The Cambodians hit us from two sides – moving in from their original ambush positions – but we were able to return their fire effectively, even using the anti-tank weapons and the mortar which, hitherto, we had tended to consider useless weight. They used arrows, blow-darts, automatic rifles, pistols and a flame-thrower which only worked for a few seconds and did us no harm. The Cossacks were not happy with this sort of warfare and as soon as there was a lull we had mounted up, packed the gear in the carts, and with sabres drawn were howling into the Khmer Stalinists (as we had been instructed to term them). Leaving them scattered and useless, we found a bit of concrete road along which we could gallop for a while. We slowed to a trot and then to a walk. The pavement was potholed and only slightly less dangerous than the jungle floor. The jungle was behind us now and seemed to have been a screen hiding the devastation ahead. The landscape was virtually flat, as if it had been bombed clean of contours, with a few broken buildings, the occasional blackened tree, and ash drifted across the road, coming sometimes up to our horses' knees. The ash was stirred by a light wind. We had witnessed scenes like it before, but never on such a scale. The almost colourless nature of the landscape was emphasised by the unrelieved brilliance of the blue sky overhead. The sun had become very hot.

Once we saw two tanks on the horizon, but they did not challenge us. We continued until early afternoon when we came to the remains of some sort of modern power installation and we made camp in the shelter of its walls. The ash got into our food and we drank more of our water than was sensible. We were all covered in the grey stuff by this time.

'We're like corpses,' said Savitsky. He resembled an heroic statue of the sort which used to be in almost every public square in the Soviet Union. 'Where are we going to find anything to eat in this?'

'It's like the end of the world,' I said.

'Have you tried the radio again?'

I shook my head. 'It isn't worth it. Napalm eats through wiring faster than it eats through you.'

He accepted this and with a naked finger began to clean off the inner rims of the goggles he (like most of us) wore as protection against sun, rain and dust. 'I could do with some orders,' he said.

'We were instructed to move into the enemy's territory. That's what we're doing.'

'Where, we were told, we would link up with American and Australian mounted units. Those fools can't ride. I don't know why they ever thought of putting them on horses. Cowboys!'

I saw no point in repeating an already stale argument. It was true, however, that the Western cavalry divisions found it hard to match our efficient savagery. I had been amused, too, when they had married us briefly with a couple of Mongolian squadrons. The Mongols had not ridden to war in decades and had become something of a laughing stock with their ancient enemies, the Cossacks. Savitsky believed that we were the last great horsemen. Actually, he did not include me, for I was a very poor rider and not a Cossack, anyway. He thought it was our destiny to survive the War and begin a new and braver civilisation: 'Free from the influence of women and Jews'. He recalled the great days of the Zaporozhian Sech, from which women had been forbidden. Even amongst the Sixth he was regarded as something of a conservative. He continued to be admired more than his opinions.

When the men had watered our horses and replaced the water bags in the cart, Savitsky and I spread the map on a piece of concrete and found our position with the help of the compass and sextant (there were no signs or landmarks). 'I wonder what has happened to Angkor,' I said. It was where we were supposed to meet other units, including the Canadians to whom, in the months to come, I was to be attached (I was to discover later that they had been in our rear all along).

'You think it's like this?' Savitsky gestured. His noble eyes began to frown. 'I mean, comrade, would you say it was worth our while making for Angkor now?'

'We have our orders,' I said. 'We've no choice. We're expected.'

Savitsky blew dust from his mouth and scratched his head. 'There's about half our division left. We could do with reinforcements. Mind you, I'm glad we can see a bit of sky at last.' We had all felt claustrophobic in the jungle.

'What is it, anyway, this Angkor? Their capital?' he asked me.

'Their Stalingrad, maybe.'

Savitsky understood. 'Oh, it has an importance to their morale. It's not strategic?'

'I haven't been told about its strategic value.'

Savitsky, as usual, withdrew into his diplomatic silence, indicating that he did not believe me and thought that I had been instructed to secrecy. 'We'd best push on,' he said. 'We've a long way to go, eh?'

After we had mounted up, Savitsky and I rode side by side for a while, along the remains of the concrete road. We were some way ahead of the long column, with its riders, its baggage-wagons, and its Makhno-style machine-gun carts. We were sitting targets for any planes and, because there was no cover, Savitsky and his men casually ignored the danger. I had learned not to show my nervousness but I was not at that moment sure how well hidden it was.

'We are the only vital force in Cambodia,' said the Division Commander with a beatific smile. 'Everything else is dead. How these yellow bastards must hate one another.' He was impressed, perhaps admiring.

'Who's to say?' I ventured. 'We don't know who else has been fighting. There isn't a nation now that's not in the War.'

'And not one that's not on its last legs. Even Switzerland.' Savitsky gave a superior snort. 'But what an inheritance for us!'

I became convinced that, quietly, he was going insane.

Chapter Three

WE CAME ACROSS an armoured car in a hollow, just off the road. One of our scouts had heard the crew's moans. As Savitsky and I rode up, the scout was covering the uniformed Khmers with his carbine, but they were too far gone to offer us any harm.

'What's wrong with 'em?' Savitsky asked the scout.

The scout did not know. 'Disease,' he said. 'Or starvation. They're not wounded.'

We got off our horses and slid down into the crater. The car was undamaged. It appeared to have rolled gently into the dust and become stuck. I slipped into the driving seat and tried to start the engine, but it was dead. Savitsky had kicked one of the wriggling Khmers in the genitals but the man did not seem to notice the pain much, though he clutched himself, almost as if he entered into the spirit of a ritual. Savitsky was saying 'Soldiers. Soldiers', over and over again. It was one of the few Vietnamese words he knew. He pointed in different directions, looking with disgust on the worn-out men. 'You'd better question them,' he said to me.

They understood my English, but refused to speak it. I tried them in French. 'What happened to your machine?'

The man Savitsky had kicked continued to lie on his face, his arms stretched along the ashy ground towards us. I felt he wanted to touch us: to steal our vitality. I felt sick as I put the heel of my boot on his hand. One of his comrades said: 'There's no secret to it. We ran out of essence.' He pointed to the armoured car. 'We ran out of essence.'

'You're a long way from your base.'

'Our base is gone. There's no essence anywhere.'

I believed him and told Savitsky who was only too ready to accept this simple explanation.

As usual, I was expected to dispatch the prisoners. I reached for my holster, but Savitsky, with rare sympathy, stayed my movement. 'Go and see what's in that can,' he said, pointing. As I waded towards the punctured metal, three shots came from the Division Commander's revolver. I wondered at his mercy. Continuing with this small farce, I looked at the can, held it up, shook it, and threw it back into the dust. 'Empty,' I said.

Savitsky was climbing the crater towards his horse. As I scrambled behind him he said: 'It's the Devil's world. Do you think we should give ourselves up to him?'

I was astonished by this unusual cynicism.

He got into his saddle. Unconsciously, he assumed the pose, often seen in films and pictures, of the noble revolutionary horseman – his head lifted, his palm shielding his eyes as he peered towards the west.

'We seem to have wound up killing Tatars again,' he said with a smile as I got clumsily onto my horse. 'Do you believe in all this history, comrade?'

'I've always considered the theory of precedent absolutely infantile,' I said.

'What's that?'

I began to explain, but he was already spurring forward, shouting to his men.

Chapter Four

ON THE THIRD day we had passed through the ash-desert and our horses could at last crop at some grass on the crest of a line of low hills which looked down on glinting, misty paddy fields. Savitsky, his field glasses to his eyes, was relieved. 'A village,' he said. 'Thank god. We'll be able to get some provisions.'

'And some exercise,' said Pavlichenko behind him. The boy laughed, pushing his cap back on his head and wiping grimy sweat from his brow. 'Shall I go down there, comrade?' Savitsky agreed, telling Pavlichenko to take two others with him. We watched the Cossacks ride down the hill and begin cautiously to wade their horses through the young rice. The sky possessed a greenish tinge here, as if it reflected the fields. It looked like the Black Sea lagoons at midsummer. A smell of foliage, almost shocking in its unfamiliarity, floated up to us. Savitsky was intent on watching the movements of his men, who had unslung their carbines and dismounted as they reached the village. With reins looped on their arms they moved slowly in, firing a few experimental rounds at the huts. One of them took a dummy grenade from his saddlebag and threw it into a nearby doorway. Peasants, already starving to the point of death it seemed, ran out. The young Cossacks ignored them, looking for soldiers. When they were satisfied that the village was clear of traps, they waved us in. The peasants began to gather together at the centre of the village. Evidently they were used to this sort of operation.

While our men made their thorough search I was again called upon to perform my duty and question the inhabitants. These, it emerged, were almost all intellectuals, part of an old Khmer Rouge re-education programme (virtually a sentence of death by

72

forced labour). It was easier to speak to them but harder to understand their complicated answers. In the end I gave up and, made
impatient by the whining appeals of the wretches, ignored them.
They knew nothing of use to us. Our men were disappointed
in their expectations. There were only old people in the village. In
the end they took the least aged of the women off and had them
in what had once been some sort of administration hut. I wondered at their energy. It occurred to me that this was something
they expected of one another and that they would lose face if they
did not perform the necessary actions. Eventually, when we had
eaten what we could find, I returned to questioning two of the
old men. They were at least antagonistic to the Cambodian troops
and were glad to tell us anything they could. However, it seemed
there had been no large movements in the area. The occasional
plane or helicopter had gone over a few days earlier. These were
probably part of the flight which had attacked us at the river. I asked
if they had any news of Angkor, but there was no radio here and
they expected us to know more than they did. I pointed towards the
purple hills on the other side of the valley. 'What's over there?'

They told me that as far as they knew it was another valley,
similar to this but larger. The hills looked steeper and were
wooded. It would be a difficult climb for us unless there was a
road. I got out the map. There was a road indicated. I pointed to
it. One of the old men nodded. Yes, he thought that road was still
there, for it led, eventually, to this village. He showed me where
the path was. It was rutted where, some time earlier, heavy vehicles had been driven along it. It disappeared into dark, green,
twittering jungle. All the jungle meant to me now was mosquitoes and a certain amount of cover from attacking planes.

Careless of leeches and insects, the best part of the division
was taking the chance of a bath in the stream which fed the paddy
fields. I could not bring myself to strip in the company of these
healthy men. I decided to remain dirty until I had the chance of
some sort of privacy.

'I want the men to rest,' said Savitsky. 'Have you any objection
to our camping here for the rest of today and tonight?'

'It's a good idea,' I said. I sought out a hut, evicted the occu-pants, and went almost immediately to sleep.

In the morning I was awakened by a trooper who brought me a metal mug full of the most delicately scented tea. I was aston-ished and accepted it with some amusement. 'There's loads of it here,' he said. 'It's all they've got!'

I sipped the tea. I was still in my uniform, with the burka on the ground beneath me and my leather jacket folded for a pillow. The hut was completely bare. I was used to noticing a few personal possessions and began to wonder if they had hidden their stuff when they had seen us coming. Then I remembered that they were from the towns and had been brought here forcibly. Perhaps now, I thought, the War would pass them by and they would know peace, even happiness, for a bit. I was scratching my ear and stretching when Savitsky came in, looking grim. 'We've found a damned burial ground,' he said. 'Hundreds of bodies in a pit. I think they must be the original inhabitants. And one or two soldiers – at least, they were in uniform.'

'You want me to ask what they are?'

'No! I just want to get away. God knows what they've been doing to one another. They're a filthy race. All grovelling and secret killing. They've no guts.'

'No soldiers, either,' I said. 'Not really. They've been preyed on by bandits for centuries. Bandits are pretty nearly the only sort of soldiers they've ever known. So the ones who want to be soldiers emulate them. Those who don't want to be soldiers treat the ones who do as they've always treated bandits. They are conciliatory until they get a chance to turn the tables.'

He was impressed by this. He rubbed at a freshly shaven chin. He looked years younger, though he still had the monumental appearance of a god. 'Thieves, you mean. They have the mental-ity of thieves, their soldiers?'

'Aren't the Cossacks thieves?'

'That's foraging.' He was not angry. Very little I said could ever anger him because he had no respect for my opinions. I was the necessary political officer, his only link with the higher, distant authority of the Kremlin, but he did not have to respect my ideas any more than he respected those which came to him from Moscow. What he respected there was the power and the fact that in some way Russia was mystically represented in our leaders. 'We leave in ten minutes,' he said.

I noticed that Pavlichenko had polished his boots for him.

By that afternoon, after we had crossed the entire valley on an excellent dirt road through the jungle and had reached the top of the next range of hills, I had a pain in my stomach. Savitsky noticed me holding my hands against my groin and said laconically, 'I wish the doctor hadn't been killed. Do you think it's typhus?' Naturally, it was what I had suspected.

'I think it's just the tea and the rice and the other stuff. Maybe mixing with all the dust we've swallowed.'

He looked paler than usual. 'I've got it, too. So have half the others. Oh, shit!'

It was hard to tell, in that jungle at that time of day, if you had a fever. I decided to put the problem out of my mind as much as possible until sunset when it would become cooler.

The road began to show signs of damage and by the time we were over the hill and looking down on the other side we were confronting scenery if anything more desolate than that which we had passed through on the previous three days. It was a grey desert, scarred by the broken road and bomb-craters. Beyond this and coming towards us was a wall of dark dust; unmistakeably an army on the move. Savitsky automatically relaxed in his saddle and turned back to see our men moving slowly up the wooded hill. 'I think they must be heading this way.' Savitsky cocked his head to one side. 'What's that?'

It was a distant shriek. Then a whole squadron of planes was coming in low. We could see their crudely painted Khmer Rouge markings, their battered fuselages. The men began to scatter off the road, but the planes ignored us. They went zooming by, seeming to be fleeing rather than attacking. I looked at the sky, but nothing followed them.

We took our field glasses from their cases and adjusted them. In the dust I saw a mass of barefoot infantry bearing rifles with fixed bayonets. There were also trucks, a few tanks, some private cars, bicycles, motorbikes, ox carts, handcarts, civilians with bundles. It was an orgy of defeated soldiers and refugees.

'I think we've missed the action.' Savitsky was furious. 'We were beaten to it, eh? And by Australians, probably!'

My impulse to shrug was checked. 'Damn!' I said a little weakly. This caused Savitsky to laugh at me. 'You're relieved. Admit it!'

I knew that I dare not share his laughter, lest it become hysterical and turn to tears, so I missed a moment of possible comradeship. 'What shall we do?' I asked. 'Go round them?'

'It would be easy enough to go through them. Finish them off. It would stop them destroying this valley, at least.' He did not, by his tone, much care.

The men were assembling behind us. Savitsky informed them of the nature of the rabble ahead of us. He put his field glasses to his eyes again and said to me: 'Infantry, too. Quite a lot. Coming on faster.'

I looked. The barefoot soldiers were apparently pushing their way through the refugees to get ahead of them.

'Maybe the planes radioed back,' said Savitsky. 'Well, it's something to fight.'

'I think we should go round,' I said. 'We should save our strength. We don't know what's waiting for us at Angkor.'

'It's miles away yet.'

'Our instructions were to avoid any conflict we could,' I reminded him.

He sighed. 'This is Satan's own country.' He was about to give the order which would comply with my suggestion when, from the direction of Angkor Wat, the sky burst into white fire. The horses reared and whinnied. Some of our men yelled and flung their arms over their eyes. We were all temporarily blinded. Then the dust below seemed to grow denser and denser. We watched in fascination as the dark wall became taller, rushing upon us and howling like a million dying voices. We were struck by the ash and forced onto our knees, then onto our bellies, yanking our frightened horses down with us as best we could. The stuff stung my face and hands and even those parts of my body protected by heavy clothing. Larger pieces of stone rattled against my goggles.

When the wind had passed and we began to stand erect, the sky was still very bright. I was astonished that my field glasses were intact. I put them up to my burning eyes and peered through swirling ash at the Cambodians. The army was running along the road towards us, as terrified animals flee a forest fire. I knew now what the planes had been escaping. Our Cossacks were in some confusion, but were already regrouping, shouting amongst themselves. A number of horses were still shying and whickering but by and large we were all calm again.

'Well, comrade,' said Savitsky with a sort of mad satisfaction, 'what do we do now? Wasn't that Angkor Wat, where we're supposed to meet our allies?'

I was silent. The mushroom cloud on the horizon was growing. It had the hazy outlines of a gigantic, spreading cedar tree, as if all at once that wasteland of ash had become promiscuously fertile. An aura of bloody red seemed to surround it, like a silhouette in the sunset. The strong, artificial wind was still blowing in our direction. I wiped dust from my goggles and lowered them back over my eyes. Savitsky gave the order for our men to mount. 'Those bastards down there are in our way,' he said. 'We're going to charge them.'

'What?' I could not believe him.

'When in doubt,' he told me, 'attack.'

'You're not scared of the enemy,' I said, 'but there's the radiation.'

'I don't know anything about radiation.' He turned in his saddle to watch his men. When they were ready he drew his sabre. They imitated him. I had no sabre to draw.

I was horrified. I pulled my horse away from the road. 'Division Commander Savitsky, we're duty-bound to conserve...'

'We're duty-bound to make for Angkor,' he said. 'And that's

what we're doing.' His perfect body poised itself in the saddle. He raised his sabre.

'It's not like ordinary dying,' I began. But he gave the order to trot forward. There was a rictus of terrifying glee on each mouth. The light from the sky was reflected in every eye.

I moved with them. I had become used to the security of numbers and I could not face their disapproval. But gradually they went ahead of me until I was in the rear. By this time we were almost at the bottom of the hill and cantering towards the mushroom cloud which was now shot through with all kinds of dark, swirling colours. It had become like a threatening hand, while the wind-borne ash stung our bodies and drew blood on the flanks of our mounts.

Yakovlev, just ahead of me, unstrapped his accordion and began to play some familiar Cossack battle-song. Soon they were all singing. Their pace gradually increased. The noise of the accordion died but their song was so loud now it seemed to fill the whole world. They reached full gallop, charging upon that appalling outline, the quintessential symbol of our doom, as their ancestors might have charged the very gates of hell. They were swift, dark shapes in the dust. The song became a savage, defiant roar.

My first impulse was to charge with them. But then I had turned my horse and was trotting back towards the valley and the border, praying that, if I ever got to safety, I would not be too badly contaminated.

The Mountain

THE LAST TWO men alive came out of the Lapp tent they had just raided for provisions.

'She's been here before us,' said Nilsson. 'It looks like she got the best of what there was.'

Hallner shrugged. He had eaten so little for so long that food no longer held any great importance for him.

He looked about him. Lapp *kata* wigwams of wood and hides were spread around the immediate area of dry ground. Valuable skins had been left out to cure, reindeer horns to bleach, the doors unfastened so that anyone might enter the deserted homes.

Hallner rather regretted the passing of the Lapps. They had had no part in the catastrophe, no interest in wars or violence or competition. Yet they had been herded to the shelters with everyone else. And, like everyone else, they had perished either by direct bombing, radiation poisoning or asphyxiation.

He and Nilsson had been in a forgotten meteorological station close to the Norwegian border. When they finally repaired their radio, the worst was over. Fall-out had by this time finished off the tribesmen in Indonesian jungles, the workers in remote districts of China, the hillbillies in the Rockies, the crofters in Scotland. Only freak weather conditions, which had been part of their reason for visiting the station earlier in the year, had so far prevented the lethal rain from falling in this area of Swedish Lappland.

They had known themselves, perhaps instinctively, to be the last two human beings alive, until Nilsson found the girl's tracks coming from the south and heading north. Who she was, how she'd escaped, they couldn't guess, but they had changed their direction from north-east to north and begun to follow. Two days later they had found the Lapp camp.

Now they stared ahead of them at the range of ancient mountains. It was 3:00 a.m., but the sun still hung a bloody spread on the horizon for it was summer – the six-week summer of the Arctic when the sun never fully set, when the snows of the mountains melted and ran down to form the rivers, lakes and marshes of the lowlands where only the occasional Lapp camp, or the muddy scar of a broad reindeer path, told of the presence of the few men who lived here during the winter months.

Suddenly, as he looked away from the range, the camp aroused some emotion akin to pity in Hallner's mind. He remembered the despair of the dying man who had told them, on his radio, what had happened to the world.

Nilsson had entered another hut and came out shaking a packet of raisins. 'Just what we need,' he said.

'Good,' said Hallner, and he sighed inaudibly. The clean, orderly nature of the little primitive village was spoiled for him by the sight he had witnessed earlier at the stream which ran through the camp. There had been simple drinking cups of clay or bone side by side with an aluminium dish and an empty Chase & Sanborn coffee jar, a cheap plastic plate and a broken toy car.

'Shall we go?' Nilsson said, and began to make his way out of the camp.

Not without certain trepidation, Hallner followed behind his friend who marched towards the mountains without looking back or even from side to side.

Nilsson had a goal and, rather than sit down, brood and die when the inescapable finally happened, Hallner was prepared to go along with him on this quest for the girl.

And, he admitted, there was a faint chance that if the winds continued to favour them, they might have a chance of life. In which case there was a logical reason for Nilsson's obsessional tracking of the woman.

His friend was impatient of his wish to walk slowly and savour the atmosphere of the country which seemed so detached and removed, uninvolved with him, disdainful. That there were things which had no emotional relationship with him had given him a slight surprise at first, and even now he walked the marshy ground with a feeling of abusing privacy, of destroying the sanctity of a place where there was so little hint of humanity; where men had been rare and had not been numerous or frequent enough visitors to have left the aura of their passing behind them.

So it was with a certain shock that he later observed the print of small rubber soles on the flat mud near a river.

'She's still ahead of us,' said Nilsson, pleased at this sign, 'and not so very far ahead. Little more than a day. We're catching up.'

Suddenly, he realised that he was displeased by the presence of the bootprints, almost resentful of Nilsson's recognition of their being there when, alone, he might have ignored them. He reflected that Nilsson's complete acceptance of the sex of the boots' wearer was entirely founded on his own wishes.

The river poured down towards the flat lake on their left, clear, bright melted snow from the mountains. Brown, sun-dried rocks stood out of it, irregularly spaced, irregularly contoured, affording them a means of crossing the swift waters.

There were many such rivers, running down the slopes of the foothills like silver veins to fill the lakes and spread them further over the marshland. There were hills on the plateau where trees crowded together, fir and silver birch, like survivors of a flood jostling for a place on the high ground. There were ridges which sometimes hid sight of the tall mountains in front of them, green with grass and reeds, studded with gorse.

He had never been so far into mountain country before and this range was one of the oldest in the world; there were no sharp peaks as in the Alps. These were worn and solid and they had lived through aeons of change and metamorphosis to have earned their right to solitude, to permanency.

Snow still spattered their sides like galaxies against the grey-green moss and rock. Snow-fields softened their lines.

Nilsson was already crossing the river, jumping nimbly from

rock to rock, his film star's profile sometimes silhouetted against the clear, sharp sky, the pack on his back like Christian's load in *The Pilgrim's Progress*. Hallner smiled to himself. Only indirectly was Nilsson heading for salvation.

Now he followed.

He balanced himself in his flat, leather-soled boots and sprang from the first rock to the second, righted his balance again and sprang to the next. The river boiled around the rocks, rushing towards the lake, to lose itself in the larger waters. He jumped again, slipped and was up to his knees in the ice-cold torrent. He raised his small knapsack over his head and, careless now, did not bother to clamber back to the rocks, but pushed on, waist-deep, through the freezing river. He came gasping to the bank and was helped to dry land by Nilsson who shook his head and laughed.

'You're hopeless!'

'It's all right,' he said, 'the sun will dry me out soon.'

But both had walked a considerable distance and both were tiring. The sun had now risen, round and hazy red in the pale, cold sky, but it was still difficult to gauge the passage of the hours. This, also, added to the detached air of timelessness which the mountains and the plateaux possessed. There was no night – only a slight alteration in the quality of the day. And although the heat was ninety degrees fahrenheit, the sky still looked cold, for it took more than the brief six weeks of summer to change the character of this wintry Jotunheim.

He thought of Jotunheim, the Land of Giants, and understood the better the myths of his ancestors with their accent on man's impermanency – the mortality of their very gods, their bleak worship of the forces of nature. Only here could he appreciate that the life-span of the world itself might be infinite, but the life-span of its denizens was necessarily subject to inevitable metamorphosis and eventual death. And, as he thought, his impression of the country changed so that instead of the feeling of invading sanctified ground, he felt as if a privilege had been granted him and he had been allowed, for a few moments of his short life, to experience eternity.

The mountains themselves might crumble in time, the planet

cease to exist, but that it would be reincarnated he was certain. And this gave him humility and hope for his own life and, for the first time, he began to think that he might have a purpose in continuing to live, after all.

He did not dwell on the idea, since there was no need to.

They came with relief to a dry place where they lighted a fire and cooked the last of their bacon in their strong metal frying pan. They ate their food and cleaned the pan with ashes from the fire, and he took it down to the nearest river and rinsed it, stooping to drink a little, not too much, since he had learned from his mistake earlier, for the water could be like a drug so that one craved to drink more and more until exhausted.

He realised, vaguely, that they had to keep as fit as possible. For one of them to come to harm could mean danger for them both. But the thought meant little. There was no sense of danger here.

He slept and, before he fell into a deep, dreamless sleep, he had a peculiar impression of being at once vast and tiny. His eyes closed, his body relaxed, he felt so big that the atoms of his body, in relation to the universe, hardly had existence, that the universe had become an unobservable electron, present but unseen. And yet, intratemporally, he had the impression that he was as small as an electron so that he existed in a gulf, a vacuum containing no matter whatsoever.

A mystic, perhaps, would have taken this for some holy experience, but he could do no more than accept it, feeling no need to interpret it. Then he slept.

Next morning, Nilsson showed him a map he had found in the village.

'That's where she's going,' he said, pointing at a mountain in the distance. 'It's the highest in this section and the second highest in the entire range. Wonder why she'd want to climb a mountain?'

Hallner shook his head.

Nilsson frowned. 'You're in a funny mood. Think you won't have a chance with the girl?' When Hallner didn't answer, Nilsson said impatiently, 'Maybe she's got some idea that she's safer on top of a mountain. With luck, we'll find out soon. Ready to go?'

Hallner nodded.

They moved on in silence.

The range was discernibly closer, now, and Hallner could look at individual mountains. Although looming over the others, the one they headed for looked squat, solid, somehow older than the rest, even.

For a while they were forced to concentrate on the ground immediately in front of them, for it had become little more than thick mud which oozed over their boots and threatened to pull them down, to join, perhaps, the remains of prehistoric saurians which lay many feet below.

Nilsson said little and Hallner was glad that no demands were made on him.

It was as if the edge of the world lay beyond the last ragged pile of mountains, or as if they had left Earth and were in a concave saucer surrounded by mountains, containing only the trees and the lakes, marshes and hills.

He had the feeling that this place was so inviolable, so invulnerable, miles from the habitation of men, that for the first time he fully realised that men had ceased to exist along with their artefacts. It was as if they had never really existed at all or that their spell of dominance had appeared and disappeared in practically the same moment of time.

But now, for the first time since he had heard the hysterical voice on the radio, he felt some stirring of his old feeling return as he stared at the great mountain, heavy and huge against the ice-blue sky. But it was transformed. Ambition had become the summit, reward the silence, the peace that waited at the peak. Curiosity was the desire to discover the cause of a freakish colouring halfway up the mountain and fear did not exist for in these enigmatic mountains there was no uncertainty. A vast, wall-less womb with the infinite sky curving above and the richly coloured scenery, blues, whites, browns and greens, surrounding them, complete, cutting them off from even the sight of the ruined outside world.

It was a snow-splashed paradise, where well-fed wolves left the carcasses of their prey to lap at the pure water of the rivers. A wilderness replete with life, with lemming, reindeer, wolverine, wolf and even bear, with lakes swarming with freshwater herring and the air a silent gulf above them to set off the smack of a hawk's wing. Night could not fall and so the potential dangers of savage wildlife, which could not be felt in the vastness of a world where there was room for everything, could never be realised.

Occasionally, they would discover a slain reindeer, bones dull and white, its hide tattered and perishing, and they would feel no horror, no emotion at all, for although its obvious killer, the wolverine, was a cruel beast, destroying often for the sake of destroying, the wolverine was not aware of its crime and therefore it was no crime at all.

Everything here was self-sufficient, moulded by fate, by circumstance, but since it did not analyse, since it accepted itself and its conditions without question, it was therefore more complete than the men who walked and stumbled across its uncompromising terrain.

At length they came to the sloping, grass-covered roots of the mountain and he trembled with emotion to see it rising so high above him, the grass fading, parting to reveal the tumbled rock and the rock vanishing higher up beneath banks of snow.

'She will have taken the easiest face,' Nilsson decided, looking at the map he had found in the camp. 'It will mean crossing two snow-fields.'

They rested on the last of the grass. And he looked down over the country through which they had passed, unable to talk or describe his feelings. It possessed no horizon, for mountains were on all sides, and within the mountains he saw rivers and lakes, tree-covered hills, all of which had taken on fresh, brighter colourings, the lakes reflecting the red of the sun and the blue of the sky and giving them subtly different qualities.

He was glad they were taking the easiest face for he felt no need, here, to test or to temper himself.

For a while he felt complete with the country, ready to climb upwards because he would rather do so, and because the view from the peak would also be different, add perhaps to the fullness of his experience.

He realised, as they got up, that this was not what Nilsson was feeling. Hallner had almost forgotten about the girl.

They began to climb. It was tiring, but not difficult for initially the slope was gradual, less than forty-five degrees. They came to the first snow-field which was slightly below them, climbed downwards carefully, but with relief.

Nilsson had taken a stick from the Lapp camp. He took a step forward, pressing the stick into the snow ahead of him, took another step, pressed the stick down again.

Hallner followed, treading cautiously in his friend's footsteps, little pieces of frozen snow falling into his boots. He knew that Nilsson was trying to judge the snow-field's thickness. Below it a deep river coursed and he thought he heard its musical rushing beneath his feet. He noted, also, that his feet now felt frozen and uncomfortable.

Very slowly they crossed the snow-field and, after a long time, they were safely across and sat down to rest for a while, preparing for the steeper climb ahead.

Nilsson eased his pack off his shoulders and leaned against it, staring back at the field.

'No tracks,' he mused. 'Perhaps she crossed further down.'

'Perhaps she didn't come here after all.' Hallner spoke with effort. He was not really interested.

'Don't be a fool.' Nilsson rose and hefted his pack onto his back again.

They climbed over the sharp rocks separating the two snow-fields and once again underwent the danger of crossing the second field.

Hallner sat down to rest again, but Nilsson climbed on. After a few moments, Hallner followed and saw that Nilsson had stopped and was frowning at the folded map in his hand.

When he reached Nilsson he saw that the mountain now curved upwards around a deep, wide indentation. Across this, a similar curve went up towards the summit. It looked a decidedly easier climb than the one which faced them.

Nilsson swore.

'The damned map's misled us – or else the position of the fields has altered. We've climbed the wrong face.'

'Should we go back down again?' Hallner asked uninterestedly.

'No – there's not much difference – we'd have still lost a lot of time.'

Where the two curves joined, there was a ridge high above them which would take them across to the face which they should have climbed. This was getting close to the peak, so that, in fact, there would be no advantage even when they reached the other side.

'No wonder we missed her tracks,' Nilsson said pettishly. 'She'll be at the summit by now.'

'How do you know she climbed this mountain?' Hallner wondered why he had not considered this earlier.

Nilsson waved the map. 'You don't think Lapps need these? No – *she* left it behind.'

'Oh…' Hallner stared down at the raw, tumbling rocks which formed an almost sheer drop beneath his feet.

'No more resting,' Nilsson said. 'We've got a lot of time to make up.'

He followed behind Nilsson who foolishly expended his energy in swift, savage ascents and was showing obvious signs of exhaustion before they ever reached the ridge.

Unperturbed by the changed situation, Hallner climbed after him, slowly and steadily. The ascent was taking longer, was more difficult and he, also, was tired, but he possessed no sense of despair.

Panting, Nilsson waited for him on a rock close to the ridge, which formed a narrow strip of jumbled rocks slanting upwards towards the peak. On one side of it was an almost sheer drop going down more than a hundred feet, and on the other the rocky sides sloped steeply down to be submerged in a dazzling expanse of faintly creaking ice – a glacier.

'I'm going to have to leave you behind if you don't move faster,' Nilsson panted.

Hallner put his head slightly on one side and peered up the mountain. Silently, he pointed.

'God! Everything's against us, today,' Nilsson kicked at a loose piece of rock and sent it out into space. It curved and plummeted down, but they could not see or hear it fall.

The mist, which Hallner had noted, came rolling swiftly towards them, obscuring the other peaks, boiling in across the range.

'Will it affect us?' Hallner asked.

'It's sure to!'

'How long will it stay?'

'A few minutes or several hours, it's impossible to tell. If we stay where we are we could very well freeze to death. If we go on there's a chance of reaching the summit and getting above it. Willing to risk it?'

This last remark was a sneering challenge.

'Why yes, of course,' Hallner said.

Now that the fact had been mentioned, he noted for the first time that he was cold. But the coldness was not uncomfortable.

They had no ropes, no climbing equipment of any kind, and even his boots were flat-soled city boots. As the mist poured in, its grey, shifting mass limiting vision almost utterly at times, they climbed on, keeping together by shouts.

Once, he could hardly see at all, reached a rock, felt about it with his boot, put his weight on the rock, slipped, clung to the rock and felt both feet go sliding free in space just as the mist parted momentarily to show him the creaking glacier far below him. And something else – a black, spread-out shadow blemishing the pure expanse of ice.

He scrabbled at the rock with his toes, trying to swing himself back to the main part of the ridge, got an insecure toehold and flung himself sideways to the comparative safety of the narrow causeway. He breathed quickly and shallowly and shook with reaction. Then he arose and continued on up the slanting ridge.

A while later, when the main thickness of the mist had rolled past and now lay above the glacier, he saw that they had crossed the ridge and were on the other side without his having realised it.

He could now see Nilsson climbing with obvious difficulty towards what he had called the 'false summit'. The real summit could not be seen, was hidden by the other, but there was now only another hundred feet to climb.

They rested on the false summit, unable to see much that was below them for, although the mist was thinner, it was thick enough to hide most of the surrounding mountains. Sometimes it would part so that they could see fragments of mountains, patches of distant lakes, but little else.

Hallner looked at Nilsson. The other man's handsome face had taken on a set, obstinate look. One hand was bleeding badly.

'Are you all right?' Hallner nodded his head towards the bleeding hand.

'Yes!'

Hallner lost interest since it was evident he could not help Nilsson in his present mood.

He noted that the mist had penetrated his thin jacket and his whole body was damp and chilled. His own hands were torn and grazed and his body was bruised, aching, but he was still not discomforted. He allowed Nilsson to start off first and then forced himself on the last stage of the climb.

By the time he reached the snowless summit, the air was bright, the mist had disappeared and the sun shone in the clear sky.

He flung himself down close to Nilsson who was again peering at his map.

He lay panting, sprawled awkwardly on the rock and stared out over the world.

There was nothing to say. The scene itself, although magnificent, was not what stopped him from talking, stopped his mind from reasoning, as if time had come to a standstill, as if the passage of the planet through space had been halted. He existed, like a monument, petrified, unreasoning, absorbing. He drank in eternity.

Why hadn't the dead human race realised this? It was only necessary to exist, not to be trying constantly to prove you existed when the fact was plain.

Plain to him, he realised, because he had climbed a mountain. This knowledge was his reward. He had not received any ability to think with greater clarity, or a vision to reveal the secret of the universe, or an experience of ecstasy. He had been given, by himself, by his own action, insensate peace, the infinite tranquillity of *existing*.

Nilsson's harsh, disappointed tones invaded this peace.

'I could have sworn she would climb up here. Maybe she did. Maybe we were too late and she's gone back down again?'

Hallner remembered the mark he had seen on the glacier. Now he knew what it had been.

'I saw something back on the ridge,' he said. 'On the glacier. A human figure, I think.'

'What? Why didn't you tell me?'

'I don't know.'

'Was she alive? Think of the importance of this – if she is alive we can start the human race all over again. What's the matter with you, Hallner? Have you gone crazy with shock or something? *Was she alive?*'

'Perhaps – I don't know.'

'You don't –' Nilsson snarled in disbelief and began scrabbling back the way he had come.

'You heartless bastard! Supposing she's hurt – injured!'

Hallner watched Nilsson go cursing and stumbling, sometimes falling, on his over-rapid descent of the mountain. He saw him rip off his pack and fling it aside, nearly staggering over the ridge as he began to climb down it.

Hallner thought dispassionately that Nilsson would kill himself if he continued so heedlessly.

Then he returned his gaze to the distant lakes and trees below him.

He lay on the peak of the mountain, sharing its existence. He was immobile, he did not even blink as he took in the view. It seemed that he was part of the rock, part of the mountain itself.

A little later there came an aching yell which died away into the silence. But Hallner did not hear it.

The Deep Fix

Chapter One

QUICKENING SOUNDS IN the early dusk. Beat of hearts, surge of blood.

Seward turned his head on the bed and looked towards the window. They were coming again. He raised his drug-wasted body and lowered his feet to the floor. He felt nausea sweep up and through him. Dizzily, he stumbled towards the window, parted the blind and stared out over the white ruins.

The sea splashed far away, down by the harbour, and the mob was again rushing through the broken streets towards the Research Lab. They were raggedly dressed and raggedly organised, their faces were thin and contorted with madness, but they were numerous.

Seward decided to activate the Towers once more. He walked shakily to the steel-lined room on his left. He reached out a grey, trembling hand and flicked down three switches on a bank of hundreds. Lights blinked on the board above the switches. Seward walked over to the monitor-computer and spoke to it. His voice was harsh, tired and cracking.

'GREEN 9/7 – O Frequency. RED 8/5 – B Frequency.' He didn't bother with the other Towers. Two were enough to deal with the mob outside. Two wouldn't harm anybody too badly.

He walked back into the other room and parted the blind again. He saw the mob pause and look towards the roof where the Towers GREEN 9/7 and RED 8/5 were already beginning to spin. Once their gaze had been fixed on the Towers, they couldn't get it away. A few saw their companions look up and these automatically shut their eyes and dropped to the ground. But the others were now held completely rigid.

One by one, then many at a time, those who stared at the Towers began to jerk and thresh, eyes rolling, foaming at the mouth, screaming (he heard their screams faintly) – exhibiting every sign of an advanced epileptic fit.

Seward leaned against the wall feeling sick. Outside, those who'd escaped were crawling round and inching down the street on their bellies. Then, eyes averted from the Towers, they rose to their feet and began to run away through the ruins.

Saved again, he thought bitterly.

What was the point? Could he bring himself to go on activating the Towers every time? Wouldn't there come a day when he would let the mob get into the laboratory, search him out, kill him, smash his equipment? He deserved it, after all. The world was in ruins because of him, because of the Towers and the other hallucimats which he'd perfected. The mob wanted its revenge. It was fair.

Yet, while he lived, there might be a way of saving something from the wreckage he had made of mankind's minds. The mobs were not seriously hurt by the Towers. It had been the other machines which had created the real damage. Machines like the Paramats, Schizomats, Engramoscopes, even Michelson's Stroboscope Type 8. A range of instruments which had been designed to help the world and had, instead, virtually destroyed civilisation.

The memory was all too clear. He wished it wasn't. Having lost track of time almost from the beginning of the disaster, he had no idea how long this had been going on. A year, maybe? His life had become divided into two sections: drug-stimulated working-period; exhausted, troubled, tranquillised sleeping-period. Sometimes, when the mobs saw the inactive Towers and charged towards the laboratory, he had to protect himself. He had learned to sense the coming of a mob. They never came individually. Mob hysteria had become the universal condition of mankind – for all except Seward who had created it.

Hallucimatics, neural stimulators, mechanical psycho-simulatory devices, hallucinogenic drugs and machines, all had been developed to perfection at the Hampton Research Laboratory under the brilliant direction of Prof. Lee W. Seward (33), psychophysicist extraordinary, one of the youngest pioneers in the field of hallucinogenic research.

Better for the world if he hadn't been, thought Seward wearily as he lowered his worn-out body into the chair and stared at the table full of notebooks and loose sheets of paper on which he'd been working ever since the result of Experiment Restoration.

Experiment Restoration. A fine name. Fine ideals to inspire it. Fine brains to make it. But something had gone wrong.

Originally developed to help in the work of curing mental disorders of all kinds, whether slight or extreme, the hallucimats had been an extension on the old hallucinogenic drugs such as CO_2, Mescalin and Lysergic Acid derivatives. Their immediate ancestor was the stroboscope and machines like it. The stroboscope, spinning rapidly, flashing brightly coloured patterns into the eyes of a subject, often inducing epilepsy or a similar disorder; the research of Burroughs and his followers into the early types of crude hallucimats, had all helped to contribute to a better understanding of mental disorders.

But, as research continued, so did the incidence of mental illness rise rapidly throughout the world.

The Hampton Research Laboratory and others like it were formed to combat that rise with what had hitherto been considered near-useless experiments in the field of Hallucimatics. Seward, who had been stressing the potential importance of his chosen field since university, came into his own. He was made Director of the Hampton Lab.

People had earlier thought of Seward as a crank and of the hallucimats as being at best toys and at worse 'madness machines', irresponsibly created by a madman.

But psychiatrists specially trained to work with them had found them invaluable aids to their studies of mental disorders. It had become possible for a trained psychiatrist to induce in himself a temporary state of mental abnormality by use of these machines. Thus he was better able to understand and help his patients. By different methods – light, sound waves, simulated brainwaves, and so on – the machines created the symptoms of dozens of basic abnormalities and thousands of permutations. They became an essential part of modern psychiatry.

The result: hundreds and hundreds of patients, hitherto virtually incurable, had been cured completely.

But the birth rate was rising even faster than had been predicted in the middle part of the century. And mental illness rose faster than the birth rate. Hundreds of cases could be cured. But there were millions to be cured. There was no mass-treatment for mental illness.

Not yet.

Work at the Hampton Research Lab became a frantic race to get ahead of the increase. Nobody slept much as, in the great big world outside, individual victims of mental illness turned into groups of – the world had only recently forgotten the old word and now remembered it again – *maniacs*.

An overcrowded, over-pressured world, living on its nerves, cracked up.

The majority of people, of course, did not succumb to total madness. But those who did became a terrible problem.

Governments, threatened by anarchy, were forced to re-institute the cruel, old laws in order to combat the threat. All over the world prisons, hospitals, mental homes, institutions of many kinds, all were turned into Bedlams. This hardly solved the problem. Soon, if the rise continued, the sane would be in a minority.

A dark tide of madness, far worse even than that which had swept Europe in the Middle Ages, threatened to submerge civilisation.

Work at the Hampton Research Laboratory speeded up and speeded up – and members of the team began to crack. Not all these cases were noticeable to the overworked men who remained sane. They were too busy with their frantic experiments.

Only Lee Seward and a small group of assistants kept going, making increasing use of stimulant-drugs and depressant-drugs to do so.

But, now that Seward thought back, they had not been sane, they had not remained cool and efficient any more than the others. They had seemed to, that was all. Perhaps the drugs had deceived them.

The fact was, they had panicked – though the signs of panic had been hidden, even to themselves, under the disciplined guise of sober thinking.

Their work on tranquillising machines had not kept up with their perfection of stimulatory devices. This was because they had had to study the reasons for mental abnormalities before they could begin to devise machines for curing them.

Soon, they decided, the whole world would be mad, well before they could perfect their tranquilomatic machines. They could see no way of speeding up this work any more.

Seward was the first to put it to his team. He remembered his words.

'Gentlemen, as you know, our work on hallucimats for the actual *curing* of mental disorders is going too slowly. There is no sign of our perfecting such machines in the near future. I have an alternative proposal.'

The alternative proposal had been Experiment Restoration. The title, now Seward thought about it, had been euphemistic. It should have been called Experiment Diversion. The existing hallucimats would be set up throughout the world and used to induce *passive* disorders in the minds of the greater part of the human race. The co-operation of national governments and World Council was sought and given. The machines were set up secretly at key points all over the globe.

They began to 'send' the depressive symptoms of various disorders. They worked. People became quiet and passive. A large number went into catatonic states. Others – a great many others, who were potentially inclined to melancholia, manic depression, certain kinds of schizophrenia – committed suicide. Rivers became clogged with corpses, roads awash with the blood and flesh of those who'd thrown themselves in front of cars. Every time a plane or rocket was seen in the sky, people expected to see at least one body come falling from it. Often, whole cargoes of people were killed by the suicide of a captain, driver or pilot of a vehicle.

Even Seward had not suspected the extent of the potential suicides. He was shocked. So was his team.

So were the World Council and the national governments. They told Seward and his team to turn off their machines and reverse the damage they had done, as much as possible.

Seward had warned them of the possible result of doing this. He had been ignored. His machines had been confiscated and the World Council had put untrained or ill-trained operators on them. This was one of the last acts of the World Council. It was one of the last rational – however ill-judged – acts the world knew.

The real disaster had come about when the bungling operators that the World Council had chosen set the hallucimats to send the full effects of the conditions they'd originally been designed to produce. The operators may have been fools – they were probably mad themselves to do what they did. Seward couldn't know. Most of them had been killed by bands of psychopathic murderers who killed their victims by the hundreds in weird and horrible rites which seemed to mirror those of prehistory – or those of the insane South American cultures before the Spaniards.

Chaos had come swiftly – the chaos that now existed.

Seward and his three remaining assistants had protected themselves the only way they could, by erecting the stroboscopic Towers on the roof of the laboratory building. This kept the mobs off. But it did not help their consciences. One by one Seward's assistants had committed suicide.

Only Seward, keeping himself alive on a series of ever-more-potent drugs, somehow retained his sanity. And, he thought ironically, this sanity was only comparative.

A hypodermic syringe lay on the table and beside it a small bottle marked M-A 19 – Mescalin-Andrenol Nineteen – a drug hitherto only tested on animals, never on human beings. But all the other drugs he had used to keep himself going had either run out or now had poor effects. The M-A 19 was his last hope of being able to continue his work on the tranquilomats he needed to perfect and thus rectify his mistake in the only way he could.

As he reached for the bottle and the hypodermic, he thought coolly that, now he looked back, the whole world had been suffering from insanity well before he had even considered Experiment Restoration. The decision to make the experiment had been just another symptom of the world-disease. Something like it would have happened sooner or later, whether by natural or artificial means. It wasn't really his fault. He had been nothing much more than fate's tool.

But logic didn't help. In a way it *was* his fault. By now, with an efficient team, he might have been able to have constructed a few experimental tranquilomats, at least.

Now I've got to do it alone, he thought as he pulled up his trouser leg and sought a vein he could use in his clammy, grey flesh. He had long since given up dabbing the area with anaesthetic. He found a blue vein, depressed the plunger of the needle and sat back in his chair to await results.

Chapter Two

THEY CAME SUDDENLY and were drastic.

His brain and body exploded in a torrent of mingled ecstasy and pain which surged through him. Waves of pale light flickered. Rich darkness followed. He rode a ferris wheel of erupting sensations and emotions. He fell down a never-ending slope of obsidian rock surrounded by clouds of green, purple, yellow, black. The rock vanished, but he continued to fall.

Then there was the smell of disease and corruption in his nostrils, but even that passed and he was standing up.

World of phosphorescence drifting like golden spheres into black night. Green, blue, red explosions. Towers rotate slowly. Towers Advance. Towers Recede. Advance. Recede. Vanish.

Flickering world of phosphorescent tears falling into the timeless, spaceless wastes of Nowhere. World of Misery. World of Antagonism. World of Guilt. Guilt – guilt – guilt...

World of hateful wonder.

Heart throbbing, mind thudding, body shuddering as M-A 19 flowed up the infinity of the spine. Shot into back-brain, shot into mid-brain, shot into fore-brain.

EXPLOSION ALL CENTRES!

No-mind – No-body – No-where.

Dying waves of light danced out of his eyes and away through the dark world. Everything was dying. Cells, sinews, nerves, synapses – all crumbling. Tears of light, fading, fading.

Brilliant rockets streaking into the sky, exploding all together and sending their multicoloured globes of light – balls on an Xmas Tree – balls on a great tree – x-mass – drifting slowly earthwards.

Ahead of him was a tall, blocky building constructed of huge chunks of yellowed granite, like a fortress. Black mist swirled around it and across the bleak, horizonless nightscape.

This was no normal hallucinatory experience. Seward felt the ground under his feet, the warm air on his face, the half-familiar smells. He had no doubt that he had entered another world.

But where was it? How had he got here?

Who had brought him here?

The answer might lie in the fortress ahead. He began to walk towards it. Gravity seemed lighter, for he walked with greater ease than normal and was soon standing looking up at the huge green metallic door. He bunched his fist and rapped on it.

Echoes boomed through numerous corridors and were absorbed in the heart of the fortress.

Seward waited as the door was slowly opened.

A man who so closely resembled the Laughing Cavalier of the painting that he must have modelled his beard and clothes on it bowed slightly and said:

'Welcome home, Professor Seward. We've been expecting you.'

The bizarrely dressed man stepped aside and allowed him to pass into a dark corridor.

'Expecting me,' said Seward. 'How?'

The Cavalier replied good-humouredly: 'That's not for me to explain. Here we go – through this door and up this corridor.' He opened the door and turned into another corridor and Seward followed him.

They opened innumerable doors and walked along innumerable corridors.

The complexities of the corridors seemed somehow familiar to Seward. He felt disturbed by them, but the possibility of an explanation overrode his qualms and he willingly followed the Laughing Cavalier deeper and deeper into the fortress, through the twists and turns until they arrived at a door which was probably very close to the centre of the fortress.

The Cavalier knocked confidently on the door, but spoke deferentially. 'Professor Seward is here at last, sir.'

A light, cultured voice said from the other side of the door: 'Good. Send him in.'

This door opened so slowly that it seemed to Seward that he was watching a film slowed down to a fraction of its proper speed. When it had opened sufficiently to let him enter, he went into the room beyond. The Cavalier didn't follow him.

It only occurred to him then that he might be in some kind of mental institution, which would explain the fortresslike nature of the building and the man dressed up like the Laughing Cavalier. But, if so, how had he got here – unless he had collapsed and order had been restored sufficiently for someone to have come and collected him. No, the idea was weak.

The room he entered was full of rich, dark colours. Satin screens and hangings obscured much of it. The ceiling was not visible. Neither was the source of the rather dim light. In the centre of the room stood a dais, raised perhaps a foot from the floor. On the dais was an old leather armchair.

In the armchair sat a naked man with a cool, blue skin.

He stood up as Seward entered. He smiled charmingly and stepped off the dais, advancing towards Seward with his right hand extended.

'Good to see you, old boy!' he said heartily.

Dazed, Seward clasped the offered hand and felt his whole arm tingle as if it had had a mild electric shock. The man's strange flesh was firm, but seemed to itch under Seward's palm.

The man was short – little over five feet tall. His eyebrows met in the centre and his shiny black hair grew to a widow's peak.

Also, he had no navel.

'I'm glad you could get here, Seward,' he said, walking back to his dais and sitting in the armchair. He rested his head in one hand, his elbow on the arm of the chair.

Seward did not like to appear ungracious, but he was worried and mystified. 'I don't know where this place is,' he said. 'I don't even know how I got here – unless...'

'Ah, yes – the drug. M-A 19, isn't it? That helped, doubtless. We've been trying to get in touch with you for ages, old boy.'

'I've got work to do – back there,' Seward said obsessionally. 'I'm sorry, but I want to get back as soon as I can. What do you want?'

The Man Without A Navel sighed. 'I'm sorry, too, Seward. But we can't let you go yet. There's something I'd like to ask you – a favour. That was why we were hoping you'd come.'

'What's your problem?' Seward's sense of unreality, never very strong here, for in spite of the world's bizarre appearance it seemed familiar, was growing weaker. If he could help the man and get back to continue his research, he would.

'Well,' smiled the Man Without A Navel, 'it's really your problem as much as ours. You see,' he shrugged diffidently, 'we want your world destroyed.'

'What!' Now something was clear, at last. This man and his kind did belong to another world – whether in space, time, or different dimensions – and they were enemies of Earth. 'You can't expect me to help you do that!' He laughed. 'You *are* joking.'

The Man Without A Navel shook his head seriously. 'Afraid not, old boy.'

'That's why you want me here – you've seen the chaos in the world and you want to take advantage of it – you want me to be a – a fifth columnist.'

'Ah, you remember the old term, eh? Yes, I suppose that is what I mean. I want you to be our agent. Those machines of yours could be modified to make those who are left turn against each other even more than at present. Eh?'

'You must be very stupid if you think I'll do that,' Seward said tiredly. 'I can't help you. I'm trying to help *them*.' Was he trapped here for good? He said weakly: 'You've got to let me go back.'

'Not as easy as that, old boy. I – and my friends – want to enter your world, but we can't until you've pumped up your machines to such a pitch that the entire world is maddened and destroys itself, d'you see?'

'Certainly,' exclaimed Seward. 'But I'm having no part of it!'

Again the Man Without A Navel smiled, slowly. 'You'll weaken soon enough, old boy.'

'Don't be so sure,' Seward said defiantly. 'I've had plenty of chances of giving up – back there. I could have weakened. But I didn't.'

'Ah, but you've forgotten the new factor, Seward.'

'What's that?'

'The M-A 19.'

'What do you mean?'

'You'll know soon enough.'

'Look – I want to get out of this place. You can't keep me – there's no point – I won't agree to your plan. Where is this world, anyway?'

'Knowing that depends on you, old boy.' The man's tone was mocking. 'Entirely on you. A lot depends on you, Seward.'

'I know.'

The Man Without A Navel lifted his head and called: 'Brother Sebastian, are you available?' He glanced back at Seward with an ironical smile. 'Brother Sebastian may be of some help.'

Seward saw the wall hangings on the other side of the room move. Then, from behind a screen on which was painted a weird, surrealistic scene, a tall, cowled figure emerged, face in shadow, hands folded in sleeves. A monk.

'Yes, sir,' said the monk in a cold, malicious voice.

'Brother Sebastian, Professor Seward here is not quite as ready to comply with our wishes as we had hoped. Can you influence him in any way?'

'Possibly, sir.' Now the tone held a note of anticipation.

'Good. Professor Seward, will you go with Brother Sebastian?'

'No.' Seward had thought the room contained only one door – the one he'd entered through. But now there was a chance of there being more doors – other than the one through which the cowled monk had come. The two men didn't seem to hear his negative reply. They remained where they were, not moving. 'No,' he said again, his voice rising. 'What right have you to do this?'

'Rights? A strange question.' The monk chuckled to himself. It was a sound like ice tumbling into a cold glass.

'Yes – rights. You must have some sort of organisation here.

Therefore you must have a ruler – or government. I demand to be taken to someone in authority.'

'But I am in authority here, old boy,' purred the blue-skinned man. 'And – in a sense – so are you. If you agreed with my suggestion, you could hold tremendous power. Tremendous.'

'I don't want to discuss that again.' Seward began to walk towards the wall hangings. They merely watched him – the monk with his face in shadow – the Man Without A Navel with a supercilious smile on his thin lips. He walked around a screen, parted the hangings – and there they were on the other side. He went through the hangings. This was some carefully planned trick – an illusion – deliberately intended to confuse him. He was used to such methods, even though he didn't understand how they'd worked this one. He said: 'Clever – but tricks of this kind won't make me weaken.'

'What on Earth d'you mean, Seward, old man? Now, I wonder if you'll accompany Brother Sebastian here. I have an awful lot of work to catch up on.'

'All right,' Seward said. 'All right, I will.' Perhaps on the way to wherever the monk was going, he would find an opportunity to escape.

The monk turned and Seward followed him. He did not look at the Man Without A Navel as he passed his ridiculous dais, with its ridiculous leather armchair.

They passed through a narrow doorway behind a curtain and were once again in the complex series of passages. The tall monk – now he was close to him, Seward estimated his height at about six feet, seven inches – seemed to flow along in front of him. He began to dawdle. The monk didn't look back. Seward increased the distance between them. Still, the monk didn't appear to notice.

Seward turned and ran.

They had met nobody on their journey through the corridors. He hoped he could find a door leading out of the fortress before someone spotted him. There was no cry from behind him.

But as he ran, the passages got darker and darker until he was careering through pitch blackness, sweating, panting and beginning to panic. He kept blundering into damp walls and running on.

It was only much later that he began to realise he was running in a circle that was getting tighter and tighter until he was doing little more than spin round, like a top. He stopped, then.

These people evidently had more powers than he had suspected. Possibly they had some means of shifting the position of the corridor walls, following his movements by means of hidden TV cameras or something like them. Simply because there were no visible signs of an advanced technology didn't mean that they did not possess one. They obviously did. How else could they have got him from his own world to this?

He took a pace forward. Did he sense the walls drawing back? He wasn't sure. The whole thing reminded him vaguely of *The Pit and the Pendulum*.

He strode forward a number of paces and saw a light ahead of him. He walked towards it, turned into a dimly lit corridor.

The monk was waiting for him.

'We missed each other, Professor Seward. I see you managed to precede me.' The monk's face was still invisible, secret in its cowl. As secret as his cold mocking, malevolent voice. 'We are almost there, now,' said the monk.

Seward stepped towards him, hoping to see his face, but it was impossible. The monk glided past him. 'Follow me, please.'

For the moment, until he could work out how the fortress worked, Seward decided to accompany the monk.

They came to a heavy, iron-studded door – quite unlike any of the other doors.

They walked into a low-ceilinged chamber. It was very hot. Smoke hung in the still air of the room. It poured from a glowing brazier at the extreme end. Two men stood by the brazier.

One of them was a thin man with a huge, bulging stomach over which his long, narrow hands were folded. He had a shaggy mane of dirty white hair, his cheeks were sunken and his nose extremely long and extremely pointed. He seemed toothless and his puckered lips were shaped in a senseless smile – like the smile of a madman Seward had once had to experiment on. He wore a stained white jacket buttoned over his grotesque paunch. On his legs were loose khaki trousers.

His companion was also thin, though lacking the stomach. He was taller and had the face of a mournful bloodhound, with sparse, highly greased, black hair that covered his bony head like a skull-cap. He stared into the brazier, not looking up as Brother Sebastian led Seward into the room and closed the door.

The thin man with the stomach, however, pranced forward, his hands still clasped on his paunch, and bowed to them both.

'Work for us, Brother Sebastian?' he said, nodding at Seward.

'We require a straightforward "Yes",' Brother Sebastian said. 'You have merely to ask the question "Will You?". If he replies "No", you are to continue. If he replies "Yes", you are to cease and inform me immediately.'

'Very well, Brother. Rely on us.'

'I hope I can.' The monk chuckled again. 'You are now in the charge of these men, professor. If you decide you want to help us, after all, you have only to say "Yes". Is that clear?'

Seward began to tremble with horror. He had suddenly realised what this place was.

'Now look here,' he said. 'You can't...'

He walked towards the monk who had turned and was opening the door. He grasped the man's shoulder. His hand seemed to clutch a delicate, birdlike structure. 'Hey! I don't think you're a man at all. What *are* you?'

'A man or a mouse,' chuckled the monk as the two grotesque creatures leapt forward suddenly and twisted Seward's arms behind him. Seward kicked back at them with his heels, squirmed in their grasp, but he might have been held by steel bands. He shouted incoherently at the monk as he shut the door behind him with a whisk of his habit.

The pair flung him onto the damp, hot stones of the floor. It smelled awful. He rolled over and sat up. They stood over him. The hound-faced man had his arms folded. The thin man with the stomach had his long hands on his paunch again. They seemed to rest there whenever he was not actually using them. It was the latter who smiled with his twisting, puckered lips, cocking his head to one side.

'What do *you* think, Mr Morl?' he asked his companion.

'I don't know, Mr Hand. After you.' The hound-faced man spoke in a melancholy whisper.

'I would suggest Treatment H. Simple to operate, less work for us, a tried and trusty operation which works with most and will probably work with this gentleman.'

Seward scrambled up and tried to push past them, making for the door. Again they seized him expertly and dragged him back. He felt the rough touch of rope on his wrists and the pain as a knot was tightened. He shouted, more in anger than agony, more in terror than either.

They were going to torture him. He knew it.

When they had tied his hands, they took the rope and tied his ankles. They twisted the rope up around his calves and under his legs. They made a halter of the rest and looped it over his neck so that he had to bend almost double if he was not to strangle.

Then they sat him on a chair.

Mr Hand removed his hands from his paunch, reached up above Seward's head and turned on the tap.

The first drop of water fell directly on the centre of his head some five minutes later.

Twenty-seven drops of water later, Seward was raving and screaming. Yet every time he tried to jerk his head away, the halter threatened to strangle him and the jolly Mr Hand and the mournful Mr Morl were there to straighten him up again.

Thirty drops of water after that, Seward's brain began to throb and he opened his eyes to see that the chamber had vanished.

In its place was a huge comet, a fireball dominating the sky, rushing directly towards him. He backed away from it and there were no more ropes on his hands or feet. He was free.

He began to run. He leapt into the air and stayed there. He was swimming through the air.

Ecstasy ran up his spine like a flickering fire, touched his back-brain, touched his mid-brain, touched his fore-brain.

EXPLOSION ALL CENTRES!

He was standing one flower among many, in a bed of tall lupines and roses which waved in a gentle wind. He pulled his roots free and began to walk.

He walked into the Lab Control Room.

Everything was normal except that gravity seemed a little heavy. Everything was as he'd left it.

He saw that he had left the Towers rotating. He went into the room he used as a bedroom and workroom. He parted the blind and looked out into the night. There was a big, full moon hanging in the deep blue sky over the ruins of Hampton. He saw its light reflected in the faraway sea. A few bodies still lay prone near the lab. He went back into the Control Room and switched off the Towers.

Returning to the bedroom he looked at the card table he had his notes on. They were undisturbed. Neatly, side by side near a large, tattered notebook, lay a half-full ampoule of M-A 19 and a hypodermic syringe. He picked up the ampoule and threw it in a corner. It did not break but rolled around on the floor for a few seconds.

He sat down.

His whole body ached.

He picked up a sheaf of his more recent notes. He wrote everything down that came into his head on the subject of tranquilomats; it helped him think better and made sure that his drugged mind and body did not hamper him as much as they might have done if he had simply relied on his memory.

He looked at his wrists. They carried the marks of the rope. Evidently the transition from the other world to his own involved leaving anything in the other world behind. He was glad. If he hadn't, he'd have had a hell of a job getting himself untied.

He tried hard to forget the questions flooding through his mind. Where had he been? Who were the people? What did they really want? How far could they keep a check on him? How did the M-A 19 work to aid his transport into the other world? Could they get at him here?

He decided they couldn't get at him, otherwise they might have tried earlier. Somehow it was the M-A 19 in his brain which allowed them to get hold of him. Well, that was simple – no more M-A 19.

With a feeling of relief, he forced himself to concentrate on his notes.

Out of the confusion, something seemed to be developing, but he had to work at great speed – greater speed than previously, perhaps, for he daren't use the M-A 19 again and there was nothing else left of much good.

His brain cleared as he once again got interested in his notes. He worked for two hours, making fresh notes, equations, checking his knowledge against the stack of earlier research notes by the wall near his camp-bed.

Dawn was coming as he realised suddenly that he was suffering from thirst. His throat was bone dry, as were his mouth and lips. He got up and his legs felt weak. He staggered, almost knocking over the chair. With a great effort he righted it and, leaning for support on the bed, got himself to the hand-basin. It was filled by a tank near the roof and he had used it sparsely. But this time he didn't care. He stuck his head under the tap and drank the stale water greedily. It did no good. His whole body now seemed cold, his skin tight, his heart thumping heavily against his ribs. His head was aching horribly and his breathing increased.

He went and lay down on the bed, hoping the feeling would leave him.

It got worse. He needed something to cure himself.

What? he asked.

M-A 19, he answered.

NO!

But – Yes, yes, yes. All he needed was a small shot of the drug and he would be all right. He knew it.

And with knowing that, he realised something else.

He was hooked.

The drug was habit-forming.

Chapter Three

H E FOUND THE half-full M-A 19 ampoule under the bed where it had rolled. He found the needle on the table where he had left it, buried under his notes. He found a vein in his forearm and shot himself full. There was no thought to Seward's action. There was just the craving and the chance of satisfying that craving.

The M-A 19 began to swim leisurely through his veins, drifting up his spine –

It hit his brain with a powerful explosion.

He was walking through a world of phosphorescent rain, leaping over large purple rocks that welcomed his feet, drew them down towards them. All was agony and startling Now.

No-time, no-space, just the throbbing voice in the air above him. It was talking to him.

DOOM, Seward. DOOM, Seward. DOOM, Seward.

'Seward is doomed!' he laughed. 'Seward is betrayed!'

Towers Advance. Towers Recede. Towers Rotate At Normal Speed.

Carnival Aktion. All Carnivals To Explode.

Up into the back-brain, into the mid-brain, on to the fore-brain.

EXPLOSION ALL CENTRES!

He was back in the torture chamber, though standing up. In the corner near the brazier the grotesque pair were muttering to one another. Mr Hand darted him an angry glance, his lips drawn over his gums in an expression of outrage.

'Hello, Seward,' said the Man Without A Navel behind him. 'So you're back.'

'Back,' said Seward heavily. 'What more do you want?'

'Only your All, Seward, old man. I remember a time in Dartford before the war...'

'Which war?'

'Your war, Seward. You were too young to share any other. You don't remember *that* war. You weren't born. Leave it to those who *do*, Seward.'

Seward turned. 'My war?' He looked with disgust at the Man Without A Navel; at his reptilian blue skin and his warm-cold, dark-light, good-evil eyes. At his small yet well-formed body.

The Man Without A Navel smiled. '*Our* war, then, old man. I won't quibble.'

'You made me do it. I think that somehow you made me suggest Experiment Restoration!'

'I said we won't quibble, Seward,' said the man in an authoritative tone. Then, more conversationally: 'I remember a time in Dartford before the war, when you sat in your armchair – one rather like mine – at your brother-in-law's house. Remember what you said, old man?'

Seward remembered well. 'If,' he quoted, 'if I had a button and could press it and destroy the entire universe and myself with it, I would. For no reason other than boredom.'

'Very good, Seward. You have an excellent memory.'

'Is that all you're going on? Something I said out of frustration because nobody was recognising my work?' He paused as he realised something else. 'You know all about me, don't you?' he said bitterly. There seemed to be nothing he didn't know. On the other hand Seward knew nothing of the man. Nothing of this world. Nothing of where it was in space and time. It was a world of insanity, of bizarre contrasts. '*How* do you know all this?'

'Inside information, Seward, old boy.'

'You're mad!'

The Man Without A Navel returned to his earlier topic. 'Are you bored now, Seward?'

'Bored? No. Tired, yes.'

'Bored, no – tired, yes. Very good, Seward. You got here later than expected. What kept you?' The man laughed.

'I kept me. I held off taking the M-A 19 for as long as I could.'

'But you came to us in the end, eh? Good man, Seward.'

'You knew the M-A 19 was habit-forming? You knew I'd have to take it, come back here?'

'Naturally.'

He said pleadingly: 'Let me go, for God's sake! You've made me. Made me...'

'Your dearest wish almost come true, Seward. Isn't that what you wanted? I made you come close to destroying the world? Is that it?'

'So you *did* somehow influence Experiment Restoration!'

'It's possible. But you haven't done very well either way. The world is in shambles. You can't reverse that. Kill it off. Let's start fresh, Seward. Forget your experiments with the tranquilomats and help us.'

'No.'

The Man Without A Navel shrugged. 'We'll see, old boy.'

He looked at the mumbling men in the corner. 'Morl – Hand – take Professor Seward to his room. I don't want any mistakes this time. I'm going to take him out of your hands. Obviously we need subtler minds put on the problem.'

The pair came forward and grabbed Seward. The Man Without A Navel opened the door and they went through it first, forcing Seward ahead of them.

He was too demoralised to resist much, this time. Demoralised by the fact that he was hooked on M-A 19. What did the junkies call it? The Habit. He had The Habit. Demoralised by his inability to understand the whereabouts or nature of the world he was on. Demoralised by the fact that the Man Without A Navel seemed to know everything about his personal life on Earth. Demoralised that he had fallen into the man's trap. Who had developed M-A 19? He couldn't remember. Perhaps the Man Without A Navel had planted it? He supposed it might be possible.

He was pushed along another series of corridors, arrived at another door. The Man Without A Navel came up behind them and unlocked the door.

Seward was shoved into the room. It was narrow and low – coffinlike.

'We'll be sending someone along to see you in a little while, Seward,' said the man lightly. The door was slammed.

Seward lay in pitch blackness.

He began to sob.

Later, he heard a noise outside. A stealthy noise of creeping feet. He shuddered. What was the torture going to be this time?

He heard a scraping and a muffled rattle. The door opened.

Against the light from the passage, Seward saw the man clearly. He was a big, fat negro in a grey suit. He wore a flowing, rainbow-coloured tie. He was grinning.

Seward liked the man instinctively. But he no longer trusted his instinct. 'What do you want?' he said suspiciously.

The huge negro raised his finger to his lips. 'Ssshh,' he whispered. 'I'm going to try and get you out of here.'

'An old Secret Police trick on my world,' said Seward. 'I'm not falling for that.'

'It's no trick, son. Even if it is, what can you lose?'

'Nothing.' Seward got up.

The big man put his arm around Seward's shoulders. Seward felt comfortable in the grip, though normally he disliked such gestures.

'Now, son, we go real quietly and we go as fast as we can. Come on.'

Softly, the big man began to tiptoe along the corridor. Seward was sure that TV cameras, or whatever they were, were following him, that the Man Without A Navel, the monk, the two torturers, the Laughing Cavalier, were all waiting somewhere to seize him.

But, very quickly, the negro had reached a small wooden door and was drawing a bolt. He patted Seward's shoulder and held the door open for him. 'Through you go, son. Make for the red car.'

It was morning. In the sky hung a golden sun, twice the size of Earth's. There was a vast expanse of lifeless rock in all directions, broken only by a white road which stretched into the distance. On the road, close to Seward, was parked a car something like a Cadillac. It was fire-red and bore the registration plates YOU 000. Whoever these people were, Seward decided, they were originally from Earth – all except the Man Without A Navel, perhaps. Possibly this was his world and the others had been brought from Earth, like him.

He walked towards the car. The air was cold and fresh. He stood by the convertible and looked back. The negro was running over the rock towards him. He dashed round the car and got into the driver's seat. Seward got in beside him.

The negro started the car, put it into gear and shoved his foot down hard on the accelerator pedal. The car jerked away and had reached top speed in seconds.

At the wheel, the negro relaxed. 'Glad that went smoothly. I didn't expect to get away with it so easily, son. You're Seward, aren't you?'

'Yes. You seem to be as well-informed as the others.'

'I guess so.' The negro took a pack of cigarettes from his shirt pocket. 'Smoke?'

'No thanks,' said Seward. 'That's one habit I don't have.'

The negro looked back over his shoulder. The expanse of rock seemed never-ending, though in the distance the fortress was disappearing. He flipped a cigarette out of the pack and put it between his lips. He unclipped the car's lighter and put it to the tip of the cigarette. He inhaled and put the lighter back. The cigarette between his lips, he returned his other hand to the wheel.

He said: 'They were going to send the Vampire to you. It's lucky I reached you in time.'

'It could be,' said Seward. 'Who are you? What part do you play in this?'

'Let's just say I'm a friend of yours and an enemy of your enemies. The name's Farlowe.'

'Well, I trust you, Farlowe – though God knows why.'

Farlowe grinned. 'Why not? I don't want your world destroyed any more than you do. It doesn't much matter, I guess, but if there's a chance of restoring it, then you ought to try.'

'Then you're from my world originally, is that it?'

'In a manner of speaking, son,' said Farlowe.

Very much later, the rock gave way to pleasant, flat countryside with trees, fields and little cottages peaceful under the vast sky. In the distance, Seward saw herds of cattle and sheep, the occasional horse. It reminded him of the countryside of his childhood, all clear and fresh and sharp with the clarity that only a child's eye can bring to a scene before it is obscured and tainted by the impressions of adulthood. Soon the flat country was behind them and they were going through an area of low, green hills, the huge sun flooding the scene with its soft, golden light. There were no clouds in the pale blue sky.

The big car sped smoothly along and Seward, in the comfortable companionship of Farlowe, began to relax a little. He felt almost happy, would have felt happy if it had not been for the nagging knowledge that somehow he had to get back and continue his work. It was not merely a question of restoring sanity to the world, now – he had also to thwart whatever plans were in the mind of the Man Without A Navel.

After a long silence, Seward asked a direct question. 'Farlowe, where is this world? What are we doing here?'

Farlowe's answer was vague. He stared ahead at the road. 'Don't ask me that, son. I don't rightly know.'

'But you live here.'

'So do you.'

'No – I only come here when – when...'

'When what?'

But Seward couldn't raise the courage to admit about the drug to Farlowe. Instead he said: 'Does M-A 19 mean anything to you?'

'Nope.'

So Farlowe hadn't come here because of the drug. Seward said: 'But you said you were from my world originally.'

'Only in a manner of speaking.' Farlowe changed gears as the road curved steeply up a hill. It rose gently above the idyllic countryside below.

Seward changed his line of questioning. 'Isn't there any sort of organisation here – no government? What's the name of this country?'

Farlowe shrugged. 'It's just a place – no government. The people in the fortress run most things. Everybody's scared of them.'

'I don't blame them. Who's the Vampire you mentioned?'

'He works for the Man.'

'What is he?'

'Why – a vampire, naturally,' said Farlowe in surprise.

The sun had started to set and the whole countryside was bathed in red-gold light. The car continued to climb the long hill.

Farlowe said: 'I'm taking you to some friends. You ought to be fairly safe there. Then maybe we can work out a way of getting you back.'

Seward felt better. At least Farlowe had given him some direct information.

As the car reached the top of the hill and began to descend Seward got a view of an odd and disturbing sight. The sun was like a flat, round, red disc – yet only half of it was above the horizon. *The line of the horizon evenly intersected the sun's disc!* It was some sort of mirage – yet so convincing that Seward looked away, staring instead at the black smoke which he could now see rolling across the valley below. He said nothing to Farlowe.

'How much further?' he asked later as the car came to the bottom of the hill. Black night had come, moonless, and the car's headlights blazed.

'A long way yet, I'm afraid, son,' said Farlowe. 'You cold?'

'No.'

'We'll be hitting a few signs of civilisation soon. You tired?'

'No – why?'

'We could put up at a motel or something. I guess we could eat anyway.'

Ahead, Seward saw a few lights. He couldn't make out where they came from. Farlowe began to slow down. 'We'll risk it,' he said. He pulled in towards the lights and Seward saw that it was a line of fuel pumps. Behind the pumps was a single-storey build-ing, very long and built entirely of timber by the look of it. Farlowe drove in between the pumps and the building. A man in overalls, the top half of his face shadowed by the peak of his cap, came into sight. Farlowe got out of the car with a signal to Seward to do the same. The negro handed his keys to the attendant. 'Fill her full and give her a quick check.'

Could this be Earth? Seward wondered. Earth in the future – or possibly an Earth of a different space-time continuum. That was the likeliest explanation for this unlikely world. The contrast between recognisable, everyday things and the grotesqueries of the fortress was strange – yet it could be explained easily if these people had contact with his world. That would explain how they had things like cars and fuel stations and no apparent organisation neces-sary for producing them. Somehow, perhaps, they just – *stole* them?

He followed Farlowe into the long building. He could see through the wide windows that it was some kind of restaurant. There was a long, clean counter and a few people seated at tables at the far end. All had their backs to him.

He and Farlowe sat down on stools. Close to them was the larg-est pin-table Seward had ever seen. Its lights were flashing and its balls were clattering, though there was no-one operating it. The coloured lights flashed series of numbers at him until his eyes lost focus and he had to turn away.

A woman was standing behind the counter now. Most of her face was covered by a yashmak.

'What do you want to eat, son?' said Farlowe, turning to him.
'Oh, anything.'

Farlowe ordered sandwiches and coffee. When the woman had gone to get their order, Seward whispered: 'Why's she wearing that thing?'

Farlowe pointed at a sign Seward hadn't noticed before. It read THE HAREM HAVEN. 'It's their gimmick,' said Farlowe.

Seward looked back at the pin-table. The lights had stopped flashing, the balls had stopped clattering. But above it suddenly appeared a huge pair of disembodied eyes. He gasped.

Distantly, he heard his name being repeated over and over again. 'Seward. Seward. Seward. Seward...'

He couldn't tell where the voice was coming from. He glanced up at the ceiling. Not from there. The voice stopped. He looked back at the pin-table. The eyes had vanished. His panic returned. He got off his stool.

'I'll wait for you in the car, Farlowe.'

Farlowe looked surprised. 'What's the matter, son?'

'Nothing – it's okay – I'll wait in the car.'

Farlowe shrugged.

Seward went out into the night. The attendant had gone but the car was waiting for him. He opened the door and climbed in.

What did the eyes mean? Were the people from the fortress following him in some way. Suddenly an explanation for most of the questions bothering him sprang into his mind. Of course – telepathy. They were probably telepaths. That was how they knew so much about him. That could be how they knew of his world and could influence events there – they might never go there in person. This comforted him a little, though he realised that getting out of this situation was going to be even more difficult than he'd thought.

He looked through the windows and saw Farlowe's big body perched on its stool. The other people in the café were still sitting with their backs to him. He realised that there was something familiar about them.

He saw Farlowe get up and walk towards the door. He came

out and got into the car, slamming the door after him. He leaned back in his seat and handed Seward a sandwich. 'You seem worked up, son,' he said. 'You'd better eat this.'

Seward took the sandwich. He was staring at the backs of the other customers again. He frowned.

Farlowe started the car and they moved towards the road. Then Seward realised who the men reminded him of. He craned his head back in the hope of seeing their faces, but it was too late. They had reminded him of his dead assistants – the men who'd committed suicide.

They roared through dimly seen towns – all towers and angles. There seemed to be nobody about. Dawn came up and they still sped on. Seward realised that Farlowe must have a tremendous vitality, for he didn't seem to tire at all. Also, perhaps, he was motivated by a desire to get as far away from the fortress as possible.

They stopped twice to refuel and Farlowe bought more sandwiches and coffee which they had as they drove.

In the late afternoon Farlowe said: 'Almost there.'

They passed through a pleasant village. It was somehow alien, although very similar to a small English village. It had an oddly foreign look which was hard to place. Farlowe pulled in at what seemed to be the gates of a large public park. He looked up at the sun. 'Just made it,' he said. 'Wait in the park – someone will come to collect you.'

'You're leaving me?'

'Yes. I don't think they know where you are. They'll look but, with luck, they won't look around here. Out you get, son. Into the park.'

'Who do I wait for?'

'You'll know her when she comes.'

'Her?' He got out and closed the door. He stood on the pavement watching as, with a cheerful wave, Farlowe drove off. He felt a tremendous sense of loss then, as if his only hope had been taken away.

Gloomily, he turned and walked through the park gates.

Chapter Four

A S HE WALKED between low hedges along a gravel path, he realised that this park, like so many things in this world, contrasted with the village it served. It was completely familiar, just like a park on his own world.

It was like a grey, hazy winter's afternoon, with the brittle, interwoven skeletons of trees black and sharp against the cold sky. Birds perched on trees and bushes, or flew noisily into the silent air.

Evergreens crowded upon the leaf-strewn grass. Cry of sparrows. Peacocks, necks craned forward, dived towards scattered bread. Silver birch, larch, elm, monkey-puzzle trees, and swaying white ferns, each one like an ostrich feather stuck in the earth. A huge, ancient, nameless trunk from which, at the top, grew an expanse of soft, yellow fungus; the trunk itself looking like a Gothic cliff, full of caves and dark windows. A grey-and-brown pigeon perched motionless on the slender branches of a young birch. Peacock chicks the size of hens pecked with concentration at the grass.

Mellow, nostalgic smell of winter; distant sounds of children playing; lost black dog looking for master; red disc of sun in the cool, darkening sky. The light was sharp and yet soft, peaceful. A path led into the distance towards a flight of wide stone steps, at the top of which was the curving entrance to an arbour, browns, blacks and yellows of sapless branches and fading leaves.

From the arbour a girl appeared and began to descend the steps with quick, graceful movements. She stopped when she reached the path. She looked at him. She had long, blonde hair and wore a white dress with a full skirt. She was about seventeen.

The peace of the park was suddenly interrupted by children rushing from nowhere towards the peacocks, laughing and shouting. Some of the boys saw the tree trunk and made for it. Others stood looking upwards at the sun as it sank in the cold air. They seemed not to see either Seward or the girl. Seward looked at her. Did he recognise her? It wasn't possible. Yet she, too, gave him a look of recognition, smiled shyly at him and ran towards him. She reached him, stood on tiptoe and gave him a light kiss on the cheek.

'Hello, Lee.'

'Hello. Have you come to find me?'

'I've been looking for you a long time.'

'Farlowe sent a message ahead?'

She took his hand. 'Come on. Where have you been, Lee?'

This was a question he couldn't answer. He let her lead him back up the steps, through the arbour. Between the branches he glanced a garden and a pool. 'Come on,' she said. 'Let's see what's for dinner. Mother's looking forward to meeting you.'

He no longer questioned how these strange people all seemed to know his name. It was still possible that all of them were taking part in the conspiracy against him.

At the end of the arbour was a house, several storeys high. It was a pleasant house with a blue-and-white door. She led him up the path and into a hallway. It was shining with dark polished wood and brass plates on the walls. From a room at the end he smelled spicy cooking. She went first and opened the door at the end. 'Mother – Lee Seward's here. Can we come in?'

'Of course.' The voice was warm, husky, full of humour. They went into the room and Seward saw a woman of about forty, very well preserved, tall, large-boned with a fine-featured face and smiling mouth. Her eyes also smiled. Her sleeves were rolled up and she put the lid back on a pan on the stove.

'How do you do, Professor Seward. Mr Farlowe's told us about you. You're in trouble, I hear.'

'How do you do, Mrs –'

'Call me Martha. Has Sally introduced herself?'

'No,' Sally laughed. 'I forgot. I'm Sally, Lee.'

Her mother gave a mock frown. 'I suppose you've been calling our guest by his first name, as usual. Do you mind, professor?'

'Not at all.' He was thinking how attractive they both were, in their different ways. The young, fresh girl and her warm, intelligent mother. He had always enjoyed the company of women, but never so much, he realised, as now. They seemed to complement one another. In their presence he felt safe, at ease. Now he realised why Farlowe had chosen them to hide him. Whatever the facts, he would *feel* safe here.

Martha was saying: 'Dinner won't be long.'

'It smells good.'

'Probably smells better than it tastes,' she laughed. 'Go into the lounge with Sally. Sally, fix Professor Seward a drink.'

'Call me Lee,' said Seward, a little uncomfortably. He had never cared much for his first name. He preferred his middle name, William, but not many others did.

'Come on, Lee,' she took his hand and led him out of the kitchen. 'We'll see what there is.' They went into a small, well-lighted lounge. The furniture, like the whole house, had a look that was half-familiar, half-alien – obviously the product of a slightly different race. Perhaps they deliberately imitated Earth culture, without quite succeeding. Sally still gripped his hand. Her hand was warm and her skin smooth. He made to drop it but, involuntarily, squeezed it gently before she took it away to deal with the drink. She gave him another shy smile. He felt that she was as attracted to him as he to her. 'What's it going to be?' she asked him.

'Oh, anything,' he said, sitting down on a comfortable sofa. She poured him a dry martini and brought it over. Then she sat demurely down beside him and watched him drink it. Her eyes sparkled with a mixture of sauciness and innocence which he found extremely appealing. He looked around the room.

'How did Farlowe get his message to you?' he said.

'He came the other day. Said he was going to try and get into the fortress and help you. Farlowe's always flitting about. I think the people at the fortress have a price on his head or something. It's exciting, isn't it?'

'You can say that again,' Seward said feelingly.

'Why are they after you?'

'They want me to help them destroy the world I come from. Do you know anything about it?'

'Earth, isn't it?'

'Yes.' Was he going to get some straightforward answers at last?

'I know it's very closely connected with ours and that some of us want to escape from here and go to your world.'

'Why?' he asked eagerly.

She shook her head. Her long, fine hair waved with the motion. 'I don't really know. Something about their being trapped here – something like that. Farlowe said something about you being a "key" to their release. They can only do what they want to do with your agreement.'

'But I could agree and then break my word!'

'I don't think you could – but honestly, I don't know any more. I've probably got it wrong. Do you like me, Lee?'

He was startled by the directness of her question. 'Yes,' he said, 'very much.'

'Farlowe said you would. Good, isn't it?'

'Why – yes. Farlowe knows a lot.'

'That's why he works against *them*.'

Martha came in. 'Almost ready,' she smiled. 'I think I'll have a quick one before I start serving. How are you feeling, Lee, after your ride?'

'Fine,' he said, 'fine.' He had never been in a position like this one – with two women both of whom were extremely attractive for almost opposite reasons.

'We were discussing why the people at the fortress wanted my help,' he said, turning the conversation back the way he felt it ought to go if he was ever going to get off this world and back to his own and his work.

'Farlowe said something about it.'

'Yes, Sally told me. Does Farlowe belong to some sort of underground organisation?'

'Underground? Why, yes, in a way he does.'

'Aren't they strong enough to fight the Man Without A Navel and his friends?'

'Farlowe says they're strong enough, but divided over what should be done and how.'

'I see. That's fairly common amongst such groups, I believe.'

'Yes.'

'What part do you play?'

'None, really. Farlowe asked me to put you up – that's all.' She sipped her drink, her eyes smiling directly into his. He drained his glass.

'Shall we eat?' she said. 'Sally, take Lee into the dining room.'

The girl got up and, somewhat possessively Seward thought, linked her arm in his. Her young body against his was distracting. He felt a little warm. She took him in. The table was laid for supper. Three chairs and three places. The sun had set and candles burned on the table in brass candelabra. She unlinked her arm and pulled out one of the chairs.

'You sit here, Lee – at the head of the table.' She grinned. Then she leaned forward as he sat down. 'Hope Mummy isn't boring you.'

He was surprised. 'Why should she?'

Martha came in with three covered dishes on a tray. 'This may not have turned out quite right, Lee. Never does when you're trying hard.'

'I'm sure it'll be fine,' he smiled. The two women sat down one either side of him. Martha served him. It was some sort of goulash with vegetables. He took his napkin and put it on his lap.

As they began to eat, Martha said: 'How is it?'

'Fine,' he said. It was very good. Apart from the feeling that some kind of rivalry for his attentions existed between mother and daughter the air of normality in the house was comforting. Here, he might be able to do some constructive thinking about his predicament.

When the meal was over, Martha said: 'It's time for bed, Sally. Say goodnight to Lee.'

She pouted. 'Oh, it's not fair.'

'Yes it is,' she said firmly. 'You can see Lee in the morning. He's had a long journey.'

'All right.' She smiled at Seward. 'Sleep well, Lee.'

'I think I will,' he said.

Martha chuckled after Sally had gone. 'Would you like a drink before you go to bed?' She spoke softly.

'Love one,' he said.

They went into the other room. He sat down on the sofa as she mixed the drinks. She brought them over and sat down next to him as her daughter had done earlier.

'Tell me everything that's been happening. It sounds so exciting.'

He knew at once he could tell her all he wanted to, that she would listen and be sympathetic. 'It's terrifying, really,' he began, half-apologetically. He began to talk, beginning with what had happened on Earth. She listened.

'I even wondered if this was a dreamworld – a figment of my imagination,' he finished, 'but I had to reject that when I went back to my own. I had rope marks on my wrists – my hair was soaking wet. You don't get that in a dream!'

'I hope not,' she smiled. 'We're different here, Lee, obviously. Our life doesn't have the – the *shape* that yours has. We haven't much direction, no real desires. We just – well – *exist*. It's as if we're waiting for something to happen. As if –' she paused and seemed to be looking down deep into herself. 'Put it this way – Farlowe thinks you're the key figure in some development that's happening here. Supposing – supposing we were some kind of – of experiment...'

'Experiment? How do you mean?'

'Well, from what you say, the people at the fortress have an advanced science that we don't know about. Supposing our parents, say, had been kidnapped from your world and – made to think – what's the word –'

'Conditioned?'

'Yes, conditioned to think they were natives of this world. We'd have grown up knowing nothing different. Maybe the Man Without A Navel is a member of an alien race – a scientist of some kind in charge of the experiment.'

'But why should they make such a complicated experiment?'

'So they could study us, I suppose.'

Seward marvelled at her deductive powers. She had come to a much firmer theory than he had. But then he thought, she might subconsciously *know* the truth. Everyone knew much more than they knew, as it were. For instance, it was pretty certain that the secret of the tranquilomat was locked somewhere down in his unconscious if only he could get at it. Her explanation was logical and worth thinking about.

'You may be right,' he said. 'If so, it's something to go on. But it doesn't stop my reliance on the drug – or the fact that the Man and his helpers are probably telepathic and are at this moment looking for me.'

She nodded. 'Could there be an *antidote* for the drug?'

'Unlikely. Drugs like that don't really need antidotes – they're not like poisons. There must be some way of getting at the people in the fortress – some way of putting a stop to their plans. What about an organised revolution? What has Farlowe tried to do?'

'Nothing much. The people aren't easy to organise. We haven't much to do with one another. Farlowe was probably hoping you could help – think of something he hasn't. Maybe one of those machines you mentioned would work against the fortress people?'

'No, I don't think so. Anyway, the hallucimats are too big to move from one place to another by hand – let alone from one world to another.'

'And you haven't been able to build a tranquilomat yet?'

'No – we have a lot of experimental machines lying around at the lab – they're fairly small – but it's a question of modifying them – that's what I'm trying to do at the moment. If I could make one that works it would solve part of my problem – it would save my world and perhaps even save yours, if you *are* in a state of conditioning.'

'It sounds reasonable,' she dropped her eyes and looked at her drink. She held the glass balanced on her knees which were pressed closely together, nearly touching him. 'But,' she said, 'they're going to catch you sooner or later. They're very powerful. They're sure to catch you. Then they'll make you agree to their idea.'

'Why are you so certain?'

'I know them.'

He let that go. She said: 'Another drink?' and got up.

'Yes please.' He got up, too, and extended his glass, then went closer to her. She put bottle and glass on the table and looked into his face. There was compassion, mystery, tenderness in her large, dark eyes. He smelled her perfume, warm, pleasant. He put his arms around her and kissed her. 'My room,' she said. They went upstairs.

Later that night, feeling strangely revitalised, he left the bed and the sleeping Martha and went and stood beside the window overlooking the silent park. He felt cold and he picked up his shirt and trousers, put them on. He sighed. He felt his mind clear and his body relax. He must work out a way of travelling from this world to his own at will – that might put a stop to the plans of the Man Without A Navel.

He turned guiltily as he heard the door open. Sally was standing there. She wore a long, white, flowing nightdress.

'Lee! I came to tell Mummy – what are you doing in here?' Her eyes were horrified, accusing him. Martha sat up suddenly.

'Sally – what's the matter!'

Lee stepped forward. 'Listen, Sally. Don't –'

Sally shrugged, but tears had come to her eyes. 'I thought you wanted *me*! Now I know – I shouldn't have brought you here. Farlowe said –'

'What did Farlowe say?'

'He said you'd want to marry me!'

'But that's ridiculous. How could he say that? I'm a stranger here. You were to hide me from the fortress people, that's all.'

But she had only picked up one word. 'Ridiculous. Yes, I suppose it is, when my own mother...'

'Sally – you'd better go to bed. We'll discuss it in the morning,' said Martha softly. 'What was it you came in about?'

Sally laughed theatrically. 'It doesn't matter now.' She slammed the door.

Seward looked at Martha. 'I'm sorry, Martha.'

'It wasn't your fault – or mine. Sally's romantic and young.'

'And jealous,' Seward sat down on the bed. The feeling of comfort, of companionship, of bringing some order out of chaos – it had all faded. 'Look, Martha, I can't stay here.'

'You're running away?'

'If you like – but – well – the two of you – I'm in the middle.'

'I guessed that. No, you'd better stay. We'll work something out.'

'Okay.' He got up, sighing heavily. 'I think I'll go for a walk in the park – it may help me to think. I'd just reached the stage where I was getting somewhere. Thanks for that, anyway, Martha.'

She smiled. 'Don't worry, Lee. I'll have everything running smoothly again by tomorrow.'

He didn't doubt it. She was a remarkable woman.

He put on his socks and shoes, opened the door and went out onto the landing. Moonlight entered through a tall, slender window at the end. He went down the two flights of stairs and out of the front door. He turned into the lane and entered the arbour. In the cool of the night, he once again was able to begin some constructive thinking.

While he was on this world, he would not waste his time, he would keep trying to discover the necessary modifications to make the tranquilomats workable.

He wandered through the arbour, keeping any thoughts of the two women out of his mind. He turned into another section of the arbour he hadn't noticed before. The turnings became numerous but he was scarcely aware of them. It was probably some sort of child's maze.

He paused as he came to a bench. He sat down and folded his arms in front of him, concentrating on his problem.

Much later he heard a sound to his right and looked up.

A man he didn't know was standing there, grinning at him.

Seward noticed at once that the man had overlong canines, that he smelled of damp earth and decay. He wore a black, polo-neck pullover and black, stained trousers. His face was waxen and very pale.

'I've been looking for you for ages, Professor Seward,' said the Vampire.

Chapter Five

S EWARD GOT UP and faced the horrible creature. The Vampire continued to smile. He didn't move. Seward felt revulsion.

'It's been a long journey,' said the Vampire in a sibilant voice like the sound of a frigid wind blowing through dead boughs. 'I had intended to visit you at the fortress, but when I got to your room you had left. I was disappointed.'

'Doubtless,' said Seward. 'Well, you've had a wasted journey. I'm not going back there until I'm ready.'

'That doesn't interest me.'

'What does?' Seward tried to stop himself from trembling.

The Vampire put his hands into his pockets. 'Only you.'

'Get away from here. You're outnumbered – I have friends.' But he knew that his tone was completely unconvincing.

The Vampire hissed his amusement. 'They can't do much, Seward.'

'What are you – some sort of android made to frighten people?'

'No.' The Vampire took a pace forward.

Suddenly he stopped as a voice came faintly from somewhere in the maze.

'Lee! Lee! Where are you?'

It was Sally's voice.

'Stay away, Sally!' Lee called.

'But I was going to warn you. I saw the Vampire from the window. He's somewhere in the park.'

'I know. Go home!'

'I'm sorry about the scene, Lee. I wanted to apologise. It was childish.'

'It doesn't matter.' He looked at the Vampire. He was standing in a relaxed position, hands in pockets, smiling. 'Go home, Sally!'

'She won't, you know,' whispered the Vampire.

Her voice was closer. 'Lee, I must talk to you.'

He screamed: 'Sally – the Vampire's here. Go home. Warn your mother, not me. Get some help if you can – but go home!'

Now he saw her enter the part of the maze he was in. She gasped as she saw them. He was between her and the Vampire.

'Sally – do what I told you.'

But the Vampire's cold eyes widened and he took one hand out of his pocket and crooked a finger. 'Come here, Sally.'

She began to walk forward.

He turned to the Vampire. 'What do you want?'

'Only a little blood – yours, perhaps – or the young lady's.'

'Damn you. Get away. Go back, Sally.' She didn't seem to hear him.

He daren't touch the cold body, the earth-damp clothes. He stepped directly between the girl and the Vampire.

He felt sick, but he reached out his hands and shoved at the creature's body. Flesh yielded, but bone did not. The Vampire held his ground, smiling, staring beyond Seward at the girl.

Seward shoved again and suddenly the creature's arms clamped around him and the grinning, fanged face darted towards his. The thing's breath disgusted him. He struggled, but could not break the Vampire's grasp.

A cold mouth touched his neck. He yelled and kicked. He felt a tiny pricking against his throat. Sally screamed. He heard her turn and run and felt a fraction of relief.

He punched with both fists as hard as he could into the creature's solar plexus. It worked. The Vampire groaned and let go. Seward was disgusted to see that its fangs dripped with blood.

His blood.

Now rage helped him. He chopped at the Vampire's throat. It gasped, tottered, and fell in a sprawl of loose limbs to the ground.

Panting, Seward kicked it in the head. It didn't move.

He bent down and rolled the Vampire over. As far as he could tell it was dead. He tried to remember what he'd read about legendary vampires. Not much. Something about a stake through its heart. Well, that was out.

But the thought that struck him most was that he had fought one of the fortress people – and had won. It was possible to beat them!

He walked purposefully through the maze. It wasn't as tortuous as he'd supposed. Soon he emerged at the arbour entrance near the house. He saw Sally and Martha running towards him. Behind them, another figure lumbered. Farlowe. He had got here fast.

'Seward,' he shouted. 'They said the Vampire had got you!'

'I got him,' said Seward as they came up and stopped.

'What?'

'I beat him.'

'But – that's impossible.'

Seward shrugged. He felt elated. 'Evidently, it's possible,' he said. 'I knocked him out. He seems to be dead – but I suppose you never know with vampires.'

Farlowe was astonished. 'I believe you,' he said, 'but it's fantastic. How did you do it?'

'I got frightened and then angry,' said Seward simply. 'Maybe you've been overawed by these people too long.'

'It seems like it,' Farlowe admitted. 'Let's go and have a look at him. Sally and Martha had better stay behind.'

Seward led him back through the maze. The Vampire was still where he'd fallen. Farlowe touched the corpse with his foot.

'That's the Vampire all right.' He grinned. 'I knew we had a winner in you, son. What are you going to do now?'

'I'm going straight back to the fortress and get this worked out once and for all. Martha gave me an idea yesterday evening and she may well be right. I'm going to try and find out anyway.'

'Better not be over-confident, son.'

'Better than being over-cautious.'

'Maybe,' Farlowe agreed doubtfully. 'What's this idea Martha gave you?'

'It's really her idea, complete. Let her explain. She's an intelligent woman – and she's bothered to think about this problem from scratch. I'd advise you to do the same.'

'I'll hear what it is, first. Let's deal with the Vampire and then get back to the house.'

'I'll leave the Vampire to you. I want to use your car.'

'Why?'

'To go back to the fortress.'

'Don't be a fool. Wait until we've got some help.'

'I can't wait that long, Farlowe. I've got other work to do back on my own world.'

'Okay,' Farlowe shrugged.

Farlowe faded.

The maze began to fade.

Explosions in the brain.

Vertigo.

Sickness.

His head ached and he could not breathe. He yelled, but he had no voice. Multicoloured explosions in front of his eyes. He was whirling round and round, spinning rapidly. Then he felt a new surface dragging at his feet. He closed his eyes and stumbled against something. He fell onto something soft.

It was his camp-bed. He was back in his laboratory.

Seward wasted no time wondering what had happened. He knew more or less. Possibly his encounter with the Vampire had sent him back – the exertion or – of course – the creature had drawn some of his blood. Maybe that was it. He felt the pricking sensation, still. He went to the mirror near the washstand. He could just see the little marks in his neck. Further proof that wherever that world was it was as real as the one he was in now.

He went to the table and picked up his notes, then walked into the other room. In one section was a long bench. On it, in various stages of dismantling, were the machines that he had been working on, the tranquilomats that somehow just didn't work. He picked up one of the smallest and checked its batteries, its lenses and its sonic agitator. The idea with this one was to use a combination of light and sound to agitate certain dormant cells in the brain. Long since, psychophysicists had realised that mental abnormality had a chemical as well as a mental cause. Just as a patient with a psychosomatic illness produced all the biological symptoms of whatever disease he thought he had, so did chemistry play a part in brain disorders. Whether the change in the brain cells came first or afterwards they weren't sure. But the fact was that the cells could be agitated and the mind, by a mixture of hypnosis and conditioning, could be made to work normally. But it was a long step from knowing this and being able to use the information in the construction of tranquilomats.

Seward began to work on the machine. He felt he was on the right track, at least.

But how long could he keep going before his need for the drug destroyed his will?

He kept going some five hours before his withdrawal symptoms got the better of him.

He staggered towards one of the drug-drawers and fumbled out an ampoule of M-A 19. He staggered into his bedroom and reached for the needle on the table.

He filled the syringe. He filled his veins. He filled his brain with a series of explosions which blew him clean out of his own world into the other.

Fire flew up his spine. Ignited back-brain, ignited mid-brain, ignited fore-brain. Ignited all centres.

EXPLOSION ALL CENTRES.

This time the transition was brief. He was standing in the part of the maze where he'd been when he'd left. The Vampire's corpse was gone. Farlowe had gone, also. He experienced a feeling of acute frustration that he couldn't continue with his work on KLTM-8 – the tranquilomat he'd been modifying when his craving for the M-A 19 took over.

But there was something to do here, too.

He left the maze and walked towards the house. It was dawn and very cold. Farlowe's car was parked there. He noticed the licence number. It seemed different. It now said YOU 009. Maybe he'd mistaken the last digit for a zero last time he'd looked.

The door was ajar. Farlowe and Martha were standing in the hall. They looked surprised when he walked in.

'I thought the Vampire was peculiar, son,' said Farlowe. 'But yours was the best vanishing act I've ever seen.'

'Martha will explain that, too,' Seward said, not looking at her. 'Has she told you her theory?'

'Yes, it sounds feasible.' He spoke slowly, looking at the floor. He looked up. 'We got rid of the Vampire. Burned him up. He burns well.'

'That's one out of the way, at least,' said Seward. 'How many others are there at the fortress?'

Farlowe shook his head. 'Not sure. How many did you see?'

'The Man Without A Navel, a character called Brother Sebastian who wears a cowl and probably isn't human either, two pleasant gentlemen called Mr Morl and Mr Hand – and a man in fancy dress whose name I don't know.'

'There are one or two more,' Farlowe said. 'But it's not their numbers we've got to worry about – it's their power!'

'I think maybe it's overrated,' Seward said.

'You may be right, son.'

'I'm going to find out.'

'You still want my car?'

'Yes. If you want to follow up behind with whatever help you can gather, do that.'

'I will.' Farlowe glanced at Martha. 'What do you think, Martha?'

'I think he may succeed,' she said. 'Good luck, Lee.' She smiled at him in a way that made him want to stay.

'Right,' said Seward. 'I'm going. Hope to see you there.'

'I may be wrong, Lee,' she said warningly. 'It was only an idea.'

'It's the best one I've heard. Goodbye.'

He went out of the house and climbed into the car.

Chapter Six

THE ROAD WAS white, the sky was blue, the car was red and the countryside was green. Yet there was less clarity about the scenery than Seward remembered. Perhaps it was because he no longer had the relaxing company of Farlowe, because his mind was working furiously and his emotions at full blast.

Whoever had designed the set-up on this world had done it well, but had missed certain details. Seward realised that one of the 'alien' aspects of the world was that everything was just a little too new. Even Farlowe's car looked as if it had just been driven off the production line.

By the early afternoon he was beginning to feel tired and some of his original impetus had flagged. He decided to move in to the side of the road and rest for a short time, stretch his legs. He stopped the car and got out.

He walked over to the other side of the road. It was on a hillside and he could look down over a wide, shallow valley. A river gleamed in the distance, there were cottages and livestock in the fields. He couldn't see the horizon. Far away he saw a great bank of reddish-looking clouds that seemed to swirl and seethe like a restless ocean. For all the *signs* of habitation, the countryside had taken on a desolate quality as if it had been abandoned. He could not believe that there were people living in the cottages and tending the livestock. The whole thing looked like the set for a film. Or a play – a complicated play devised by the Man Without A Navel and his friends – a play in which the fate of a world – possibly two worlds – was at stake.

How soon would the play resolve itself? he wondered, as he turned back towards the car.

*

A woman was standing by the car. She must have come down the hill while he was looking at the valley. She had long, jet-black hair and big, dark eyes. Her skin was tanned dark gold. She had full, extraordinarily sensuous lips. She wore a well-tailored red suit, a black blouse, black shoes and black handbag. She looked rather sheepish. She raised her head to look at him and as she did so a lock of her black hair fell over her eyes. She brushed it back.

'Hello,' she said. 'Am I lucky!'

'Are you?'

'I hope so. I didn't expect to find a car on the road. You haven't broken down, have you?' She asked this last question anxiously.

'No,' he said. 'I stopped for a rest. How did you get here?'

She pointed up the hill. 'There's a little track up there – a cattle track, I suppose. My car skidded and went into a tree. It's a wreck.'

'I'll have a look at it for you.'

She shook her head. 'There's no point – it's a write-off. Can you give me a lift?'

'Where are you going?' he said unwillingly.

'Well, it's about sixty miles that way,' she pointed in the direction he was going. 'A small town.'

It wouldn't take long to drive sixty miles on a road as clear as this with no apparent speed limit. He scratched his head doubtfully. The woman was a diversion he hadn't expected and, in a way, resented. But she was very attractive. He couldn't refuse her. He hadn't seen any cart tracks leading off the road. This, as far as he knew, was the only one, but it was possible he hadn't noticed since he didn't know this world. Also, he decided, the woman evidently wasn't involved in the struggle between the fortress people and Farlowe's friends. She was probably just one of the conditioned, living out her life completely unaware of where she was and why. He might be able to get some information out of her.

'Get in,' he said.

'Oh, thanks.' She got in, seeming rather deliberately to show him a lot of leg. He opened his door and slid under the wheel. She sat uncomfortably close to him. He started the engine and moved the car out onto the road again.

'I'm a stranger here,' he began conversationally. 'What about you?'

'Not me – I've lived hereabouts all my life. Where do you come from – stranger?'

He smiled. 'A long way away.'

'Are they all as good-looking as you?' It was trite, but it worked. He felt flattered.

'Not any more,' he said. That was true. Maniacs never looked very good. But this wasn't the way he wanted the conversation to go, however nice the direction. He said: 'You're not very heavily populated around here. I haven't seen another car, or another person for that matter, since I set off this morning.'

'It does get boring,' she said. She smiled at him. That and her full body, her musky scent and her closeness, made him breathe more heavily than he would have liked. One thing about this world – the women were considerably less inhibited than on his own. It was a difference in population, perhaps. In an overcrowded world your social behaviour must be more rigid, out of necessity.

He kept his hands firmly on the wheel and his eyes on the road, convinced that if he didn't he'd lose control of himself and the car. The result might be a sort of femme fatality. His attraction towards Sally and Martha had not been wholly sexual. Yet this woman radiated a purely animal attraction that he had never felt before. He glanced at her. Did she understand how she affected him?

It said a lot for the woman if she could take his mind so completely off his various problems.

'My name's Magdalen,' she smiled. 'A bit of a mouthful. What's yours?'

It was a relief to find someone here who didn't already know his name. He rejected the unliked Lee and said: 'Bill – Bill Ward.'

'Short and sweet,' she said. 'Not like mine.'

He grunted vaguely, consciously fighting the emotions rising in him. There was a word for them. A simple word – short and sweet – lust. He rather liked it. He'd been somewhat repressed on his home world and had kept a tight censorship on his feelings. Here it was obviously different.

A little later, he gave in. He stopped the car and kissed her. He was surprised at the ease with which he did it. He forgot about the tranquilomats, about the M-A 19, about the fortress. He forgot about everything except her, and that was maybe why he did what he did.

It was as if he was drawn into yet another world – a private world where only he and she had any existence. An enclosed world consisting only of their desire and their need to satisfy it.

Afterwards he felt gloomy, regretful and guilty. He started the car savagely. He knew he shouldn't blame her, but he did. He'd wasted time. Minutes were valuable, even seconds. He'd wasted hours.

Beside him she took a headscarf from her bag and tied it over her hair. 'You're in a hurry.'

He pressed the accelerator as far down as he could.

'What's the problem?' she shouted as the engine thudded noisily.

'I've wasted too much time already. I'll drop you off wherever it is you want.'

'Oh, fine. Just one of those things, eh?'

'I suppose so. It was my fault, I shouldn't have picked you up in the first place.'

She laughed. It wasn't a nice laugh. It was a mocking laugh and it seemed to punch him in the stomach.

'Okay,' he said, 'okay.'

He switched on the headlamps as dusk became night. There was no milometer on the dashboard so he didn't know how far they'd travelled, but he was sure it was more than sixty miles.

'Where is this town?' he said.

'Not much further.' Her voice softened. 'I'm sorry, Lee. But what *is* the matter?'

Something was wrong. He couldn't place it. He put it down to his own anger.

'You may not know it,' he said, 'but I suspect that nearly all the people living here are being deceived. Do you know the fortress?'

'You mean that big building on the rock wastes?'

'That's it. Well, there's a group of people there who are duping you and the rest in some way. They want to destroy practically the whole of the human race by a particularly nasty method – and they want me to do it for them.'

'What's that?'

Briefly, he explained.

Again she laughed. 'By the sound of it, you're a fool to fight this Man Without A Navel and his friends. You ought to throw in your lot with them. You could be top man.'

'Aren't you angry?' he said in surprise. 'Don't you believe me?'

'Certainly. I just don't share your attitude. I don't understand you turning down a chance when it's offered. I'd take it. As I said, you could be top man.'

'I've already been top man,' he said, 'in a manner of speaking. On my own world. I don't want that kind of responsibility. All I want to do is save something from the mess I've made of civilisation.'

'You're a fool, Lee.'

That was it. She shouldn't have known him as Lee but as Bill, the name he'd introduced himself by. He stopped the car suddenly and looked at her suspiciously. The truth was dawning on him and it made him feel sick at himself that he could have fallen for her trap.

'You're working for him, aren't you? The Man?'

'You seem to be exhibiting all the symptoms of persecution mania, Seward. You need a good psychiatrist.' She spoke coolly and reached into her handbag. 'I don't feel safe with you.'

'It's mutual,' he said. 'Get out of the car.'

'No,' she said quietly. 'I think we'll go all the way to the fortress together.' She put both hands into her bag. They came out with two things. One was a half bottle of brandy.

The other was a gun.

'Evidently my delay tactics weren't effective enough,' she mocked. 'I thought they might not be, so I brought these. Get out, yourself, Seward.'

'You're going to kill me?'

'Maybe.'

'But that isn't what the Man wants, is it?'

She shrugged, waving the gun.

Trembling with anger at his own gullibility and impotence, he got out. He couldn't think clearly.

She got out, too, keeping him covered. 'You're a clever man, Seward. You've worked out a lot.'

'There are others here who know what I know.'

'What do they know?'

'They know about the set-up – about the conditioning.'

She came round the car towards him, shaking her head. Still keeping him covered, she put the brandy bottle down on the seat.

He went for the gun.

He acted instinctively, in the knowledge that this was his only chance. He heard the gun go off, but he was forcing her wrist back. He slammed it down on the side of the car. She yelled and dropped it. Then he did what he had never thought he could do. He hit her, a short, sharp jab under the chin. She crumpled.

He stood over her, trembling. Then he took her headscarf and tied her limp hands behind her. He dragged her up and dumped her in the back of the car. He leaned down and found the gun. He put it in his pocket.

Then he got into the driving seat, still trembling. He felt something hard under him. It was the brandy bottle. It was what he needed. He unscrewed the cap and took a long drink.

His brain began to explode even as he reached for the ignition.

It seemed to crackle and flare like burning timber. He grabbed the door handle. Maybe if he walked around...

He felt his knees buckle as his feet touched the ground. He strained to keep himself upright. He forced himself to move round the car. When he reached the bonnet, the headlamps blared at him, blinded him.

They began to blink rapidly into his eyes. He tried to raise his hands and cover his eyes. He fell sideways, the light still blinking. He felt nausea sweep up and through him. He saw the car's licence plate in front of him.

YOU 099

YOU 100

YOU 101

He put out a hand to touch the plate. It seemed normal. Yet the digits were clocking up like the numbers on an adding machine.

Again his brain exploded. A slow, leisurely explosion that subsided and brought a delicious feeling of well-being.

Green clouds like boiled jade, scent of chrysanthemums. Swaying lilies. Bright lines of black and white in front of his eyes. He shut them and opened them again. He was looking up at the blind in his bedroom.

As soon as he realised he was back, Seward jumped off the bed and made for the bench where he'd left the half-finished tranquilomat. He remembered something, felt for the gun he'd taken off the girl. It wasn't there.

But he felt the taste of the brandy in his mouth. Maybe it was as simple as that, he thought. Maybe all he needed to get back was alcohol.

There was sure to be some alcohol in the lab. He searched through cupboards and drawers until he found some in a jar. He filled a vial and corked it. He took off his shirt and taped the vial under his armpit – that way he might be able to transport it from his world to the other one.

Then he got down to work.

Lenses were reassembled, checked. New filters went in and old ones came out. He adjusted the resonators and amplifiers. He was recharging the battery which powered the transistorised circuits, when he sensed the mob outside. He left the little machine on the bench and went to the control board. He flicked three switches down and then, on impulse, flicked them off again. He went back to the bench and unplugged the charger. He took the machine to the window. He drew the blind up.

It was a smaller mob than usual. Evidently some of them had learned their lesson and were now avoiding the laboratory.

Far away, behind them, the sun glinted on a calm sea. He opened the window.

There was one good way of testing his tranquilomat. He rested it on the sill and switched it to ATTRACT. That was the first necessary stage, to hold the mob's attention. A faint, pleasant humming began to come from the machine. Seward knew that specially shaped and coloured lenses were whirling at the front. The mob looked up towards it, but only those in the centre of the group were held. The others dived away, hiding their eyes.

Seward felt his body tightening, growing cold. Part of him began to scream for the M-A 19. He clung to the machine's carrying handles. He turned a dial from Zero to 50. There were 100 units marked on the indicator. The machine was now sending at half-strength. Seward consoled himself that if anything went wrong he could not do any more harm to their ruined minds. It wasn't much of a consolation.

He quickly saw that the combined simulated brainwaves, sonic vibrations and light patterns were having some effect on their minds. But what was the effect going to be? They were certainly responding. Their bodies were relaxing, their faces were no longer twisted with insanity. But was the tranquilomat actually doing any constructive good – what it had been designed to do? He upped the output to 75 degrees.

His hand began to tremble. His mouth and throat were tight and dry. He couldn't keep going. He stepped back. His stomach ached. His bones ached. His eyes felt puffy. He began to move towards the machine again. But he couldn't make it. He moved towards the half-full ampoule of M-A 19 on the table. He filled the blunt hypodermic. He found a vein. He was weeping as the explosions hit his brain.

Chapter Seven

THIS TIME IT was different.

He saw an army of machines advancing towards him. An army of malevolent hallucimats. He tried to run, but a thousand electrodes were clamped to his body and he could not move. From nowhere, needles entered his veins. Voices shouted SEWARD! SEWARD! SEWARD! The hallucimats advanced, shrilling, blinking, buzzing – *laughing*. The machines were laughing at him.

SEWARD!

Now he saw Farlowe's car's registration plate.

YOU 110

YOU 111

YOU 119

SEWARD!

YOU!

SEWARD!

His brain was being squeezed. It was contracting, contracting. The voices became distant, the machines began to recede. When they had vanished he saw he was standing in a circular room in the centre of which was a low dais. On the dais was a chair. In the chair was the Man Without A Navel. He smiled at Seward.

'Welcome back, old boy,' he said.

Brother Sebastian and the woman, Magdalen, stood close to the dais. Magdalen's smile was cool and merciless, seeming to anticipate some new torture that the Man and Brother Sebastian had devised.

But Seward was jubilant. He was sure his little tranquilomat had got results.

'I think I've done it,' he said quietly. 'I think I've built a workable tranquilomat – and, in a way, it's thanks to you. I had to speed
my work up to beat you – and I did it!'

They seemed unimpressed.

'Congratulations, Seward,' smiled the Man Without A Navel.
'But this doesn't alter the situation, you know. Just because you
have an antidote doesn't mean we have to use it.'

Seward reached inside his shirt and felt for the vial taped under his
arm. It had gone. Some of his confidence went with the discovery.

Magdalen smiled. 'It was kind of you to drink the drugged
brandy.'

He put his hands in his jacket pocket.

The gun was back there. He grinned.

'What's he smiling at?' Magdalen said nervously.

'I don't know. It doesn't matter. Brother Sebastian, I believe you
have finished work on your version of Seward's hypnomat?'

'I have,' said the sighing, cold voice.

'Let's have it in. It is a pity we didn't have it earlier. It would
have saved us time – and Seward all his efforts.'

The curtains behind them parted and Mr Hand, Mr Morl and the
Laughing Cavalier wheeled in a huge, bizarre machine that
seemed to have a casing of highly polished gold, silver and platinum. There were two sets of lenses in its domed, headlike top.
They looked like eyes staring at Seward.

Was this a conditioning machine like the ones they'd probably
used on the human populace? Seward thought it was likely. If they
got him with that, he'd be finished. He pulled the gun out of his
pocket. He aimed it at the right-hand lens and pulled the trigger.

The gun roared and kicked in his hand, but no bullet left the
muzzle. Instead there came a stream of small, brightly coloured
globes, something like those used in the attraction device on the
tranquilomat. They sped towards the machine, struck it, exploded.
The machine buckled and shrilled. It steamed and two discs, like
lids, fell across the lenses. The machine rocked backwards and
fell over.

The six figures began to converge on him, angrily.

Suddenly, on his left, he saw Farlowe, Martha and Sally step from behind a screen.

'Help me!' he cried to them.

'We can't!' Farlowe yelled. 'Use your initiative, son!'

'Initiative?' He looked down at the gun. The figures were coming closer. The Man Without A Navel smiled slowly. Brother Sebastian tittered. Magdalen gave a low, mocking laugh that seemed – strangely – to be a criticism of his sexual prowess. Mr Morl and Mr Hand retained their mournful and cheerful expressions respectively. The Laughing Cavalier flung back his head and – laughed. All around them the screens, which had been little more than head-high were lengthening, widening, stretching up and up.

He glanced back. The screens were growing.

He pulled the trigger of the gun. Again it bucked, again it roared – and from the muzzle came a stream of metallic-grey particles which grew into huge flowers. The flowers burst into flame and formed a wall between him and the six.

He peered around him, looking for Farlowe and the others. He couldn't find them. He heard Farlowe's shout: 'Good luck, son!' He heard Martha and Sally crying goodbye.

'Don't go!' he yelled.

Then he realised he was alone. And the six were beginning to advance again – malevolent, vengeful.

Around him the screens, covered in weird designs that curled and swirled, ever-changing, were beginning to topple inwards. In a moment he would be crushed.

Again he heard his name being called. SEWARD! SEWARD! Was it Martha's voice? He thought so.

'I'm coming,' he shouted, and pulled the trigger again.

The Man Without A Navel, Magdalen, Brother Sebastian, the Laughing Cavalier, Mr Hand and Mr Morl – all screamed in unison and began to back away from him as the gun's muzzle spouted a stream of white fluid which floated into the air.

Still the screens were falling, slowly, slowly.

The white fluid formed a net of millions of delicate strands. It drifted over the heads of the six. It began to descend. They looked up and screamed again.

'Don't, Seward,' begged the Man Without A Navel. 'Don't, old man – I'll make it worth your while.'

Seward watched as the net engulfed them. They struggled and cried and begged.

It did not surprise him much when they began to shrink.

No! *They* weren't shrinking – he was growing. He was growing over the toppling screens. He saw them fold inwards. He looked down and the screens were like cards folding neatly over the six little figures struggling in the white net. Then, as the screens folded down, the figures were no longer in sight. It got lighter. The screens rolled themselves into a ball.

The ball began to take on a new shape.

It changed colour. And then, there it was – a perfectly formed human skull.

Slowly, horrifyingly, the skull began to gather flesh and blood and muscles to itself. The stuff flowed over it. Features began to appear. Soon, in a state of frantic terror, Seward recognised the face.

It was his own.

His own face, its eyes wide, its lips parted. A tired, stunned, horrified face.

He was back in the laboratory. And he was staring into a mirror.

He stumbled away from the mirror. He saw he wasn't holding a gun in his hand but a hypodermic needle. He looked round the room.

The tranquilomat was still on the window sill. He went to the window. There, quietly talking among the ruins below, was a group of sane men and women. They were still in rags, still gaunt. But they were sane. That was evident. They were saner than they had ever been before.

He called down to them, but they didn't hear him.

Time for that later, he thought. He sat on the bed, feeling dazed and relieved. He dropped the needle to the floor, certain he wouldn't need to use it again.

It was incredible, but he thought he knew where he had been. The final image of his face in the mirror had given him the last clue.

He had been inside his own mind. The M-A 19 was merely an hallucinogenic after all. A powerful one, evidently, if it could give him the illusion of rope marks on his wrists, bites on his neck and the rest.

He had escaped into a dreamworld.

Then he wondered – but why? What good had it done?

He got up and went towards the mirror again.

Then he heard the voice. Martha's voice.

SEWARD! SEWARD! Seward, listen to me!

No, he thought desperately. No, it can't be starting again. There's no need for it.

He ran into the laboratory, closing the door behind him, locking it. He stood there, trembling, waiting for the withdrawal symptoms. They didn't come.

Instead he saw the walls of the laboratory, the silent computers and meters and dials, begin to blur. A light flashed on above his head. The dead banks of instruments suddenly came alive. He sat down in a big chrome, padded chair which had originally been used for the treating of test-subjects.

His gaze was caught by a whirling stroboscope that had appeared from nowhere. Coloured images began to form in front of his eyes. He struggled to get up but he couldn't.

YOU 121

YOU 122

YOU 123

Then the first letter changed to a V.

VOU 127

SEWARD!

His eyelids fell heavily over his eyes.

'Professor Seward.' It was Martha's voice. It spoke to someone else. 'We may be lucky, Tom. Turn down the volume.'

He opened his eyes.

'Martha.'

The woman smiled. She was dressed in a white coat and was leaning over the chair. She looked very tired. 'I'm not – Martha – Professor Seward. I'm Doctor Kalin. Remember?'

'Doctor Kalin, of course.'

His body felt weaker than it had ever felt before. He leaned back in the big chair and sighed. Now he was remembering.

It had been his decision to make the experiment. It had seemed to be the only way of speeding up work on the development of the tranquilomats. He knew that the secret of a workable machine was imbedded in the deepest level of his unconscious mind. But, however much he tried – hypnosis, symbol-association, word-association – he couldn't get at it.

There was only one way he could think of – a dangerous experiment for him – an experiment which might not work at all. He would be given a deep-conditioning, made to believe that he had brought disaster to the world and must remedy it by devising a tranquilomat. Things were pretty critical in the world outside, but they weren't as bad as they had conditioned him to believe. Work on the tranquilomats *was* falling behind – but there had been no widespread disaster, *yet*. It was bound to come unless they could devise some means of mass-cure for the thousands of neurotics and victims of insanity. An antidote for the results of mass-tension.

So, simply, they conditioned him to think his efforts had destroyed civilisation. He must devise a working tranquilomat. They had turned the problem from an intellectual one into a personal one.

The conditioning had apparently worked.

He looked around the laboratory at his assistants. They were all alive, healthy, a bit tired, a bit strained, but they looked relieved.

'How long have I been under?' he asked.

'About fourteen hours. That's twelve hours since the experiment went wrong.'

'Went wrong?'

'Why, yes,' said Doctor Kalin in surprise. 'Nothing was happening. We tried to bring you round – we tried every darned machine and drug in the place – nothing worked. We expected catatonia. At least we've managed to save you. We'll just have to go on using the ordinary methods of research, I suppose.' Her voice was tired, disappointed.

Seward frowned. But he *had* got the results. He knew exactly how to construct a working tranquilomat. He thought back.

'Of course,' he said. 'I was only conditioned to believe that the world was in ruins and I had done it. There was nothing about – about – the *other* world.'

'What other world?' Macpherson, his Chief Assistant asked the question.

Seward told them. He told them about the Man Without A Navel, the fortress, the corridors, the tortures, the landscapes seen from Farlowe's car, the park, the maze, the Vampire, Magdalen… He told them how, in what he now called Condition A, he had believed himself hooked on a drug called M-A 19.

'But we don't have a drug called M-A 19,' said Doctor Kalin.

'I know that now. But I didn't know that and it didn't matter. I would have found something to have made the journey into – the other world – a world existing only in my skull. Call it Condition B, if you like – or Condition X, maybe. The unknown. I found a fairly logical means of making myself *believe* I was entering another world. That was M-A 19. By inventing symbolic characters who were trying to stop me, I made myself work harder. Unconsciously I knew that Condition A was going wrong – so I escaped into Condition B in order to put right the damage. By acting out the drama I was able to clear my mind of its confusion. I had, as I suspected, the secret of the tranquilomat somewhere down there all the time. Condition A failed to release that secret – Condition B succeeded. I can build you a workable tranquilomat, don't worry.'

'Well,' Macpherson grinned. 'I've been told to use my imagination in the past – but you *really* used yours!'

'That was the idea, wasn't it? We'd decided it was no good just using drugs to keep us going. We decided to use our drugs and hallucimats directly, to condition me to believe that what we feared will happen *had* happened.'

'I'm glad we didn't manage to bring you back to normality, in that case,' Doctor Kalin smiled. 'You've had a series of classic – if more complicated than usual – nightmares. The Man Without A Navel, as you call him, and his "allies" symbolised the elements in you that were holding you back from the truth – diverting you. By "defeating" the Man, you defeated those elements.'

'It was a hell of a way to get results,' Seward grinned. 'But I got them. It was probably the only way. Now we can produce as many tranquilomats as we need. The problem's over. I've – in all modesty –' he grinned, 'saved the world before it needed saving. It's just as well.'

'What about your "helpers", though,' said Doctor Kalin helping him from the chair. He glanced into her intelligent, mature face. He had always liked her.

'Maybe,' he smiled, as he walked towards the bench where the experimental tranquilomats were laid out, 'maybe there was quite a bit of wish-fulfilment mixed up in it as well.'

'It's funny how you didn't realise that it wasn't real, isn't it?' said Macpherson behind him.

'Why is it funny?' He turned to look at Macpherson's long, worn face. 'Who knows what's real, Macpherson? This world? That world? Any other world? I don't feel so adamant about this one, do you?'

'Well...' Macpherson said doubtfully. 'I mean, you're a trained psychiatrist as well as everything else. You'd think you'd recognise your own symbolic characters?'

'I suppose it's possible.' Macpherson had missed his point. 'All the same,' he added. 'I wouldn't mind going back there some day. I'd quite enjoy the exploration. And I liked some of the people. Even though they were probably wish-fulfilment figures. Farlowe – father – it's possible.' He glanced up as his eye fell on a meter. It consisted of a series of code-letters and three digits. VOU 128 it said now. There was Farlowe's number-plate. His mind had turned the V into a Y. He'd probably discover plenty of other symbols around, which he'd turned into something else in the other world. He still couldn't think of it as a dreamworld. It had seemed so real. For him, it was still real.

'What about the woman – Martha?' Doctor Kalin said. 'You called *me* Martha as you were waking up.'

'We'll let that one go for the time being,' he grinned. 'Come on, we've still got a lot of work to do.'

The Frozen Cardinal

M OLDAVIA. S. POLE. 1/7/17
Dear Gerry,

I got your last, finally. Hope this reaches you in less than a year. The supply planes are all robots now and are supposed to give a faster service. Did I tell you we were being sent to look over the southern pole? Well, we're here. Below zero temperatures, of course, and at present we're gaining altitude all the time. At least we don't have to wear breathing equipment yet. The Moldavian poles have about twice the volume of ice as those of Earth, but they're melting. As we thought, we found the planet at the end of its Ice Age. I know how you hate statistics and you know what a bore I can be, so I won't go into the details. To tell you the truth, it's a relief not to be logging and measuring.

It's when I write to you that I find it almost impossible to believe how far away Earth is. I frequently have a peculiar sense of closeness to the home planet, even though we are light years from it. Sometimes I think Earth will appear in the sky at 'dawn' and a rocket will come to take me to you. Are you lying to me, Gerry? Are you really still waiting? I love you so much. Yet my reason cautions me. I can't believe in your fidelity. I don't mean to make you impatient but I miss you desperately sometimes and I'm sure you know how strange people get in these conditions. I joined the expedition, after all, to give you time by yourself, to reconsider our relationship. But when I got your letter I was overjoyed. And, of course, I wish I'd never signed up for Moldavia. Still, only another six months to go now, and another six months home. I'm glad your mother recovered from her accident. This time next year we'll be spending all my ill-gotten gains in the Seychelles. It's what keeps me going.

We're perfectly safe in our icesuits, of course, but we get terribly tired. We're ascending a series of gigantic ice terraces which seem to go on for ever. It takes a day to cross from one terrace to the wall of the next, then another day or so to climb the wall and move the equipment up. The small sun is visible throughout an entire cycle of the planet at this time of year, but the 'day', when both suns are visible, is only about three hours. Then everything's very bright, of course, unless it's snowing or there's a thick cloud cover, and we have to protect our eyes. We use the brightest hours for sleeping. It's almost impossible to do anything else. The vehicles are reliable, but slow. If we make any real speed we have to wait a consequently longer interval until they can be recharged. Obviously, we recharge during the bright hours, so it all works out reasonably well. It's a strangely orderly planet, Gerry: everything in its place. Those creatures I told you about were not as intelligent as we had hoped. Their resemblance to spiders is remarkable, though, even to spinning enormous webs around their nests; chiefly, it seemed to us, for decoration. They ate the rations we offered and suffered no apparent ill effects, which means that the planet could probably be opat-gen in a matter of years. That would be a laugh on Galtman. Were you serious, by the way, in your letter? You couldn't leave your USSA even to go to Canada when we were together! You wouldn't care for this ice. The plains and jungles we explored last year feel almost deserted, as if they were once inhabited by a race which left no mark whatsoever. We found no evidence of intelligent inhabitants, no large animals, though we detected some weirdly shaped skeletons in caves below the surface. We were told not to excavate, to leave that to the follow-up team. This is routine official work; there's no romance in it for me. I didn't expect there would be, but I hadn't really allowed for the boredom, for the irritation one begins to feel with one's colleagues. I'm so glad you wrote to say you still love me. I joined to find myself, to let you get on with your life. I hope we both will be more stable when we meet again.

The gennard is warmed up and I'm being signalled, so I'll close this for the time being. We're about to ascend another wall, and that means only one of us can skit to see to the hoist, while the others go up the hard way on the lines. Helander's the leader on this particular op. I must say he's considerably easier going than old I.P. whom you'll probably have seen on the news by now, showing off his eggs. But the river itself is astonishing, completely encircling the planet; fresh water and Moldavia's only equivalent to our oceans, at least until this Ice Age is really over!

8/7/17 'Dawn'

A few lines before I fall asleep. It's been a hard one today. Trouble with the hoists. Routine stuff, but it doesn't help morale when it's this cold. I was dangling about nine hundred metres up, with about another thousand to go, for a good hour, with nothing to do but listen to Fisch's curses in my helmet, interspersed with the occasional reassurance. You're helpless in a situation like that! And then, when we did all get to the top and started off again across the terrace (the ninth!) we came almost immediately to an enormous crevasse which must be half a kilometre across! So here we are on the edge. We can go round or we can do a horizontal skit. We'll decide that in the 'evening'. I have the irrational feeling that this whole section could split off suddenly and engulf us in the biggest landslide a human being ever witnessed. It's silly to think like that. In relationship to this astonishing staircase we are lighter than midges. Until I got your last letter I wouldn't have cared. I'd have been excited by the idea. But now, of course, I've got something to live for. It's peculiar, isn't it, how that makes cowards of the best of us?

9/7/17

Partridge is down in the crevasse at this moment. He thinks we can bridge, but wants to make sure. Also our instruments have picked up something odd, so we're duty-bound to investigate. The rest of us are hanging around, quite glad of the chance to do nothing. Fedin is playing his music and Simons and Russell are fooling about on the edge, kicking a ration-pack about, with the crevasse as the goal. You can hardly make out the other side.

Partridge just said he's come across something odd imbedded in the north wall. He says the colours of the ice are beautiful, all dark greens and blues, but this, he says, is red. 'There shouldn't be anything red down here!' He says it's probably rock but it resembles an artefact. Maybe there have been explorers here before us, or even inhabitants. If so, they must have been here relatively recently, because these ice-steps are not all that old, especially at the depth Partridge has reached. Mind you, it wouldn't be the first practical joke he's played since we arrived.

Later

Partridge is up. When he pushed back his visor he looked pale and said he thought he was crazy. Fedin gave him a check-up immediately. There are no extraordinary signs of fatigue. Partridge says the outline he saw in the ice seemed to be a human figure. The instruments all suggest it is animal matter, though of course there are no life functions. 'Even if it's an artefact,' said Partridge, 'it hasn't got any business being there.' He shuddered. 'It seemed to be looking at me. A direct, searching stare. I got frightened.' Partridge isn't very imaginative, so we were all impressed. 'Are we going to get it out of there?' asked Russell. 'Or do we just record it for the follow-up team, as we did with those skeletons?' Helander was uncertain. He's as curious as the rest of us. 'I'll take a look for myself,' he said. He went down, said something under his breath which none of us could catch in our helmets, then gave the order to be hoisted up again. 'It's a Roman Catholic cardinal,' he said. 'The hat, the robes, everything. Making a benediction!' He frowned. 'We're going to have to send back on this and await instructions.'

Fedin laughed. 'We'll be recalled immediately. Everyone's warned of the hallucinations. We'll be hospitalised back at base for months while the bureaucrats try to work out why we went mad.'

'You'd better have a look,' said Helander. 'I want you to go down one by one and tell me what you see.'

Partridge was squatting on his haunches, drinking something

hot. He was trembling all over. He seemed to be sweating. 'This is ridiculous,' he said, more than once.

Three others are ahead of me, then it's my turn. I feel perfectly sane, Gerry. Everything else seems normal – as normal as it can be. And if this team has a failing it is that it isn't very prone to speculation or visual hallucinations. I've never been with a duller bunch of fact-gatherers. Maybe that's why we're all more scared than we should be. No expedition from Earth could ever have been to Moldavia before. Certainly nobody would have buried a Roman Catholic cardinal in the ice. There is no explanation, how-ever wild, which fits. We're all great rationalists on this team. Not a hint of mysticism or even poetry among us. The drugs see to that if our temperaments don't!

Russell's coming up. He's swearing, too. Chang goes down. Then it's my turn. Then Simons. Then Fisch. I wish you were here, Gerry. With your intelligence you could probably think of something. We certainly can't. I'd better start kitting up. More when I come up. To tell you the absolute truth I'm none too happy about going down!

Later

Well, I've been down. It's dark. The blues and greens glow as if they give off an energy of their own, although it's only reflec-tions. The wall is smooth and opaque. About four metres down and about half a metre back into the ice of the face you can see him. He's tall, about fifty-five, very handsome, clean-shaven and he's looking directly out at you. His eyes seem sad but not at all malevolent. Indeed, I'd say he seemed kind. There's something noble about him. His clothes are scarlet and fall in folds which suggest he became frozen while standing naturally in the spot he stands in now. He couldn't, therefore, have been dropped, or the clothing would be disturbed. There's no logic to it, Gerry. His right hand is raised and he's making some sort of Christian sign. You know I'm not too hot on anthropology. Helander's the expert.

His expression seems to be one of forgiveness. It's quite over-whelming. You almost find your heart going out to him while at the same time you can't help thinking you're somehow responsible for his being there! Six light years from Earth on a planet which was only catalogued three years ago and which we are supposedly the first human beings to explore. Nowhere we have been has anyone discovered a shred of evidence that man or anything resembling man ever explored other planets. You know as well as I do that the only signs of intelligent life anyone has found have been negligible and certainly we have never had a hint that any other creature is capable of space travel. Yet here is a man dressed in a costume which, at its latest possible date, is from the twentieth century.

I tried to stare him down. I don't know why. Eventually I told them to lift me up. While Simons went down, I waited on the edge, sipping ade and trying to stop shaking. I don't know why all of us were so badly affected. We've been in danger often enough (I wrote to you about the lavender swamps) and there isn't anyone on the team who hasn't got a sense of humour. Nobody's been able to raise a laugh yet. Helander tried, but it was so forced that we felt sorry for him. When Simons came up he was in exactly the same state as me. I handed him the rest of my ade and then returned to my biv to write this. We're to have a conference in about ten minutes. We haven't decided whether to send back information yet or not. Our curiosity will probably get the better of us. We have no specific orders on the question, but we're pretty sure we'll get a hands-off if we report now. The big skeletons were one thing. This is quite another. And yet we know in our hearts that we should leave well alone.

'Dawn'

The conference is over. It went on for hours. Now we've all decided to sleep on it. Helander and Partridge have been down for another look and have set up a carver in case we decide to go ahead. It will be easy enough to do. Feeling very tired. Have the notion that if we disturb the cardinal we'll do something cataclysmic. Maybe the whole planet will dissolve around us. Maybe this enormous mountain will crumble to nothing. Helander says that what he would like to do is send back on the cardinal but say that he is already carving, since our instruments suggest the crevasse is unstable and could close. There's no way it could close in the next week! But it would be a good enough excuse. You might never get this letter, Gerry. For all we're told personal mail is uninspected I don't trust them entirely. Do you think I should? Or if someone else is reading this, do they think I should have trusted to the law? His face is in my mind's eye as I write. So tranquil. So sad. I'm taking a couple of deegs, so will write more tomorrow.

10/7/17

Helander has carved. The whole damned thing is standing in the centre of the camp now, like a memorial. A big square block of ice with the cardinal peering out of it. We've all walked round and round the thing. There's no question that the figure is human. Helander wanted to begin thawing right away, but bowed to Simons, who doesn't want to risk the thing deteriorating. Soon he's going to vacuum-cocoon it. Simons is cursing himself for not bringing more of his archaeological gear along with him. He expected nothing like this, and our experience up to now has shown that Moldavia doesn't *have* any archaeology worth mentioning. We're all convinced it was a living creature. I even feel he may still be alive, the way he looks at me. We're all very jittery, but our sense of humour has come back and we make bad jokes about the cardinal really being Jesus Christ or Mahomet or somebody. Helander accuses us of religious illiteracy. He's the only one with any real knowledge of all that stuff. He is behaving oddly. He snapped at Russell a little while ago, telling him he wasn't showing proper reverence.

Russell apologised. He said he hadn't realised Helander was superstitious. Helander has sent back, saying what he's done and telling them he's about to thaw. A fait accompli. Fisch is unhappy. He and Partridge feel we should replace the cardinal and get on with 'our original business'. The rest of us argue that this *is* our original business. We are an exploration team. 'It's follow-up work,' said Fisch. 'I'm anxious to see what's at the top of this bloody great staircase.' Partridge replied: 'A bloody great Vatican, if you reason it through on the evidence we have.' That's the trouble with the kind of logic we go in for, Gerry. Well, we'll all be heroes when we get back to Earth, I suppose. Or we'll be disgraced, depending on what happens next. There's not a lot that can happen to me. This isn't my career, the way it is for the others. I'll be only too happy to be fired, since I intend to resign as soon as I'm home. Then it's the Seychelles for us, my dear. I hope you haven't changed your mind. I wish you were here. I feel the need to share what's going on – and I can think of nobody better to share it than you. Oh, God, I love you so much, Gerry. More, I know, than you'll ever love me; but I can bear anything except separation. I was reconciled to that separation until you wrote your last letter. I hope the company is giving you the yellow route now. You deserve it. With a clean run through to Maracaibo there will be no stopping the old gaucho, eh? But those experiments are risky, I'm told. So don't go too far. I think I know you well enough to be pretty certain you won't take unnecessary risks. I wish I could reach out now and touch your lovely, soft skin, your fine fair hair. I must stop this. It's doing things to me which even the blunn can't control! I'm going out for another walk around our frozen friend.

Later

Well, he's thawed. And it is human. Flesh and blood, Gerry, and no sign of deterioration. A man even taller than Helander. His clothes are all authentic, according to the expert. He's even wearing a pair of old-fashioned cotton underpants. No protective clothing. No sign of having had food with him. No sign of transport. And our instruments have been scouring a wider and wider area. We have the little beeps on automatic, using far more energy than they should. The probes go everywhere. Helander says that this is important. If we can find a vehicle or a trace of habitation, then at least we'll have the beginnings of an answer. He wants something to send back now, of course. We've had an acknowledgement and a hold-off signal. There's not much to hold-off from, currently. The cardinal stands in the middle of the camp, his right arm raised in benediction, his eyes as calm and sad and resigned as ever. He continues to make us jumpy. But there are no more jokes, really, except that we sometimes call him 'padre'. Helander says all expeditions had one in the old days: a kind of psych-medic, like Fedin. Fedin says he thinks the uniform a bit unsuitable for the conditions. It's astonishing how we grow used to something as unbelievable as this. We look up at the monstrous ice-steps ahead of us, the vast gulf behind us, at an alien sky with two suns in it; we know that we are millions upon millions of miles from Earth, across the vacuum of interstellar space, and real-ise we are sharing our camp with a corpse dressed in the costume of the sixteenth century and we're beginning to take it all for granted... I suppose it says something for human resilience. But we're all still uncomfortable. Maybe there's only so much our brains can take. I wish I was sitting on a stool beside you at the Amset having a beer. But things are so strange to me now that *that* idea is hard to accept. This has become normality. The probes bring in nothing. We're using every instrument we've got. Noth-ing. We're going to have to ask for the reserve stuff at base and get them to send something to the top. I'd like to be pulled back, I think, and yet I remain fascinated. Maybe you'll be able to tell me if I sound mad. I don't feel mad. Nobody is behaving badly. We're all under control, I think. Only Helander seems profoundly affected. He spends most of his time staring into the cardinal's face, touching it.

Later

Helander says the skin feels warm. He asked me to tell him if I agreed. I stripped off a glove and touched the fingers. They cer-tainly feel warm, but that could just be the effect of sun. Nevertheless, the arm hasn't moved, neither have the eyes. There's no breathing. He stares at us tenderly, blessing us, forgiving us. I'm beginning to resent him. What have I done that he should for-give me? I now agree with those who want to put him back. I suppose we can't. We've been told to sit tight and wait for base to send someone up. It will take a while before they come.

*

11/7/17

Russell woke me up. I kitted up fast and went out. Helander was kneeling in front of the cardinal and seemed to be mumbling to himself. He refused to move when we tried to get him to stand up. 'He's weeping,' he said. 'He's weeping.'

There did seem to be moisture on the skin. Then, even as we watched, blood began to trickle out of both eyes and run down the cheeks. The cardinal was weeping tears of blood, Gerry!

'Evidently the action of the atmosphere,' said Fedin, when we raised him. 'We might have to refreeze him, I think.'

The cardinal's expression hadn't changed. Helander became impatient and told us to go away. He said he was communicating with the cardinal. Fedin sedated him and got him back to his biv. We heard his voice, even in sleep, mumbling and groaning. Once, he screamed. Fedin pumped some more stuff into him, then. He's quiet now.

Later

We've had word that base is on its way. About time, too, for me. I'm feeling increasingly scared.

'Dusk'

I crawled out of my biv thinking that Helander was crying again or that Fedin was playing his music. The little, pale sun was high in the sky, the big one was setting. There was a reddish glow on the ice. Everything seemed red, in fact. I couldn't see too clearly, but the cardinal was still standing there, a dark silhouette. And the sounds were coming from him. He was singing, Gerry. There was no-one else up. I stood in front of the cardinal. His lips were moving. Some sort of chant. His eyes weren't looking at me any longer. They were raised. Someone came to stand beside me. It was Helander. He was a bit woozy, but his face was ecstatic. He began to join in the song. Their singing seemed to fill the sky, the planet, the whole damned universe. The music made me cry, Gerry. I have never heard a more beautiful voice. Helander turned to me once. 'Join in,' he said. 'Join in.' But I couldn't because I didn't know the words. 'It's Latin,' said Helander. It was like a bloody choir. I found myself lifting my head like a dog. There were resonances in my throat. I began to howl. But it wasn't howling. It was chanting, the same as the cardinal. No words. Just music. It was the most exquisite music I have ever heard in my life. I became aware that the others were with me, standing in a semi-circle, and they were singing too. And we were so full of joy, Gerry. We were all weeping. It was incredible. Then the sun had set and the music gradually faded and we stood looking at one another, totally exhausted, grinning like coyotes, feeling complete fools. And the cardinal was looking at us again, with that same sweet tolerance. Helander was kneeling in front of him and mumbling, but we couldn't hear the words. Eventually, after he'd been on the ice for an hour, Fedin decided to sedate him. 'He'll be dead at this rate, if I don't.'

Later

We've just finished putting the cardinal back in the crevasse, Gerry. I can still hear that music in my head. I wish there was some way I could play you the recordings we've made, but doubt-less you'll hear them in time, around when you get this letter. Base hasn't arrived yet. Helander said he was going to let it be their responsibility. I'm hoping we'll be relieved for those medical tests we were afraid of at first. I want to get away from here. I'm terrified, Gerry. I keep wanting to climb into the crevasse and ask the cardinal to sing for me again. I have never known such absolute release, such total happiness, as when I sang in harmony with him. What do you think it is? Maybe it's all hallucination. Some-one will know. Twice I've stood on the edge, peering down. You can't see him from here, of course. And you can't see the bottom. I haven't the courage to descend the lines.

I want to jump. I would jump, I think, if I could get the chance just once more to sing with him. I keep thinking of eternity. For the first time in my life I have a glimmering of what it means.

Oh, Gerry, I hope it isn't an illusion. I hope you'll be able to hear that voice on the tapes and know what I felt when the frozen cardinal sang. I love you, Gerry. I want to give you so much. I wish I could give you what I have been given. I wish I could sing for you the way the cardinal sang. There isn't one of us who hasn't been weeping. Fedin keeps trying to be rational. He says we are more exhausted than we know, that the drugs we take have side effects which couldn't be predicted. We look up into the sky from time to time, waiting for base to reach us. I wish you were here, Gerry. But I can't possibly regret now that I made the decision I made. I love you, Gerry. I love you all.

Wolf

WHOSE LITTLE TOWN are you, friend? Who owns you here? Wide and strong, you have an atmosphere of detached impermanence as you sit in the shallow valley with your bastion of disdainful pines surrounding you; with your slashed, gashed earth roads and your gleaming graveyards, cool under the sun. Here I stand in your peaceful centre, among the low houses, looking for your owner. Night is looming in my mind's backwaters.

I stop a long-jawed man with down-turned, sensuous lips. He rocks on his feet and stares at me in silence, his grey eyes brooding.

'Who owns this town?' I ask him.

'The people,' he says. 'The residents.'

I laugh at the joke, but he refuses to join me, does not even smile. 'Seriously – tell me. Who owns this town?'

He shrugs and walks off. I laugh louder: 'Who owns this town, friend? Who owns it?' Does he hate me?

Without a mood, what is a man, anyway? A man has to have some kind of mood, even when he dreams. Scornfully, I laugh at the one who refused to smile and I watch his back as he walks stiffly and self-consciously over a bridge of wood and metal which spans soft water, full of blossom and leaves, flowing in the sunlight.

In my hand is a cool silver flask loaded with sweet fire. I know it is there. I lift it to my mouth and consume the fire, letting it consume me, also. Blandly, we destroy each other, the fire and I.

My stomach is full of flame and my legs are tingling, as soft as soda water, down to where my feet ache. *Don't leave me, sweetheart, with your hair of desire and your mockeries hollow in the moaning dawn. Don't leave me with the salt rain rushing down my cold face.* I laugh again and repeat the man's words: 'The people – the residents!' Ho ho ho! But there is no-one to hear my laughter now unless there are inhabitants in the white town's curtained dwellings. *Where are you, sweetheart – where's your taunting body, now, and the taste of your fingernails in my flesh?*

Harsh smoke drowns my sight and the town melts as I fall slowly down towards the cobbles of the street and a pain begins to inch its way through my stinging face.

Where's the peace that you seek in spurious godliness of another man – a woman? Why is it never there?

I regain my sight and look upwards to where the blue sky fills the world until it is obscured by troubled sounds which flow from a lovely face dominated by eyes asking questions which make me frustrated and angry, since I cannot possibly answer them. Not one of them. I smile, in spite of my anger and say, cynically: 'It makes a change, doesn't it?' The girl shakes her head and the worried noises still pour from her mouth. Lips as red as blood – splashed on slender bones, a narrow, delicate skull. 'Who –? Why are you –? What happened to you?'

'That's a very personal question, my dear,' I say patronisingly. 'But I have decided not to resent it.'

'Thank you,' says she. 'Are you willing to rise and be helped somehow?'

Of course I am, but I would not let her know just yet. 'I am seeking a friend who came this way,' I say. 'Perhaps you know her? She is fat with my life – full of my soul. She should be easy to recognise.'

'No – I haven't...'

'Ah – well, if you happen to notice her, I would appreciate it if you would let me know. I shall be in the area for a short while. I have become fond of this town.' A thought strikes me; 'Perhaps you own it?'

'No.'

'Please excuse the question if you are embarrassed by it. I, personally, would be quite proud to own a town like this. Is it for sale, do you think?'

'Come, you'd better get up. You might be arrested. Up you get.'

There is a disturbing reluctance on the part of the residents to tell me the owner of the town. Of course, I could not afford to buy it – I asked cunningly, in the hope of discovering who the owner was. Maybe she is too clever for me. The idea is not appealing.

'You're like a dead bird,' she smiles, 'with your wings broken.'

I refuse her hand and get up quickly. 'Lead the way.'

She frowns and then says: 'Home I think.' So off we go with her walking ahead. I point upwards: 'Look – there's a cloud the shape of a cloud!' She smiles and I feel encouraged to such a degree that I want to thank her.

We reach her house with its green door opening directly onto the street. There are windows with red and yellow curtains and the white paint covering the stone is beginning to flake. She produces a key, inserts it into the large black iron lock and pushes the door wide open, gesturing gracefully for me to enter before her. I incline my head and walk into the darkened hallway of the house. It smells of lavender and is full of old polished oak and brass plates, horse brasses, candlesticks with no candles in them. On my right is a staircase which twists up into gloom, the stairs covered by dark red carpet.

There are ferns in vases, placed on high shelves. Several vases of ferns are on the window sill by the door.

'I have a razor if you wish to shave,' she informs me. Luckily for her, I am self-critical enough to realise that I need a shave. I thank her and she mounts the stairs, wide skirt swinging, leading me to the upstairs floor and a small bathroom smelling of perfume and disinfectant.

She switches on the light. Outside, the blue of the sky is deepening and the sun has already set. She shows me the safety-razor, soap, towel. She turns a tap and water gushes out into her cupped hand. 'Still hot,' she says, turning and closing the door behind her. I am tired and make a bad job of shaving. I wash my hands as an afterthought and then go to the door to make sure it isn't locked. I open the door and peer out into the lighted passage. I shout: 'Hey!' and her head eventually comes into sight around another door at the far end of the passage. 'I've shaved.'

'Go downstairs into the front room,' she says. 'I'll join you there in a few minutes.' I grin at her and my eyes tell her that I know she is naked beneath her clothes. They all are. Without their clothes and their hair, where would they be? *Where is she? She came this way – I scented her trail right here, to this town. She could even be hiding inside this woman – fooling me. She was always clever in her own way. I'll break her other hand, listen to the bones snap, and they won't catch me. She sucked my life out of me and they blamed me for breaking her fingers. I was just trying to get at the ring I gave her. It was hidden by the blaze of the others.*

She turned me into a sharp-toothed wolf.

I thunder down the stairs, deliberately stamping on them, making them moan and creak. I locate the front room and enter it. Deep leather chairs, more brass, more oak, more ferns in smoky glass of purple and scarlet. A fireplace without a fire. A soft carpet, multicoloured. A small piano with black and white keys and a picture in a frame on top of it.

There is a white-clothed table with cutlery and plates for two. Two chairs squat beside the table.

I stand with my back to the fireplace as I hear her pointed-heeled shoes tripping down the stairs. 'Good evening,' I say politely when she comes in, dressed in a tight frock of dark blue velvet, with rubies around her throat and at her ears. There are dazzling rings on her fingers and I shudder, but manage to control myself.

'Please sit down.' She repeats the graceful gesture of the hand, indicating a leather chair with a yellow cushion. 'Do you feel better now?' I am suspicious and will not answer her. It might be a trick question, one never knows. 'I'll get dinner,' she tells me, 'I won't be long.' Again I've defeated her. She can't win at this rate.

I consume the foreign meal greedily and only realise afterwards that it might have been poisoned. Philosophically I reflect that it is too late now as I wait for coffee. I will test the coffee and see if it smells of bitter almonds. If it does, I will know it contains poison. I try to remember if any of the food I have already eaten tasted of bitter almonds. I don't think so. I feel comparatively safe.

She brings in the coffee smoking in a big brown earthenware pot. She sits down and pours me a cup. It smells good and, relievedly, I discover it does not have the flavour of bitter almonds. Come to think of it, I am not altogether sure what bitter almonds smell like.

'You may stay the night here, if you wish. There is a spare room.'

'Thank you,' I say, letting my eyes narrow in a subtle question, but she looks away from me and reaches a slim hand for the coffee pot. 'Thank you,' I repeat. She doesn't answer me. What's her game? She takes a breath, is about to say something, looks quickly at me, changes her mind, says nothing. I laugh softly, leaning back in my chair with my hand clasped around my coffee cup.

'There are wolves and there are sheep,' I say, as I have often said. 'Which do you think you are?'

'Neither,' says she.

'Then you are sheep,' say I. 'The wolves know what they are – what their function is. I am wolf.'

'Really,' she says and it is obvious that she is bored by my philosophy, not understanding it. 'You had better go to bed now – you are tired.'

'If you insist,' I say lightly. 'Very well.'

She shows me up to the room overlooking the unlit street and bids me goodnight. Closing the door, I listen carefully for the sound of a key turning, but the sound doesn't come. The room contains a high, old-fashioned bed, a standard lamp with a parchment shade with flowers pressed between two thicknesses, an empty bookcase and a wooden chair, beautifully carved. I feel the chair with my fingertips and shiver with delight at the sensation I receive. I pull back the quilt covering the bed and inspect the sheets which are clean and smell fresh. There are two white pillows, both very soft. I extract myself from my suit, taking off my

169

shoes and socks and leaving my underpants on. I switch off the light and, trembling a little, get into the sheets, I am soon asleep, but it is still very early. I am convinced that I shall wake up at dawn.

I open my eyes in the morning and pale sunshine forces its way between gaps in the curtains. I lie in bed trying to go back to sleep, but cannot. I push away the covers, which have slipped partly off the bed, and get up. I go to the window and look down into the street.

Incredibly, a huge hare is loping along the pavement, its nose twitching. A lorry roars past, its gears grating, but the hare continues its imperturbable course. I am tensed, excited. I open my door and run along the passage to the woman's room, entering with a rush. She is asleep, one arm sprawled outwards, the hand dangling over the edge of her bed, her shoulders pale and alive. I take hold of one shoulder in a strong grip designed to hurt her into wakefulness. She cries out, sits up quivering.

'Quick,' I say – 'Come and see. There is a hare in the street!'

'Go away and let me sleep,' she tells me, 'let me sleep.'

'No! You must come and look at the big hare in the street. How did it get there?'

She rises and follows me back to my room. I leap towards the window and see with relief that the hare is still there. 'Look!' I point towards it and she joins me at the window. She, too, is amazed. 'Poor thing,' she gasps. 'We must save it.'

'Save it?' I am astounded. 'Save it? No, I will kill it and we can eat it.'

She shudders. 'How could you be so cruel?' The hare disappears around a corner of the street. I am furious and all the nerves of my body are taut. 'It has gone!'

'It will probably be all right,' she says in a self-conciliatory tone and this makes me more angry. I begin to sob with frustration. She puts a hand on my arm. 'What is the matter?' I shrug off the hand, then think better of it, I begin to cry against her breast. She pats me on the back and I feel better. 'Let me come to bed with you,' I plead.

'No,' she says quietly. 'You must rest.'

'Let me sleep with *you*,' I insist, but she breaks from my grasp and backs towards the door. 'No! Rest.'

I follow her, my eyes hot in my skull, my body full. 'You owe me something,' I tell her viciously. 'You all do.'

'Go away,' she says threateningly, desperate and afraid of me. I continue to move towards her, beyond the door, along the passage. She starts to run for her room but I run also, and catch her. I catch her before she reaches the room. She screams. I clutch at her fingers. I bend them back slowly, putting my other hand over her mouth to stop her horrible noises. The bones snap in the slim, pale flesh. Not all at once.

'You made me wolf.' I snarl. 'And sheep must die.' My teeth seek her pounding jugular, my nose scents the perfume of her throat. I slide my sharp teeth through skin and sinew. Blood oozes into my mouth. As I kill her, I sob.

Why did she suck the soul of me from the wounds she made? Why am I wolf because of her? Or did it always lurk there, needing only the pain she made to release the ferocity?

But she is dead.

I had forgotten. I had sought her in this pleasant town.

Ah, now the other is dead, too.

Let murder drown me until I am nothing but a snarling speck, harmless and protected by my infinitesimal size.

Oh, God, my bloody darling...

The Pleasure Garden of Felipe Sagittarius

THE AIR WAS still and warm, the sun bright and the sky blue above the ruins of Berlin as I clambered over piles of weed-covered brick and broken concrete on my way to investigate the murder of an unknown man in the garden of Police Chief Bismarck.

My name is Minos Aquilinas, Metatemporal Investigator, Europe, and this job was going to be a tough one, I knew.

Don't ask me the location or the date. I never bother to find out things like that. They only confuse me. With me it's instinct, win or lose.

They'd given me all the information there was. The dead man had already had an autopsy. Nothing unusual about him except that he had paper lungs – disposable lungs. That pinned him down a little. The only place I knew of where they still used paper lungs was Rome. What was a Roman doing in Berlin? Why was he murdered in Police Chief Bismarck's garden? He'd been strangled, that I'd been told. It wasn't hard to strangle a man with paper lungs; it didn't take long. But who and why were harder questions to answer right then.

It was a long way across the ruins to Bismarck's place. Rubble stretched in all directions and only here and there could you see a landmark – what was left of the Reichstag, the Brandenburg Gate, the Brechtsmuseum and a few other places like that.

I stopped to lean on the only remaining wall of a house, took off my jacket and loosened my tie, wiped my forehead and neck with my handkerchief and lit a Black Cat. The wall gave me some shade and I felt a little cooler by the time I was ready to get going again.

As I mounted a big heap of brick on which a lot of blue weeds grew I saw the Bismarck place ahead. Built of heavy, black-veined marble, in the kind of Valhalla/Olympus mixture they went in for, it was fronted by a smooth, green lawn and backed by a garden surrounded by such a high wall I only glimpsed the leaves of some of the foliage even though I was looking down on the place. The thick Graecian columns flanking the porch were topped by a baroque façade covered in bas-reliefs showing hairy men in horned helmets killing dragons and one another apparently indiscriminately.

I picked my way down to the lawn and walked across it, then up some steps until I reached the front door. It was big and heavy, bronze I guessed, with more bas-reliefs, this time of clean-shaven characters in ornate and complicated armour with two-handed swords and riding horses. Some had lances and axes. I pulled the bell and waited.

I had plenty of time to study the pictures before one of the doors swung open and an old man in a semi-military suit, holding himself straight by an effort, raised a white eyebrow at me.

I told him my name and he let me into a cool, dark hall full of the same kinds of armour the men outside had been wearing. He opened a door on the right and told me to wait. The room was all iron and leather – weapons on the walls and hide-covered furniture on the carpet.

Thick velvet curtains were drawn back from the window and I stood looking out over the quiet ruins, smoked another stick, popped the butt in a green pot and put my jacket back on.

The old man came in again and I followed him out of that room, along the hall, up one flight of the wide stairs and into a huge, less cluttered room where I found the guy I'd come to see.

He stood in the middle of the carpet. He was wearing a heavily ornamented helmet with a spike on the top, a deep blue uniform covered in badges, gold and black epaulettes, shiny jackboots and steel spurs. He looked about seventy and very tough. He had bushy grey eyebrows and a big, carefully combed moustache. As I came in he grunted and one arm sprang into a horizontal position, pointing at me.

'Herr Aquilinas. I am Otto von Bismarck, Chief of Berlin's police.'

I shook the hand. Actually it shook me, all over.

'Quite a turn up,' I said. 'A murder in the garden of the man who's supposed to prevent murders.'

His face must have been paralysed or something because it didn't move except when he spoke, and even then it didn't move much.

'Quite so,' he said. 'We were reluctant to call you in, of course. But I think this is your speciality. Devilish work.'

'Maybe. Is the body still here?'

'In the kitchen. The autopsy was performed here. Paper lungs – you know about that?'

'I know. Now, if I've got it right, you heard nothing in the night –'

'Oh, yes, I did hear something – the barking of my wolfhounds. One of the servants investigated but found nothing.'

'What time was this?'

'Time?'

'What did the clock say?'

'About two in the morning.'

'When was the body found?'

'About ten – the gardener discovered it in the vine grove.'

'Right – let's look at the body and then talk to the gardener.'

He took me to the kitchen. One of the windows was opened onto a lush garden, full of tall, brightly coloured shrubs of every possible shade. An intoxicating scent came from the garden. It made me feel horny. I turned to look at the corpse lying on a scrubbed deal table covered in a sheet.

I pulled back the sheet. The body was naked. It looked old but strong, deeply tanned. The head was big and its most noticeable feature was the heavy grey moustache. The body wasn't what it had been. First there were the marks of strangulation around the throat, as well as swelling on wrists, forearms and legs which seemed to indicate that the victim had also been tied up recently. The whole of the front of the torso had been opened for the

175

autopsy and whoever had stitched it up again hadn't been too careful.

'What about clothes?' I asked the Police Chief.

Bismarck shook his head and pointed to a chair standing beside the table. 'That was all we found.'

There was a pair of neatly folded paper lungs, a bit the worse for wear. The trouble with disposable lungs was that while you never had to worry about smoking or any of the other causes of lung disease, the lungs had to be changed regularly. This was expensive, particularly in Rome where there was no State-controlled Lung Service as there had been in most of the European City-States until a few years before the war when the longer-lasting polythene lung had superseded the paper one. There was also a wristwatch and a pair of red shoes with long, curling toes.

I picked up one of the shoes. Middle Eastern workmanship. I looked at the watch. It was heavy, old, tarnished and Russian. The strap was new, pigskin, with 'Made in England' stamped on it.

'I see why they called us,' I said.

'There *were* certain anachronisms,' Bismarck admitted.

'This gardener who found him, can I talk to him?

Bismarck went to the window and called: 'Felipe!'

The foliage seemed to fold back of its own volition and a cadaverous dark-haired man came through it. He was tall, long-faced and pale. He held an elegant watering can in one hand. He was dressed in a dark green high-collared shirt and matching trousers. I wondered if I had seen him somewhere.

We looked at one another through the window.

'This is my gardener Felipe Sagittarius,' Bismarck said.

Sagittarius bowed, his eyes amused. Bismarck didn't seem to notice.

'Can you let me see where you found the body?' I asked.

'Sure,' said Sagittarius.

'I shall wait here,' Bismarck told me as I went towards the kitchen door.

'Okay.' I stepped into the garden and let Sagittarius show me the way. Once again the shrubs seemed to part on their own.

The scent was still thick and erotic. Most of the plants had dark, fleshy leaves and flowers of deep reds, purples and blues. Here and there were clusters of heavy yellow and pink.

The grass I was walking on felt like it crawled under my feet and the weird shapes of the trunks and stems of the shrubs didn't make me want to take a snooze in that garden.

'This is all your work is it, Sagittarius?' I asked.

He nodded and kept walking.

'Original,' I said. 'Never seen one like it before.'

Sagittarius turned then and pointed a thumb behind him. 'This is the place.'

We were standing in a little glade almost entirely surrounded by thick vines that curled about their trellises like snakes. On the far side of the glade I could see where some of the vines had been ripped and the trellis torn and I guessed there had been a fight. I still couldn't work out why the victim had been untied before the murderer strangled him – it must have been before, or else there wouldn't have been a fight. I checked the scene, but there were no clues. Through the place where the trellis was torn I saw a small summerhouse, built to represent a Chinese pavilion, all red, yellow and black lacquer with highlights picked out in gold. It didn't fit with the architecture of the house.

'What's that?' I asked the gardener.

'Nothing,' he said sulkily, evidently sorry I'd seen it.

'I'll take a look at it anyway.'

He shrugged but did not offer to lead on. I moved between the trellises until I reached the pavilion. Sagittarius followed slowly. I took the short flight of wooden steps up to the verandah and tried the door. It opened. I walked in. There seemed to be only one room, a bedroom. The bed needed making and it looked as if two people had left it in a hurry. There was a pair of nylons tucked half under the pillow and a pair of man's underpants on the floor. The sheets were very white, the furnishings very oriental and rich.

Sagittarius was standing in the doorway.

'Your place?' I said.

'No.' He sounded offended. 'The Police Chief's.'

I grinned.

Sagittarius burst into rhapsody. 'The languorous scents, the very menace of the plants, the *heaviness* in the air of the garden, must surely stir the blood of even the most ancient man. This is the only place he can relax. This is what I'm employed for.

'He gives me my head. I give him his pleasures.'

'Has this,' I said, pointing to the bed, 'anything to do with last night?'

'He was probably here when it happened, but I...' Sagittarius shook his head and I wondered if there was anything he'd meant to imply which I'd missed.

I saw something on the floor, stooped and picked it up. A pendant with the initials E.B. engraved on it in Gothic script.

'Who's E.B.?' I said.

'Only the garden interests me, Herr Aquilinas. I do not know who she is.'

I looked out at the weird garden. 'Why does it interest you – what's all this for? You're not doing it to his orders, are you? You're doing it for yourself.'

Sagittarius smiled bleakly. 'You are astute.' He waved an arm at the warm foliage that seemed more reptilian than plant and more mammalian, in its own way, than either. 'You know what I see out there? I see deep-sea canyons where lost submarines cruise through a silence of twilit green, threatened by the waving tentacles of predators, half-fish, half-plant, and watched by the eyes of long-dead mermen whose blood went to feed their young; where squids and rays fight in a graceful dance of death, clouds of black ink merging with clouds of red blood, drifting to the surface, sipped at by sharks in passing, where they will be seen by mariners leaning over the rails of their ships; maddened, the mariners will fling themselves overboard to sail slowly towards those distant plant-creatures already feasting on the corpse of squid and ray. This is the world I can bring to the land – that is my ambition.'

He stared at me, paused, and said: 'My skull – *it's like a monstrous fish bowl!*'

I nipped back to the house to find Bismarck had returned to his room. He was sitting in a plush armchair, a hidden hi-fi playing, of all things, a Ravel string quartet.

'No Wagner?' I said and then: 'Who's E.B.?'

'Later,' he said. 'My assistant will answer your questions for the moment. He should be waiting for you.'

There was a car parked outside the house – a battered Volkswagen containing a neatly uniformed man of below average height. He had a small toothbrush moustache, a stray lock of black hair falling over his forehead, black gloves on his hands which gripped a military cane in his lap. When he saw me come out he smiled, said, 'Aha,' and got briskly from the car to shake my hand with a slight bow.

'Adolf Hitler,' he said. 'Captain of Uniformed Detectives in Precinct XII. Police Chief Bismarck has put me at your service.'

'Glad to hear it. Do you know much about him?'

Hitler opened the car door for me and I got in. He went round the other side, slid into the driving seat.

'The Chief?' He shook his head. 'He is somewhat remote. I do not know him well – there are several ranks between us. Usually my orders come from him indirectly. This time he chose to see me himself.'

'What were they, his orders, this time?'

'Simply to help you in this investigation.'

'There isn't much to investigate. You're completely loyal to your chief, I take it?'

'Of course.' Hitler seemed honestly puzzled. He started the car and we drove down the drive and out along a flat, white road, surmounted on both sides by great heaps of overgrown rubble.

'The murdered man had paper lungs, eh?' he said.

'Yes. Guess he must have come from Rome. He looked a bit like an Italian.'

'Or a Jew, eh?'

'I don't think so. What made you think that?'

'The Russian watch, the Oriental shoes – the nose. That was a big nose he had. And they still have paper lungs in Moscow, you know.'

179

His logic seemed a bit offbeat to me but I let it pass. We turned a corner and entered a residential section where a lot of buildings were still standing. I noticed that one of them had a bar in its cellar. 'How about a drink?' I said.

'Here?' He seemed surprised, or maybe nervous.

'Why not?'

So he stopped the car and we went down the steps into the bar. A girl was singing. She was a plumpish brunette with a small, good voice. She was singing in English and I caught the chorus:

> Nobody's grievin' for Steven,
> And Stevie ain't grievin' no more,
> For Steve took his life in a prison cell,
> And Johnny took a new whore.

It was 'Christine', the latest hit in England. We ordered beers from the bartender. He seemed to know Hitler well because he laughed and slapped him on the shoulder and didn't charge us for the beer. Hitler seemed embarrassed.

'Who was that?' I asked.

'Oh, his name is Weill. I know him slightly.'

'More than slightly, it looks like.'

Hitler seemed unhappy and undid his uniform jacket, tilted his cap back on his head and tried unsuccessfully to push back the stray lock of hair. He looked a sad little man and I felt that maybe my habit of asking questions was out of line here. I drank my beer and watched the singer. Hitler kept his back to her but I noticed she kept looking at him.

'What do you know about this Sagittarius?' I asked.

Hitler shrugged. 'Very little.'

Weill turned up again behind the bar and asked us if we wanted more beer. We said we didn't.

'Sagittarius?' Weill spoke up brightly. 'Are you talking about that crank?'

'He's a crank, is he?' I said.

'That's not fair, Kurt,' Hitler said. 'He's a brilliant man, a biologist –'

'Who was thrown out of his job because he was insane!'

'That is unkind, Kurt,' Hitler said reprovingly. 'He was investigating the potential sentience of plant life. A perfectly reasonable line of scientific enquiry.'

From the corner of the room someone laughed jeeringly. It was a shaggy-haired old man sitting by himself with a glass of schnapps on the little table in front of him.

Weill pointed at him. 'Ask Albert. He knows about science.'

Hitler pursed his lips and looked at the floor. 'He's just an embittered old mathematics teacher – he's jealous of Felipe,' he said quietly, so that the old man wouldn't hear.

'Who is he?' I asked Weill.

'Albert? A *really* brilliant man. He has never had the recognition he deserves. Do you want to meet him?'

But the shaggy man was leaving. He waved a hand at Hitler and Weill. 'Kurt, Captain Hitler – good day.'

'Good day, Doctor Einstein.' Hitler turned to me. 'Where would you like to go now?'

'A tour of the places that sell jewellery, I guess,' I said, fingering the pendant in my pocket. 'I may be on the wrong track altogether, but it's the only track I can find at the moment.'

We toured the jewellers. By nightfall we were nowhere nearer finding who had owned the thing. I'd just have to get the truth out of Bismarck the next day, though I knew it wouldn't be easy. He wouldn't like answering personal questions. Hitler dropped me off at the Precinct House where a cell had been converted into a bedroom for me.

I sat on the hard bed smoking and brooding. I was just about to get undressed and go to sleep when I started to think about the bar we'd been in earlier. I was sure someone there could help me. On impulse I left the cell and went out into the deserted street. It was still very hot and the sky was full of heavy clouds. Looked like a storm was due.

I got a cab back to the bar. It was still open.

Weill wasn't serving there now. He was playing the piano-accordion for the same girl singer I'd seen earlier. He nodded to me as I came in. I leaned on the bar and ordered a beer from the barman.

When the number was over, Weill unstrapped his accordion and joined me. The girl followed him.

'Adolf not with you?' he said.

'He went home. He's a good friend of yours, is he?'

'Oh, we met years ago in Austria. He's a nice man, you know. He should never have become a policeman. He's too mild.'

'That's the impression I got. Why did he ever join in the first place?'

Weill smiled and shook his head. He was a short, thin man, wearing heavy glasses. He had a large, sensitive mouth. 'Sense of duty, perhaps. He has a great sense of duty. He is very religious, too – a devout Catholic. I think that weighs on him. You know these converts, they accept nothing, are torn by their consciences. I never yet met a happy Catholic convert.'

'He seems to have a thing about Jews.'

Weill frowned. 'What sort of thing? I've never really noticed. Many of his friends are Jews. I am, and Sagittarius...'

'Sagittarius is a friend of his?'

'Oh, more an acquaintance I should think. I've seen them together a couple of times.'

It began to thunder outside. Then it started to rain.

Weill walked towards the door and pulled down the blind. Through the noise of the storm I heard another sound, a strange, metallic grinding. A crunching.

'What's that?' I called. Weill shook his head and walked back towards the bar. The place was empty now. 'I'm going to have a look,' I said.

I went to the door, opened it, and climbed the steps.

Marching across the ruins, illuminated by rapid flashes of gunfire, I saw a gigantic metal monster, as big as a tall building. Supported on four telescopic legs, it lumbered at right angles to the street. From its huge body and head the snouts of guns stuck out in all directions. Lightning sometimes struck it and it made an ear-shattering bell-like clang, paused to fire upwards at the source of the lightning, and march on.

I ran down the steps and flung open the door. Weill was tidying up the bar. I described what I'd seen.

'What is it, Weill?'

The short man shook his head. 'I don't know. At a guess it is something Berlin's conquerors left behind.'

'It looked as if it was made here...'

'Perhaps it was. After all, who conquered Berlin –?'

A woman screamed from a back room, high and brief.

Weill dropped a glass and ran towards the room. I followed.

He opened a door. The room was homely. A table covered by a thick, dark cloth, laid with salt and pepper, knives and forks, a piano near the window, a girl lying on the floor.

'Eva!' Weill gasped, kneeling beside the body.

I gave the room another once-over. Standing on a small coffee table was a plant. It looked at first rather like a cactus of unpleasantly mottled green, though the top curved so that it resembled a snake about to strike. An eyeless, noseless snake – with a mouth. There was a mouth. It opened as I approached. There were teeth in the mouth – or rather thorns arranged the way teeth are. One thorn seemed to be missing near the front. I backed away from the plant and inspected the corpse. I found the thorn in her wrist. I left it there.

'She is dead,' Weill said softly, standing up and looking around. 'How?'

'She was bitten by that poisonous plant,' I said.

'Plant...? I must call the police.'

'That wouldn't be wise at this stage maybe,' I said as I left. I knew where I was going.

Bismarck's house. And the pleasure garden of Felipe Sagittarius.

It took me time to find a cab and I was soaked through when I did. I told the cabby to step on it.

I had the taxi stop before we got to the house, paid it off and walked across the lawns. I didn't bother to ring the doorbell. I let myself in by the window, using my glass-cutter.

I heard voices coming from upstairs. I followed the sound until I located it – Bismarck's study. I inched the door open.

Hitler was there. He had a gun pointed at Otto von Bismarck who was still in full uniform. They both looked pale. Hitler's hand was shaking and Bismarck was moaning slightly.

Bismarck stopped moaning to say pleadingly, 'I wasn't blackmailing Eva Braun, you fool – she liked me.'

Hitler laughed curtly, half hysterically. 'Like *you* – a fat old man.'

'She liked fat old men.'

'She wasn't that kind of girl.'

'Who told you this, anyway?'

'The investigator told me some. And Weill rang me half an hour ago to tell me some more – also that Eva had been killed. I thought Sagittarius was my friend. I was wrong. He is your hired assassin. Well, tonight I intend to do my own killing.'

'Captain Hitler – I am your superior officer!'

The gun wavered as Bismarck's voice recovered some of its authority. I realised that the hi-fi had been playing quietly all the time. Curiously it was Bartók's Fifth String Quartet.

Bismarck moved his hand. 'You are completely mistaken. That man you hired to follow Eva here last night – he was Eva's ex-lover!'

Hitler's lip trembled.

'You knew,' said Bismarck.

'I suspected it.'

'You also knew the dangers of the garden, because Felipe had told you about them. The vines killed him as he sneaked towards the summerhouse.'

The gun steadied. Bismarck looked scared.

He pointed at Hitler. 'You killed him – not I!' he screamed. 'You sent him to his death. You killed Stalin – out of jealousy. You hoped he would kill me and Eva first. You were too frightened, too weak, to confront any of us openly!'

Hitler shouted wordlessly, put both hands to the gun and pulled the trigger several times. Some of the shots went wide, but one hit Bismarck in his Iron Cross, pierced it and got him in the heart.

He fell backwards. As he did so his uniform ripped apart and his helmet fell off. I ran into the room and took the gun from Hitler who was crying. I checked that Bismarck was dead. I saw what had caused the uniform to rip open. He had been wearing a corset – one of the bullets must have cut the cord. It was a heavy corset and had a lot to hold in.

I felt sorry for Hitler. I helped him sit down as he sobbed. He looked small and wretched.

'What have I killed?' he stuttered. 'What have I killed?'

'Did Bismarck send that plant to Eva Braun to silence her? Was I getting too close?'

Hitler nodded, snorted and started to cry again.

I looked towards the door. A man hesitated there.

I put the gun on the mantelpiece.

It was Sagittarius.

He nodded to me.

'Hitler's just shot Bismarck,' I explained.

'So it appears.' He touched his thin lips.

'Bismarck had you send Eva Braun that plant, is that so?' I said.

'Yes. A beautiful cross between a common cactus, a Venus Fly-trap and a rose – the venom was curaré, of course.'

Hitler got up and walked from the room. We watched him leave. He was still sniffling.

'Where are you going?' I asked.

'To get some air,' I heard him say as he went down the stairs.

'The repression of sexual desires,' said Sagittarius seating himself in an armchair and resting his feet comfortably on Bismarck's corpse. 'It is the cause of so much trouble. If only the passions that lie beneath the surface, the desires that are locked in the mind could be allowed to range free, what a better place the world would be.'

'Maybe,' I said.

'Are you going to make any arrests, Herr Aquilinas?'

'It's my job to file a report on my investigation, not to make arrests,' I said.

'Will there be any repercussions over this business?'

I laughed. 'There are always repercussions,' I told him.

From the garden came a peculiar barking noise.

'What's that?' I asked. 'The wolfhounds?'

Sagittarius giggled. 'No, no – the dog-plant, I fear.'

I ran out of the room and down the stairs until I reached the kitchen. The sheet-covered corpse was still lying on the table. I was going to open the door onto the garden when I stopped and pressed my face to the window instead.

The whole garden was moving in what appeared to be an agitated dance. Foliage threshed about and, even with the door closed, the strange scent was unbearable.

I thought I saw a figure struggling with some thick-boled shrubs. I heard a growling noise, a tearing sound, a scream and a long-drawn-out groan.

Suddenly the garden was motionless.

I turned. Sagittarius stood behind me, his hands folded on his chest, his eyes staring down at the floor.

'It seems your dog-plant got him,' I said.

'He knew me – he knew the garden.'

'Suicide maybe?'

'Very likely.' Sagittarius unfolded his hands and looked up at me. 'I liked him, you know. He was something of a protégé. If you had not interfered none of this might have happened. He might have gone far with me to guide him.'

'You'll have other protégés,' I said.

'Let us hope so.' His voice was cold as the stars.

The sky outside began to lighten imperceptibly. The rain was now only a drizzle, falling on the thirsty leaves of the plants.

'Are you going to stay here?' I asked him.

'Yes – I have the garden to work on. Bismarck's servants will look after me.'

'I guess they will,' I said.

I went back up the stairs and I walked away from that house into a cold and desolate dawn. I tried to light my last Black Cat and failed. Then I threw the damp cigarette into the rubble, turned up the collar of my coat and began to make my way slowly across the ruins.

The Real Life Mr Newman

Chapter One

THE LONDON FOG was lifting. In Charing Cross Gardens black skeletons of trees became visible and Newman could now make out the shadowy buildings beyond them. As the fog dispersed he got up from the bench. He did not welcome the change in the weather.

He seemed to be the only person about. What time was it?

London was still silent as he swung his huge body, swaddled in its thick, tan overcoat, towards the Embankment, plodded through the gates of the Gardens and out into the main road. Running across the road he noticed the stationary bus and wondered briefly why the passengers sat so still. Then he leaned on the Embankment wall and peered down into the river.

He thought for a moment that the Thames, too, was petrified. But he had been mistaken. It was moving, very sluggishly; alive with bobbing refuse, stained with oil. Turning his head to his right, Newman saw the ugly railway bridge, rusted steel and peeling green paint, a suburban train clanking across it. On his left marked by its orange lights was white Waterloo Bridge, curving over the water like a graceful sea-beast. And across the river, marked only by patches of light breaking through the fog, was the Festival Hall. Newman turned and put his back against the wall, staring across the road at the entrance to Embankment Underground Station. He was disappointed. He had expected the fog to last much longer. He was never afraid in the fog.

Near the Underground entrance a few vague shapes moved.

Grey figures emerged from the fog and became black silhouettes in the light of the station foyer.

He crossed the road in a lumbering run, skipped hastily onto the pavement, as a hooting taxi narrowly missed him, and rushed into the lobby. He paused, fumbling in his coat for change. He put his money into a machine, took his ticket from the slot and walked slowly to the barrier. The attendant ignored him as he went through.

He had gone past the barrier and was about to step onto the downward escalator when he paused and began to tremble. He could not calm the trembling which rapidly became violent.

For a few seconds he fought to conquer his fear, but it was hopeless. He could not take a single step towards the escalator. It was well lit; he could see to the bottom where a short tunnel led to the platform. The layout of the station was familiar to him. There was no danger. But he could go no further. He turned and stumbled back through the barrier, out of the station by its other entrance and up Villiers Street, still dark and silent, towards Trafalgar Square.

As the fog dispersed Newman's peace of mind evaporated. He now felt troubled, persecuted. He ran faster when he reached the Strand and turned towards Trafalgar Square.

He stopped dead again at what he thought he saw.

Nelson's Column had grown to gigantic size, seeming to fill the whole square with its grimy masonry, stretching above him into the remnants of the rising fog. He shut his eyes and rubbed them – for him, a normal habit. When he opened them again the column had grown even larger. He raced down the Strand away from it, colliding with several people.

Now the rest of the buildings began to increase in size. Even passers-by seemed larger. Vast walls of concrete towered higher and higher – no longer buildings, but sheer, cave-studded sides of immense black cliffs. He charged on through canyons that appeared to fold in upon him. Blurs of light – red, blue, green, orange – darted like fireflies before his eyes. There were noises; distant roars and shrieks. He felt the sensation of blows on his body, and everywhere the smell of iodine and almonds. Vibrating lines attacked his face, veering off as he raised his pale hands against them. His lungs were filled with a million tiny, stabbing icicles, his stomach was hollow, painful; his legs liquid, without bone or muscle.

The solid, thrumming note of a drum filled his skull – the sound of his maddened pulse as his heart sought to free itself from its restraining flesh and ribs. His breathing was a series of huge gasps – he could not get enough of the thin air. Booted feet ached, thighs and groin throbbed; hands waved on bruised arms – hands like peeled sticks waving in a high wind.

As a boy in England and later in Virginia, where his mother had gone with her American husband, Newman had admired trees more than anything else. He liked them green and golden and rustling in summer; he liked them stark and black and brittle in winter. He rarely broke a branch or stripped a twig of its bark or its leaves. He liked sometimes to climb them in summer, particularly when climbing helped him breathe in their sweetness and look down at a surging sea of foliage. But most of the time he had liked simply to walk among their trunks or lie in their shade, his back to the grass. He had resented it if he had been called away from the woods, where he would have drowned among trees if it had been possible.

'Sebastian!' his mother used to call in her half-English accent. 'Are you there?'

'Come on, Seb!' The good-natured voice of his stepfather, slightly embarrassed by the authority over her child which marrying Sebastian's mother had given him.

Usually Sebastian would come when called. He was an obedient child. But sometimes he would hide, or creep deeper into the woods that went on without end at the back of the house. He had fancied sometimes that the house stood on the edge of civilisation – beyond it, endless forests without houses or human beings. He didn't need to populate this forest of his imagination; the forest was enough.

He had been a cheerful boy, lonely by choice. He had mixed

well enough at school, sometimes playing with the neighbour-hood children. He had been personable and clever, though he absorbed knowledge intuitively rather than consciously. Exams would release facts he did not know he knew. Blindly and amiably, he followed his stepfather into the Air Force when he left college – he had majored in physics – and became an efficient, mildly liked officer. He was one of the men selected to go up in a space cap-sule when the Special Space Project got under way.

Col. Sebastian Newman, USAF, ran blindly through the trans-formed streets of a terrifying London. Since his flight was silent, he was cursed rather than restrained by the people he bumped into. He did not look very different from a commuter late for his train. He ran down the Strand, past Aldwych, where cars braked as he crossed their paths, up Fleet Street until, exhausted, he stopped, drained of adrenaline. The aural and visual sensations diminished and disappeared. His physical sensations remained. His mouth was dry and he was wet with sweat.

He looked up at the *Daily Express* building. It had the appear-ance of a monstrous, Edwardian public lavatory and wash-house, covered in shiny tiles. He knew then that he was in Fleet Street. He had not come particularly far, but could not remember how he had got here. He guessed something like this had happened several times already. He looked at his watch. It had stopped. He pulled up his coat collar, wiping the sweat from his face. No-one seemed to be looking at him, so he decided that his behaviour had not been too abnormal. He hailed a taxi, climbed in and gave the address.

A towering, glowering, twisted London went past as the driver took him towards Notting Hill. Nothing looked man-made. Everything had the appearance of a strange, natural landscape – canyons and crags, grey and black, with dim lights gleaming here and there. Asymmetrical and organic, it had an air of being as yet only partly formed, waiting for a shape that would be given it. The shape, Newman felt, would not be that of the London he knew.

The sense of menace increased as the taxi sped on and he con-trolled his urge to tell the driver to stop.

Above all, Newman thought, it was bleak; it was a wasteland. It had never been alive.

Yet there was life there – life in it, like the maggots in a corpse. Life in the tall, brooding cliffs, hollowed by a million burrows. Life full of misery and disease and hopeless repetition of senseless actions. Life neurotic. Nothing could make it worse than it was, and only total destruction, perhaps, could improve it.

Part of one of the burrows was his; in the miserable slum he would once have recognised as North Kensington, which apart from being a shade or two darker was now little different from anywhere else.

The taxi stopped. Newman paid, looking up at the distorted face of the immense cliff and trying to remember which entrance at the base he should crawl through to find his burrow.

Habit guided him. He clambered up obsidian slopes to enter the cave mouth.

It was dark and smelled of damp and old age. A switch clicked beneath his hand but the place remained dark. He headed upwards, climbing slowly, gripping a balustrade he felt rather than saw.

At last he reached his room. Turning on the light, he reeled, for the walls appeared to be at odd angles, and there were too many surfaces. He made out the gas-fire and the ring and the meter, the divan bed, the chest of drawers and the cane-seated chair.

He knew he paid thirty shillings a week for the room and he had lived in it for seven weeks since checking out of a nearby American servicemen's club where he had stayed for a weekend. He had told the club that he was going on to Italy. Perhaps they were looking for him there.

As an astronaut, Newman was a hero and on indefinite leave for having circled Mars umpteen times with his co-pilot, who had died. A steel capsule, cluttered with noisy instruments and his spacesuited body lying in a semi-horizontal position.

He had had to work hard to get permission to travel around incognito. He had skipped his shadow when he had left the club. He had grown a full beard and let his hair grow longer. He wore dark glasses. His accent was American, but especially unnoticed in the area where he'd chosen to live. Here, nothing about him was particularly peculiar.

Not even his madness, he thought. He was undoubtedly mad, he supposed. For some reason he had the feeling that he was observing things as they actually were. His vision had distorted everything since his return from space, and yet the suspicion persisted that, when landing, he had seen everything clearly for the first time.

Yet the London out there was a madman's London – a dark dream, an ultra-subjective impression and not, as he had sometimes supposed, a super-objective impression.

He staggered towards the bed. Tomorrow he must go out and try to find someone who could help him but would not betray him to the US authorities, who were looking for him. Perhaps others were looking for him, too?

Was all this hallucination? he wondered. Or was it absolute reality – not the apparent reality of conscious life but the reality of the unconscious, the reality responsible for affecting events and controlling society? Was he seeing it as well as sensing it? Or had his senses turned themselves in such a way that images appeared to his conscious mind exactly as they did to his unconscious?

Taking off his overcoat, he lay down on the bed and slept. The London he dreamed of was the London he had passed through in the taxi.

Chapter Two

I T IS POSSIBLE that Sebastian Newman was mad, but when he woke up next morning it was with a feeling of tranquillity. Outside, the sun had risen, its pale light reflected on the huge, crooked cliffs that had been the buildings of London. This morning they looked solid and permanent. Newman no longer doubted their reality.

He got off the bed and made his way across the angular room to the gas-fire. He lit that and the gas-ring and filled a large kettle with water from the tap. When it had boiled he washed himself and felt even more relaxed.

Having breakfasted on milk and cereal, he dressed and went down the twisted stairs and out into the street, now a gleaming ribbon reminiscent of frozen lava running between the cliffs. A few people passed, their faces quite blank. When he accidentally knocked into one, the man did not seem to notice. When Newman apologised, the man did not hear him.

They were like zombies, Newman thought. Like marionettes.

Though the buildings had changed, the general plan of the city had not, and Newman headed towards the Bayswater Road, walking up the narrow, winding gully that had been Portobello Road. He hardly noticed the girl who walked past him dressed in a farthingale – returning home, possibly, from a late fancy-dress party.

Before he reached the end of the street he heard the clang of metal on metal and wondered where the sound came from. Until now he had not realised that the silence had been so complete. He turned into a court, smelling fire and hot steel, and there, in a workshop like a blacksmith's forge, a little man hammered at a beautifully engraved breastplate from a suit of armour. The man was engrossed in this and Newman watched as he hammered, expertly turning the breastplate on the anvil with a pair of tongs held in his left hand. The burnished steel shone and glinted in the red light from the fire that burned in the wide grate to the left of the workshop. The armour was covered in small, intricate designs of flowers, crosses and little figures in pastoral settings. It was the design for a lady's sampler rather than for a suit of armour, and the combination of the delicate, embroiderylike design and the martial nature of the thing seemed odd to Newman.

Evidently satisfied at last, the old man straightened up to become almost as tall as Newman. His shoulders were stooped and his face had a pink, healthy appearance. He wore glasses and his hair, like his old-fashioned moustache, was thick and white. He gave Newman a genial nod and began to strip off the heavy leather gloves he had worn when working the breastplate. His apron was also leather, and he now wiped his hands down it to get rid of the sweat.

'Good morning,' Newman said. 'I didn't know anyone like you worked around here.'

'You didn't?' The old man smiled. 'Good morning. You aren't a customer, by the look of you.'

'How can you tell?'

'I can tell a man who needs armour.'

'You're an armourer?'

'That's my trade.'

'But surely no-one wears armour these days. Only a few ceremonial regiments maybe. Do they employ you?'

The old man shrugged. 'Anyone may employ me. Many do. I restore old armour and I make new armour – armour of all kinds, you know. My name is Schweitzer.'

'Mine's Newman, Mr Schweitzer. How do you do?'

'How do you do? Would you like a cup of tea? My wife should have one ready.'

'Thanks.'

Newman followed the old man through the workshop and entered a dark room behind it – a parlour. It contained a solid table covered with a thick, tasselled tablecloth with a rich, Indian design in purple and gold. An earthenware teapot in a knitted cosy stood on it, steam curling from the spout. There was a small window with dark, velvet curtains and heavy net; a dresser in dark oak held crockery primarily of Willow Pattern. Mr Schweitzer indicated one of two leather armchairs and Newman sat down while Mr Schweitzer poured the tea into two large mugs.

When they were both sitting, Mr Schweitzer said: 'You seem to have a problem, Mr Newman. Can I help?'

'I don't think so,' Newman said. 'I have been confused for some time now, ever since I returned to Earth, but this morning I feel calm. I've a feeling of detachment. You know, of peace – certainty, if you like.'

'A very valuable feeling. If all were like you I should be out of work.' Mr Schweitzer smiled and sipped his tea.

'I don't follow you,' Newman said.

'I make armour of many sorts, Mr Newman. Many sorts.' Mr Schweitzer stretched his arm towards the table and put down his cup. 'Would you like to see some of the armour I make?'

Newman admitted that he was curious and the old man led him from the parlour, up a narrow staircase and into a storeroom, very neatly arranged. Here were shelves and racks bearing a strange assortment of things. There were cards full of pairs of sunglasses, hats with veils, helmets with visors, a suit of city clothes – black coat, pinstripe trousers, bowler hat, briefcase and umbrella – on a dummy. There were masks, plain and embroidered and fashioned into grotesque faces; there were Chinese fans, suits of armour from every period of history and every age; there were costumes – crinolines in brown and black, broadcloth suits in black. There were no bright colours among the suits and dresses.

'This is only one section of my stock of armour,' Mr Schweitzer told him. 'Call them travelling caves, portable fortresses. But my main stock cannot really be seen.'

Puzzled, Newman asked what it was.

'I trade in tangible intangibles, if you like.' Schweitzer smiled.

'Intangibles that have tangible effects, to be more precise.' He went to a bureau and pulled out a drawer full of books. Taking them from the drawer, he spread them before Newman. They were religious books. A Bible, a Qur'an, the Vestas – all kinds of works by religious thinkers, including modern works.

'I don't understand,' said Newman. 'This is armour?'

'The most lasting kind, Mr Newman. It is the armour of *ideas* and of *ritual*. Mental armour to shut out those other ideas...'

'Those are?'

'The ideas we fear, that we refuse to investigate unless swathed in armour. What if there were no purpose to existence, Mr Newman, other than to exist?'

Newman shrugged. 'What of it? That idea does not disturb me.'

'I told you I did not think you were a customer of mine. You have the manner of a man who has retreated so far that he has circled right back to the thing he fears – approaching it from the rear, as it were, and finding it not so fearsome as he felt. But that is an unfair judgement. I do not know you.'

'You may be right or you may be wrong,' Newman answered carelessly. 'Even now it occurs to me that I may be totally insane and that you are a figment of my imaginings.'

'What of it? Am I not as real as anything you have known in the past?'

'More so, in many ways.'

'Well, then?'

Newman nodded. 'I see your point. But could not all this – that transformed city out there, this shop, yourself – could they not be a monstrous suit of armour I have constructed for myself?'

'I am an armourer. I have been in the trade for longer than I would like to say. I know a customer when I see one. You are no customer for me.'

'Already you give me reassurance.' Newman smiled. 'You comfort me with your words – you ease my mind.'

'If you say so. There is a difference between self-confidence and self-deception.'

'Fair enough.' Newman paced around the storeroom, looking

at everything. Now that Schweitzer had mentioned it, he could see that it was armour – all of it. It disturbed him that people should go to such lengths to embellish it, to put all their arts and skills into producing it.

There were more books, also – books of attractive, comforting philosophy.

'Antidotes, do you see, Mr Newman. My job is not to effect cures.'

'Just the diving suits,' Newman said, picking up a heavy diver's helmet. 'So that the depths can be visited but never really explored. And you sell all these?'

'I do not sell them, Mr Newman. Call me a philanthropist. I give them away.' Schweitzer moved towards another door. 'This way.'

In the next room were large, old-fashioned bottles of the kind once used for keeping sweets. Newman stared at some of the labels. They read: *Cynicism* (J); *Hatred* (M); *Idealism* (R5); *Despair* (12). And so on.

'All armour?' Newman asked.

'Just so. Like the knight who wore that breastplate you saw me working earlier, people lumber around in their heavy suits and their actions becoming cruder, their movements more sluggish, the longer they wear them. But what can one do? Needs must when the devil drives...'

'And what is the devil, Mr Schweitzer?'

'Fear. Let us go back to the parlour and see if the tea is still hot enough for a second cup.'

While they sat drinking their tea in silence, Newman thought a little about the things he had seen in Mr Schweitzer's storerooms. A short time later, the door from the workshop opened and a girl came in. She was very tall and beautiful, wearing no make-up and with long, dark hair framing her face. She wore an ankle-length dress of crimson and both hands held leashes. At the end of one leash was a lyre-bird, very tame and confident, and on the other a peacock with its tail at its peak of splendour, sweeping the ground behind it as it walked beside the girl.

'Good morning, Mr Schweitzer,' she said with a friendly smile. 'Is it all right to pop in?'

'Of course, Fanny.'

Newman got up.

'This is Miss Fanny Patrick,' Schweitzer said. 'Mr Newman.'

The girl transferred one leash to her left hand and shook hands, giving him the same open smile she had given Schweitzer. 'How do you do, Mr Newman?'

For the first time it struck Newman, not very seriously, that he might have died and entered some previously unimagined heaven or hell – or, more likely, purgatory – since his experiences so far had not affected him particularly strongly in any direction. Fanny Patrick, however, could have come from a dream, for she appeared to be his ideal woman.

He even liked her choice of pets.

'You're not a Londoner, Mr Newman,' she was saying.

'I was born here,' he said. 'But I went to the States as a kid. I was a space-pilot. I came back to Europe because –' he laughed self-deprecatingly – 'because I was looking for some roots, I guess.'

'Roots, eh?' She raised an eyebrow. 'Geographical?'

'That's what I thought. It all sounds so phoney. Psychological, maybe.'

'Have you found them?'

'I'm not sure. Almost, perhaps.'

'That's fine. I'm lunching up the road. Why don't you join me?'

'I'd like to.'

'I'd really come to ask Mr Schweitzer if he felt like an early lunch out,' she said, turning to the old man. 'What do you say, Mr Schweitzer?'

'No, thank you.' Mr Schweitzer smiled. 'I've some work to get on with. I'm being kept pretty busy at the moment. I'll see you again, Mr Newman.'

Newman and the girl said goodbye and left through the work-shop. The sun was bright and the sky cloudless as they sauntered up the canyon towards a café with a striped awning that jutted out from the cliff-wall on their right. They sat down at one of the tables under the awning and an old, black-clad waiter took their order with a nod of greeting to Fanny Patrick.

'What's your first name?' she asked as they waited for their food.

'Sebastian.'

'Well, there are so few of us here that we tend to get on first-name terms right away. Is that all right by you?'

'Suits me.' Newman smiled. 'Ah, I feel as though I'm on holiday.'

'You've just got in, have you?'

'I don't quite follow you.'

She smiled. 'I mean, things have changed recently. Your surroundings – that sort of thing.' She watched as her two birds, which she had freed from their leashes, ran among the tables pecking at scraps of food.

'That's right.'

'It happened to me. I was in a mental hospital for quite a while. Then, one day, everything seemed to sort itself out. The images, that I'd kept glimpsing, suddenly solidified, if you know what I mean. And here I was. I like it here.'

A thought struck Newman. 'Do you ever get the feeling you should be *doing* something here?'

She shook her head. 'I just take it easy,' she said. 'There's nothing to do – unless you're someone like Mr Schweitzer, working for the outside people.'

'Who are they?'

'Almost everybody,' she said. 'Look, you see that young man walking this way.'

Newman looked and saw him. He was fair-haired, sallow, and his face was somehow tight yet devoid of expression. He walked mechanically, like the people Newman had seen earlier. The other noticeable thing about him was that he was dressed in Edwardian clothes.

Fanny Patrick got up and walked towards the young man. She shouted 'Good morning', but he didn't seem to hear her. She walked alongside him, peering into his face, tapping him gently on the shoulder. A suggestion of vague irritation crossed his brow but he walked on without looking at her. She shrugged, spread her hands and came back to the table.

The young man turned a corner and was gone.

'That's the outside people for you, Sebastian,' she said as she sat down. 'Now do you know what I mean?'

'I suppose so. What makes them like that?'

'Oh, too many things.'

The lunch came. Newman had ordered schnitzel and noodles; Fanny had a Steak Diane.

'Those people are still living in the world we knew, is that it?' Newman suggested.

'I suppose it is,' she said. 'They go in and out of houses, along streets, buy things in shops that are still there as far as they're concerned. Yet we can see that they're not. Two kinds of reality, you see – coexisting. It still comes down to the question, if you care to ask it and worry about it: is it the minority or the majority who are really insane? Or are all insane?'

Chapter Three

DRINKING COFFEE AFTER lunch, Fanny Patrick glanced at her watch.

'I'm sailing for Paris this afternoon,' she said. 'Mustn't miss the ship.'

'Paris.' Newman was disappointed. 'So you're going away.'

'Why don't you come, too?' she suggested with a quick smile. 'You'd enjoy the voyage. And you've nothing else on, I gather.'

'No,' he said. 'I haven't. But I don't have much money with me and I'd need clothes...' He'd already made up his mind to go if he could.

'Don't worry about either. We don't use money. There's so few of us and we've everything we need. You can get some clothes there.'

'All right,' He grinned. 'I'll come.'

'Good. We'll pop back to my place; get my bag, make sure the birds are looked after. That was one reason for calling on Mr S. – his wife usually takes care of them for me while I'm away. Then we'll be off.'

They left the restaurant and walked round the corner to where a pale section of cliff, like a sandstone butte, stood alone. This was her house. Inside it was spacious, with white walls and red carpets, the furniture of light wood and upholstered in blue. He waited for her in a room which looked out over a landscaped garden with a fountain in the middle. She wasn't long. She came into the room with her bag in her hand, the lyre-bird and the peacock running behind her.

He took the bag.

'I've got a dog-cart ready at the side of the house,' she said.

He followed her out to where a scarlet-and-gold dog-cart, with a palomino pony between its shafts, was waiting for them. She climbed into the seat and lifted the placid birds into the back. Newman got up beside her. She jiggled the reins and the pony moved off.

After they'd left the birds with the pale, pleasant-voiced Mrs Schweitzer, Fanny headed east.

'Where's the boat docked?' he asked.

'Port o' London,' she said. 'Sailing with the next tide.'

London, in spite of its transformation, still seemed brooding and repressive as they made their way through it, but the sun was bright and their mood was good. They passed a few cars, with marionettes at their wheels, and two old people cycling along, the man in plus fours, the woman in a long, divided skirt. They waved to them cheerfully.

'Not outside people,' Newman said, holding on to his seat as the cart gathered speed.

'No, I suppose not. The trouble is, of course, that not so many people of our age seem to get through. They're mostly children or elderly, and the children don't stay long. It's a shame, isn't it?'

'Yes, it is. What about people born here?'

'Children born here are usually taken from their parents after a while. They go outside. Some stay – not many. It's one of the big tragedies – one of the main sacrifices of people who live here.'

'It's strange when you think of it,' Newman said as they left the canyon that had been Oxford Street and entered another which was High Holborn. 'There are traffic jams and jostling crowds here, yet we can't see them and they can't see us. Yet we both exist – we're both solid and real.'

'I've often wondered about it,' she said. 'Are we ghosts? Or do we have an existence in both worlds, just as so many of the outside people do? Perhaps we're corpses lying somewhere in the out-world, eh?'

'I don't like the idea. I can't believe it.'

'Neither can I. There's no need to look for explanations, really.

Look at that!' She pointed as a man in wig and clothes of the mid-eighteenth century was carried past in a sedan chair by two automata wearing twentieth-century clothes. 'Have you noticed how time is so mixed up? This is still the twentieth century in most respects, but some people speak and dress like people from as far back as the sixteenth. And here and there you meet people who seem to be from a short way into the future.'

'It is surprising,' Newman agreed. 'It's as if time has sorted itself out into zones where, perhaps, the true mood or event is shown – not in the sequence, or apparent sequence, of the history we knew, but into... well, zones of *influence*, if you like. You know those historians who divide history up into the Age of this and the Age of that. Maybe all the people in this world are from an age where a particular psychological mood prevailed, dating from around the Renaissance in this case.'

'Psychic time zones.' She smiled. 'Where the nature of the psyche changes very slightly – perhaps even a lot – from zone to zone.'

Newman laughed. 'Something like that. It all sounds a bit queer.' It was odd, he thought, how a conversation like this would not have come at all naturally to him in his other life, yet here it seemed normal.

The pony trotted on through Stepney. The cliffs were blacker and gloomier than ever, with an atmosphere of decay and menace about them. Newman half-expected ghoulish, flying creatures to come flapping and squawking from their eyries, and to see misshapen troglodytes scuttling into cave mouths, hurling poison-tipped flint spears before disappearing. The sound of the pony's hoofs echoed hollowly and Fanny seemed to sense the mood, for she gave the animal its head. It galloped along, and soon the docks were in sight.

The docks were grim and grey, with jagged cliffs stretching along one side and the black river on the other. But the single ship floating at anchor there was in positive contrast to its surroundings. She was a great white clipper ship, her beams bound in bright brass, shining like gold; her sails, as pale as her paint, loose on her four tall masts.

Etched in gold letters on her side was the name, *White Lass*. The dog-cart trundled onto the dockside beside the clipper's main gangplank. An Asiatic sailor, dressed in trim blue jacket and trousers, called to them from the rail.

'Hurry aboard, there – we're sailing within the next five minutes.'

They climbed down and walked up the gangplank, Fanny leading the way, Newman behind carrying her bag.

A man in a merchant captain's uniform from around the turn of the century, a clipboard under one arm, came towards them along the deck. He gave them a cheerful salute. He was middle-aged, weather-tanned, and with an imperial beard. His nose was strong and aquiline, his mouth firm and sensitive.

'Good afternoon, captain.' Fanny smiled. 'Can you take another passenger? This is Mr Sebastian Newman.'

'Good afternoon, Miss Patrick – Mr Newman. Yes, we've plenty of room aboard. You're welcome, sir.'

He spoke with a faint foreign accent; a deep voice with a permanent note of warm irony.

'This is Captain Conrad,' said Fanny, introducing them. Newman shook hands with him.

'The cabin next to yours is empty,' Conrad said. 'I think it will suit Mr Newman, Miss Patrick. You'll excuse me while I get back to work – we're sailing almost at once.' He beckoned a white-coated steward who had just emerged from below deck. 'Will you put Mr Newman in the cabin next to Miss Patrick's, please?'

The steward took Fanny's bag from Newman and led them back the way he had come, down a short companionway into a passage which had six doors leading off it, three on each side.

'This is the passenger section,' Fanny explained. 'The ship is mainly a cargo vessel.'

The steward opened one door and took the bag in. Fanny and Newman followed. The cabin was comfortable, with a wide bunk against one bulkhead, a large porthole, washing facilities, a writing desk and a cane chair bolted to the deck under the porthole and a heavier armchair opposite them.

The steward took Newman out of this cabin and into the one next to it. This was furnished similarly.

'Will that be all, sir?' asked the steward.

'Yes, thanks.'

The steward left.

Fanny sauntered into Newman's cabin. 'Not bad, eh?' she said. 'She's a beautiful ship. You'll realise that most of all when we're on the open sea.'

Newman heard shouts above them, felt the ship list very slightly, then right herself.

'They've cast off,' Fanny said excitedly. 'Come on. Let's go up on deck.'

The sails billowed and the ship was soon moving rapidly down-river, speeding past the cliffs that were warehouses and rotting buildings, towards open countryside and then the sea.

They joined the captain on the poop deck. He was leaning on a rail and staring down the long river. He looked up with a smile. 'Cabins all right?'

'Couldn't be better,' said Newman.

'Good.'

Newman noticed the silence of the ship as it sailed – just the faint creaking of the rigging. The perpetual noise and smell of even the best steamers was noticeably absent and it seemed a shame to Newman that the clippers, which could match many steamships for speed and capacity, had been abandoned. The slender ship slipped through the water of the river so smoothly that it was almost impossible to tell that they were moving, save for the scenery going past on both sides. Newman saw the helmsman in the wheelhouse behind him, guiding the clipper down the winding strip of water. A bell sounded. Sailors ran about tidying the ship, making lines fast, checking the sails and fastening hatches. The ship was bright, clean and trim, yet with an air of sturdiness about her. She was a fine-looking ship, but it was evident that she could stand hard work, too.

They reached the sea as evening came, the cold, watery flats of

MICHAEL MOORCOCK

the Thames mouth racing by in the waning light; the reeds waving, making the land a parody of the sea.

Now at sea, they left the deck to join the captain in his cabin for supper.

As they ate, Newman said: 'This is rather a long way of getting to Paris, isn't it, captain? Normally ships bound for France leave Dover, I thought.'

The captain smiled. 'Outside, they do, Mr Newman. But here there are so few ships, and we suit ourselves. It is a longer voyage, but we use the rivers as much as we can. On this trip, for instance, we shall be going all the way to Paris, up the Seine. It is longer but simpler, since there are difficulties in getting overland transportation for our cargo and passengers sometimes.'

'I can understand now.' Newman smiled. 'It is a nice way to travel.'

'I agree,' Fanny said. 'We'll cross the sea at night and by morning should have reached the mouth of the Seine. Here, it is possible for ships of this size to sail the big rivers.'

In the morning, Newman was awakened by a knock on his door. He called, 'Come in,' and Fanny entered with some clothes in her arms. There was a pair of jeans and a white shirt, a black, roll-neck jumper and some underwear.

'Captain Conrad managed to sort these out for you,' she said. 'Will they do? I think they'll fit.'

'That's good of him,' Newman replied. 'They'll be fine.'

'I'll see you on deck for breakfast in about half an hour,' she said as she left.

Newman got up. There was warm water in the taps of the washbasin and he washed himself all over before drying off and climbing into the clothes Fanny had left. They were a good fit, the waist of the jeans being a little loose, but a broad leather belt answered that problem.

On deck, a small table and two chairs had been set out. Coffee and rolls were on it and Fanny was pouring herself a cup of coffee as he sat down.

The sea was bright blue and the sun exceptionally warm. There was a light wind, sufficient to refresh him and fill the sails of the clipper. Ahead he could see the coast. Captain Conrad called from the poop deck. 'Good morning, you two. Sleep well?'

'Very well,' Newman shouted amiably back. 'And thanks for the clothes, captain.'

'Join me as soon as you've finished breakfast.' Conrad disappeared.

The food was good and the coffee delicious. Completing breakfast, they climbed up to the captain's bridge. Conrad handed Fanny his field glasses and she peered through them towards the coast.

'You can just see the mouth of the river.' Conrad pointed.

Fanny passed the glasses to Newman, who now saw the river mouth clearly, the tide swirling amongst sandbanks.

'It looks difficult to negotiate.' He returned the glasses to Conrad.

'Not when you know it well.' The captain frowned.

'How long have you been sailing this route?' Newman asked.

'A long time, I should think, Mr Newman. It is difficult to judge the passing of time in this world. The days are of the same duration, but few people bother to count them. The seasons are the same; the tides are the same. Nature does not change, and neither do men and women in this world. They make few attempts to change nature and nature makes few attempts to change them. Time means little here.'

'You can't remember when you arrived?'

'About 1912, I should say.'

'And you were the same age then as you are now?'

'I suppose so. I am like a kind of Flying Dutchman, eh?' Conrad laughed. 'Except I am very happy with my situation.'

'You feel no regret – no boredom?'

'I don't think so. I was once a man of action. I played my part in the world, as you did. But not any more. Perhaps I should feel uncomfortable about the kind of life I lead now, but I don't.'

'But you play a part in this world. What is this world?'

'It is the real world as seen by the inner mind, Mr Newman. The real world as seen by the outer mind is the one you left. In my opinion the inner mind is the true mirror of human history. It is the inner mind that creates the ideas that produce the great events, the outer mind translates them into action – deals with the details, you might say. Yet when the outer mind tries to interpret these events that it has helped produce, it always fails. It always finds anomalies, puzzles – while to the inner mind everything is clear. That is the irony of it.'

'The outer mind needs the inner mind, then?'

'They are complementary. We know which governs what, but the important thing is which controls the individual. Most people pay too little attention to the inner mind, allowing their judgements to be swayed by the apparent logic of the outer mind.'

'But aren't we just as guilty, obeying the inner mind too completely?'

'Perhaps. I only know what I prefer to do.'

Newman was in a quandary for the first time since he had come here.

'Has this world no future, then?' he asked. 'No future of its own?'

'Apparently not. A few things change from time to time, depending on where you are, but there is no progress in the terms of the outer mind. It's strange, really, for only the inner mind is unaffected by the passing of time – or affected very little, at least. Yet only the inner mind can predict, in general ways, the future as it is likely to be. It can plot a rough course; it can even judge which winds are likely to change, and when. But it does not care. That is left to the outer mind, for the outer mind produces the actions after the inner mind has supplied the original impulse.'

'Then should there not be a balance?' said Newman.

'Ideally, Mr Newman. But this is not an ideal world. We are lucky, the few of us here, to have the choice.'

The Seine flowed through rich countryside which was picturesque even for the season. It was entirely rural, with no towns sighted until Paris came in view.

Newman had expected something similar to London, but he had been wrong.

Paris was a city of coloured crystal, a dazzling piece of gigantic yet delicate jewellery from which light blazed. Newman was delighted. 'Magnificent!' he said to Fanny, who stood beside him by the rail of the main deck. 'I never imagined anything so beautiful. It's like a heavenly city.' He laughed. 'Will Saint Peter let us in, do you think?'

She smiled back, tucking her arm in his. 'I don't think there'll be much difficulty, Sebastian.'

The *White Lass* sailed into Paris a short while later, her whole deck alive with the light from the city, the water sparkling with a thousand reflected colours. Tall poplars grew along the banks of the river and the buildings were not the bleak cliffs of London but great structures of multicoloured crystal, with tall spires and turrets and domes.

They docked. Fanny and Newman thanked Captain Conrad and disembarked.

'They love glory, the French.' Fanny grinned as they walked through the avenues while the city seemed almost to sing with colour and light. 'This city is like so much of their music – delightful yet, you suspect, insubstantial. Romantic, rather grandiose, beautiful but artificial. Yet, like their philosophy and their art,' she smiled, pretending to shade her eyes, 'it is dazzling.'

'You seem to have a great affection for the French.'

'So I have. They treat serious things lightly and light things seriously. This makes them amusing and, to the Anglo-Saxon, refreshing. Take existentialism. What other race could make a profound philosophy of the obvious?'

Chapter Four

THE CRYSTAL CITY was entrancing. They wandered through it hand in hand as Fanny showed Newman the sights.

Although the faceted structures were not recognisable as any buildings Newman had ever known, they had the grace and inspiration of great architecture. Yet, like London's black stone cliffs, they seemed natural phenomena rather than man-made. They were, at least in one sense, man-made, for, like London, they represented an ideal of a city. Newman wondered why the average Londoner would prefer to inhabit his cave dwellings and gloomy abysses when Paris, alive with colour and light, was there as an example. The broad avenues were tree-lined and there were a few more people about than there had been in London, though the marionette population from the 'outside' was still in evidence.

Having lunched inside one of the crystal buildings – all gilt, plush and big mirrors, with waiters in the white aprons and black suits of the '90s – Newman and Fanny wandered out until they came to a wide square full of topiary animals and birds, cathedrals and famous figures from French history, all exquisitely cut from the shrubs. In miniature lakes, fountains of ormolu and precious metals, marble and delicately painted enamel, played water coloured like rainbows. Some distance away, from a small pavilion, its little roof of red, white and blue stripes, its supports of gilded iron, twisted like barley sugar sticks, bunting looped between them, came music.

A string quartet with a French horn player, their music on stands in front of them, were playing Mozart's *E-Flat Quintet* for French horn and strings, its wit and humanity at once blending and contrasting with the surroundings.

The performers were dressed in the clothes of Mozart's time:

fine silk coats, embroidered waistcoats, lace-trimmed shirts and elaborate wigs. They might have been performing for the last of the Bourbons at Versailles.

A few people, one or two dressed like the performers but most of them in different styles of the twentieth century, stood around the pavilion listening to the music. Newman and Fanny joined them.

When the piece was finished the performers stood up and bowed as the listeners applauded. They had played magnificently. They stepped down from the pavilion and began to chat with the others. Newman had expected to hear them talking in the flowery speech of eighteenth-century France. Instead, he was astonished at their accents, which were evidently American.

Newman approached the horn player. 'Are you from the States?' he asked in English.

'Sure, man.' The horn player nodded. 'But we'd better talk French here, if it's okay with you. These guys don't like anything else.'

'You played very well,' Newman said in French. 'That was the best Mozart chamber music I ever heard.'

'Good of you to say so. They seem to like our way of playing too. Excuse me.' The horn player pointed across the park to where a Renault had drawn up. The driver was waving to them. 'We've got another engagement. Hope to see you again.'

The musicians, their instruments and music under their arms, walked through the park to the car, climbed in and the car drove away.

At length, almost everyone else had gone, apart from three men, who stopped to chat with Fanny. One of them was dressed in the elaborate clothes of the eighteenth century; another wore the heavy, respectably high-crowned hat, frock-coat and dark trousers of the Second Empire, while the third had on black, tight-fitting trousers, a black pullover and a black beret on his thick hair. A cigarette hung from his lower lip. He looked a caricature of an *apache*.

'I think I prefer Debussy,' the man in the bright silk coat was saying. 'There is something just a trifle *heavy*, even in Mozart.'

'I can't say I agree,' Fanny replied with a smile. 'This is my friend, Sebastian Newman. He's an American, too.'

'Delighted,' said the three men as they shook hands with Newman.

'What did you think of your cousins' performance?' asked the man in the top hat.

'Brilliant,' said Newman. 'No doubt about it.'

'Mmm, perhaps. Myself, I felt it was rather insufficiently restrained.'

'You would think that, Berger,' said the man in the beret, slapping him on the back. 'Restraint in all things for you, eh?'

'Just so, Monsieur Alfred.'

'I wonder if Monsieur Sol agrees,' Berger said, turning to the man in the eighteenth-century finery. 'What do you think, Sol? Not restrained enough for you – the performance?'

'It was too restrained. A little more flair was called for, I felt,' Sol replied with a faint smile.

They could have been brothers. Their complexions were dark, their lower lips protuberant, their noses large, their eyelids heavy and expressions deliberately controlled. With an exchange of clothes they might have been the same man.

'Ah, well.' Alfred smiled. 'Enough of this. Let's have some wine at my place. Will you join us, mademoiselle, monsieur?'

'Certainly,' said Fanny, 'if you'll have us.'

'Come, then.'

They all followed Alfred from the park and up an avenue, in through a door of rosé glass into a passageway lined with gilt-framed mirrors that were a little fly-specked and their gilt rather faded.

A quaint lift cage of rococo ironwork took them up several storeys and then they were in Alfred's room. It was lit by a large skylight that almost covered one wall and the roof. A mattress lay against the far wall, its blankets untidy. On it lay a girl staring blankly upwards. A table was covered with pages of manuscript and books. Several bottles of wine stood on it.

'Oh, Alfred!' Berger said, pointing at the girl. 'How could you do that?'

Newman thought Berger was shocked at finding a woman in Alfred's room, but then he noticed that the girl had the dazed, set expression of an 'outsider'.

'Why not?' Alfred said lightly. 'After all, we can manipulate them sometimes if we wish to. Yesterday I wished to. And what will she know about it?'

'It is not done to disturb these people,' M. Sol said. 'You know that, Alfred. Who do you think you are to justify this? How would you justify it? With the logic of a de Sade?'

Alfred shrugged. 'I'll get rid of her, then. Take care of the wine, will you, Sol?' He stooped, lifted the girl in his arms and carried her out.

Sol gave them all wine and, when Alfred returned, handed him a glass.

The atmosphere was strained for a while, but the wine helped to restore everyone to better spirits.

'Is this your first visit to Paris, Monsieur Newman?' Berger asked. He had taken off his top hat and placed it on a chair beside him.

'The first under these conditions,' Newman replied. 'I'm impressed. In London I was convinced that the images that reached the... the "inner mind" were wholly depressing. I was wrong. Paris is a miracle.'

'And what do you think of France in general?'

'I have only been here a few hours.'

'But the French,' M. Sol said, waving a hand at the window as if the French were waiting outside to hear Newman's judgement. 'The French. You must have an opinion of us. Everyone has.'

'Just as we have an opinion of everyone,' said Alfred with a smile.

Rising to the occasion, Newman said: 'I find the French charming, the architecture breathtaking and the public transport bewildering. The museums are magnificent, the exhibits, on the whole, mediocre. The French are absolutely courteous – and absolutely ill-mannered.'

'Never "absolute"!' whispered M. Sol in mock horror. 'Never that!'

'What do you mean?'

Fanny laughed. 'Yes, what do you mean, Monsieur Sol?'

'The Frenchman knows of the absolute, mademoiselle, but he despises it,' Alfred interjected.

'Exactly,' said Sol. 'It is the curse of the French that they will go to extremes. We declare a republic and then worship an emperor. We have been doing it for nearly two hundred years. Republic, emperor – republic, emperor. Sometimes we call them by different names. Yet the Frenchman claims to avoid extremes and never to approach the absolute. But we are a nation of enthusiasts. When an idea fires us we put all we have into it. When it bores us we abandon it. We are not sufficiently obsessive to stick at one thing for long. Our ambitions are short-lived. We have become afraid of excess, m'sieu. Monsieur Berger, as you noticed this afternoon, distrusts any hint of it. Yet give him a mission for a day or so and he would show you what excess really meant!' Sol laughed.

'Nonsense,' said Berger, looking embarrassed.

Alfred laughed, too. Drunkenly. He swayed around the room, refilling everyone's glass. He kept blinking.

'Do not drink so much,' Berger said to him. 'You will go back.'

'My will is too strong.' Alfred bellowed as he fell onto his mattress.

'We shall see,' Berger murmured.

Newman began to feel uncomfortable. He looked at Fanny, trying to see if she were ready to leave, but she made no sign. She seemed to be enjoying herself.

Alfred shook his head dazedly. 'I am an intellectual,' he said. 'I am the lifeblood of France.'

'Nonsense,' Berger said. 'It is the intellectuals who have ruined France. It is the bourgeoisie who have tried to sustain her.'

'It is the aristocrats who have managed to,' Sol put in. 'Every time France flounders she finds a new élite. The Bourbons, Napoleon, de Gaulle and so on... What else do you expect of a paternalistic nation? It must be so.'

Alfred rose, staggered to his desk, opened a drawer and took out a revolver. 'And so must this be so!' He shouted and waved the gun.

'Not these days, surely,' Sol murmured sardonically.

Fanny got up. 'Monsieur Alfred, is the gun loaded?'

'It is, ma'amoiselle,' he said with a drunken bow. He pointed it at his head. She reached out hastily to take it, but he staggered back, his arm falling. Again he began to blink rapidly. His other hand went to his temple and squeezed it. 'Ah! You are right, Berger. I must stop drinking.'

'Why do you do it – this drinking to excess?' Berger seemed perturbed and worried for his friend. 'And the girl. Why are you so irresponsible about your own fate and everyone else's?'

'Curiosity,' Sol remarked. 'Isn't that so, Alfred? Curiosity?'

'Yes, yes.' Alfred wandered back to the mattress.

'He is not merely content to be in this ideal world,' Sol said, turning to Newman and Fanny. 'He must investigate it always – test it. He ruins what could be a perfectly good and long life. Can you believe it?'

Newman felt some sympathy with Alfred. He was the first man he had met here who seemed to be dissatisfied with the 'inner world'.

'There could be something in what he is trying to do,' Newman suggested. 'Living here is like a perpetual holiday. There's nothing to do when you get here. It's nice for a while, but...'

'But then you want to start spoiling it,' Berger said heatedly. 'Others have tried without success. Most of them have died or gone back. Think of that! Dying and leaving heaven!'

'Be content,' Sol said. 'Relax and be content. It is this contentedness which should mark us from the others "outside".'

'It makes us superior?' Newman asked.

'Of course it does. Have you something against superiority?'

'I don't believe it.'

'Do not try to pursue your American ideal of equality here, my friend,' Sol mocked.

'Surely,' Newman said, 'the only difference between us and them is that we recognise and control the inner mind? But those out there still possess inner minds – and they still represent a force to be reckoned with, for they can take action. What sort of action can be taken here that will affect the destiny of mankind?'

'Mankind has no destiny but to exist.' Alfred had risen from the mattress again, the revolver still in his hand. 'All that the inner mind is, is a survival mechanism that controls his actions, makes them fit the pattern of the universe, though this is not always observable in the outer world. The inner mind makes him behave in accordance with the laws of nature, though his outer mind would attempt to thwart those laws and thus destroy him. The inner mind is in tune with the rhythm of the spheres, gentlemen. As individuals we are nothing and as a race we simply exist. That is our only purpose. Why should we seek another? The inner mind does not seek another. We do not seek another here.'

'And if one cannot believe it?' Newman enquired.

'Then you have no business being here!' Sol stood up. 'He is right. You know he is right.'

'He is right, Sebastian,' said Fanny. 'I'm sure of it.'

'So am I,' Newman said. 'And I suspect anything I'm so sure of. I think of Mr Schweitzer's armour.'

'You are in a worse position than Alfred,' Berger said with a sidelong glance at Sol. He winked.

There was a shot. Alfred was falling, the gun clattering to the floor, his eyes staring as he pitched forward.

'The fool,' Sol said casually. 'He has denied his purpose. He has thwarted his destiny. He has ceased to exist!'

Fanny began to sob and Newman tried to comfort her.

M. Sol sighed. 'What do we do now, Berger? This is upsetting. I feel a trifle uncomfortable. What does one do in such a time of crisis?'

Berger began to take off his jacket. 'Change clothes, Monsieur Sol. It is all there is to do.'

Beside the corpse of Alfred, the two men began to strip off their clothes and trade them. Soon Sol was dressed in Berger's frock-coat, trousers and top hat, and Berger wore Sol's silks and lace. Newman was horrified by the charade and watched speechlessly as Fanny sobbed on and the pair left the room.

'Let's get away from here, Sebastian,' Fanny said a little later. 'Poor Monsieur Alfred. It was so unexpected.'

Newman helped her out to the lift. As they descended, he said, 'Do you want to leave Paris altogether, then?'

'Don't you?'

'I wouldn't mind.'

'I have a car near here. We can leave right away.'

'Where shall we go?'

'I don't care. Just drive.'

The car was a big, old Citroën limousine. Newman found it easy to handle. He drove through the streets of the Crystal City, Fanny staring blankly ahead.

Soon they were in the countryside, heading north.

Chapter Five

NEWMAN DROVE FOR more than a day along a wide, straight road that went on and on between flat fields. He did not know where it led, and he did not care. He was trying to think and finding thinking difficult.

It was on the second day of living off raw vegetables found in the fields and sleeping in the car that they saw a van ahead of them, driving in the same direction.

By this time Fanny had cheered up a little. When she saw the van she brightened even more.

'Sebastian! It's Mr Schweitzer's van. I wonder where he's going.'

Relieved at the prospect of seeing a familiar face, Newman accelerated, passing the van with a wave as he saw Mr Schweitzer in the cabin.

Looking a trifle puzzled Schweitzer smiled and pulled in to the side of the road.

Newman backed the Citroën up to the van and helped Fanny out. They reached the van as Mr Schweitzer climbed down.

'What are you two doing here?' he asked. 'I thought you'd gone to Paris.'

'We decided to leave,' Newman told him. He described what had happened.

Schweitzer shook his head and pursed his lips, sighing.

'Yes, yes. That sometimes does happen. They shun my wares there, you know, but they need them, really...'

'They need something,' said Fanny earnestly.

'Where does this road lead?' Newman asked. 'We've no idea.'

'It leads to Berlin, Mr Newman. I don't think you want to go there.'

'Why not?'

'It's an unpleasant place at the best of times. A strange place. My biggest single customer, you know. Why don't you turn round – go back to Paris or take a side road to Amsterdam or Hamburg and see if you can find a ship to get you to London?'

'I'm curious now.' Newman smiled. 'I think I'd like the experience of Berlin, Mr Schweitzer.'

'I suppose it can do you little harm, Mr Newman. Very well. If you'd like to keep pace with my old van, we'll travel together.'

They followed the road for the rest of the day and at night camped beside it. Mr Schweitzer was well equipped with a primus stove and provisions. They ate well for the first time since they had left Paris.

They slept in the tent Mr Schweitzer lent them and at dawn were on the road again.

A few hours later they saw Berlin.

A vast wall surrounded the city and it was really this they sighted. Berlin itself was completely hidden by the wall.

Its black, basalt sides were high and smooth and small gateways led through from the roads.

As they neared it, Newman could make out figures high above on the top of the wall. The figures were encased in full medieval armour with sub-machine guns cradled in their arms.

'Here the whole city is populated by those who see with the inner eye,' Schweitzer explained. 'But what their inner eye sees – its terrible ideal... Oh dear! This Berlin – it is the City of Fear. Such a strange people – so perceptive yet so terrified. They warp their perceptions even as they find them. A dreadful mix-up, I'm afraid.'

The guards seemed to recognise Schweitzer's van, for the doors of the gateway swung open and they passed through into the city.

Berlin was smaller than London in every respect, but what Newman had not noticed was that the whole city had a roof, stretching from wall to wall. The roof was of heavy, smoked glass, or something similar, and it let in little light.

Many of the buildings looked like huge, round boulders with tiny entrances, just about big enough for a man to crawl through.

The streets, like the tunnels of some stone maze, were full. Lumbering horses bore the great, clumsy weight of armoured men, while others, on the pavements, wore masks or heavy hoods to hide their faces.

Unable to negotiate the narrow streets, the van was forced to stop in a small square.

They got out. A man in a 1914–18 flying suit, with fur jacket, boots and gauntlets, but wearing a Gothic helmet on his head, the visor covering his face, walked towards Schweitzer, hand held out.

When he spoke in German, a language which Newman understood only imperfectly, his voice was an echo in the helmet. After shaking hands with the man, Schweitzer introduced Newman and Fanny as English.

'Herr von Richthofen, eh?' Newman said. 'Any relation to the Baron?'

Von Richthofen shrugged. 'We don't use those titles in our Germany, Herr Newman. Would you like to come back to my house for some refreshment?'

The house was one of a number of boulders on the far side of the square. Stooping through the small doorway, they entered. Inside it was, if anything, gloomier than outside. A few torches illuminated a fairly large hall and a fire glimmered in a grate. A stone staircase led upwards and von Richthofen climbed it until they entered a smaller, slightly more hospitable room, heated by some sort of steam apparatus. Newman sat down on a wet chair, coughing as the hot, damp air entered his lungs. The place was like a Turkish bath and there was a faint smell of salt.

'Some food will be brought to us,' von Richthofen said. 'Well, Herr Schweitzer, what have you got this time? Heavier stuff than last, I hope. The fashions change so rapidly and now one must wear an even thicker plate than ever if one is to fit in.' He reached up and lifted off his ornate steel helmet. The face revealed was of a man of about thirty-five – handsome, self-indulgent, faintly cynical.

'That's better,' he said. 'Only in here do I feel comfortable with it off.'

Newman looked around. There were no windows in the room. It seemed very strange to him and he could not imagine why people should choose to live in such places.

The food arrived. Dull, German food – sausages, sauerkraut, bread, but good coffee.

When they had eaten, von Richthofen leaned back in his wooden armchair.

'Have you just come from England, Herr Newman?'

'I was in Paris first.'

'A wonderful city. Very romantic. You liked it?'

'In general. It seems strange that you should like it, Herr von Richthofen, when your own taste in architecture is so different.'

'Aha! So very different, eh? But *secure*, do you see, Herr Newman? Strong, invincible, able to withstand anything.'

Newman was puzzled. 'But why should it be? Are you expecting trouble? Who'd attack you?'

'Better safe than sorry, eh?'

Newman, the damp having penetrated his clothing, shifted uncomfortably on his chair. 'I suppose so.'

Von Richthofen seemed to notice his discomfort. He laughed. 'You get used to that. Oh, we know all about freedom and beautiful surroundings making beautiful minds. All that sort of thing. But we have made a conscious sacrifice. A study of history will show you that a race which holds firmly together, building heavy walls, survives longer than one which lives in idyllic surroundings. Look at Greece. Compare it with Rome. You see what I mean?'

Newman did not. He thought von Richthofen was misguided. He could see no logic in what the man was saying.

'I should have thought that here, in the inner world, you would not need such walls or such ideas. Your walls are built because you fear something – something which you do not know exists. Living in this world, you surely realise this?'

'We realise that you are probably right. But there is a possibility that you are wrong. It is that possibility we prepare for, Herr Newman. The Berliner is capable of mental detachment more than anyone.

'But you use this detachment to escape, it seems to me,' Newman said. 'Some people read adventure stories. You invent complicated systems of metaphysics. And you achieve the same end. You leave reality.'

'Is not our reality the same as yours – on the inner or the outer plane?'

'It borders on it. But is your fortified city "realistic" in this world? Is your fashion for wearing heavier armour "realistic"? Surely these are totally subjective things. I find it very difficult to understand how these things, so typical of the outer world, can exist in the inner world. I remember reading of some Crusaders once who went across the desert to fight a battle. They refused to dispense with their armour, in spite of crippling heat and utter weariness. They rode for days, until all sense of reality was driven from them. Finally, harried all the way by Saracens, they reached their battleground and were trapped and massacred. If only they had taken their armour off to cross the desert they would have done so at greater speed and arrived fresh. Because of their *need* for their armour – which *reason* told them they did not need – they perished. Their armour killed them, in fact.'

Von Richthofen pursed his lips ironically. 'A nice little moral tale, Herr Newman. But we are different. We see things in a far bigger way. We do not just take the world view – we take the universal view.'

'How does that bear on what we're discussing?'

'It has every bearing. Every bearing.'

Von Richthofen got up. 'I would like some time to show you what Athens has become.'

'I've never been to Athens,' Fanny put in. 'What has it become?'

Von Richthofen put his hand to his chin. 'You want to know? Very well, I will fly you there myself. Tomorrow. When we have seen what Mr Schweitzer has to offer us. How would you like that?'

Newman was willing to take any opportunity to leave Berlin as speedily as possible. 'Suits me,' he said. 'I'd like to go to Greece. It's one of my favourite countries.'

'Is it, Herr Newman? Is it? Good.'

Chapter Six

V ON RICHTHOFEN'S PLANE was very modern. It lay on an air-field outside the walls of Berlin. It resembled an American Phantom fighter-bomber in almost every detail. On its wings and fuselage, however, were painted large swastikas.

'They are just for old times' sake,' von Richthofen said with a laugh as he led them up to the plane. They were all dressed in pressure suits. They had just said goodbye to Mr Schweitzer. 'A joke, you know,' Richthofen added. 'I feel no embarrassment these days. Do you?'

Newman said nothing. He helped Fanny into the big cockpit, wider than a Phantom's. It could take three – two in the front and one just behind. Expertly, he settled himself into his own seat. He had flown similar aircraft before he began training for space.

Von Richthofen started the engine and at length the plane began to move off down the long runway. They were quickly air-borne and von Richthofen, for Fanny's sake, kept them down to just over the speed of sound.

They flashed through the peaceful sky at four thousand feet, heading south-east for Greece.

They landed on a long airstrip just outside Athens. There were none of the usual airport buildings, just the tarmac with grassy slopes on either side.

Newman was surprised to see that Athens was not the modern city but the ancient one transformed. Graceful villas, widely spaced, surrounded tree-lined squares. Here and there were larger buildings, like the Parthenon and the Acropolis. Most of the people wore togas or linen jerkins tied loosely at the waist. The women wore the flowing robes that Newman had previously only seen represented on statues, paintings or bas-reliefs. But there were several who wore the clothes of other periods, including Newman's own.

The sun was warm and the mood of the city leisurely. A few people waved cheerfully to them, but most were gathered in little groups, lazing in the sun, drinking wine and eating fruit and talking all the time. The hum of conversation filled the city.

'It hasn't been changed,' Newman said to von Richthofen. 'Why is that?'

'There has been no need, my friend. This Athens is the Athens of the Golden Age, altered in only minor details. Here the idea and the actuality are one. Here, the inner mind and the outer mind merged to produce an ideal. It happens rarely. The cities you have seen so far – London, Paris, Berlin – are transformed because the idea the builders had of them was never fulfilled in actuality. Only an approximation was produced. Not so with the Athenians. It took later ages to spoil the ideal city – later events. But events have not altogether changed the Greeks as they changed us Northerners. Time has not "moved on" so much.' Von Richthofen laughed unpleasantly. 'But they are not strong, Herr Newman – Fräulein Patrick.'

'They don't need to be *strong*,' Fanny said in bewilderment, putting her arm through Newman's. 'What have they to fear here?'

'Only the inconsistent – only some arbitrary action disobeying the fundamental laws of existence. We of the inner world all recognise these laws, I believe.'

'And they are?' Fanny said.

'Simple. That nature follows a pattern – a simple cycle of birth, death and rebirth. Everything obeys this law, from the tiniest particles to the suns and galaxies of the infinite universe. But, basically, everything remains the same – everything is consistent, fixed for ever according to the pattern.'

'It simply exists, is that it?' Newman said, remembering the words of the late M. Alfred. 'It had no purpose but to exist.'

'Exactly. So your Parisians exist in their crystal city, in their still somewhat artificial way. Here, in Athens people exist in a simpler, more natural way. This is right, you say; this is proper. This obeys the law of the universe.'

'Fair enough,' said Fanny. 'But what are you driving at?'

'I am trying to tell you what we Berliners protect ourselves against in this perfect inner world, Fräulein Patrick. All you have seen here so far – apart from our Berlin – have accepted that to live without fear, without protection and suspicion, is *moral* – that is, it accords with the true pattern of existence.'

'Okay,' said Newman. 'What about it?'

'Have you never considered that detachment of the kind we have might recognise that law, might understand the essential morality of our Greek friends here – but decide coolly, out of pure whim, *to disobey the law and live immorally*? A man or a group of men might decide to "throw a spanner in the works", *ja*? Out of boredom, perhaps – out of despair or out of curiosity? We are ultimately bound by the law, Herr Newman, but that does not stop us from *consciously* disobeying it. To recognise the invulnerable and eternal law is not automatically to obey it. Do you see? We are conscious, reasoning beings – we can *decide* to disobey.'

'But what point would there be in doing that?' Fanny asked, bemused. 'In the outer world the law is broken all the time – insensately, out of fear and greed and bewilderment. That's understandable. But here, who would break the law?'

'You ask what point is there in doing such a thing.' Von Richthofen smiled. 'But there again what point is there in existence? None. To make one's mark, however small, one can only behave illogically in an ultimately logical universe. Who are the great myth figures of our history? Disrupters all! Even where they preached the law they succeeded in producing more chaos than had existed before they came. Here, in this inner world, we are all equal. Supposing a man achieved this plan and refused to accept what he found. Suppose he deliberately offended against the law of the universe. What then?'

'This is the possibility you fear in Berlin?' Newman said quietly. 'This?'

'Why should we not fear it in Berlin? Haven't we sufficient cause to do so? Is not our history full of the servants of chaos?'

'And of order, too. Your composers, your poets, your novelists –'

'Just so. We have the ability, as I told you, to *see* – but there are those amongst us who are not content with seeing – they wish to take action in a world that denies action, other than those necessary for existence alone, and demands the status quo.'

'You sound like one yourself.' Newman smiled half-heartedly.

Von Richthofen shrugged. 'I am not the stuff of the Antichrist,' he said. 'I only try to illustrate what Berlin still fears; detachment, vision, knowledge do not bring an automatic absence of danger.'

'You mean that what people say in the outer world – that if everyone could achieve detachment, control over emotion, everything would be better? You mean that's not necessarily true?' said Fanny.

'Why should it be?'

'Why, indeed…' Newman agreed. 'But you serve no good to yourselves or others by wrapping yourselves in stone and metal, and hiding.'

Richthofen smiled. 'It is our duty. We obey the universal, fundamental law.'

'How?' Newman asked.

'We exist – and we see to it that we continue to exist. But enough of this. I came here not only to tell you what I meant, but to illustrate my point.' He took something from the pocket of his flying suit. Then he threw back his arm and flung the object towards the Parthenon. 'Witness,' he said. 'The arbitrary action.'

He must have thrown a grenade.

The Parthenon blew up, bodies were scattered, many torn to pieces. Greeks came hurrying onto the scene, absolutely shocked, almost incapable of action. Slowly, a few began to go to the aid of the wounded.

Newman and Fanny were horrified. 'Murder…' whispered Newman.

'Murder, yes. Call it what you will. Suppose such a man as myself came to Berlin. He would do little harm.'

Von Richthofen turned around with a crooked smile on his face and began to walk casually away from the destruction. Nobody tried to stop him.

'I'm returning to Berlin now,' he said. 'Do you want to come? You'll be welcome.'

'I'll take my chances,' Newman said grimly, his mind reeling. 'What about you, Fanny?'

'Me, too,' she said.

Around them, Athens was fading and soon all they could see was the ruin of the Parthenon. The airfield had gone; so had von Richthofen and his jet.

'We're back,' Fanny said faintly. 'Aren't we, Sebastian?'

'I think so.'

'What do we do now?'

'We've got to do something,' he said. 'I suppose.' They walked away from the ruin of the Parthenon towards that other Athens.

The Cairene Purse

For Robert Nye

Chapter One
Her First Fond Hope of Eden Blighted

O N THE EDGE of the Nile's fertile shadow, pyramids merged with the desert and from the air seemed almost two-dimensional in the steady light of late morning. Spreading now beyond the town of Giza, Cairo's forty million people threatened to engulf, with their old automobiles, discarded electronics and every dusty non-degradable of the modern world, the grandiose tombs of their ancestors.

Though Cairo, like Calcutta, was a monument to the enduring survival of our race, I was glad to leave. I had spent only as much time as I needed, seeking information about my archaeologist sis-ter and discovering that everyone in the academic community thought she had returned to England at least a year ago. The noise had begun to seem as tangible as the haze of sand which hung over the crowded motorways, now a mass of moving flesh, of camels, donkeys, horses, mules and humans hauling every variety of vehicle and cargo, with the occasional official electric car or, even rarer, petrol-driven truck.

I suppose it had been a tribute to my imagined status that I had been given a place on a plane, rather than having to take the river or the weekly train to Aswan. Through the porthole of the little VW8 everything but the Nile and its verdant borders were the colours of sand, each shade and texture of which still held mean-ing for the nomad Arab, the Bedouin who had conquered the First

Kingdom and would conquer several others down the millennia. In the past only the Ptolomies, turning their backs on the Nile and the Sahara, ever truly lost the sources of Egypt's power.

My main reason for accepting the assignment was personal rather than professional. My sister had not written for some months and her letters before that had been disconnected, hinting at some sort of emotional disturbance, perhaps in connection with the dig on which I knew she had been working. An employee of UNEC, I had limited authority in Egypt and did not expect to discover any great mysteries at Lake Nasser, which continued to be the cause of unusual weather. The dam's builders somewhat typically had refused to anticipate this. They had also been warned by our people in the 1950s that the New High Dam would eventually so poison the river with bilharzia that anyone using its water would die. The rain, some of it acid, had had predictable effects, flooding quarries and washing away towns. The local Nubians had long since been evicted from their valleys to make way for the lake. Their new settlements, traditionally built, had not withstood the altered environment, so the government had thrown up concrete shells for them. The road to Aswan from the airport was lined with bleak, half-built structures of rusted metal girders and cinder blocks. Today's Egyptians paid a high price for regulated water.

From the airport my horse-drawn taxi crossed the old English dam with its sluices and gigantic gauges, a Victorian engineer's dream of mechanical efficiency, and began the last lap of the journey into town. Aswan, wretched as much of it is, has a magic few Nile settlements now possess, rising from the East Bank to dominate the coppery blue waters and glinting granite islands of the wide river where white-sailed feluccas cruise gracefully back and forth, ferrying tourists and townspeople between the two sides. The heights, massive grey boulders, are commanded by a beautiful park full of old eucalyptus, poplars and monkey-puzzle trees. Above this, the stately Edwardian glory of Cook's Cataract Hotel is a marvellous example of balconied and shuttered rococo British orientalism at its finest.

The further upriver one goes the poorer Aswan becomes, though even here the clapboard and corrugated iron, the asbestos sheeting and crumbling mud walls are dominated by a splendid hilltop mosque in the grand Turkish style. I had asked to be billeted at a modest hotel in the middle of town, near the souk. From the outside, the Hotel Osiris, with its pale pink and green pseudo-neon, reminded me of those backstreet Marseilles hotels where once you could take your partner for a few francs an hour. It had the same romantic attraction, the same impossible promises. I found that, once within its tiny fly-thick lobby – actually the communal hallway leading directly to the courtyard – I was as lost to its appeal as any pop to his lid. I had discovered a temporary spiritual home.

The Osiris, though scarcely more than a bed-and-breakfast place by London standards, boasted four or five porters, all of them eager to take my bag to the rooms assigned me by a Hindu lady at the desk. I let one carry my canvas grip up two flights of dirty stairs to a little tiled, run-down apartment looking into the building's central well where two exhausted dogs, still coupled, panted on their sides in the heat. Giving him a five-pound note, I asked my porter on the off-chance if he had heard of an Englishwoman called Noone or Pappenheim living in Aswan. My sister had used the poste restante and, when I had last been here, there were few Europeans permanently living in town. He regretted that he could not help. He would ask his brother, who had been in Aswan several months. Evidently, now that I had as it were paid for the information in advance he felt obliged to me. The *bakshish* custom is usually neither one of bribery nor begging in any European sense, but has a fair amount to do with smooth social intercourse. There is always, with legitimate *bakshish*, an exchange. Some measure of mutual respect is also usual. Most Arabs place considerable emphasis on good manners and are not always tolerant of European coarseness.

I had last been in Egypt long before the great economic convulsion following that chain reaction of destruction or near-exhaustion of so many resources. Then Aswan had been the final port of call for the millions of tourists who cruised the Nile from dawn to dusk, the sound of their dance music, the smell of their barbecues, drifting over fields and mud villages which had remained unchanged for five thousand years.

In the '80s and '90s of the last century Aswan had possessed, among others, a Hilton, a Sheraton, a Ritz-Carlton and a Holiday Inn, but now the luckiest local families had requisitioned the hotels and only the State-owned Cataract remained, a place of pilgrimage for every wealthy enthusiast of 1930s detective stories or autobiographies of the twentieth-century famous. Here, during wartime, secret meetings had been held and mysterious bargains struck between unlikely participants. Today on the water below the terrace some tourists still sailed, the Israelis and the Saudis on their own elegant *schoomers*, while other boats carried mixtures of Americans, Italians and Germans, French, English, Swedes, Spaniards, Japanese and Hungarians, their women dressed and painted like pagan temptresses of the local soap operas, displaying their bodies naked on the sundecks of vast slow-moving windliners the size of an earlier era's ocean-going ships, serving to remind every decent Moslem exactly what the road to hell looked like. No eighteenth-century English satirist could have provided a better image.

As an officer of the UN's Conservation and Preservation Department I knew all too well how little of Egypt's monuments were still visible, how few existed in any recognisable state. Human erosion, the dam raising the water table, the volume of garbage casually dumped in the river, the activities of archaeologists and others, of tourists encouraged in their millions to visit the great sites and bring their hard currency, the two-year Arabian war, all had created a situation where those monuments still existing were banned to everyone but the desperate restorers. Meanwhile replicas had been made by the Disney Corporation and located in distant desert settlements surrounded by vacation towns, artificial trees and vast swimming pools, built by French and German experts and named 'Rameses City', 'Land of the Gods' or 'Tutankhamen World'. I was sure that this was why my sister had been secretive about her team's discoveries, why it was important to try to avoid the circumstances which now made Abu Simbel little more than a memory of two great engineering miracles.

When I had washed and changed I left the Osiris and strolled through busy alleys in the direction of the corniche, the restored Victorian riverfront promenade which reminded me more than anywhere of the old ocean boulevard at Yalta. Without her earlier weight of tourists, Aswan had developed a lazy, decayed glamour. The foodstalls, the fake antiquities, the flimsy headdresses and gelabeas sold as traditional costume, the souvenir shops and post-card stands, the 'cafetrias' offering 'Creme Teas' and 'Mix Grile', were still patronised by a few plump Poles and tomato-coloured English who had been replaced in the main by smaller numbers of blond East Africans, Swedes and Nigerians affecting the styles and mannerisms of thirty or forty years earlier and drawn here, I had heard, by a Holy Man on the outskirts of Aswan who taught a peculiar mixture of orthodox Sunni Islam and his own brand of mysticism which accepted the creeds of Jews and Christians as well as the existence of other planetary populations, and spoke of a 'pure' form of Islam practised in other parts of the galaxy.

Aswan's latter-day hippies, wearing the fashions of my own youthful parents, gave me a queer feeling at first, for although Egypt offers several experiences akin to time travel, these images of recent history, perhaps of a happier period altogether, were somehow more incongruous than a broken-down VW, for instance, being dragged behind a disgusted camel. There was a greater preponderance of charm-sellers and fortune-tellers than I remembered, together with blank-eyed European men and women, some of them with babies or young children, who begged me for drug-money on the street. With the rise of Islamic-Humanism, the so-called Arab Enlightenment, coupled to the increasing power of North Africa and the Middle East in world politics, the drug laws, introduced originally to placate foreign tour operators and their governments, had been relaxed or for-mally abolished. Aswan, I had heard, was now some kind of

Mecca for privileged youngsters and visionary artists, much as Haight-Ashbury or Ladbroke Grove had been in the 1960s. Romanticism of that heady, exaggerated, rather mystical variety was once again loose in the world and the comforts it offered seemed to me almost like devilish temptations. But I was of that puritanical, judgemental generation which had rejected the abstractions of its parents in favour of more realistic, as we saw it, attitudes. A good many of us had virtually rejected the entire Western Enlightenment itself and retreated into a kind of liberal medievalism not incompatible with large parts of the Arab world. In my own circles I was considered something of a radical.

I had to admit however that I found these new Aswanians attractive. In many ways I envied them. They had never known a time when Arabia had not been a major power. They came here as equals with everyone and were accepted cheerfully by the Nubians who treated them with the respect due to richer pilgrims and potential converts to the divine revelation of Islam.

Again in common with my generation, I was of a secular disposition and saw only damaging, enslaving darkness in any religion. We had even rejected the received wisdoms of Freud, Jung, Marx and their followers and embraced instead a political creed which had as its basis the eminent likelihood of ecological disaster and the slight possibility of an economic miracle. They called us the Anaemic Generation now; a decade or more that was out of step with the progress of history as it was presently interpreted. It suited me to know that I was an anachronism; it afforded me a special kind of security. Very few people took me seriously.

An Egyptian army officer marched past me as I crossed to the river-side of the corniche to look down at the half-completed stairways, the crumbling, poorly mixed concrete and the piles of rat-infested rubble which the Korean engineers, who had put in the lowest tender for the work, had still neither repaired nor cleared. The officer glanced at me as if he recognised me but then went past, looking, with his neatly trimmed moustache and rigid shoulders, the perfect image of a World War Two English Guards captain. Even his uniform was in the English style. I suppose Romans coming to fifth-century Britain after some lapse of time would have been equally impressed to see a Celt striding through the streets of Londinium, impeccable in a slightly antiquated centurion's kit. The whole casual story of the human race seemed to be represented in the town as I paused to look at the hulks of converted pleasure boats, home to swarms of Nubian families impoverished by the altered climate and the shift of tourism towards the Total Egypt Experience found in the comfort of Fort Sadat and New Memphis. Despite the piles of filthy garbage along the shore, Aswan had acquired the pleasant, nostalgic qualities of unfashionable British resorts like Morecambe or Yarmouth, a local population careless of most strangers save sometimes for the money they brought.

About halfway along the corniche I stopped at a little café and sat down on a cane chair, ordering mint tea from a proprietor whose ancient tarboosh might have escaped from the costume department of a touring production of *Death on the Nile*. He addressed me as '*effendi*' and his chosen brand of English seemed developed from old British war movies. Like me, I thought, he was out of step with the times. When he brought the tea I told him to keep the change from a pound and again on the off-chance asked after my sister. I was surprised by the enthusiasm of his response. He knew the name Pappenheim and was approving when I told him of our relationship. 'She is very good,' he said. 'A tip-top gentlewoman. But now, I think, she is unwell. It is hard to see the justice of it.'

Pleased and a little alarmed, I asked if he knew where she lived.

'She lived in *Sharri al Sahahaldeen*, just off the *Sharri al Souk*.' He pointed with his thumb back into town. 'But that was more than a year ago. Oh, she is very well known here in Aswan. The poor people like her immensely. They call her *Saidneh Duukturah*.'

'Doctor?' My sister had only rudimentary medical training. Her doctorate had been in archaeology. 'She treats the sick?'

'Well, not so much any more. Now only if the hospitals refuse help. The Bisharim, in particular, love her. You know those nomads. They trust your sister only. But she moved from Sahahaldeen Street after some trouble. I heard she went to the English House over on the West Bank, but I'm not so sure. Perhaps you should ask the Bisharim.' He raised his hand in welcome to a small man in a dark blue gelabea who walked briskly into the darkness of the shop's interior. 'A customer.' From his pocket he took a cut-throat razor. '*Naharak sa'id*,' he called and, adopting the swagger of the expert barber, waved farewell to me and entered his shop.

'*Fi amani 'llah.*' Picking up my hat I crossed to a rank where the usual two or three ill-used horses stood between the shafts of battered broughams, still the commonest form of taxi in Aswan. I approached the first driver, who stood flicking at flies with his ragged whip while he smoked a cigarette and chatted with his fellows. He wore an American sailor's hat, a faded T-shirt advertising some Russian artpopper, a pair of traditional baggy trousers exposing ulcerated calves and, on his feet, pink and black Roos. From the state of his legs I guess he had retained the habit, against all current warnings, of wading into the Nile to urinate. I asked him to take me first to the dam's administration office where, for courtesy's sake, I presented myself and made an appointment with my old acquaintance Georges Abidos, the Chief Press Officer, who had been called out to the northern end of the lake. His secretary said he was looking forward to seeing me tomorrow and handed me a welcoming note. I then asked the calash driver if he knew the Bisharim camp on the outskirts of town. I had heard that in recent years the tribe had returned to its traditional sites. He was contemptuous. 'Oh, yes, sir. The barbarians are still with us!' I told him I would give him another ten pounds to take me there and return. He made to bargain but then accepted, shrugging and gesturing for me to get in his carriage. I guessed he was maintaining some kind of face for himself. In my travels I had grown used to all kinds of mysterious body language, frequently far harder to interpret than any spoken tongue.

We trotted back to town and jogged beside a river strewn with old plastic water bottles, with all the miscellaneous filth from the boats that no legislation appeared able to limit, past flaking quasi-French façades still bearing the crests of Farouk and his ancestors and each now occupied by twenty or thirty families whose washing hung over the elaborate iron balconies and carved stone sphinxes like bunting celebrating some joyous national holiday. We passed convents and churches, mosques and graveyards, shanties, monuments, little clumps of palm trees sheltering donkeys and boys from a sun which as noon approached grew steadily more intense.

We went by the English holiday villas where hippies nowadays congregated; we passed the burned-out shells of warehouses and storerooms, victims of some forgotten riot, the stained walls sprayed with the emerald-coloured ankh of the Green Jihad, and eventually, turning inland again, reached the old Moslem necropolis, almost a mile long and half a mile across, surrounded by a low, mud wall and filled with every shape and size of stone or sarcophagus. Beyond this, further up the hill, I made out clumps of palms and the dark woollen tents of the Bisharim.

My driver reined in his horse some distance from the camp, beside a gate into the graveyard. 'I will wait for you here,' he said significantly.

Chapter Two

Ah, Whence, and Whither Flown Again, Who Knows?

T HE NOMAD CAMP, showing so few outward signs of Western influence, had the kind of self-contained dignity which city Arabs frequently manage to re-create in their homes and yet which is not immediately noticed by those visitors merely disgusted by, for instance, Cairo's squalor.

Sheikh Khamet ben Achmet was the patriarch of this particular clan. They had come in a month ago, he said, from the Sudan, to trade horses and camels. They all knew my sister but she had disappeared. He employed a slow, classical Arabic which was easy for me to understand and in which I could easily respond. 'God has perhaps directed thy sister towards another vocation,' he suggested gently. 'It was only a short time since she would visit us whenever we put down our tents here. She had a particularly efficient cure for infections of the eye, but it was the women who went to her, chiefly.' He looked at me with quiet amusement. 'The best type of Englishwoman, as we say. Sometimes God sends us his beneficence in strange forms.'

'Thou has no knowledge of her present dwelling?' I sipped the coffee a servant brought us. I was glad to be in the cool tent. Outside it was now at least thirty-five degrees. There was little danger of freak rain today.

He looked up at me from his ironic grey eyes. 'No,' he said. 'She always visits us. When we needed her we would send messages to the Copt's house. You know, the carpenter who lives on the street leading from the great mosque to the souk.'

I did not know him, I said.

'He is as gold-haired as thou. They nickname him The German, but I know he is a Copt from Alexandria. I think he is called Iskander. I know that he is easily found.'

'Thou knowest my sister was an archaeologist?' I was a little hesitant.

'Indeed, I do! We discussed all manner of ancient things together and she had the courtesy to say that I was at least as informative as the great Egyptian Museum in Cairo!' He was amused by what he perceived as elegant flattery. My sister, if I still knew her, had done no more than to state her direct opinion.

It would have been ill-mannered of me to have left as soon as I had the information I sought, so I spent two further hours answering the sheikh's questions about current American and European politics. I was not surprised that he was well-informed. I had seen his short-wave radio (doubtless full of piles noires) standing on the ivory-inlaid chest on the far side of the tent. I was also unsurprised by his interpretations of what he had learned. They were neither cynical nor unintelligent, but they were characteristic of certain desert Arabs who see everything in terms of power and opportunity and simply cannot grasp the reverence for political institutions we have in the West. For a few minutes I foolishly tried to re-educate him until it became clear I must give offence. Recalling my old rules, I accepted his terms. As a result we parted friends. Any South African apologist for apartheid could not have been more approving of my good manners.

When I got up to leave, the old man took my arm and wished me God's grace and help in finding my sister. 'She was associated with Jews.' He spoke significantly. 'Those who did not like her said that she was a witch. And it is true that two of my women saw her consorting with the spell-seller from the souk. The one called Lallah Zenobia. The black woman. Thou and I art men of the world and understand that it is superstitious folly. But thou knowest how women are. And they are often,' he added in an even lower tone, 'susceptible to Yehudim flattery and lies.'

It was by no means the first time I had to accept such sentiments from the mouth of one who was otherwise hospitality, tolerance and kindness personified. To persuade a desert Arab that Jews are not in direct and regular touch with Satan and all his minions is still no easier than persuading a Dixie Baptist that the doors of a Catholic Church are not necessarily a direct gateway to hell. One is dealing with powerful survival myths which only direct experience will disprove. In such circumstances I never mention my mother's family. I said I would visit Iskander the Carpenter. At this point a braying, bellowing and snorting chorus grew so loud I could barely hear his elaborate goodbyes. The stock was being beaten back from the water. As I emerged from the tent I saw my driver in the distance. He was sitting on the wall of the cemetery feinting with his whip at the boys and girls who flowed like a tide around him, daring one another to run within his range.

Chapter Three

Crystal to the Wizard Eye

I HAD NO difficulty in discovering Iskander the Carpenter. He was a slight man wearing a pair of faded denim overalls. Sanding off a barley sugar chairleg, he sat just inside his workshop, which was open to the street and displayed an entire suite of baroque bedroom and living-room furniture he had almost completed. He chose to speak in French. 'It is for a couple getting married this weekend. At least they are spending their money on furniture rather than the wedding itself!' He put down his chairleg and shook my hand. He was fair-skinned and blond, as Sheikh Achmet had said, though I could not have taken him for anything but Egyptian. His features could have come straight from the Egyptian Museum's clay statue displays of ancient tradespeople. He might have been a foreman on a Middle Kingdom site. He turned up a chair which still had to have the upholstery over its horsehair seat, indicated that I should sit and sent his son to get us a couple of bottles of Pyramid beer.

'Of course I know Saidneh Duukturah. She was my friend. That one,' he pointed to his disappearing boy, 'owes his life to her. He was poisoned. She treated him. He is well. It is true I knew where she lived and would get messages to her. But for a year or more she went away from us. Until recently she was staying at the English House. There are many rumours. Most of them are simply stupid. She is no witch. She was a woman blessed by God with the healing touch. The other woman, now, is undoubtably a witch. My wife heard that your sister fell in love and went to the Somalin, Zenobia, for a philtre. Certainly, by chance, my wife saw her handing Zenobia a heavy purse. A Cairene purse, she was sure.'

'I do not know what that is.' I moved further into the shade.

Outside, Aswan had fallen into a doze as the population closed its shutters until mid-afternoon. The yellow walls of the houses were now almost blistering to the touch.

'A purse of money, that's all. It used to mean a bag of gold. About twenty sovereigns. That is what a witch demands for a very powerful spell. Something very valuable, my friend.'

'My sister was buying a charm from a spell-seller?'

'A powerful one, yes. That negress has been involved with the police more than once. She was suspected of killing a rival suitor at the behest of another, of being responsible for the death of a man who was owed over a thousand pounds by another man. Now, if your sister was disposed to witchcraft, why would she go to a witch and pay her a healthy sum for a job she could as readily do herself?'

I agreed it was unlikely my sister was a witch. I asked how the matter had come to official attention.

'The police went to see her, I think. My wife's friend – friend no more – gossiped. They arrested Zenobia, then let your sister go. You should visit the *mamur* at the *markaz*, the police department. The *mamur* here is a very just man. He never accepts money unless he can do whatever it is he promises. His name is Inspector el-Bayoumi. If anyone knows where your sister is living in Aswan he probably will.'

By the time I had discussed the affairs of the day and thanked the carpenter for the beer, it was already cooler and I walked down to the *Sharri al Souk* which was beginning to open for business again, filling with women in black lacy *milayum* which barely revealed the vivid colours of their house dresses beneath, clutching bright plastic shopping bags and going about their weekend buying. Because it was Friday afternoon the butchers were displaying their calves' heads and bullock tails, their sheep's hearts and heads, their divided carcasses, all protected from an unforgiving sun by the thick coating of black flies which also covered the fish and offal on other stalls. Sellers of turkeys, pigeons and chickens took water in their mouths to force between the beaks of their wares so that they would not dehydrate before they were sold, and seemed to be kissing, tenderly, each one. Cheerful greengrocers called out the virtues of their squash, mangoes, potatoes or green beans. Gas lorries, electro-scoots, bicycles and a few official cars moved in slow competition with rickshaws, donkeys, mules or camels through alleys where, every so often, a bright sign would advertise in English the virtues of unobtainable Panasonic televisions or Braun refrigerators and others would, almost pathetically, alert the passer-by to the Color Xerox machine or Your Local Fax Office. Like every similar souk in the Arab world, the tools and artefacts of the centuries were crowded side by side and functioning in perfect compatibility. Aswan had adapted, far more readily and more cheerfully, to modern energy restraints than had London, for instance, where it had taken an Act of Parliament to reintroduce the public horse trough.

I made my way to the northern end of the street where the police station, the *markaz*, resembling an old British garrison, was guarded by two boys in serge khaki who were armed with the Lee-Enfield .303s with which Lawrence had armed his men for the Desert War and which had, then, been an Arab's prized possession. Now it was unlikely any reliable ammunition existed for these antiques. I understood only the crack militia was allowed to sport the old Kalashnikovs or M16s issued to regular infantry. With the end of international arms trading, almost any well-made gun was valuable, if only as status.

I had no appointment and was informed by the bright young civilian woman on the duty desk that Inspector el-Bayoumi would be back from New Town, the concrete development near the airport, in about an hour. I gave my name, my business, and said I would be back at about five-thirty. Courteously she assured me that the inspector would await me.

Chapter Four

Her Heart All Ears and Eyes, Lips Catching the Avalanche of the Golden Ghost

I HAD FORGOTTEN how much time one had to spend on enquiries of this kind. I returned to my apartment to find an envelope pushed under my door. It was not, as I had hoped, from my sister, but a letter welcoming me to Aswan, a short personal note from my friend Georges, a list of appointments with various engineers and officials, some misleading publicity about the dam, consisting mainly of impressive photographs, a variety of press releases stressing the plans for 'an even better dam' and so on. I went out again having glanced at them. I was obsessed with all the mysteries with which I had been presented in a single day. How had my sister metamorphosed from a dedicated archaeologist to some kind of local Mother Theresa?

Disturbed by my own speculations I forced myself to think about the next day's work when I would be discussing methods of reducing pollution in all its varieties and rebuilding the dam to allow silt down to the arable areas. The signs of serious 'redesertization', as ugly official jargon termed it, were now found everywhere in the Nile valley. In other words, the Aswan Dam was now seriously contributing to ecological damage as well as helping to wipe out our most important links with the remote past. I could not believe how intelligent scientists, who were not those industrial developers motivated only by greed, failed to accept the dreadful psychic damage being done to people whose whole identities were bound up with a particular and very specific landscape. My own identity, for instance, was profoundly linked to a small Oxfordshire village which had remained unchanged for hundreds of years after successfully resisting developers wanting to surround it with high-quality modern properties instead of its existing beeches and oaks.

Few Egyptians were in such comfortable circumstances or could make any choice but the one promising the most immediate benefit, yet they had the same understanding of their tribal homes and what values they represented, and still resisted all attempts to force them to lose their traditional clothes, language and attitudes and make them modern citizens of their semi-democratic society. Unfortunately, this attitude also extended to a dam now much older than many of its staff and never at any time an engineering miracle. UNEC had plans for a replacement. Currently they and the Rajhidi government were arguing over the amounts each would contribute. Happily, that was not my problem.

With a slightly clearer head, I walked to the post office on the corner of Abdel el Taheer Street. Though almost fifty years had passed since the First Revolution, the building still bore the outlines of earlier royal insignia. The elaborate cast-ironwork on doors and windows was of that 'Oriental' pattern exported from the foundries of Birmingham to adorn official buildings throughout the Empire east of Gibraltar. Even by the 1970s the stuff was still available from stock, during the brief period after the death of Britain's imperial age and before the birth of that now much-despised and admittedly reckless Thatcher period known ironically as 'the Second Empire', the period which had shaped my own expectations of life as well as those of uncounted millions of my fellows, the period in which my uncle had died, a soldier in the Falklands cause.

I entered the main door's cool archway and walked through dusty shafts of light to a tiled counter where I asked to speak to the Post Master. After a moment's wait I was shown into his little gloomy mahogany office, its massive fan constantly stirring piles of documents which moved like a perpetually unsettled flight of doves. A small, handsome Arab entered and closed the door carefully behind him. His neat, Abraham Lincoln beard suggested religious devotion. I told him that my name was Pappenheim and I was expecting mail. I handed him an envelope I had already prepared. On the outside was my name and occupation. Inside was the conventional 'purse' – actually another envelope containing a few pounds. I said I would appreciate his personal interest in my mail and hoped he could ensure it was available to me the moment it arrived. Absently, he took the envelope and put it in his trouser pocket. He had brightened at the sound of my name. 'Are you related to that woman of virtue whom we know here in Aswan?' He spoke measured, cultured Arabic with the soft accents of Upper Egypt.

'My sister.' I was trying to locate her, I said. Perhaps her mail was delivered here?

'It has not been collected, Si Pappenheim, for several months. Yet she has been seen in Aswan recently. There was a small scandal. I understand that El Haj Sheikh Ibrahim Abu Halil intervened. Have you asked him about your sister?'

'Is he the governor?'

He laughed. Clearly the idea of the governor intervening on behalf of an ordinary member of the public amused him. 'No. Sheikh Abu Halil is the gentleman so many come to Aswan to see these days. He is the great Sufi now. We are blessed in this. God sends us everything that is good, even the rain. So much more grows and blooms. People journey to us from all over the world. Here, God has chosen to reveal a glimpse of paradise.'

I was impressed by his optimism. I told him I would go to see Sheikh Abu Halil as soon as possible. Meanwhile I had an appointment with the police chief. At this his face grew a little uncertain, but his only response was some conventional greeting concerning Allah's good offices.

Police Inspector el-Bayoumi was one of those suave career officers produced by the new academies. His manners were perfect, his hospitality generous and discreet, and when I had replied to his question, telling him where I had been born in England, he confessed affectionate familiarity with another nearby Cotswold village. Together, we deplored the damage tourism had done to the environment and confessed it to be a major problem in both our countries, which depended considerably on the very visitors who contributed to the erosion. He sighed. 'I think the human race has rather foolishly cancelled many of its options.'

Since he preferred to speak it, I replied in English. 'Perhaps our imaginative resources are becoming as scarce as our physical ones?'

'There has been a kind of psychic withering,' he agreed. 'And its worst symptom, in my view, Mr Pappenheim, is found in the religious and political fundamentalism to which so many subscribe. As if, by some sort of sympathetic magic, the old, simpler days will return. We live in complicated times with complicated problems. It's a sad fact that they require sophisticated solutions.'

I admitted I had been schooled in many of those fundamentalist notions and sometimes found them difficult to resist. We chatted about this for a while. Coffee was brought, together with a selection of delicious *gurrahiya* pastries, whose secret the Egyptians inherited from the Turks, and we talked for another half-hour, during which time we took each other's measure and agreed the world would be a better place if civilised people like ourselves were allowed a greater voice. Whereupon, in that sometimes abrupt change of tone Arabs have, which can mislead Europeans into thinking they have somehow given offence, Inspector el-Bayoumi asked what he could do for me.

'I'm looking for my sister. She's an economic archaeologist who came here two and a half years ago with the Burbank College Project. It was an international team. Only about half were from California and those returned the next year, after the big earthquake. Most of them, of course, had lost relatives. My sister stayed on with the remaining members.' I did not mention her talk of a wonderful discovery out in the Western Sahara. Their sonavids had picked up a New Kingdom temple complex almost perfectly preserved but buried some hundred feet under the sand. My sister had been very excited about it. It was at least on a par with the discovery of the Tutankhamen treasures and probably of far greater historical importance. She and the team kept the discovery quiet, of course, especially since so many known monuments had suffered. Naturally, there were some conflicts of interest. There was little she could tell me in a letter and most of that was a bit vague, making reference to personal or childhood incidents whose relevance escaped me. I added delicately. 'You know about the discovery, naturally.'

He smiled as he shook his handsome head. 'No, Mr Pappenheim, I don't. I think an elaborate dig would not escape my notice.' He paused, asking me if he might smoke. I told him I was allergic to cigarette smoke and he put his case away. Regretfully, he said: 'I should tell you that your sister is a little disturbed. She was arrested by us about a year ago. There was something we had to follow up. An outbreak of black magic amongst the local people. We don't take such things very seriously until it's possible to detect a cult growing. Then we have to move to break it up as best we can. Such things are not a serious problem in London, but for a policeman in Aswan they are fairly important. We arrested a known witch, a Somali woman they call Madame Zenobia, and with her an Englishwoman, also rumoured to be practising. That was your sister, Mr Pappenheim. She was deranged and had to be given a sedative. Eventually, we decided against charging her and released her into the custody of Lady Roper.'

'The Consul's wife?'

'He's the Honorary Consul here in Aswan now. They have a large house on the West Bank, not far from the Ali Khan's tomb. You can't see it from this side. It is our miracle. Locally, it's called the English House. More recently they've called it the Rose House. You'll find no mysteries there!'

'That's where my sister's staying?'

'No longer. She left Aswan for a while. When she came back she joined the community around Sheikh Abu Halil and I understand her to be living in the old holiday villas on the Edfu road, near the racecourse. I'll gladly put a man to work on the matter. We tend not to pursue people too much in Aswan. Your sister is a good woman. An honest woman. I hope she has recovered herself.'

Thanking him I said I hoped my search would not involve the time of a hard-working police officer. I got up to leave. 'And what happened to Madame Zenobia?'

'Oh, the courts were pretty lenient. She got a year, doing

quarry work for the Restoration Department in Cairo. She was a fit woman. She'll be even fitter now. Hard labour is a wonderful cure for neurosis! And far more socially useful than concocting love potions or aborting cattle.'

He sounded like my old headmaster. As an afterthought, I said, 'I gather Sheikh Abu Halil took an interest in my sister's case.'

He flashed me a look of intelligent humour. 'Yes, he did. He is much respected here. Your sister is a healer. The Sufi is a healer. He sometimes makes an accurate prophecy. He has a following all over the world, I believe.'

I appreciated his attempt at a neutral tone, given his evident distaste for matters psychic and mystical. We shared, I think, a similar outlook.

I found myself asking him another question. 'What was the evidence against my sister, inspector?'

He had hoped I would not raise the matter, but was prepared for it. 'Well,' he began slowly, 'for instance, we had a witness who saw her passing a large bag of money to the woman. The assumption was that she was paying for a spell. A powerful one. A love philtre, possibly, but it was also said that she wanted a man dead. He was the only other member of her team who had remained behind. There was some suggestion, Mr Pappenheim,' he paused again, 'that he made her pregnant. But this was all the wildest gossip. He did in fact die of a heart attack shortly after the reported incident. Sometimes we must treat such cases as murder. But we only had circumstantial evidence. The man was a drug addict and apparently had tried to force your sister to give him money. There was just a hint of blackmail involved in the case, you see. These are all, of course, the interpretations of a policeman. Maybe the man had been an ex-lover, no more. Maybe she wanted him to love her again?'

'It wasn't Noone, was it?'

'It was not her estranged husband. He is, I believe, still in New Zealand.'

'You really think she got tangled up in black magic?'

'When confused, men turn to war and women to magic. She

was not, as the Marrakshim say, with the caravan.' He was just a little sardonic now. 'But she was adamant that she did not wish to go home.'

'What did she tell you?'

'She denied employing the witch. She claimed the Somali woman was her only friend. Otherwise she said little. But her manner was all the time distracted, as if she imagined herself to be surrounded by invisible witnesses. We were not unsympathetic. The psychiatrist from the German hospital came to see her. Your sister is a saintly woman who helped the poor and the sick and asked for no reward. She enriched us. We were trying to help her, you know.'

He had lost his insouciance altogether now and spoke with controlled passion. 'It could be that your sister had an ordinary breakdown. Too much excitement in her work, too much sun. Caring too much for the hardships of others. She tried to cure the whole town's ills and that task is impossible for any individual. Her burden was too heavy. You could see it written in every line of her face, every movement of her body. We wanted her to recover. Some suspected she was in the witch's power, but in my own view she carried a personal weight of guilt, perhaps. Probably pointlessly, too. You know how woman are. They are kinder, more feeling creatures than men.'

Chapter Five

The Seasons of Home – Aye, Now They are Remembered!

THAT EVENING, WHILE there was still light, I took the felucca across the Nile, to the West Bank. The ferryman, clambering down from his high mast where he had been reefing his sail, directed me through the village to a dirt road winding up the hillside a hundred yards or so from the almost austere resting place of the Ali Khan. 'You will see it,' he assured me. 'But get a boy.'

There were a couple of dozen children waiting for me on the quay. I selected a bright-looking lad of about ten. He wore a ragged Japanese T-shirt with the inscription I LOVE SEX WAX, a pair of cut-off jeans and Adidas trainers. In spite of the firmness with which I singled him out, we were followed by the rest of the children all the way to the edge of the village. I had a couple of packs of old electronic watches which I distributed, to a pantomime of disappointment from the older children. Watches had ceased to be fashionable currency since I had last been in Aswan. Now, from their requests, I learned it was 'real' fountain pens. They showed me a couple of Sheaffers some tourist had already exchanged for their services as guides and companions of the road.

I had no fountain pen for the boy who took me to the top of the hill and pointed down into the little valley where, amongst the sand and the rocks, had been erected a large two-storey house, as solidly Edwardian as any early-twentieth-century vicarage. Astonishingly, it was planted with cedars, firs and other hardy trees shading a garden to rival anything I had ever seen in Oxfordshire. There were dozens of varieties of roses, of every possible shade, as well as hollyhocks, snapdragons, foxgloves, marigolds and all the flowers one might find in an English July garden. A peculiar wall about a metre high surrounded the entire mirage and I guessed that it disguised some kind of extraordinarily expensive watering and sheltering apparatus which had allowed the owners to do the impossible and bring a little bit of rural England to Upper Egypt. The grounds covered several acres. I saw some stables, a garage, and a woman on the front lawn. She was seated in a faded deckchair watching a fiche-reader or a video which she rested in her left hand. With her right hand she took a glorious drink from the little table beside her and sipped through the straw. As I drew nearer, my vision was obscured by the trees and the wall, but I guessed she was about sixty-five, dressed in a thoroughly unfashionable Marks and Ashley smock, a man's trilby hat and a pair of rubber-tyre sandals. She looked up as I reached the gate and called 'Good afternoon'. Happy with cash, my boy departed.

'Lady Roper?'

She had a quick, intelligent, swarthy face, her curls all grey beneath the hat, her long hands expressive even when still. 'I'm Diana Roper.'

'My name's Paul Pappenheim. I'm Beatrice's brother.'

'The engineer!' She was full of welcome. 'My goodness, you know, I think Bea could foretell the future. She *said* you'd be turning up here about now.'

'I wrote and told her!' I was laughing as the woman unlocked the gate and let me in. 'I knew about this job months ago.'

'You're here on business.'

'I'm going through the rituals of sorting out a better dam and trying to do something about the climatic changes. I got sent because I know a couple of people here – and because I asked to come. But there's little real point to my being here.'

'You don't sound very hopeful, Mr Pappenheim.' She led me towards the back of the house, to a white wrought-iron conservatory which was a relatively recent addition to the place and must have been erected by some forgotten imperial dignitary of the last century.

'I'm always hopeful that people will see reason, Lady Roper.'

We went into the sweet-smelling anteroom, whose glass had been treated so that it could admit only a certain amount of light, or indeed reflect all the light to perform some needed function elsewhere. Despite its ancient appearance, I guessed the house to be using up-to-date EE technologies and to be completely self-sufficient. 'What an extraordinary garden,' I said.

'Imported Kent clay.' She offered me a white basket chair. 'With a fair bit of Kenyan topsoil, I understand. We didn't have it done. We got it all dirt cheap. It takes such a long time to travel anywhere these days, most people don't want the place. It belonged to one of the Fayeds, before they all went off to Malaysia. But have you looked carefully at our roses, Mr Pappenheim? They have a sad air to them, a sense of someone departed, someone mourned. Each bush was planted for a dead relative, they say.' Her voice grew distant. 'Of course, the new rain has helped enormously. I've survived because I know the rules. Women frequently find their intuition very useful in times of social unrest. But things are better now, aren't they? We simply refuse to learn. We refuse to learn.'

Grinning as if enjoying a game, a Nubian girl of about sixteen brought us a tray of English cakes and a pot of Assam tea. I wondered how I had lost the thread of Lady Roper's conversation.

'We do our best,' I said, letting the girl take tongs to an éclair and with a flourish pop it on my plate. 'I believe Bea lived here for a while.'

'My husband took quite a fancy to her. As did I. She was a sweetie. And so bright. Is that a family trait? Yes, we shared a great deal. It was a luxury for me, you know, to have such company. Not many people have been privileged as she and I were privileged.' She nodded with gentle mystery, her eyes in the past. 'We were friends of your uncle. That was the funny thing we found out. All at Cambridge together in the late '60s. We thought conservation an important subject *then*. What? Fifty years ago, almost? Such a jolly boy. He joined up for extremely complicated reasons, we felt. Did you know why?'

I had never really wondered. My picture of my mother's

brother was of the kind of person who would decide on a military career, but evidently they had not been acquainted with that man at all. Finding this disturbing, I attempted to return to my subject. 'I was too young to remember him. My sister was more curious than I. Did she seem neurotic to you, while she was here?'

'On the contrary. She was the sanest of us all! Sound as a bell upstairs, as Bernie always said. Sharp intelligence. But, of course, she had been there, you see. And could confirm everything we had been able to piece together at this end.'

'You're referring to the site they discovered?'

'That, of course, was crucial. Especially at the early stages. Yes, the site was extraordinary. We went out to see it with her, Bernie and I. What a mind-blower, Paul! Amazing experience. Even the small portion they had excavated. Four mechanical sifters just sucking the sand gradually away. It would have taken years in the old days. Unfortunately three of the operators left after the earthquake and the sifters were recalled for some crucial rescue work over in Sinai. And then, of course, everything changed.'

'I'm not sure I'm...'

'After the ship came and took Bea.'

'A ship? On the Nile?'

She frowned at me for a moment and then her tone changed to one of distant friendliness. 'You'll probably want a word with Bernie. You'll find him in his playroom. Nadja will take you. And I'm here if you need to know anything.'

She glanced away, through the glass walls of the conservatory and was at once lost in melancholy reflection of the roses and their guardian trees.

Chapter Six

The Smoke Along the Track

A TAPE OF some antique radio programme was playing as I knocked on the oak door and was admitted by a white-haired old man wearing a pair of overalls and a check shirt, with carpet slippers on his feet. His skin had the healthy sheen of a sun-baked reptile and his blue eyes were brilliant with trust. I was shocked enough to remain where I was, even as he beckoned me in. He turned down his stereo, a replica of some even older audio contraption, and stood proudly to display a room full of books and toys. One wall was lined with glass shelves on which miniature armies battled amidst a wealth of tiny trees and buildings. 'You don't look much like a potential playmate!' His eyes strayed towards the brilliant jackets of his books.

'And you're not entirely convincing as Mr Dick, sir.' I stood near the books, which were all well-ordered, and admired his illustrated Dickens. The temperature in the room was, I guessed, thoroughly controlled. Should the power fail for just a few hours the desert would fade and modify this room as if it had been a photograph left for an hour in the sun.

My retort seemed to please him. He grinned and came forward. 'I'm Bernie Roper. While I have no immediate enemies, I enjoy in this room the bliss of endless childhood. I have my lead soldiers, my bears and rabbits, my model farm, and I read widely. *Treasure Island* is very good, as are the "William" books, and Edgar Rice Burroughs and, as you say, Charles Dickens, though he's a bit on the scary side sometimes. E. Nesbit and H.G. Wells and Shaw. I enjoy so much. For music I have the very best of *Children's Favourites* from the BBC – a mixture of comic songs, Gilbert and Sullivan, "Puff, the Magic Dragon", "The Laughing Policeman", popular classics and light opera. Flanders and Swann, Danny Kaye, *Sparky's Magic Piano*, *Peter and the Wolf* and *Song of the South*. Do you know any of those? But I'm a silly chap! You're far too young. They'd even scrapped *Children's Hour* before you were born. Oh, dear. Never to enjoy *Larry the Lamb* or Norman and Henry Bones, the Boy Detectives! Oh!' he exclaimed with a knowing grin. 'Calamity!' Then he returned his attention to his toys for a moment. 'You think I should carry more responsibility?'

'No.' I had always admired him as a diplomat. He deserved the kind of retirement that suited him.

'I feel sorry for the children,' he said. 'The pleasures of childhood are denied to more and more of them as their numbers increase. Rajhid and Abu Halil are no real solution, are they? We who remember the Revolution had hoped to have turned the desert green by now. I plan to die here, Mr –?'

'My name's Pappenheim. I'm Bea's brother.'

'My boy! Thank goodness I offered an explanation. I'm not nearly as eccentric as I look! "Because I could not stop for Death, He kindly stopped for me. We shared a carriage, just we two, and Immortality." Emily Dickinson, I believe. But I could also be mis-remembering. "The child is Father to the Man", you know. And the lost childhood of Judas. Did you read all those poems at school?'

'I was probably too young again,' I said. 'We didn't do poetry as such.'

'I'm so sorry. All computer studies nowadays, I suppose.'

'Not all, sir.' The old-fashioned courtesy surprised us both. Sir Bernard acted as one cheated and I almost apologised. Yet it was probably the first time I had used the form of address without irony. I had, I realised, wanted to show respect. Sir Bernard had come to the same understanding. 'Oh, well. You're a kind boy. But you'll forgive me, I hope, if I return to my preferred world.'

'I'm looking for my sister, Sir Bernard. Actually, I'm pretty worried about her.'

Without irritation, he sighed. 'She was a sweet woman. It was terrible. And nobody believing her.'

'Believing what, Sir Bernard?'

'About the spaceship, you know. But that's Di's field, really. Not my area of enthusiasm at all. I like to make time stand still. We each have a different way of dealing with the fact of our own mortality, don't we?' He strolled to one of his displays and picked up a charging 17th Lancer. 'Into the Valley of Death rode the six hundred.'

'Thank you for seeing me, Sir Bernard.'

'Not at all, Paul. She talked about you. I liked her. I think you'll find her either attending Abu Halil's peculiar gymnasium or at the holiday homes. Where those Kenyan girls and boys are now living.'

'Thank you. Goodbye, sir.'

'Bye, bye!' Humming some stirring air, the former Director General of the United Nations hovered, contented, over his miniature Death-or-Glory Boys.

Chapter Seven

Another Relay in the Chain of Fire

LADY ROPER HAD remained in her conservatory. She rose as I entered. 'Was Bernie able to help?'

'I could be narrowing things down.' I was anxious to get back to the East Bank before dark. 'Thank you for your kindness. I tried to find a phone number for you.'

'We're not on the phone, lovey. We don't need one.'

'Sir Bernard mentioned a spaceship.' I was not looking forward to her reply.

'Oh, dear, yes,' she said. 'The flying-saucer people. I think one day they will bring us peace, don't you? I mean one way or another. This is better than death for me, at any rate, Paul. But perhaps they have a purpose for us. Perhaps an unpleasant one. I don't think anybody would rule that out. What could we do if that were the case? Introduce a spy? That has not proved a successful strategy. We know that much, sadly. It's as if all that's left of Time is here. A few shreds from a few ages.'

Again I was completely nonplussed and said nothing.

'I think you share Sir B.'s streak of pessimism. Or realism is it?'

'Well, we're rather different, actually...' I began to feel foolish.

'He was happier as Ambassador, you know. Before the UN. And then we were both content to retire here. We'd always loved it. The Fayeds had us out here lots of times, for those odd parties. We were much younger. You probably think we're both barking mad.' When I produced an awkward reply she was sympathetic. 'There *is* something happening here. It's a *centre*. You can feel it everywhere. It's an ideal place. Possibly we shall be the ones left to witness the birth of the New Age.'

At that moment all I wished to do was save my sister from that atmosphere of half-baked mysticism and desperate faith, to get her back to the relative reality of London and a doctor who would know what was wrong with her and be able to treat it.

'Bea was never happier than when she was in Aswan, you know,' said Lady Roper.

'She wrote and told me as much.'

'Perhaps she risked a bit more than was wise. We all admire her for it. What I don't understand is why she was so thick with Lallah Zenobia. The woman's psychic, of course, but very unsophisticated.'

'You heard about the witness? About the purse?'

'Naturally.'

'And you, too, are sure it was a purse?'

'I suppose so. It's Cairo slang, isn't it, for a lot of money? The way the Greeks always say "seven years" when they mean a long time has passed. Bernie's actually ill, you realise? He's coherent much of the time. A form of P.D., we were told. From the water when we were in Washington. He's determined to make the best of it. He's sweet, isn't he?'

'He's an impressive man. You don't miss England?'

She offered me her hand. 'Not a bit. You're always welcome to stay if you are bored over there. Or the carping materialism of the Old Country gets to you. Simplicity's the keynote at the Rose House. Bernie says the British have been sulking for years, like the Lost Boys deprived of their right to go a-hunting and a-pirating at will. I'm afraid, Paul, that we don't think very much of home any more.'

Chapter Eight

And All These in Their Helpless Days...

THE GREAT EGYPTIAN sun was dropping away to the horizon as, in the company of some forty blue-cowled Islamic school-girls and a bird-catcher, I sailed back to the East. Reflected in the Nile the sky was the colour of blood and saffron against every tone of dusty blue; the rocks, houses and palms dark violet silhouettes, sparkling here and there as lamps were lit, signalling the start of Aswan's somewhat orderly nightlife. Near the landing stage I ate some *mulakhiya*, rice and an antique salad at Mahommeds' Cafetria, drank some mint tea and went back to the Osiris, half expecting to find that my sister had left word, but the Hindu woman had no messages and handed me my key with a quick smile of encouragement.

I slept poorly, kept awake by the constant cracking of a chemical 'equaliser' in the basement and the creak of the all but useless wind-generator on the roof. It was ironic that Aswan, so close to the source of enormous quantities of electricity, was as cruelly rationed as everyone.

I refused to believe that my sister, who was as sane as I was and twice as intelligent, had become entangled with a black-magic flying-saucer cult. Her only purpose for associating with such people would be curiosity, perhaps in pursuit of some anthropological research connected with her work. I was, however, puzzled by her secrecy. Clearly, she was deliberately hiding her whereabouts. I hoped that, when I returned the next day, I would know where she was.

My meetings were predictably amiable and inconsequential. I had arrived a little late, having failed to anticipate the levels of security at the dam. There were police, militia and security people everywhere, both on the dam itself and in all the offices and operations areas. I had to show my pass to eleven different people. The dam was under increased threat from at least three different organisations, the chief being Green Jihad. Our main meetings were held in a large, glass-walled room overlooking the lake. I was glad to meet so many staff, though we all knew that any decisions about the dam would not be made by us but by whoever triumphed in the Geneva negotiations. It was also good to discover that earlier attitudes towards the dam were changing slightly and new thinking was being done. Breakfasted and lunched, I next found myself guest of honour at a full-scale Egyptian dinner which must have taken everyone's rations for a month, involved several entertainments and lastly a good deal of noisy toasting, in cokes and grape juice, our various unadmired leaders.

At the Hotel Osiris, when I got back that night, there was no note for me so I decided next day to visit the old vacation villas before lunching as arranged at the Cataract with Georges Abidos, who had told me that he was retiring as Public Relations officer for the dam. I had a hunch that my sister was probably living with the neo-hippies. The following morning I ordered a calash to pick me up and sat on the board beside the skinny, cheerful driver as his equally thin horse picked her way slowly through busy Saturday streets until we were on the long, cracked concrete road with the railway yards on one side and the river on the other, flanked by dusty palms, which led past the five-storey Moorish-style vacation complex, a tumble of typical tourist architecture of the kind once found all around the Mediterranean, Adriatic and parts of the Black and Red Seas. The white stucco was patchy and the turquoise trim on window frames and doors was peeling, but the new inhabitants, who had occupied it when the Swedish owners finally abandoned it, had put their stamp on it. Originally the place had been designed for Club Med, but had never sustained the required turnover, even with its special energy dispensations, and had been sold several times over the past ten years. Now garishly dressed young squatters from the wealthy

African countries, from the Australias, North and South America, as well as Europe and the Far East, had covered the old complex with their sometimes impressive murals and decorative graffiti. I read a variety of slogans. LET THE BLOOD CONSUME THE FIRE, said one. THE TYGERS OF THE MIND RULE THE JUNGLE OF THE HEART, said another. I had no relish for such undisciplined nonsense and did not look forward to meeting the occupants of this bizarre New New Age fortress. Psychedelia, even in its historical context, had never attracted me.

As I dismounted from the calash I was greeted by a young woman energetically cleaning the old Club Med brass plate at the gate. She had those startling green eyes in a dark olive skin which one frequently comes across everywhere in Egypt and are commonly believed to be another inheritance from the Pharaonic past. Her reddish hair was braided with multicoloured ribbons and she wore a long green silk smock which complemented her eyes.

'Hi!' Her manner was promiscuously friendly. 'I'm Lips. Which is short for Eclipse, to answer your question. Don't get the wrong idea. You're here to find a relative, right?' Her accent was Canadian with a trace of something else, possibly Ukrainian. 'What's your name?'

'Paul,' I said. 'My sister's called Bea. Are the only people who visit you trying to find relatives?'

'I just made an assumption from the way you look. I'm pretty good at sussing people out.' Then she made a noise of approving excitement. 'Bea Porcupine, is it? She's famous here. She's a healer and an oracle. She's special.'

'Could you take me to her apartment?' I did my best not to show impatience with the girl's nonsense.

'Lips' answered me with a baffled smile. 'No. I mean, sure I could take you to one of her rooms. But she's not here now.'

'Do you know where she went?'

The girl was vaguely apologetic. 'Mercury? Wherever the ship goes.'

My irritation grew more intense. But I controlled myself. 'You've no idea when the ship gets back?'

'Now? Yesterday? There's so much time-bending involved. No. You just have to hope.'

I walked past her into the complex.

Chapter Nine

Fast Closing Toward the Undelighted Night...

B Y THE TIME I had spoken to a dozen or so *enfants des fleurs* I
had found myself a guide who introduced himself as Magic
Mungo and wore brilliant face-paint beneath his straw hat. He
had on an old pair of glitterjeans which whispered and flashed as
he walked. His jacket announced in calligraphic Arabic phonetic
English: THE NAME IS THE GAME. He was probably no older than
thirteen. He asked me what I did and when I told him he said he,
too, planned to become an engineer 'and bring back the power'.
This amused me and restored my temper. 'And what will you do
about the weather?' I asked.

'It's not the weather,' he told me, 'not Nature – it's the ships.
And it's not the dam, or the lake, that's causing the storms and
stuff. It's the Reens.'

I misheard him. I thought he was blaming the Greens. Then I
realised, belatedly, that he was expressing a popular notion amongst
the New New Agers, which by the time I had heard it several times
more had actually begun to improve my mood. The Reens, the
flying-saucer people, were used by the hippies as an explanation
for everything they couldn't understand. In rejecting Science, they
had substituted only a banal myth. Essentially, I was being told that
the gods had taken my sister. In other words they did not know
where she was. At last, after several further short but keen conver-
sations, in various rug-strewn galleries and cushion-heavy
chambers smelling strongly of kif, incense and patchouli, I met a
somewhat older woman, with grey streaks in her long black hair
and a face the colour and texture of well-preserved leather.

'This is Ayesha.' Mungo gulped comically. 'She-who-must-be-
obeyed!' He ran to the woman who smiled a perfectly ordinary

smile as she embraced him. 'We encourage their imaginations,' she said. 'They read books here and everything. Are you looking for Bea?'

Warily expecting more Reen talk, I admitted that I was trying to find my sister.

'She went back to Aswan. I think she was at the Medrasa for a bit – you know, with the Sufi – but after that she returned to town. If she's not there, she's in the desert again. She goes there to medi-tate, I'm told. If she's not there, she's not anywhere. Around here, I mean.'

I was relieved by the straightforward nature of her answer. 'I'm greatly obliged. I thought you, too, were going to tell me she was taken into space by aliens!'

Ayesha joined in my amusement. 'Oh, no, of course not. That was more than a year ago!'

Chapter Ten

Thoughts of Too Old a Colour Nurse My Brain

I DECIDED TO have a note delivered to the Sufi, El Haj Ibrahim Abu Halil, telling him that I planned to visit him next day, then, with a little time to spare before my appointment, I strolled up the corniche, past the boat-ghetto at the upper end, and along the more fashionable stretches where some sporadic attempt was made to give the railings fresh coats of white paint and where a kiosk, closed since my first time here, advertised in bleached Latin type the *Daily Telegraph*, *Le Monde* and the *New York Herald Tribune*. A few thin strands of white smoke rose from the villages on Elephantine Island; and from *Gazirat-al-Bustan*, Plantation Island, whose botanical gardens, begun by Lord Kitchener, had long since mutated into marvellously exotic jungle, came the laughter of the children and teenagers who habitually spent their free days there.

Outside the kiosk stood an old man holding a bunch of faded and ragged international newspapers under one arm and *Al Misr* under the other. 'All today!' he called vigorously in English, much as a London coster shouted 'All fresh!' A professional cry rather than any sort of promise. I bought an *Al Misr*, only a day old, and glanced at the headlines as I walked up to the park. There seemed nothing unusually alarming in the paper. Even the E.C. rate had not risen in the last month. As I tried to open the sheet a gust came off the river and the yellow-grey paper began to shred in my hands. It was low-density recyke, unbulked by the sophisticated methods of the West. Before I gave up and dumped the crumpled mess into the nearest reclamation bin I had glimpsed references to the UNEC conference in Madagascar and something about examples of mass hysteria in Old Paris and Bombay, where a group called *Reincarnation* was claiming its leader to be a newly born

266

John Lennon. There were now about as many reincarnated Lennons abroad as there had been freshly risen Christs in the early Middle Ages.

I stopped in the park to watch the gardeners carefully tending the unsweet soil of the flower beds, coaxing marigolds and nasturtiums to bloom at least for a few days in the winter, when the sun would not burn them immediately they emerged. The little municipal café was unchanged since British days and still served only ice-creams, tea, coffee or soft drinks, all of them made with non-rationed ingredients and all equally tasteless. Pigeons wandered hopelessly amongst the débris left by customers, occasionally pecking at a piece of wrapping or a sliver of *Sustenance* left behind by some poor devil who had been unable to force his stomach to accept the high-concentrate nutrients we had developed at UNEC for his benefit.

The Cataract's entrance was between pillars which, once stately, Egyptianate and unquestionably European, were now a little the worse for wear, though the gardens on both sides of the drive were heavy with freshly planted flowers. Bougainvillaeas of every brilliant variety covered walls behind avenues of palms leading to a main building the colour of Nile clay, its shutters and ironwork a dark, dignified green, the kind of colour Thomas Cook himself would have picked to represent the security and solid good service which established him as one of the Empire's noblest champions.

I walked into the great lobby cooled by massive carved mahogany punkahs worked on hidden ropes by screened boys. Egypt had had little trouble implementing many of the UN's mandatory energy-saving regulations. She had either carried on as always or had returned, perhaps even with relief, to the days before electricity and gas had become the necessities rather than the luxuries of life.

I crossed the lobby to the wooden verandah where we were to lunch. Georges Abidos was already at our table by the rail looking directly over the empty swimming pool and, beyond that, to the river itself. He was drinking a cup of Lipton's tea and I remarked on it, pointing to the label on the string dangling from his tiny metal pot. 'Indeed!' he said. 'At ten pounds the pot why shouldn't the Cataract offer us Lipton's, at least!' He dropped his voice. 'Though my guess is the teabag has seen more than one customer through the day's heat. Would you like a cup?'

I refused. He hadn't, I said, exactly sold me on the idea. He laughed. He was a small, attractively ugly Greek from Alexandria. Since the flooding, he had been driven, like so many of his fellow citizens, to seek work inland. At least half the city had not been thought worth saving as the sea-level had steadily risen to cover it.

'Can't you,' he asked, 'get your American friends to do something about this new embargo? One misses the cigarettes and I could dearly use a new John B.' He indicated his stained Planter's straw and then picked it up to show me the label on the mottled sweatband so that I might verify it was a genuine product of the Stetson Hat Co. of New Jersey. 'Size seven and a quarter. But don't get anything here. The Cairo fakes are very close. Very good. But they can't fake the finish, you see.'

'I'll remember,' I promised. I would send him a Stetson next time I was in the USA.

I felt we had actually conducted our main business before we sat down. The rest of the lunch would be a social affair with someone I had known both professionally and as a close personal acquaintance for many years.

As our mixed hors d'oeuvres arrived, Georges Abidos looked with a despairing movement of his mouth out towards the river. 'Well, Paul, have you solved any of our problems?'

'I doubt it,' I said. 'That's all going on in Majunga now. I'm wondering if my function isn't as some kind of minor smokescreen.'

'I thought you'd volunteered.'

'Only when they'd decided that one of us had to come. It was a good chance, I thought, to see how my sister was. I had spare relative allowance and lots of energy and travel owing, so I got her a flight out with me. It took for ever! But I grew rather worried. The last note I had from her was three months ago and very disjointed. It didn't tell me anything. I'd guessed that her husband had turned up. It was something she said. That's about all I know which would frighten her that much. My mistake, it's emerged. Then I wondered if she wasn't pregnant. I couldn't make head nor tail of her letters. They weren't like her at all.'

'Women are a trial,' said Georges Abidos. 'My own sister has divorced, I heard. But then,' as if to explain it, 'they moved to Kuwait.' He turned his eyes back to the river which seemed almost to obsess him. 'Look at the Nile. An open sewer running through a desert. What has Egypt done to deserve rescue? She gave the world the ancestors who first offered Nature a serious challenge. Should we be grateful for that? From Lake Nasser to Alexandria the river remains undrinkable and frequently unusable. She once replenished the earth. Now, what with their fertilisers and sprays, she helps poison it.' It was as if all the doubts he had kept to himself as a publicity officer were now being allowed to emerge. 'I listen to Blue Danube Radio from Vienna. The English station. It's so much more reliable than the World Service. We are still doing less than we could, they say, here in Egypt.'

The tables around us had begun to fill with Saudis and wealthy French people in fashionable silk shifts, and the noise-level rose so that it was hard for me to hear my acquaintance's soft tones.

We discussed the changing nature of Aswan. He said he would be glad to get back to Cairo where he had a new job with the Antiquities Department raising money for specific restoration or reconstruction projects.

We had met at the reopening of the Cairo Opera House in 1989, which had featured the Houston Opera Company's *Porgy and Bess*, but had never become more than casual friends, though we shared many musical tastes and he had an extraordinary knowledge of modern fiction in English. His enthusiasm was for the older writers like Gilchrist or DeLillo, who had been amongst my own favourites at college.

We were brought some wonderfully tasty Grönburgers and I remarked that the cuisine had improved since I was last here. 'French management,' he told me. 'They have one of the best teams outside of Paris. They all came from Nice after the troubles. Lucky for us. I might almost be tempted to stay! Oh, no! I could not. Even for that! Nubian music is an abomination!'

I told him about my sister, how I was unable to find her and how I was beginning to fear the worst. 'The police suggested she was mad.'

Georges was dismissive of this. 'A dangerous assumption at any time, Paul, but especially these days. And very difficult for us to define here, in Egypt, just as justice is at once a more brutal and a subtler instrument in our interpretation. We never accepted, thank God, the conventional wisdoms of psychiatry. And madness here, as elsewhere, is defined by the people in power, usually calling themselves the State. Tomorrow those power-holders could be overthrown by a fresh dynasty, and what was yesterday simple common sense today becomes irresponsible folly. So I do not like to make hasty judgements or pronounce readily on others' moral or mental conditions – lest, indeed, we inadvertently condemn ourselves.' He paused. 'They say this was not so under the British, that it was fairer, more predictable. Only real troublemakers and criminals went to jail. Now it isn't as bad as it was when I was a lad. Then anyone was liable to arrest. If it was better under the British, then that is our shame.' And he lowered his lips to his wine-glass.

We had slipped, almost automatically, into discussing the old, familiar topics. 'It's sometimes argued,' I said, 'that the liberal democracies actually stopped the flow of history. A few hundred years earlier, as feudal states, we would have forcibly Christianised the whole of Islam and changed the entire nature of the planet's power struggle. Indeed, all the more childish struggles might have been well and truly over by now!'

'Or it might have gone the other way,' Georges suggested dryly, 'if the Moors had reconquered France and Northern Europe. After all, Islam did not bring the world to near-ruin. What has the European way achieved except the threat of death for all?'

I could not accept an argument which had already led to massive conversions to Islam amongst the youth of Europe, America and Democratic Africa, representing a sizeable proportion of the vote. This phenomenon had, admittedly, improved the tenor of world politics, but I still deplored it.

'Oh, you're so thoroughly out of step, my friend.' Georges Abidos smiled and patted my arm. 'The world's changing!'

'It'll die if we start resorting to mystical Islamic solutions.'

'Possibly.' He seemed unconcerned. I think he believed us unsaveable.

A little drunk, I let him take me back to the Osiris in a calash. He talked affectionately of our good times, of concerts and plays we had seen in the world's capitals before civilian flight had become so impossibly expensive, of the Gilbert and Sullivan season we had attended in Bangkok, of Wagner in Bayreuth and Britten in Glyndebourne. We hummed a snatch from *Iolanthe* before we parted.

When I got up to my room all the shutters had been drawn back to give the apartment the best of the light. I recognised the subtle perfume even as my sister came out of the bathroom to laugh aloud at my astonishment.

Chapter Eleven
Saw Life to Be a Sea Green Dream

B EATRICE HAD CUT her auburn hair short and her skin was paler than I remembered. While her blue eyes and red lips remained striking, she had gained an extra beauty. I was overjoyed. This was the opposite of what I had feared to find.

As if she read my mind, she smiled. 'Were you expecting the Mad Woman of Aswan?' She wore a light blue cotton skirt and a darker blue shirt.

'You've never looked better.' I spoke the honest truth.

She took both my hands in hers and kissed me. 'I'm sorry I didn't write. It began to seem such as sham. I couldn't write for a while. I got your letters today, when I went to the post office. What a coincidence, I thought – my first sally into the real world and here comes good old Paul to help me. If anyone understands reality, you do.'

I was flattered and grinned in the way I had always responded to her half-mocking praise. 'Well, I'm here to take you back to it, if you want to go. I've got a pass for you on the Cairo plane in four days' time, and from there we can go to Geneva or London or anywhere in the Community.'

'That's marvellous,' she said. She looked about my shabby sitting room with its cracked foam cushions, its stained tiles. 'Is this the best you get at your rank?'

'This is the best for any rank, these days. Most of us don't travel at all and certainly not by plane.'

'The *schoomers* are still going out of Alex, are they?'

'Oh, yes. To Genoa, some of them. Who has the time?'

'That's what I'd thought of, for me. But here you are! What a bit of luck!'

I was immensely relieved. 'Oh, Bea. I thought you might be dead – you know, or worse.'

'I was selfish not to keep you in touch, but for a while, of course, I couldn't. Then I was out there for so long...'

'At your dig, you mean?'

She seemed momentarily surprised, as if she had not expected me to know about the dig. 'Yes, where the dig was. That's right. I can't remember what I said in my letters.'

'That you'd made a terrific discovery and that I must come out the first chance I got. Well, I did. This really was the first chance. Am I too late? Have they closed down the project completely? Are you out of funds?'

'Yes,' she smiled. 'You're too late, Paul. I'm awfully sorry. You must think I've brought you on a wild-goose chase.'

'Nonsense. That wasn't why I really came. Good Lord, Bea, I care a lot for you!' I stopped, a little ashamed. She was probably in a more delicate condition than she permitted me to see. 'And, anyway, I had some perks coming. It's lovely here, still, isn't it? If you ignore the rubbish tips. You know, and the sewage. And the Nile!' We laughed together.

'And the rain and the air,' she said. 'And the sunlight! Oh, Paul! What if this really is the future?'

Chapter Twelve

A Man in the Night Flaking Tombstones

S HE ASKED IF I would like to take a drive with her beside the evening river and I agreed at once. I was her senior by a year but she had always been the leader, the initiator and I admired her as much as ever.

We went up past the ruins of the Best Western and the Ramada Inn, the only casualties of a shelling attack in '02, when the Green Jihad had attempted to hole the dam and six women had died. We stopped near the abandoned museum and bought a drink from the ice-stall. As I turned, looking out at the river, I saw the full moon, huge and orange, in the cloudless night. A few desultory mosquitoes hung around our heads and were easily fanned away as we continued up the corniche, looking out at the lights from the boats, the flares on the far side, the palms waving in the soft breeze from the north.

'I'm quitting my job,' she said. 'I resigned, in fact, months ago. I had a few things to clear up.'

'What will you do? Get something in London?'

'Well, I've my money. That was invested very sensibly by Jack before our problems started. Before we split up. And I can do free-lance work.' Clearly, she was unwilling to discuss the details. 'I could go on living here.'

'Do you want to?'

'No,' she said. 'I hate it now. But is the rest of the world any better, Paul?'

'Oh, life's still a bit easier in England. And Italy's all right. And Scandinavia, of course, but that's closed off, as far as residency's concerned. The population's dropping quite nicely in Western Europe. Not everything's awful. The winters are easier.'

She nodded slowly as if she were carefully noting each observation. 'Well,' she said, 'anyway, I don't know about Aswan. I'm
not sure there's much point in my leaving Egypt. I have a permanent visa, you know.'

'Why stay, Bea?'

'Oh, well,' she said. 'I suppose it feels like home. How's Daddy?
Is everything all right in Marrakech?'

'Couldn't be better, I gather. He's having a wonderful time.
You know how happy he always was there. And with the new government! Well, you can imagine.'

'And Mother?'

'Still in London. She has a house to herself in West Hampstead.
Don't ask me how. She's installed the latest EE generators and
energy storers. She's got a TV set, a pet option and a gas licence.
You know Mother. She's always had the right contacts. She'll be
glad to know you're okay.'

'Yes. That's good, too. I've been guilty of some awfully selfish
behaviour, haven't I? Well, I'm putting all that behind me and getting on with my life.'

'You sound as if you've seen someone. About whatever it was.
Have you been ill, Bea?'

'Oh, no. Not really.' She turned to reassure me with a quick
smile and a hand out to mine, just as always. I nearly sang with
relief. 'Emotional trouble, you know.'

'A boyfriend?'

'Well, yes, I suppose so. Anyway, it's over.'

'All the hippies told me you'd been abducted by a flying saucer!'

'Did they?'

I recognised her brave smile. 'What's wrong? I hadn't meant to
be tactless.'

'You weren't. There are so many strange things happening
around here. You can't blame people for getting superstitious, can
you? After all, we say we've identified the causes, yet can do virtually nothing to find a cure.'

'Well, I must admit there's some truth in that. But there are still
things we can do.'

'Of course there are. I didn't mean to be pessimistic, old Paul.' She punched me on the arm and told the driver to let his horse trot for a bit, to get us some air on our faces, since the wind had dropped so suddenly.

She told me she would come to see me at the same time tomorrow and perhaps after that we might go to her new flat. It was only a temporary place while she made up her mind. Why didn't I just go to her there? I said. Because, she said, it was in a maze. You couldn't get a calash through and even the schoolboys would sometimes mislead you by accident. Write it down, I suggested, but she refused with an even broader smile. 'You'll see I'm right. I'll take you there tomorrow. There's no mystery. Nothing deliberate.'

I went back into the damp, semi-darkness of the Osiris and climbed through black archways to my rooms.

Chapter Thirteen

You'll Find No Mirrors in that Cold Abode

I HAD MEANT to ask Beatrice about her experience with the Somali woman and the police, but her mood had swung so radically I had decided to keep the rest of the conversation as casual as possible. I went to bed at once more hopeful and more baffled than I had been before I left Cairo.

In the morning I took a cab to the religious academy, or Medrasa, of the famous Sufi, El Haj Sheikh Ibrahim Abu Halil, not because I now needed his help in finding my sister, but because I felt it would have been rude to cancel my visit without explanation. The Medrasa was out near the old obelisk quarries. Characteristically Moslem, with a tower and a domed mosque, it was reached on foot or by donkey, up a winding, artificial track that had been there for at least two thousand years. I climbed to the top, feeling a little dizzy as I avoided looking directly down into the ancient quarry and saw that the place was built as a series of stone colonnades around a great courtyard with a fountain in it. The fountain, in accordance with the law, was silent.

The place was larger than I had expected and far more casual. People, many obviously drugged, of every age and race sat in groups or strolled around the cloisters. I asked a pale young woman in an Islamic burqa where I might find Sheikh Abu Halil. She told me to go to the office and led me as far as a glass door through which I saw an ordinary business layout of pens and paper, mechanical typewriters, acoustic calculators and, impressively, an EMARGY console. I felt as if I were prying. My first job, from which I had resigned, was as an Energy Officer. Essentially the work involved too much peeping-tomism and too little real progress.

A young black man in flared Mouwes and an Afghan jerkin signalled for me to enter. I told him my business and he said, 'No problem, man.' He asked me to wait in a little room furnished like something still found in any South London dentist's. Even the magazines looked familiar and I did not intend to waste my battery ration plugging in to one. A few minutes later the young man returned and I was escorted through antiseptic corridors to the Sufi's inner sanctum.

I had expected some rather austere sort of Holy Roller's Executive Suite, and was a trifle shocked by the actuality which resembled a scene from *The Arabian Nights*. The Sufi was clearly not celibate, and was an epicurean rather than ascetic. He was also younger than I had expected. I guessed he was no more than forty-five. Dressed in red silks of a dozen shades, with a massive scarlet turban on his head, he lay on cushions smoking from a silver-and-brass hookah while behind him on rich, spangled divans lolled half a dozen young women, all of them veiled, all looking at me with frank, if discreet, interest. I felt as if I should apologise for intruding on someone's private sexual fantasy, but the Sufi grinned, beckoned me in, then fell to laughing aloud as he stared into my face. All this, of course, only increased my discomfort. I could see no reason for his amusement.

'You think this a banal piece of play-acting?' He at once became solicitous. 'Pardon me, *Herr Doktor*. I misunderstood your expression for a moment. I thought you were an old friend.' Now he was almost grave. 'How can I help you?'

'Originally,' I said, 'I was looking for my sister Beatrice. I believe you know her.' Was this my sister's secret? Had she involved herself with a charismatic charlatan to whom even I felt drawn? But the banality of it all! True madness, like true evil, I had been informed once, was always characterised by its banality.

'That's it, of course. Bea Porcupine was the name the young ones used. She is a very good friend of mine. Are you looking for her no longer, Dr Porcupine?'

I pointed out that Pappenheim was the family name. The hippies had not made an enormously imaginative leap.

'Oh, the children! Don't they love to play? They are blessed. Think how few of us in the world are allowed by God to play.'

'Thou art most tolerant indeed, sidhi.' I used my best classical Arabic, at which he gave me a look of considerable approval and addressed me in the same way.

'Doth God not teach us to tolerate, but not to imitate, all the ways of mankind? Are we to judge God, my compatriot?' He had done me the honour, in his own eyes, of addressing me as a co-religionist. When he smiled again his expression was one of benign happiness. 'Would you care for some coffee?' he asked in educated English. 'Some cakes and so on? Yes, of course.' And he clapped his hands, whispering instructions to the nearest woman who rose and left. I was so thoroughly discomforted by this outrageously old-fashioned sexism, which, whatever their private practices, few sophisticated modern Arabs were willing to admit to, that I remained silent.

'And I trust that you in turn will tolerate my stupid self-indulgence,' he said. 'It is a whim of mine – and these young women – to lead the life of Haroun-el-Raschid, eh? Or the great chiefs who ruled in the days before the Prophet. We are all nostalgic for that, in Egypt. The past, you know, is our only escape. You don't begrudge it us, do you?'

I shook my head, although by training and temperament I could find no merit in his argument. 'These are changing times,' I said. 'Your past is crumbling away. It's difficult to tell good from evil or right from wrong, let alone shades of intellectual preference.'

'But I can tell you really do still think there are mechanical solutions to our ills.'

'Don't you, sidhi?'

'I do. I doubt though that they're much like a medical man's.'

'I'm an engineer, not a doctor of medicine.'

'Pardon me. It's my day for gaffs, eh? But we're all guilty of making the wrong assumptions sometimes. Let us open the shutters and enjoy some fresh air.' Another of the women went to fold back the tall wooden blinds and let shafts of sudden sunlight down upon the maroons, burgundies, dark pinks, bottle-greens and royal blues of that luxurious room. The woman sank into the shadows and only Sheikh Abu Halil remained with half his face in light, the other in shade, puffing on his pipe, his silks rippling as he moved a lazy hand. 'We are blessed with a marvellous view.'

From where we sat it was possible to see the Nile, with its white sails and flanking palms, on the far side of an expanse of glaring granite.

'My sister –' I began.

'A remarkable woman. A saint, without doubt. We have tried to help her, you know.'

'I believe you're responsible for getting her out of police custody, sidhi.'

'God has chosen her and has blessed her with unusual gifts. Dr Pappenheim, we are merely God's instruments. She has brought a little relief to the sick, a little consolation to the despairing.'

'She's coming home with me. In three days.'

'A great loss for Aswan. But perhaps she's more needed out there. Such sadness, you know. Such deep sadness.' I was not sure if he described my sister or the whole world. 'In Islam, you see,' an ironic twitch of the lip, 'we share our despair. It is a democracy of misery.' And he chuckled. 'This is blasphemy I know, in the West. Especially in America.'

'Well, in parts of the North maybe.' I smiled. My father was from Mississippi and settled first in Morocco, then in England after he came out of the service. He said he missed the old, bittersweet character of the US South. The New South, optimistic and, in his view, Yankified, no longer felt like home. He was more in his element in pre-Thatcher Britain. When she, too, began a programme of 'Yankification' of her own he retreated into fantasy, leaving my mother and going to live in a working-class street in a run-down north-eastern town where he joined the Communist Party and demonstrated against closures in the mining, fishing and steel industries. My mother hated it when his name appeared in the papers or, worse in her view, when he wrote intemperate letters to the weekly journals or the heavy dailies. But 'Jim

Pappenheim' was a contributor to *Marxism Today* and, later, *Red is Green* during his brief flirtation with Trotskyist Conservationism. He gave that up for anarcho-socialism and disappeared completely into the world of the abstract. He now wrote me letters describing the 'Moroccan experiment' as the greatest example of genuinely radical politics in action. I had never completely escaped the tyranny of his impossible ideals. This came back to me, there and then, perhaps because in some strange way I found this sufi as charming as I had once found my father. 'We say that misery loves company. Is that the same thing?' I felt I was in some kind of awful contest. 'Is that why she wanted to stay with you?'

'I knew her slightly before it all changed for her. Afterwards, I knew her better. She seemed very delicate. She came back to Aswan, then went out to the dig a couple more times, then back here. She was possessed of a terrible restlessness she would allow nobody here to address and which she consistently denied. She carried a burden, Dr Pappenheim.' He echoed the words of Inspector el-Bayoumi. 'But perhaps we, even we, shall never know what it was.'

Chapter Fourteen

On Every Hand – The Red Collusive Stain

S HE ARRIVED AT the Osiris only a minute or two late. She wore a one-piece worksuit and a kind of bush-hat with a veil. She also carried a briefcase which she displayed in some embarrassment. 'Habit, I suppose. I don't need the maps or the notes. I'm taking you into the desert, Paul. Is that okay?'

'We're not going to your place?'

'Not now.'

I changed into more suitable clothes and followed her down to the street. She had a calash waiting which carried us to the edge of town, to a camel camp where, much to my dismay, we transferred to grumbling dromedaries. I had not ridden a camel for ten years, but mine proved fairly tractable once we were moving out over the sand.

I had forgotten the peace and the wonderful smell of the desert and it was not long before I had ceased to pay attention to the heat or the motion and had begun to enjoy a mesmeric panorama of dunes and old rock. My sister occasionally used a compass to keep course but sat her high saddle with the confidence of a seasoned drover. We picked up speed until the heat became too intense and we rested under an outcrop of red stone which offered the only shade. It was almost impossible to predict where one would find shade in the desert. A year ago this rock might have been completely invisible beneath the sand; in a few months it might be invisible again.

'The silence is seductive,' I said after a while.

My sister smiled. 'Well, it whispers to me, these days. But it is wonderful, isn't it? Here you have nothing but yourself, a chance to discover how much of your identity is your own and how much is actually society's. And the ego drifts away. One becomes a virgin beast.'

'Indeed!' I found this a little too fanciful for me. 'I'm just glad to be away from all that...'

'You're not nervous?'

'Of the desert?'

'Of getting lost. Nothing comes out here, ever, now. Nomads don't pass by and it's been years since a motor vehicle or plane was allowed to waste its E.R. on mere curiosity. If we died, we'd probably never be found.'

'This is a bit morbid, isn't it, Bea? It's only a few hours from Aswan, and the camels are healthy.'

'Yes.' She rose to put our food and water back into their saddlebags, causing a murmuring and an irritable shifting of the camels. We slept for a couple of hours. Bea wanted to be able to travel at night, when we would make better time under the full moon.

The desert at night will usually fill with the noises of the creatures who waken as soon as the sun is down, but the region we next entered seemed as lifeless as the Bical flats, though without their aching mood of desolation. The sand still rose around our camels' feet in silvery gasps and I wrapped myself in the other heavy woollen gelabea Beatrice had brought. We slept again, for two or three hours, before continuing on until it was almost dawn and the moon faint and fading in the sky.

'We used to have a gramophone and everything,' she said. 'We played those French songs mainly. The old ones. And a lot of classic Rai. It was a local collection someone had brought with the machine. You wouldn't believe the mood of camaraderie that was here, Paul. Like Woodstock must have been. We had quite a few young people with us – Egyptian and European mostly – and they all said the same. We felt privileged.'

'When did you start treating the sick?' I asked her.

'Treating? Scarcely that! I just helped out with my First Aid kit and whatever I could scrounge from a pharmacy. Most of the problems were easily treated, but not priorities as far as the hospitals are concerned. I did what I could whenever I was in Aswan. But the kits gradually got used and nothing more was sent. After the quake, things began to run down. The Burbank Foundation needed its resources for rebuilding at home.'

'But you still do it. Sometimes. You're a legend back there. Ben Achmet told me.'

'When I can, I help those nomads cure themselves, that's all. I was coming out here a lot. Then there was some trouble with the police.'

'They stopped you? Because of the Somali woman?'

'That didn't stop me.' She raised herself in her saddle suddenly. 'Look. Can you see the roof there? And the pillars?'

They lay in a shallow valley between two rocky cliffs and they looked in the half-light as if they had been built that very morning. The decorated columns and the massive flat roof were touched a pinkish gold by the rising sun and I could make out hieroglyphics, the blues and ochres of the Egyptian artist. The building, or series of buildings, covered a vast area. 'It's a city,' I said. I was still disbelieving. 'Or a huge temple. My God, Bea! No wonder you were knocked out by this!'

'It's not a city or a temple, in any sense *we* mean.' Though she must have seen it a hundred times, she was still admiring of the beautiful stones. 'There's nothing like it surviving anywhere else. No record of another. Even this is only briefly mentioned and, as always with Egyptians, dismissively as the work of earlier, less exalted leaders, in this case a monotheistic cult which attempted to set up its own god-king and, in failing, was thoroughly destroyed. Pragmatically, the winners in that contest re-dedicated the place to Sekhmet and then, for whatever reasons – probably economic – abandoned it altogether. There are none of the usual signs of later uses. By the end of Nyusere's reign no more was heard of it at all. Indeed, not much more was heard of Nubia for a long time. This region was never exactly the centre of Egyptian life.'

'It was a temple to Ra?'

'Ra, or a sun deity very much like him. The priest here was

represented as a servant of the sun. We call the place Onu'us, after him.'

'Four thousand years ago? Are you sure this isn't one of those new Dutch repros?' My joke sounded flat, even to me.

'Now you can see why we kept it dark, Paul. It was an observatory, a scientific centre, a laboratory, a library. A sort of university, really. Even the hieroglyphics are different. They tell all kinds of things about the people and the place. And, it had a couple of other functions.' Her enthusiasm died and she stopped, dismounting from her camel and shaking sand from her hat. Together we watched the dawn come up over the glittering roof. The pillars, shadowed now, stood only a few feet out of the sand, yet the brilliance of the colour was almost unbelievable. Here was the classic language of the Fifth Dynasty, spare, accurate, clean. And it was obvious that the whole place had only recently been refilled. Elsewhere churned, powdery earth and overturned rock spoke of vigorous activity by the discovering team; there was also, on the plain which stretched away from the southern ridge, a considerable area of fused sand. But even this was now covered by that desert tide which would soon bury again and preserve this uncanny relic.

'You tried to put the sand back?' I felt stupid and smiled at myself.

'It's all we could think of in the circumstances. Now it's far less visible than it was a month ago.'

'You sound very proprietorial.' I was amused that the mystery should prove to have so obvious a solution. My sister had simply become absorbed in her work. It was understandable that she should.

'I'm sorry,' she said. 'I must admit...'

For a moment, lost in the profound beauty of the vision, I did not realise she was crying. Just as I had as a little boy, I moved to comfort her, having no notion at all of the cause of her grief, but assuming, I suppose, that she was mourning the death of an important piece of research, the loss of her colleagues, the sheer disappointment at this unlucky end to a wonderful adventure. It was plain, too, that she was completely exhausted.

She drew towards me, smiling an apology. 'I want to tell you everything, Paul. And only you. When I have, that'll be it. I'll never mention it again. I'll get on with some sort of life. I'm sick of myself at the moment.'

'Bea. You're very tired. Let's go home to Europe where I can coddle you for a bit.'

'Perhaps,' she said. She paused as the swiftly risen sun outlined sunken buildings and revealed more of a structure lying just below the surface, some dormant juggernaut.

'It's monstrous,' I said. 'It's the size of the large complex at Luxor. But this is different. All the curved walls, all the circles. Is that to do with sun worship?'

'Astronomy, anyway. We speculated, of course. When we first mapped it on the sonavids. This is the discovery to launch a thousand theories, most of them crackpot. You have to be careful. But it felt to us to be almost a contrary development to what was happening at roughly the same time around Abu Ghurab, although of course there were sun-cults there, too. But in Lower Egypt the gratification and celebration of the Self had reached terrible proportions. All those grandiose pyramids. This place had a mood to it. The more we sifted it out the more we felt it. Wandering amongst those light columns, those open courtyards, was marvellous. All the turquoises and reds and bright yellows. This had to be the centre of some ancient Enlightenment. Far better preserved than Philae, too. And no graffiti carved anywhere, no Christian or Moslem disfigurement. We all worked like maniacs. Chamber after chamber was opened. Gradually, of course, it dawned on us! You could have filled this place with academic people and it would have been a functioning settlement again, just as it was before some petty Pharaoh or local governor decided to destroy it. We felt we were taking over from them after a gap of millennia. It gave some of us a weird sense of responsibility. We talked about it. They knew so much, Paul.'

'And so little,' I murmured. 'They only had limited information to work with, Bea...'

'Oh, I think we'd be grateful for their knowledge today.' Her manner was controlled, as if she desperately tried to remember how she had once talked and behaved. 'Anyway, this is where it all happened. We thought at first we had an advantage. Nobody was bothering to come out to what was considered a very minor find and everyone involved was anxious not to let any government start interfering. It was a sort of sacred trust, if you like. We kept clearing. We weren't likely to be found. Unless we used the emergency radio nobody would waste an energy unit on coming out. Oddly, we found no monumental statuary at all, though the engineering was on a scale with anything from the Nineteenth Dynasty – not quite as sophisticated, maybe, but again far in advance of its own time.'

'How long did it take you to uncover it all?'

'We never did. We all swore to reveal nothing until a proper international preservation order could be obtained. This government is as desperate for cruise-*schoomer* dollars as anyone...'

I found myself interrupting her. 'This was all covered by hand, Bea?'

'No, no.' Again she was amused. 'No, the ship did that, mostly. When it brought me back.'

A sudden depression filled me. 'You mean a spaceship, do you?'

'Yes,' she said. 'A lot of people here know about them. And I told Di Roper, as well as some of the kids, and the Sufi. But nobody ever believes us – nobody from the real world, I mean. And that's why I wanted to tell you. You're still a real person, aren't you?'

'Bea – you could let me know everything in London. Once we're back in a more familiar environment. Can't we just enjoy this place for what it is? Enjoy the world for what it is?'

'It's not enjoyable for me, Paul.'

I moved away from her. 'I don't believe in spaceships.'

'You don't believe in much, do you?' Her tone was unusually cool.

I regretted offending her, yet I could not help but respond. 'The nuts and bolts of keeping this ramshackle planet running somehow. That's what I believe in, Bea. I'm like that chap in the first version of *The African Queen*, only all he had to worry about was a

World War and a little beam-engine. Bea, you were here alone and horribly overtired. Surely...?'

'Let me talk, Paul.' There was a note of aching despair in her voice which immediately silenced me and made me lower my head in assent.

We stood there, looking at the sunrise pouring light over that dusty red and brown landscape with its drowned architecture, and I listened to her recount the most disturbing and unlikely story I was ever to hear.

The remains of the team had gone into Aswan for various reasons and Bea was left alone with only a young Arab boy for company. Ali worked as a general servant and was as much part of the team as anyone else, with as much enthusiasm. 'He, too, understood the reasons for saying little about our work. Phil Springfield had already left to speak to some people in Washington and Professor al-Bayumi, no close relative of the inspector, was doing what he could in Cairo, though you can imagine the delicacy of his position. Well, one morning, when I was cleaning the dishes and Ali had put a record on the gramophone, this freak storm blew up. It caused a bit of panic, of course, though it was over in a minute or two. And when the sand settled again there was the ship – there, on that bluff. You can see where it came and went.'

The spaceship, she said, had been a bit like a flying saucer in that it was circular, with deep sides and glowing horizontal bands at regular intervals. 'It was more drum-shaped, though there were discs – I don't know, they weren't metal, but seemed like visible electricity, sort of protruding from it, half on the inside, half on the outside. Much of that moved from a kind of hazy gold into a kind of silver. There were other colours, too. And, I think, sounds. It looked a bit like a kid's tambourine – opaque, sparkling surfaces top and bottom – like the vellum on a drum. And the sides went dark sometimes. Polished oak. The discs, the flange things, went scarlet. They were its main information sensors.'

'It was organic?'

'It was a bit. You'd really have to see it for yourself. Anyway, it stood there for a few minutes and then these figures came out. I thought they were test pilots from that experimental field in Libya and they'd made an emergency landing. I was going to offer them a cup of tea when I realised they weren't human. They had dark bodies that weren't suits exactly but an extra body you wear over your own. Well, you've seen something like it. We all have. It's Akhenoton and Nefertiti. Those strange abdomens and elongated heads, their hermaphroditic quality. They spoke a form of very old-fashioned English. They apologised. They said they had had an instrument malfunction and had not expected to find anyone here. They were prepared to take us with them, if we wished to go. I gathered that these were standard procedures for them. We were both completely captivated by their beauty and the wonder of the event. I don't think Ali hesitated any more than I. I left a note for whoever returned, saying I'd had to leave in a hurry and didn't know when I'd be back. Then we went with them.'

'You didn't wonder about their motives?'

'Motives? Yes, Paul, I suppose hallucinations have motives. We weren't the only Earth-people ever to go. Anyway, I never regretted the decision. On the dark side of the moon the main ship was waiting. That's shaped like a gigantic dung-beetle. You'll laugh when I tell you why. I still find it funny. They're furious because their bosses won't pay for less antiquated vessels. Earth's not a very important project. The ship was designed after one of the first organisms they brought back from Earth, to fit in with what they thought was a familiar form. Apparently their own planet has fewer species but many more different sizes of the same creature. They haven't used the main ship to visit Earth since we began to develop sensitive detection equipment. Their time is different, anyway, and they still find our ways of measuring and recording it very hard to understand.'

'They took you to their planet?' I wanted her story to be over. I had heard enough to convince me that she was in need of immediate psychiatric help.

'Oh, no. They've never been there. Not the people I know. Others have been back, but we never communicated with them.

They have an artificial environment on Mercury.' She paused, noticing my distress. 'Paul, you know me. I hated that von Däniken stuff. It was patently rubbish. Yet this was, well, horribly like it. Don't think I wasn't seriously considering I might have gone barmy. When people go mad, you know, they get such ordinary delusions. I suppose they reflect our current myths and apocrypha. I felt foolish at first. Then, of course, the reality grew so vivid, so absorbing, I forgot everything. I could not have run away, Paul. I just walked into it all and they let me. I'm not sure why, except they know things – even circumstances, if you follow me – and must have felt it was better to let me. They hadn't wanted to go underwater and they'd returned to an old location in the Sahara. They'd hoped to find some spares, I think. I know it sounds ridiculously prosaic.

'Well, they took us with them to their base. If I try to pronounce their language it somehow sounds so ugly. Yet it's beautiful. I think in their atmosphere it works. I can speak it, Paul. They can speak our languages, too. But there's no need for them. Their home planet's many light years beyond the Solar System which is actually very different to Earth, except for some colours and smells, of course. Oh, it's so lovely there, at their base. Yet they complain all the time about how primitive it is and long for the comforts of home. You can imagine what it must be like.

'I became friends with a Reen. He was exquisitely beautiful. He wasn't really a he, either, but an androgyne or something similar. There's more than one type of fertilisation, involving several people, but not always. I was completely taken up with him. Maybe he wasn't so lovely to some human eyes, but he was to mine. He was golden-pale and looked rather negroid, I suppose, like one of those beautiful Masai carvings you see in Kenya, and his shape wasn't altogether manlike, either. His abdomen was permanently rounded – most of them are like that, though in the intermediary sex I think there's a special function. My lover was of that sex, yet he found it impossible to make me understand how he was different. Otherwise they have a biology not dissimilar to ours, with similar organs and so on. It was not hard for me to adapt. Their food is delicious, though they moan about that, too. It's sent from home. Where they can grow it properly. And they have extraordinary music. They have recordings of English TV and radio – and other kinds of recordings, too. Earth's an entire department, you see. Paul,' she paused as if regretting the return of the memory, 'they have recordings of events. Like battles and ceremonies and architectural stuff. He – my lover – found me an open-air concert at which Mozart was playing. It was too much for me. An archaeologist, and I hadn't the nerve to look at the past as it actually was. I might have got round to it. I meant to. I'd planned to force myself, you know, when I settled down there.'

'Bea, don't you know how misanthropic and nuts that sounds?'

'They haven't been "helping" us or anything like that. It's an observation team. We're not the only planet they're keeping an eye on. They're academics and scientists like us.' She seemed to be making an effort to convince me and to repeat the litany of her own faith, whatever it was that she believed kept her sane. Yet the creatures she described, I was still convinced, were merely the inventions of an overtaxed, isolated mind. Perhaps she had been trapped somewhere under ground?

'I could have worked there, you see. But I broke the rules.'

'You tried to escape?' Reluctantly I humoured her.

'Oh, no!' Her mind had turned backward again and I realised then that it was not any far-off interstellar world but her own planet that had taken her reason. I was suddenly full of sorrow.

'A flying saucer, Bea!' I hoped that my incredulity would bring her back to normality. She had been so ordinary, so matter-of-fact, when we had first met.

'Not really,' she said. 'The hippies call them Reens. They don't know very much about them, but they've made a cult of the whole thing. They've changed it. Fictionalised it. I can see why that would disturb you. They've turned it into a story for their own purposes. And Sheikh Abu Halil's done the same, really. We've had arguments. I can't stand the exploitation, Paul.'

'That's in the nature of a myth.' I spoke gently, feeling foolish and puny as I stood looking down on that marvellous construction.

I wanted to leave, to return to Aswan, to get us back to Cairo and from there to the relative sanity of rural Oxfordshire, to the village where we had lived with our aunt during our happiest years.

She nodded her head. 'That's why I stopped saying anything.

'You can't imagine how hurt I was at first, how urgent it seemed to talk about it. I still thought I was only being taught a lesson and they'd return for me. It must be how Eve felt when she realised God wasn't joking.' She smiled bitterly at her own naïveté, her eyes full of old pain. 'I was there for a long time, I thought, though when I got back it had only been a month or two and it emerged that nobody had ever returned here from Aswan. There had been that Green Jihad trouble and everyone was suddenly packed off back to Cairo and from there, after a while, to their respective homes. People assumed the same had happened to me. If only it had! But really Paul I wouldn't change it.'

I shook my head. 'I think you were born in the wrong age, Bea. You should have been a priestess of Amon, maybe. Blessed by the gods.'

'We asked them in to breakfast, Ali and me.' Shading her eyes against the sun, she raised her arm to point. 'Over there. We had a big tent we were using for everything while the others were away. Our visitors didn't think much of our C-Ral and offered us some of their own rations which were far tastier. It was just a scout, that ship. I met my lover later. He had a wonderful sense of irony. As he should, after a thousand years on the same shift.'

I could bear no more of this familiar modern apocrypha. 'Bea. Don't you think you just imagined it? After nobody returned, weren't you anxious? Weren't you disturbed?'

'They weren't away long enough. I didn't know they weren't coming back, Paul. I fell in love. That wasn't imagination. Gradually, we found ourselves unable to resist the mutual attraction. I suppose I regret that.' She offered me a sidelong glance I might have thought cunning in someone else. 'I don't blame you for not believing it. How can I prove I'm sane? Or that I was sane then?'

I was anxious to assure her of my continuing sympathy. 'You're not a liar, Bea. You never were.'

'But you think I'm crazy.' All at once her voice became more urgent. 'You know how terribly dull madness can be. How conventional most delusions are. You never think you could go mad like that. Then maybe it happens. The flying saucers come down and take you off to Venus, or paradise, or wherever, where war and disease and atmospheric disintegration are long forgotten. You fall in love with a Venusian. Sexual intercourse is forbidden. You break the law. You're cast out of paradise. You can't have a more familiar myth than that, can you, Paul?' Her tone was disturbing. I made a movement with my hand, perhaps to silence her.

'I loved him,' she said. 'And then I watched the future wither and fade before my eyes. I would have paid any price, done anything, to get back.'

That afternoon, as we returned to Aswan, I was full of desperate, bewildered concern for a sister I knew to be in immediate need of professional help. 'We'll sort all this out,' I reassured her, 'maybe when we get to Geneva. We'll see Frank.'

'I'm sorry, Paul.' She spoke calmly. 'I'm not going back with you. I realised it earlier, when we were out at the site. I'll stay in Aswan, after all.'

I resisted the urge to turn away from her, and for a while I could not speak.

Chapter Fifteen

Whereat Serene and Undevoured He Lay...

T HE FLIGHT WAS leaving in two days and there would be no other ticket for her. After she went off, filthy and withered from the heat, I rather selfishly used my whole outstanding water allowance and bathed for several hours as I tried to separate the truth from the fantasy. I thought how ripe the world was for Bea's revelation, how dangerous it might be. I was glad she planned to tell no-one else, but would she keep to that decision? My impulse was to leave, to flee from the whole mess before Bea started telling me how she had become involved in black magic. I felt deeply sorry for her and I felt angry with her for not being the strong leader I had looked up to all my life. I knew it was my duty to get her back to Europe for expert attention.

'I'm not interested in proving what's true or false, Paul,' she had said after agreeing to meet me at the Osiris next morning. 'I just want you to *know*. Do you understand?'

Anxious not to upset her further, I had said that I did.

That same evening I went to find Inspector el-Bayoumi in his office. He put out his cigarette as I came in, shook hands and, his manner both affable and relaxed, offered me a comfortable leather chair. 'You've found your sister, Mr Pappenheim. That's excellent news.'

I handed him a 'purse' I had brought and told him, in the convoluted manner such occasions demand, that my sister was refusing to leave, that I had a ticket for her on a flight and that it was unlikely I would have a chance to return to Aswan in the near future. If he could find some reason to hold her and put her on the plane, I would be grateful.

With a sigh of regret – at my folly, perhaps – he handed back the envelope. 'I couldn't do it, Mr Pappenheim, without risking the peace of Aswan, which I have kept pretty successfully for some years. We have a lot of trouble with Green Jihad, you know. I am very short-staffed as a result. You must convince her, my dear sir, or you must leave her here. I assure you, she is much loved and respected. She is a woman of considerable substance and will make her own decisions. I promise, however, to keep you informed.'

'By the mail packet? I thought you wanted me to get her out of here!'

'I had hoped you might *persuade* her, Mr Pappenheim.'

I apologised for my rudeness. 'I appreciate your concern, inspector.' I put the money back in my pocket and went out to the corniche, catching the first felucca across to the West Bank where this time I paid off my guides before I reached the English House.

The roses were still blooming around the great brick manor and Lady Roper was cutting some of them, laying them carefully in her bucket. 'Really, Paul, I don't think you must worry, especially if she doesn't want to talk about her experiences. *We* all know she's telling the truth. Why don't you have a man-to-man with Bernie? There he is, in the kitchen.'

Through the window, Sir Bernard waved with his cocoa cup before making a hasty and rather obvious retreat.

Chapter Sixteen

Your Funeral Bores Them with Its Brilliant Doom

Awaking at dawn the next morning I found it impossible to return to sleep. I got up and tried to make some notes but writing down what my sister had told me somehow made it even more difficult to understand. I gave up. Putting on a cotton gelabea and some slippers I went down to the almost empty street and walked to the nearest corner café where I ordered tea and a couple of rolls. All the other little round tables were occupied and from the interior came the sound of a scratched Oum Kalthoum record. The woman's angelic voice, singing the praises of God and the joys of love, reminded me of my schooldays in Fèz, when I had lived with my father during his brief entrepreneurial period, before he had returned to England to become a Communist. Then Oum Kalthoum had been almost a goddess in Egypt. Now she was as popular again, like so many of the old performers who had left a legacy of 78 rpms which could be played on spring-loaded gramophones or the new clockworks which could also play a delicate LP but which few Egyptians could afford. Most of the records were re-pressed from ancient masters purchased from Athenian studios which, fifty years earlier, had mysteriously manufactured most Arabic recordings. The quality of her voice came through the surface noise as purely as it had once sounded through fractured stereos or on crude pirate tapes in the days of licence and waste. 'Inte el Hob', wistful, celebratory, thoughtful, reminded me of the little crooked streets of Fèz, the stink of the dyers and tanners, the extraordinary vividness of the colours, the pungent mint bales, the old men who loved to stand and declaim on the matters of the day with anyone who would listen, the smell of fresh saffron, of lavender carried on the backs of donkeys driven by little boys crying '*balek!*' and insulting, in the vocabulary of a professional soldier, anyone who refused to move aside for them. Life had been sweet then, with unlimited television and cheap air-travel, with any food you could afford and any drink freely available for a few dirhams, and every pleasure in the reach of the common person. The years of Easy, the years of Power, the paradise from which our lazy greed and hungry egos banished us to eternal punishment, to the limbo of the Age of Penury, for which we have only ourselves to blame! But Fèz was good, then, in those good, old days.

A little more at peace with myself, I walked down to the river while the muezzin called the morning prayer and I might have been back in the Ottoman Empire, leading the simple, steady life of a small landowner or a civil servant in the family of the Bey. The débris of the river, the ultimate irony of the Nile filling with all the bottles which had held the water needed because we had polluted the Nile, drew my attention. It was as if the water industry had hit upon a perfect means of charging people whatever they wanted for a drink of *eau naturelle*, while at the same time guaranteeing that the Nile could never again be a source of free water. All this further reinforced my assertion that we were not in the Golden Age those New New Aquarians so longed to re-create. We were in a present which had turned our planet into a single, squalid slum, where nothing beautiful could exist for long, unless in isolation, like Lady Roper's rose garden. We could not bring back the Golden Age. Indeed we were now paying the price of having enjoyed one.

I turned away from the river and went back to the café to find Sheikh Abu Halil sitting in the chair I had recently occupied. 'What a coincidence, Dr Pappenheim. How are you? How is your wonderful sister?' He spoke educated English.

I suspected for a moment that he knew more than he allowed but then I checked myself. My anxiety was turning into paranoia. This was no way to help my sister.

'I was killing time,' he said, 'before coming to see you. I didn't want to interrupt your beauty sleep or perhaps even your breakfast, but I guessed aright. You have the habits of Islam.' He was flattering me and this in itself was a display of friendship or, at least, affection.

'I've been looking at the rubbish in the river.' I shook his hand and sat down in the remaining chair. 'There aren't enough police to do anything about it, I suppose.'

'Always a matter of economics.' He was dressed very differently today in a conservative light-and-dark blue gelabea, like an Alexandrian businessman. On his head he wore a discreet, matching cap. 'You take your sister back today, I understand, Dr Pappenheim.'

'If she'll come.'

'She doesn't want to go?' The Sufi's eyelid twitched almost raffishly, suggesting to me that he had been awake most of the night. Had he spent that time with Bea?

'She's not sure now,' I said. 'She hates flying.'

'Oh, yes. Flying is a very difficult and unpleasant thing. I myself hate it and would not do it if I could.'

I felt he understood far more than that and I was in some way relieved. 'You couldn't persuade her of the wisdom of coming with me, I suppose, sidhi?'

'I have already told her what I think, Paul. I think she should go with you. She is unhappy here. Her burden is too much. But she would not and will not listen to me. I had hoped to congratulate you and wish you Godspeed.'

'You're very kind.' I now believed him sincere.

'I love her, Paul.' He gave a great sigh and turned to look up at the sky. 'She's an angel! I think so. She will come to no harm from us.'

'Well –' I was once again at a loss. 'I love her too, sidhi. But does she want our love, I wonder?'

'You are wiser than I thought, Paul. Just so. Just so.' He ordered coffee and sweetac for us both. 'She knows only the habit of giving. She has never learned to receive. Not here, anyway. Especially from you.'

'She was always my best friend.' I said. 'A mother sometimes. An alter ego. I want to get her to safety, Sheikh Abu Halil.'

'Safety?' At this he seemed sceptical. 'It would be good for her to know the normality of family life. She has a husband.'

'He's in New Zealand. They split up. He hated what he called her "charity work".'

'If he was unsympathetic to her calling, that must be inevitable.'

'You really think she has a vocation?' The coffee came and the oversweetened breakfast cakes which he ate with considerable relish. 'We don't allow these at home. All those chemicals!' There was an element of self-mockery in his manner now that he was away from his Medrasa. 'Yes. We think she has been called. We have many here who believe that of themselves, but most are self-deluding. Aswan is becoming a little over-stocked with mystics and wonder-workers. Eventually, I suppose, the fashion will change, as it did in Nepal, San Francisco or Essaouira. Your sister, however, is special to us. She is so sad, these days, doctor. There is a chance she might find happiness in London. She is spending too long in the desert.'

'Isn't that one of the habitual dangers of the professional mystic?' I asked him.

He responded with quiet good humour. 'Perhaps of the more old-fashioned type, like me. Did she ever tell you what she passed to Lallah Zenobia that night?'

'You mean the cause of her arrest? Wasn't it money? A purse. The police thought it was.'

'But if so, Paul, what was she buying?'

'Peace of mind, perhaps,' I said. I asked him if he really believed in people from space, and he said that he did, for he believed that God had created and populated the whole universe as He saw fit.

'By the way,' he said, 'are you walking up towards the Cataract? There was some kind of riot near there an hour or so ago. The police were involved and some of the youngsters from the holiday villas. Just a peaceful demonstration, I'm sure. That would be nothing to do with your sister?'

I shook my head.

'You'll go back to England, will you, Dr Pappenheim?'

'Eventually,' I told him. 'The way I feel at the moment I might retire. I want to write a novel.'

'Oh, your father was a vicar, then?'

I was thoroughly puzzled by this remark. Again he began to laugh. 'I do apologise. I've always been struck by the curious fact that so much enduring English literature has sprung, as it were, from the loins of the minor clergy. I wish you luck, Dr Pappenheim, in whatever you choose to do. And I hope your sister decides to go with you tomorrow.' He kissed me three times on my face. 'You both need to discover your own peace. *Sabah el Kher.*'

'*Allah yisabbe'h Kum bil-Kher.*'

The holy man waved a dignified hand as he strolled down towards the corniche to find a calash.

By now the muezzin was calling the mid-morning prayer. I had been away from my hotel longer than planned. I went back through the crowds to the green-and-white entrance of the Osiris and climbed slowly to my room. It was not in my nature to force my sister to leave and I felt considerably ashamed of my attempt to persuade Inspector el-Bayoumi to extradite her. I could only pray that, in the course of the night, she had come to her senses. My impulse was to seek her out but I still did not know her address.

I spent the rest of the morning packing and making official notes until, at noon, she came through the archway, wearing a blue cotton dress and matching shawl. I hoped this was a sign she was preparing for the flight back to civilisation. 'You haven't eaten, have you?' she said.

She had booked a table on the Mut, a floating restaurant moored just below the Cataract. We boarded a thing resembling an Ottoman pleasure barge, all dark green trellises, scarlet fretwork and brass ornament, while inside it was more luxurious than the Sufi's 'harem'. 'It's hardly used, of course, these days,' Bea said. 'Not enough rich people wintering in Aswan any more. But the atmosphere's nice still. You don't mind? It's not against your puritan nature, is it?'

'Only a little.' I was disturbed by her apparent normality. We might never have ridden into the desert together, never have talked about aliens and spaceships and ancient Egyptian universities. I wondered, now, if she were not seriously schizophrenic.

'You do seem troubled, though.' She was interrupted by a large man in a dark yellow gelabea smelling wildly of garlic who embraced her with affectionate delight. 'Beatrice! My Beatrice!' We were introduced. Mustafa shook hands with me as he led us ecstatically to a huge, low table looking over the Nile, where the feluccas and great sailing barges full of holidaymakers came close enough to touch. We sat on massive brocaded foam cushions.

I could not overcome my depression. I was faced with a problem beyond my scope. 'You've decided to stay, I take it?'

The major-domo returned with two large glasses of Campari-soda. 'Compliments of the house.' It was an extraordinary piece of generosity. We saluted him with our glasses, then toasted each other.

'Yes.' She drew her hair over her collar and looked towards the water. 'For a while, anyway. I won't get into any more trouble, Paul, I promise. And I'm not the suicide type. That I'm absolutely sure about.'

'Good.' I would have someone come out to her as soon as possible, a psychiatrist contact in MEDAC who could provide a professional opinion. 'You'll tell me your address?'

'I'm moving. Tomorrow. I'll stay with the Ropers if they'll have me. Any mail care of them will be forwarded. I'm not being deliberately mysterious, dear, I promise. I'm going to write. And meanwhile, I've decided to tell you the whole of it. I want you to remember it, perhaps put it into some kind of shape that I can't. It's important to me that it's recorded. Do you promise?'

I could only promise that I would make all the notes possible.

'Well, there's actually not much else.'

I was relieved to know I would not for long have to suffer those miserably banal inventions.

'I fell in love, you see.'

'Yes, you told me. With a spaceman.'

'We knew it was absolutely forbidden to make love. But we

couldn't help ourselves. I mean, with all his self-discipline he was as attracted to me as I was to him. It was important, Paul.'

I did my best to give her my full attention while she repeated much of what she had already told me in the desert. There was a kind of biblical rhythm to her voice. 'So they threw me out. I never saw my lover again. I never saw his home again. They brought me back and left me where they had found me. Our tents were gone and everything was obviously abandoned. They let their engines blow more sand over the site. Well, I got to Aswan eventually. I found water and food and it wasn't too hard. I'm not sure why I came here. I didn't know then that I was pregnant. I don't think I knew you could get pregnant. There isn't a large literature on sexual congress with semi-males of the alien persuasion. You'd probably find him bizarre, but for me it was like making love to an angel. All the time. It was virtually our whole existence. Oh, Paul!' She pulled at her collar. She smoothed the tablecloth between her knife and fork. 'Well, he was wonderful and he thought I was wonderful. Maybe that's *why* they forbid it. The way they'd forbid a powerful habit-forming stimulant. Do you know I just this second thought of that?'

'That's why you were returned here?' I was still having difficulty following her narrative.

'Didn't I say? Yes. Well, I went to stay with the Ropers for a bit, then I stayed in the commune and then the Medrasa, but I kept going out to the site. I was hoping they'd relent, you see. I'd have done almost anything to get taken back, Paul.'

'To escape from here, you mean?'

'To be with him. That's all. I was – I am – so lonely. Nobody could describe the void.'

I was silent, suddenly aware of her terrible vulnerability, still convinced she had been the victim of some terrible deception.

'You're wondering about the child,' she said. She put her hand on mine where I fingered the salt. 'He was born too early. He lived for eight days. I had him at Lallah Zenobia's. You see, I couldn't tell what he would look like. She was better prepared, I thought. She even blessed him when he was born so that his soul might go

to heaven. He was tiny and frail and beautiful. His father's colouring and eyes. My face, I think, mostly. He would have been a
wunderkind, I shouldn't be surprised. Paul…' Her voice became a
whisper. 'It was like giving birth to the Messiah.'

With great ceremony, our meal arrived. It was a traditional
Egyptian *meze* and it was more and better food than either of us
had seen in years. Yet we hardly ate.

'I took him back to the site.' She looked out across the water
again. 'I'd got everything ready. I had some hope his father would
come to see him. Nobody came. Perhaps it needed that third sex
to give him the strength? I waited, but there was not, as the kids
say, a Reen to be seen.' This attempt at humour was hideous. I
took firm hold of her hands. The tears in her eyes were barely
restrained.

'He died.' She released her hands and looked for something in
her bag. I thought for a frightening moment she was going to
produce a photograph. 'Eight days. He couldn't seem to get
enough nourishment from what I was feeding him. He needed
that – whatever it was he should have had.' She took a piece of
linen from her bag and wiped her hands and neck. 'You're thinking I should have taken him to the hospital. But this is Egypt, Paul,
where people are still arrested for witchcraft and here was clear
evidence of my having had congress with an *ifrit*. Who would
believe my story? I was aware of what I was doing. I'd never
expected the baby to live or, when he did live, to look the way he
did. The torso was sort of pear-shaped and there were several
embryonic limbs. He was astonishingly lovely. I think he belonged
to his father's world. I wish they had come for him. It wasn't fair
that he should die.'

I turned my attention to the passing boats and controlled my
own urge to weep. I was hoping she would stop, for she was, by
continuing, hurting herself. But, obsessively, she went on. 'Yes,
Paul. I could have gone to Europe as soon as I knew I was pregnant and I would have done if I'd had a hint of what was coming,
but my instincts told me he would not live or, if he did live, it
would be because his father returned for him. I don't think that

was self-deception. Anyway, when he was dead I wasn't sure what to do. I hadn't made any plans. Lallah Zenobia was wonderful to me. She said she would dispose of the body properly and with respect. I couldn't bear to have some future archaeologist digging him up. You know, I've always hated that. Especially with children. So I went to her lean-to in Shantytown. I had him wrapped in a shawl – Mother's lovely old Persian shawl – and inside a beautiful inlaid box. I put the box in a leather bag and took it to her.'

'That was the Cairene Purse? Or did you give her money, too?'

'Money had nothing to do with it. Do the police still think I was paying her? I offered Zenobia money but she refused. "Just pray for us all," was what she said. I've been doing it every night since. The Lord's prayer for everyone. It's the only prayer I know. I learned it at one of my schools.'

'Zenobia went to prison. Didn't you try to tell them she was helping you?'

'There was no point in mentioning the baby, Paul. That would have constituted another crime, I'm sure. She was as good as her word. He was never found. She made him safe somewhere. A little funeral boat on the river late at night, away from all the witnesses, maybe. And they would have found him if she had been deceiving me, Paul. She got him home somehow.'

Dumb with sadness, I could only reach out and stroke her arms and hands, reach for her unhappy face.

We ate so as not to offend our host, but without appetite. Above the river the sun was at its zenith and Aswan experienced the familiar, unrelenting light of an African afternoon.

She looked out at the river with its day's flow of débris, the plastic jars, the used sanitary towels, the paper and filth left behind by tourists and residents alike.

With a deep, uneven sigh, she shook her head, folded her arms under her breasts and leaned back in the engulfing foam.

All the *fhouls* and the marinated salads, the *ruqaq* and the meats lay cold before us as, from his shadows, the proprietor observed us with discreet concern.

There came a cry from outside. A boy perched high on the

single mast of his boat, his white gelabea tangling with his sail so that he seemed all of a piece with the vessel, waved to friends on the shore and pointed into the sky. One of our last herons circled overhead for a moment and then flew steadily south, into what had been the Sudan.

My sister's slender body was moved for a moment by some small, profound anguish.

'He could not have lived here.'

THE END. Chapter Quotes: 1 Hood; 2 Khayyám/FitzGerald; 3 AE; 4 Dylan Thomas; 5 Wheldrake; 6 Yokum; 7 Aeschylus/ MacNeice; 8 Vachel Lindsay; 9 F. Thompson; 10 Peake; 11 Treece; 12 Duffy; 13 Nye; 14 C.D. Lewis; 15 E. St V. Millay; 16 Nye.

Acknowledgements

'Casablanca' first appeared in *Casablanca*, Gollancz, 1989.

'Going to Canada' and 'Leaving Pasadena' first appeared in *My Experiences in the Third World War*, Savoy Books, 1980.

'Crossing into Cambodia' first appeared in *Twenty Houses of the Zodiac*, edited by Maxim Jakubowski, New English Library, 1979.

'The Mountain' first appeared (in French) in NOCTURNE No. 1, ed. Jakubowski, 1964, and (in English, as by 'James Colvin') in NEW WORLDS No. 147, edited by Michael Moorcock, February 1965.

'The Deep Fix' first appeared (as by Colvin) in SCIENCE FANTASY No. 64, edited by John Carnell, April 1964.

'The Frozen Cardinal' first appeared in *Other Edens*, edited by Christopher Evans & Robert Holdstock, Unwin, 1987.

'Wolf' and 'The Real Life Mr Newman' first appeared in *The Deep Fix* (as by Colvin), Compact Books, 1966.

'The Pleasure Garden of Felipe Sagittarius' first appeared (as by Colvin) in NEW WORLDS No. 154, ed. Moorcock, September 1965.

'The Cairene Purse' first appeared in *Zenith 2*, edited by David S. Garnett, Orbit, 1990.

MICHAEL MOORCOCK (1939-) is one of the most important figures in British SF and Fantasy literature. The author of many literary novels and stories in practically every genre, he has won and been shortlisted for numerous awards including the Hugo, Nebula, World Fantasy, Whitbread and Guardian Fiction Prize. He is also a musician who performed in the seventies with his own band, the Deep Fix; and, as a member of the space-rock band, Hawkwind, won a platinum disc. His tenure as editor of NEW WORLDS magazine in the sixties and seventies is seen as the high watermark of SF editorship in the UK, and was crucial in the development of the SF New Wave. Michael Moorcock's literary creations include Hawkmoon, Corum, Von Bek, Jerry Cornelius and, of course, his most famous character, Elric. He has been compared to, among others, Balzac, Dumas, Dickens, James Joyce, Ian Fleming, J.R.R. Tolkien and Robert E. Howard. Although born in London, he now splits his time between homes in Texas and Paris.

For a more detailed biography, please see Michael Moorcock's entry in *The Encyclopedia of Science Fiction* at: http://www.sf-encyclopedia.com/

For further information about Michael Moorcock and his work, please visit www.multiverse.org, or send S.A.E. to The Nomads Of The Time Streams, Mo Dhachaidh, Loch Awe, Dalmally, Argyll, PA33 1AQ, Scotland, or P.O. Box 385716, Waikoloa, HI 96738, USA.